THE GORDIAN KNOT

Robert A Gore
12/7/00

THE GORDIAN KNOT

▼

A Novel

Robert A. Gore

Writers Club Press
San Jose New York Lincoln Shanghai

The Gordian Knot
A Novel

Writers Club Press
an imprint of iUniverse.com, Inc.

For information address:
iUniverse.com, Inc.
5220 S 16th, Ste. 200
Lincoln, NE 68512
www.iuniverse.com

ISBN: 0-595-14685-6

Printed in the United States of America

To Roberta, my wife, inspiration, supporter and friend, and Austin, may you grow up to be a Joe Tolleson.

CONTENTS

According to ancient Greek legend, an oracle revealed that a complex knot tied by King Gordius of Phrygia would be undone only by the future master of Asia. Alexander the Great made one futile attempt to untie the knot, drew his sword and cut it in half. Before he died in India at the age of thirty-three, he had conquered most of the Middle East.

CHAPTER 1

▼

SILHOUETTE

Massive bronze doors loomed before the youth, twin sentries barring his entry into the old church. Not that he was interested in entering the church. If so, he could pick the lock on the door in the back, by the parsonage. Its modern design would be an uncomplicated arrangement of either wafers or pins. He wanted to pick the hundred–year–old front door lock, an ancient configuration unlike anything he had tinkered with in his father's hardware store.

The twilight shadows of autumn lengthened as evening slid into night. The youth had stood at the church doors for an hour, but soon it would be too dark for him to continue. Stymied, he acknowledged another defeat—for over a year he had puzzled over this unyielding lock. He gathered the lock picks he had "borrowed" from his father and stepped down the church steps. He stopped, considered a new idea, and returned to the doors. Using an instrument with a long stem and a flat, spade-shaped blade, he probed the keyhole. Whenever he encountered resistance, he moved the instrument left and right, pressing each side of the blockage. Toward the back of the keyhole, he felt a small release, and he pushed the instrument in farther than before, into a series of up and down levers.

He manipulated the levers until he heard the drop of the bar uniting the two doors. He pulled one of the heavy doors open and entered the church's dimly lit vestibule. He would not tell anyone that he had solved the mystery of the old church lock; it was enough that he had done it. His eyes adjusted to the light as he looked around the vestibule. He had not been in the church for over four years. The same tapestries hung on the walls and the same red carpet partially covered the granite floor, emitting a musty scent. A cross, a guest book and a pile of programs were set on a table located against the wall between the two entrances into the nave. On the left side of the vestibule a stairway led up to the organ and choir loft.

He walked into the nave. Spread before him were countless rows of pews, illuminated by twilight rays filtered through stained-glass windows. Two long aisles ran to the transept before the chancel. The transept, perpendicular to the nave, gave the church the shape of a cross. Alcoves at the ends of the transept were hidden behind veils of darkness. He glanced towards the left alcove then looked away; its veil seemed to obscure some sort of threat. Through the dim light he saw the outlines of the pulpit and altar. Ornate brass candlestick holders stood on either side of the altar. Above them hung oversize Biblical tapestries, four on each side. High above the altar, red and blue light emanated from a giant stained-glass cross. He glanced along the smaller stained-glass windows set above the repeating pillars and arches, which extended down both sides of the nave. Shadows hid the walkways behind the pillars.

The sixteen-year-old walked halfway up the aisle and stopped. The giant cross loomed before him—a challenge. He looked up, but darkness hid the high vaulted ceiling. His stomach tightened. The church's immensity, the cold stone floor, the heavy air, and the stained-glass rays melting into darkness felt oppressive, even constricting. He walked back down the aisle, suddenly conscious of a noise that might have been occurring for some time. A low rhythmic creaking, the sound of timber under a periodic stress, came from the choir loft in the back of the church. It was too dark to see the loft and pipe organ at the rear of the loft. He left the nave.

The youth's curiosity about the noise overcame his distaste for the church and he climbed the stairs to the choir loft. The landing was dark. He ran his hands along the walls until he found a switch and flipped on the light. He tiptoed down a short, narrow hall to the choir loft door. The creaking came from behind the door, which he opened.

The outline of a girl's body traced a silhouette against the stained-glass cross. Suspended from a wooden ceiling rafter by a long length of rope, the twisting body on the cross resembled a crucifix. Horrified, but fascinated, the youth stepped down the stairs of the loft towards the girl. Bulging eyes, the puffed up skin covering the noose around her neck, and the fetid odor of waste and death told him that she was not alive. The naked body hung above a white plastic sheet. There was a small pile of clothes on the floor nearby. As he got closer to the girl, he saw moistness on her inner thighs, glistening in the light from the door.

Suddenly, there was no light from the door—it had been shut. In the near darkness, the youth sensed a tall presence moving towards him, but he could not see the apparition's face. The youth backed down the choir loft steps, past the body and into the guardrail beyond the last row of seats. As the apparition advanced towards him, the youth recognized the minister of the church, his face a mask of malice.

Physically, the youth was no match for the minister. As the minister closed in, lunging at him, the youth flipped backwards over the rail. He was lucky—he landed in an aisle, on the floor instead of a pew, and he landed on his feet, so although pain shot up from the balls of his feet to his hips, there were no broken bones. The minister, in his early fifties, was unwilling to make the same leap. The youth, recovering from the pain, looked up towards the choir loft. In a measured baritone the minister spoke from the darkness. "Only those who forsake their lives for my sake will know life everlasting." The voice went flat. "Welcome to hell, Joseph, you're about to see why I'm the Very Reverend Silas Wayne." Too frightened to ponder the significance of the minister's quote or his prophecy, Joseph ran from the church, into the night.

CHAPTER 2

▼

INTIMIDATION

Sergeant Albert Ruprecht, second in command of the Hidden Falls Police Department, sat at his small desk, sipping a cup of coffee and reading a magazine for gun enthusiasts. A half-eaten turkey sandwich rested on a sheet of wax paper. The police station was empty except for Ruprecht and the chief, Bill Marsh. On an autumn Friday night virtually everyone, including most of the police department, attended the high school football game. Tonight was the first game of the playoffs. Ruprecht looked forward to a quiet night, at least until the game was over.

"Excuse me."

Ruprecht peered over his magazine. Standing before his desk was Alice and Jack Tolleson's boy, Joe. Sweat poured from Joe's disheveled mop of straight blond hair and down his oval face, glistening on his clear, fair skin.

His eyes—white circles surrounding deep blue irises, punctuated by the dark periods of his pupils—were wide. He rocked back and forth on his heels and he was panting.

"What can I do for you?" Ruprecht said.

"There's been a murder."

Ruprecht dropped his magazine.

"At the old church. I saw a body hanging in the choir loft. It was a girl and she might have been raped, too. I think Reverend Wayne did it, because he was there, and he tried to catch me. If we hurry back, he might still be there with the body."

Ruprecht's eyes narrowed. "Come with me, this is something the chief has to hear."

Joe followed Ruprecht to Chief Marsh's office, and Ruprecht opened the door. Marsh was putting papers in his briefcase, preparing to leave and meet his family at the football game. He greeted Ruprecht with a look of annoyance. "What is it?"

"I know you're going to the game, but you have to hear this. Joe Tolleson says he's seen a murder out at the old church."

"Bring him in."

They walked into the office. Marsh motioned for Joe to sit in a chair in front of his large, uncluttered desk. The desk's gray metal matched that of the file cabinets lining the office walls. Above the cabinets on one wall hung certificates of professional accomplishment and a diploma from Kentfield, a religiously affiliated college ninety miles from Hidden Falls. Venetian blinds covered the window that looked out on the station. There were no photographs.

Marsh slowly lowered his large frame into the chair behind his desk. His physical strength and courage, and a shrewdness born of both intelligence and experience had made him an excellent street cop. The horizontal lines on his forehead were the only seams on his beefy face. His brown hair, combed back, had scattered streaks of gray. Heavy jowls pulled the corners of his mouth into a permanent frown. Stolid gray eyes directed the professionally impassive gaze of a blackjack dealer or a coroner. He looked through people and was pleased when they were intimidated.

"Start at the beginning, and tell us what you saw. Don't leave anything out." He wrote Tolleson's name, the date and time on a yellow legal pad. Albert Ruprecht sat in a chair behind the chief. His balding head, long, thin, curved nose and close-set, sunken dark eyes gave him the look of a predatory bird.

"I was in the old church—" Joe said.

"How did you get in the church? The Reverend Wayne usually has it locked," Marsh said.

"I pick locks. I taught myself…at my dad's hardware store."

"Do you use your dad's tools?"

"Yeah."

"He's supposed to keep those locked up. Does he know you use them?"

"No."

"I see. Go ahead."

"Today I figured out the lock. I went inside the church and I heard this noise coming from the choir loft. It sounded like wood creaking, but I couldn't see what it was because it was too dark. I went upstairs to the choir loft.

When I opened the door there was a girl's body hanging from a rope, twisting around."

"If it was so dark up there, how could you see that it was a girl's body?"

"I had turned on a light in the hall outside the choir loft and left the door open. I walked towards the body. It was naked and there was a plastic sheet on the floor under it. As I got closer to it I could tell it was a girl's. I could see her face—it was starting to puff up. Also," he said, hesitating, "she had breasts. She might have been raped, too."

"Why do you say that?"

"There was fluid on the inside of her thighs. Just as I got to the body, though, the door closed and it was dark again."

"Who closed the door?"

Joe swallowed hard. He had returned Marsh's unwavering stare, but now he looked away, towards Ruprecht, as he said, "the Reverend Wayne." The sergeant examined him as a hawk examines a field mouse.

"How did you know it was the Reverend Wayne?" Marsh asked.

"At first, all I could see was that it was somebody tall. But as he came down the stairs I could tell it was him. He backed me into the railing and lunged at me. I threw myself back over the rail and landed on the floor."

"Did the man you claim was the Reverend Wayne say anything to you?"

"Yes. When I was on the floor he said: `Only those who forsake their lives for me will know life everlasting. Welcome to hell, Joseph, you're about to find out why I'm the Very Reverend Silas Wayne.' Then I ran out and didn't stop until I got here."

"Is that first sentence from the Bible?"

"I don't know. What difference does it make? Are you going to the church?"

Marsh stared at Joe for a long time. Joe had contained his agitation while telling his story, but he squirmed in his seat through Marsh's silent inspection. Joe returned Marsh's stare, but the chief's face offered no clue as to what he was thinking.

"Would you step into the hall for a moment?" Marsh said.

Ruprecht rose from his chair, stepped to the door and opened it for Joe. Joe left the office and Ruprecht shut the door. Joe sat on a chair in the hall outside the office. He could make out snatches of Ruprecht and Marsh's conversation. He heard Ruprecht say, "investigate." There was an unintelligible rumble from Marsh, until Joe heard "this kid's say so." Another Marsh rumble, and Joe caught the name "Harvey Roach." Ruprecht's unintelligible response seemed to make Marsh angry. Marsh's voice rose and Joe heard the phrase "weirdo," then "I don't give a damn how smart he is." Marsh's voice abruptly dropped and Joe heard nothing more.

After several minutes, the door opened and Ruprecht motioned for Joe to return. Joe sat down. Marsh again stared at him. His gaze never wavered, but his eyes widened in a ferocious glare.

"Son, I've got no idea why you would tell a story like that about the Reverend Wayne, but if you ever tell it again I'll arrest you for trespassing and breaking and entering at the old church. I'm going to do you a favor and forget that you were ever in here. So is Sergeant Ruprecht." Ruprecht nodded. "What you said here will go no farther than this office—I won't even tell your parents. The sergeant will show you to the door and you'd better not pull another stunt like this again. That's all." Marsh nodded in dismissal.

Sergeant Ruprecht shoved Joe to the front of the police station. He gave him a final shove at the station door and said, "good riddance, you little shit," as Joe stumbled down the street. Reentering the station, he encountered the chief, who was leaving for the football game.

Marsh turned to him as they passed in the hall and said, "I did that kid a favor."

CHAPTER 3

▼

THE FIFTH COMMANDMENT

It was a point of pride with Alice Tolleson that she could usually decipher the minute twitches that played across her son's poker face. A slight narrowing of his eyes indicated anger or contempt. When surprised or pleased, he raised his eyebrows enough to form crinkles in his forehead. A barely perceptible widening of his tight, small mouth on the left side was a signal of amusement, usually over something apparent to nobody else. His "sad" look caused her the most problems. When Joe was deep in thought, his eyes drooped, he frowned, and she detected a certain wistfulness. It had taken her a long time to accept his explanation that he was thinking, and that whatever he was thinking about caused him no particular dismay or grief.

Tonight was one of the few times when her son's face was an open window on his emotions. Looking up from her cooking as he entered the kitchen, she saw his confused anguish. Her reproach for delaying the family's dinner died on her lips. Instead, she reached out to embrace him. It was a rare moment of physical contact between them. They stood silently for several moments and then she spoke.

"Something's happened."

Joe nodded.

She put her arm around her son, and they walked into the living room. Jack Tolleson was sitting on a beige sofa, reading a newspaper. His straw blond hair was thinning, and prosperity had brought a few extra pounds, but most people would have been surprised to learn that he had recently hit the mid-century mark. They would have been astonished to find out that his wife had only a few months to go. They sat next to each other and Joe sank into a matching sofa opposite them. Joe told his parents what he had seen at the old church and what had happened at the police station afterwards. His voice occasionally quavered. His parents did not interrupt. After Joe finished his story, Jack turned towards Alice, awaiting her response.

She twice opened her mouth without saying anything. She looked at her husband, then her son and then back at her husband. They expected her to say something, but she could not. Finally Jack broke the silence.

"Joe, when you saw the body, did you actually touch it?"

"No."

"And when the Reverend Wayne tried to attack you, did he actually touch you?"

"No."

There was another long silence.

"You say you didn't touch the body?" Alice asked.

No, Mom."

"And Silas didn't touch you?"

"No, Mom. Why do you repeat the same questions, do you think I'm making this up?"

"I think you believe you saw what you said you saw."

"Joe," Jack said, "it may not be a question of believing or not believing you, it may be a question of what we can do about it. I think that Chief Marsh and Sergeant Ruprecht's reaction is typical of how most people in this town would react if you told them what you saw. You know the Reverend Wayne. If you're going to make an accusation against him, you have to have some sort of proof."

Alice suddenly sprang from the sofa and began pacing in front of the living room's large picture window, agitated. "I don't believe," she stammered, her voice high and brittle, "I don't believe that Silas would do what you said he did. I simply don't believe it."

"Mom, I know what I saw."

"No, I'm not sure you do. Think about it. You were out at the church around nightfall, weren't you?"

"Yes."

"As much as I love that old church, at twilight it's spooky when the lights aren't on. You were brave to wander around the church, but you must have been a little scared. Sometimes, when people are scared, their minds play tricks on them. They see visions in the shadows and invent things to fulfill their fears."

"Mom, I saw a girl's body hanging above the choir loft, and I saw the minister."

She walked over to the couch on which Joe was sitting and sat down beside him. She squeezed his hand. "Honey, so many things happen that we don't understand. Your father and I love you and we're proud of you. However, we can't always believe what we think we see. When we're

young, there doesn't seem to be any limit on what we can
do. As you get older, you'll discover your limits. There's so
much more than we can ever grasp with our senses."

Joe turned to his father. "Dad, do you believe this?"

Jack met Joe's steady gaze. "Son, I agree with your
mother that in a place like that old church, your mind can
play tricks on you. I don't think you're making this up, but
I think she's right, what you think you saw might not be
what actually happened. It's hard to believe that the
Reverend Wayne would do something like this."

"Joe, your father and I have known Silas for thirty
years. He married us. He baptized you. I've never met a
kinder, more caring person." Jack nodded. "Everybody in
this town could tell you about something Silas has done
for them. I can't believe that he could do the things you
say he's done." She squeezed her son's hand again. "I know
you won't agree with this, but it could be that you're being
tested. You're very proud and you've rejected our religion.
However, just because you've forgotten God doesn't mean
that he's forgotten you. Perhaps what you think you saw in
the church is part of God's plan to show you that you've
made a mistake."

"How?"

"I don't know. He works in ways that we don't always
understand."

Joe slumped.

"Joe," his father said, "if anything happened out at the
old church, it won't stay hidden for long. If there was a
dead girl, she had to have a name and a family. We can
come forward if something turns up. Until it does, the
police obviously won't help us and neither will anyone
else. You can't accuse the Reverend Wayne without being

able to prove what you say." An unmistakable sternness crept into his voice. "For the time being, it's best that you don't say anything to anybody."

"I think that's a good idea," Alice said.

Joe closed his eyes for several moments, choking down his disgust while gathering his strength. He stood and slowly walked towards the stairs leading up to his bedroom. He turned towards his parents.

"The police use force and intimidation and you use faith and love. Either way, you're not going to keep me quiet." He went up the stairs.

Alice and Jack stared silently at each other for a long time. Finally, Alice stood and walked through the living room and entryway. She looked, as she always did, at her wavy blonde hair, sparkling blue eyes and homecoming queen face in the entryway mirror. She went into a small bathroom. Jack absently reached for the remote control for the big screen television, turned it on and switched to the news channel. Perplexed by his son's story, he paid no attention to the stories on a new trade treaty, the plight of the homeless, and the pending divorce of a famous actor and actress.

Alice emerged from the bathroom, went into the kitchen, finished preparing dinner, and set the table. Although Jack called upstairs to Joe for dinner, Joe did not come.

"Should I go get him?" Jack asked.

"Maybe it's best if you don't."

They sat at the dinner table and ate in silence. Finally, Jack took a drink of milk, wiped his mouth with his napkin and cleared his throat.

"You know, honey, you hear about these priests and ministers and how they've done all sorts of terrible things. Do you think it's possible that Silas did what Joe said he did?"

Alice placed her fork on her plate. Jack had never seen the severe, completely closed expression his wife's face now assumed. There was a long moment of silence.

"No."

They ate the rest of their meal without speaking.

*   *   *

A point—the basic geometric unit, indivisible, the smallest space greater than nothing. A line—a series of contiguous points. A plane—a surface that completely contains every straight line joining any two points lying in it. A cell—a series of contiguous, parallel planes. A crystal—a three dimensional structure consisting of periodically repeated, identically constituted, congruent unit cells. The complexity of a crystal is reducible to its constituent elements—cells, planes, lines and points. As an ordered array, crystalline structure can be defined by the symbolic logic of mathematics. The equations of physics describe how the path of light will be reflected and refracted by a crystal.

Joe thought of his own mind as a crystal—mental constructs built of less complicated elements reducible to their integral components; thoughts structured in a logical progression; the path of information ordered as life was arranged into an algorithmic code of premises and conclusions. The essence of understanding was simplification. $E=MC^2$—the universe described by an equation. That was the way his mind worked—the complex reduced to its simplest possible representation.

As he lay in bed that night, his crystal was shattered—bombarded by a kaleidoscopic chaos of images, sensations and random emotions. Whether he opened or closed his eyes, he saw the old church, the hanging corpse, Silas Wayne, Marsh's indifference, Ruprecht's hostility, his mother's anxiety, and his father's confused deference. Bathed in a pool of sweat, alternately feverish and chilled, several times he thought he would vomit. He could smell and taste the choir loft odor of waste and death. Tears trickled down his face as wave after wave of terror, anxiety and anger overwhelmed him.

Only after hours of emotional turmoil was he conscious of fragments of thought—mostly questions. Why did Wayne do it? Who was the girl? How could the police refuse to consider his story? Why didn't his parents believe him? Was it possible that he hadn't seen what he thought he had seen? Could he trust his senses? This last troubling question he kept repeating to himself.

Long after midnight a semblance of order returned to his thinking. Could he trust his senses? If he didn't, how could he survive? There were optical illusions, but what he had seen was no illusion. Yes, the church was a frightening place, but he hadn't conjured up imaginary horrors. If he'd been that frightened, he wouldn't have gone up to the choir loft. But what was he to do about what he had seen there? His mother's attempt to induce doubt about his perceptions frightened him. He did not question his rationality, but hers. How did she survive if she actually believed what she had said?

He would not forget what he had seen. He had to expose the truth about Silas Wayne. Tired, overwrought and unable to formulate a plan, he nevertheless felt more composed as the early morning light poked through his window. The night's terror and confusion had been replaced by grim determination. Somehow, he would find the proof his father said they needed. And if his parents wanted silence from him, that's what they'd get. His eyes felt puffy, but they were wide open as he stared at the ceiling. It would be difficult to develop the case against Silas Wayne. The preacher had some power over the people of Hidden Falls that he did not understand.

His father knocked on his door. Every Saturday they went to the hardware store together. Joe dressed and went downstairs to eat breakfast with his father. They did not speak at breakfast or as they drove to the store; Joe rebuffed his father's attempts to make conversation. At the store he numbly went through the motions of an interminable day. He misstocked several items and twice rang up the wrong price on the cash register. Finally the day came to an end and Joe and Jack drove home, again without speaking. Ignoring his mother's anxious inquiries, Joe skipped dinner and went to his room. Exhausted, he barely managed to take off his clothes before he fell into bed and slept—his first respite from the previous day.

CHAPTER 4

THE SABBATH

"Let us pray."

The Very Reverend Silas Wayne stood at his pulpit. The gigantic stained-glass cross loomed above him. The church's tall stone walls and vaulted ceiling made the congregation look small, although people filled most of the high-backed, unpadded wooden pews. Multicolored light rays from stained-glass windows illuminated dust motes, suspended high in the air. Forty members of the choir and the organist sat in the choir loft above and behind the congregation. Behind them, on the back wall, the pipes of the organ gleamed.

"Our Father who art in Heaven, hallowed be thy name."

The minister surveyed the bowed heads of his congregation while he led them in the Lord's Prayer. They were bound to him by gossamer skeins—all those who told him their troubled secrets, accepted his consolation and then his advice, and were gently prodded down the path of righteousness. He crept about his web, spinning silken strands, vigilant, aware of any disturbance in a carefully constructed, delicately balanced world. As the prayer drew to a close, he found Sergeant Albert Ruprecht of the Hidden Falls Police Department, in his customary seat in the third row. Silas smiled.

Fifteen years ago, when Ruprecht was a sophomore in high school, he attended a church picnic. He wandered off with another boy to an isolated spot by the river. Silas happened upon the two while Ruprecht was performing fellatio on the other boy. Silas said nothing, but later he offered to give Ruprecht a ride home from the picnic. They rode in silence for some time; Ruprecht was terrified.

"Albert," Silas said, "at your age everyone is confused by sex and what's happening to their bodies. It seems as if things are out of control. That's why God is so important to you now; he can help you understand yourself and what you're going through. What happened today by the river will stay our secret. I'm sure the fellow you were with won't say anything. However, the Bible condemns homosexuality, Albert, because it's a sin. You're going to need help dealing with this. I want you to know that I'll help you— we can work this thing out."

Ruprecht's eyes widened. Perhaps the only thing he actually heard Silas say was that what he had done would stay a secret. "Yes, sir," he stammered, ashamed but grateful. "I know what I did was wrong. I don't want to do anything like that again."

The problem was that he did want to do what he had done—again and again. He guiltily admitted this to the

Reverend Wayne about a year after their initial conversation. He could not stop thinking about it, no matter how frequently he prayed and followed the minister's other prescriptions. Eventually a tacit bargain was struck. While Silas could not condone sin, he told Ruprecht that his secret would be safe as long as Ruprecht settled in Hidden Falls, but relieved his sexual tensions elsewhere. Ruprecht left Hidden Falls for college and, afraid to challenge Wayne's implicit threat, returned to a position that the preacher arranged for him in the police training program.

"For thine is the kingdom, and the power, and the glory forever. Amen. Now please turn to hymn 267, 'Gladly the Cross I'd Bear'."

Silas led a sea of uplifted faces in song. "Amen," the minister intoned, when the last strains of the hymn died in the torpid church air. "Brother Hodges will read today's scripture, from Matthew, chapter eight, verses one through 33." A middle-aged gentleman stepped up from the first row and walked to the pulpit. Silas moved to the side of the altar.

The scripture was an illustration of Silas's favorite theme—the necessity and power of faith. Hodges read verses about Jesus healing a leper, a paralyzed boy and the apostle Peter's feverish mother-in-law; Jesus calming the rising waters and then casting demons into a herd of pigs. When he finished, Silas stepped to the pulpit.

"Thank you, Brother Hodges." He paused to allow Hodges to return to his seat. After arranging his papers on the pulpit, he began his sermon. His topic that morning followed that of the scripture passage—faith. In his magnificently sonorous baritone, he talked of the conflict between selfish desires and God's plans, highlighting his theme as it applied to the choice of a person's career. He admonished his flock to abandon "popular magazine conceptions of self-esteem and happiness" by striving to attain the impossible standard of Christian selflessness. To address inevitable doubts, he counseled unswerving faith in a "higher logic that accepts God's will."

Silas had preached variants of this sermon many times and almost had it memorized. Several times he looked up and scanned his flock. Where was Alice? Alice, whose life had been a great, albeit still incomplete, triumph of God's will. Sometimes poor Alice felt that she was working at cross-purposes with herself. The necessity and power of faith. He could not find Alice; she was not in the pew towards the back where she and Jack usually sat.

"Those who ask about earthly pleasure and happiness are asking the wrong questions. Rather, your concern should be with the fate of your souls through eternity. We turn to faith as our answer to the question of our brief, often empty life on this earth. We are afraid, and faith allows us to surmount our fears. We are afraid of ourselves and our capacity to sin, we are afraid of separation from the flock, and we are afraid of death. Christ teaches us that the denial, rather than the assertion, of ourselves—the acceptance of God's plan for our life—is the key to our chances for life everlasting."

He paused and again looked out at the congregation. He finally spotted Alice, sitting more towards the front than where she usually sat. He felt an odd sense of relief. And there was Jack. And Joseph. What the hell was he doing here?

Joe had surprised his parents that morning by asking to attend the church service. Now he sat with them, intently watching Silas. The minister was looking their way and his and Joe's eyes briefly met. Slowly, deliberately, Joe turned his head and looked towards the choir loft. When he turned back, Silas had looked away. Joe thought he detected a waver in Silas's voice as the minister continued his sermon. A small victory for Joseph—he had thrown down the gauntlet.

Silas regained his form and Joe's attention wandered. Even with the stress of his recent confrontation with the minister, church bored him. He had been baptized as an infant, but had not been brought to a regular service until he was five years old. He had instinctively rejected everything he had witnessed. The assembled congregation seemed to be engaged in a ritual of mass self-abasement. The term "worship" was distasteful to him—subordinating one's self to an unseen God. Watching the heads bowed in a prayer of confession and pleading, he had felt a visceral disgust. He was just discovering his own capabilities, exploring life's possibilities. He was too young to formulate metaphysical criticisms, but he had detested the tone of servility and sorrow and vowed never to become a part of it.

Now he looked around the church. Silas's melodic baritone held the worshippers in a kind of trance. Themes were stated and recapitulated as his voice waxed and waned. He would build to a crescendo, gradually increasing his volume and intensity as he made his point. Then he would diminish the tension with a few summary sentences in a soothing tone, his voice low, yet still powerful. Joe turned towards his mother and father. Her eyes shined and his were half closed as his head nodded slowly back and forth. Joe tried concentrating on Silas's sermon, but it was a senseless exercise, like hearing poetry in a foreign language. He recognized the beauty and rhythmic order of the words, but they conveyed no meaning to him. Silas's words were to be felt, not considered. As a child, Joe had usually fallen asleep during sermons. Now, seeking logic in the illogical, his eyelids grew heavy. Yielding to his old narcosis, he recalled the quote about the "opiate of the masses" and fell asleep.

The closing hymn awakened him. He rubbed his eyes and wondered if anyone had noticed that he had slept, and then decided that he did not care if they had. The last note of the last verse died and the congregation slowly filed out of the church. The Reverend Wayne was there to greet them. He smiled at Alice and Jack as he clasped their hands. Then, shaking Joe's hand, he said, "I hope you found the sermon instructive, Joseph."

Joe looked directly into the killer's gray-green eyes. "Very enlightening," he said. He pulled his hand away and proceeded down the church steps.

                *   *   *

Sunday evening, Alice stood at the deluxe stove in the Tolleson's spacious, state-of-the-art kitchen, preparing dinner. She smiled. Jack and Joe would never waste an afternoon watching football games. Jack was at one of his car dealerships, and Joe was at the hardware store. She tried to maintain the dinner hour as a focal point for her family, the one time of day when they were together. Sunday dinner was usually the most elaborate meal of the week. Tonight she had prepared all their old favorites— roast beef, potatoes and gravy, corn on the cob and a cherry cobbler. This meal would be a small step towards restoring her family to normalcy.

She heard her husband's Cadillac pull into the driveway.

He entered from the garage.

"Hello dear," he said, walking over to her and lightly kissing her on the cheek. He grabbed a beer from the refrigerator and sat down at the kitchen table.

"Hello, darling. How did it go today?"

"Pretty busy for a Sunday. Mostly lookers, though. People still aren't opening their wallets."

"Well, it'll pick up." A subconscious irritant, hitherto unnoticed, suddenly pushed to the forefront of her consciousness. "Say, Jack, was something wrong with Silas this morning?"

"I didn't notice."

"He looked over at us and then he looked away, but after he looked away it seemed as if he had a little trouble with the sermon."

"Did he see Joe? Did Joe do anything?"

"I don't know, I wasn't watching Joe."

They heard the front door opening.

"Joe," Jack shouted, "is that you? Dinner's almost ready, go wash up."

A short while later the family sat down for dinner. Serving several slices of roast beef, Alice said to Joe, "thank you for coming to services this morning."

"Sure."

Joe's confusion about his parents had metastasized into rage. They'd get nothing but monosyllables tonight.

"How were things at the hardware store?" his father asked.

"Slow."

"Yeah, it always slows down at the end of the fall. We won't start selling winter merchandise until next month. By now, everybody's bought their rakes and lawn mowers."

He looked directly at his father. They either thought he was lying or they were willing to ignore a murder and a rape. Which was worse? His respect for them was dying and he felt like crying. He winced—his thoughts were starting to sound like bad country music.

"Uh huh."

Joe ate less than usual and quickly excused himself. He picked up the *Hidden Falls Herald* from the living room coffee table and went upstairs to his bedroom.

Flipping through the newspaper, he noticed a grainy photograph under a headline entitled "Newcomers to Hidden Falls." The man's face in the photograph was the one of the ugliest he had ever seen—heavy jowls, bulging dark eyes, two scars on his forehead and a prominent nose that appeared to have been broken repeatedly, pointing in a different direction than the rest of his face. His neck was wider than his head—the hallmark of football players, wrestlers and body-builders.

No surprise then, that the man had indeed been a football player. Joe read the blurb accompanying the photograph. His name was Gary Benewski. He had played tackle in college, until a career ending knee injury. He had gone to law school, and then to the district attorney's office in Tyler City, in the southern part of the state. He had left shortly after conducting an investigation into political corruption. Benewski was a law school classmate of Mike Devore, the local district attorney, and had recently moved to Hidden Falls to join Devore's staff.

Joe examined the picture. The unyielding scowl, bull mastiff jowls and direct, intently focused stare—it was an intimidating face. Being new to Hidden Falls, Benewski probably didn't know Silas Wayne. Joe was unsure of how responsibility was divided in the criminal justice system. Perhaps the district attorney's office could conduct an investigation independently of the police department. He would call Benewski in the morning.

CHAPTER 5

▼

INVESTIGATION

Joe called Gail Smathers, Gary Benewski's secretary, early the next day and made an appointment. After school, he drove past the town hall and parked two blocks away. The police department was also in the town hall and he did not want to take a chance on his car being recognized in the parking lot. He was greeted in an outer office by Smathers and after a brief wait, was shown into Benewski's office. He told his story to Benewski, who betrayed no reaction while he recounted the events of the previous Friday. Benewski asked several questions, taking notes on the answers.

While Benewski wrote, Joe studied his face. The newspaper photograph didn't do him justice; he was much uglier in person. His mangled nose was more misshapen than in the photograph and he had numerous small scars, which had not been visible. He had probably shaved for that picture, but now, towards the end of the day, he had a dark five o'clock shadow.

"Is there anything else?" Benewski asked.

Joe hesitated. "Do you believe me?"

"Joe, I'll open an investigation. That's all I can say. If you need to talk to me, here's my card with my phone number."

It was one notch better than being peremptorily dismissed, but Joe still felt disappointed. He had one other question.

"Do you have to notify the police department that you are conducting an investigation?"

"No."

Joe felt better. He even smiled slightly as he exchanged pleasantries with Ms. Smathers on the way out.

It was a weird, unfortunate coincidence that he left the office at the same time as Sergeant Ruprecht came out of the men's room across the hall. They almost ran into each other. Joe felt a knot form in his stomach. Ruprecht looked down at Joe and Joe could see the surprise on his face dissolving to anger. Ruprecht hurried away.

Walking back to his car, Joe reflected bitterly on the uselessness of his precaution in parking away from the town hall. Now Ruprecht knew that he had talked to someone in the district attorney's office.

Back in his office, Benewski leaned back in his chair, analyzing what he had just heard. Children and adolescents could fabricate a story, especially if they believed it was what adults wanted to hear. However, Joe had told his story with quiet gravity, demonstrating maturity beyond his sixteen years. He had met the simple test of being able to look Benewski in the eye as he talked, although there were times when he could not hide his distress. It would not be the first time that a religious figure had committed a crime. There was also the question of Joe's motivation. Why would he make up that kind of story about the minister?

A suspicion was a hypothesis, not a fact. He needed information about both Silas Wayne and Joe Tolleson and he needed physical evidence, especially the body. He picked up the phone and spoke to his boss, Mike Devore.

"Mike, do you have a minute? I need to talk to you."

"Sure, come on over."

Everything through channels. There would be no more Tyler Citys—he needed this job. He walked to Devore's office, next door to his.

The assistant district attorney was aware of his boss's alert scrutiny as he settled his bulk into the chair across from his desk. Devore was a much smaller man than Benewski and it seemed odd that their positions at the desk were not reversed. Devore was slender, five feet eight inches tall. Out of a sense of professionalism, rather than vanity, he was quite conscious of his appearance. It was important, he had once told Benewski, to convey the right impression to judges and juries. His expensive, tailored suit was an understated charcoal gray, with a burgundy tie and white shirt. He was 37 years old and beginning to acquire the valuable signs of maturity. His short dark brown hair, which he combed back, was turning gray at the temples. Tiny crow's feet wrinkles had made their appearance around his alert blue eyes. Horn-rimmed glasses accentuated the owlish effect of his narrow face. His examined Benewski with intent, unwavering concentration.

"What can I do for you?"

"Who is Silas Wayne?"

Devore took off his glasses and carefully placed them on his desk. From the inside breast pocket of his suit coat (he seldom took off his coat) he removed a neatly folded cloth and placed it beside his glasses. He unfolded the cloth, fold by fold, and then picked up his glasses. He breathed on one of the lenses and cleaned it with the cloth. He repeated this ritual on the other lens and inspected both lenses. After putting his glasses back on, he folded the cloth, fold by fold, and put it back in his coat pocket.

"If you asked a lot of people in this town to draw God, you'd get a picture of the Reverend Wayne. You've seen the massive old church as you first come into town?" Benewski nodded. "Silas Wayne is the minister of that church. You can't help running into him once in a while. He's tall and gaunt, with dark, graying hair and a stern face, in his mid-fifties. He's the most influential person in town and his influence is expanding beyond Hidden Falls. Last year he became the chairman of the denominational regional conference. He's a good friend of Bert Weathin, the TV evangelist. They were seminary classmates. Why do you ask?"

"I just finished talking with a kid, Joe Tolleson, who says he saw the corpse of a girl strung up in the choir loft of Wayne's church last Friday. He thinks the girl was raped. He said that Wayne was in the choir loft when he found the body. Wayne tried to catch him, but he jumped out of the choir loft. He also says that the police threatened to charge him with trespassing at the church if he told anyone else his story, and that his own parents don't believe him."

Devore slowly nodded his head. He leaned back in his chair, folded his hands and rested them on his stomach. "What did you think of Tolleson?"

"He's pretty smart. Sincerity's the easiest thing to fake, but I think he could be telling the truth."

"'Pretty smart' is an understatement. He's got an IQ that's off the charts and he was born to the right parents. His mother is still the prettiest woman in town. His father owns a number of local businesses and is quite wealthy. Who did he talk to in the police department?"

"Chief Marsh and a Sergeant Ruprecht."

"And he says they told him to be quiet and go away?"

"That's about it. He says they wouldn't even go out to the church to investigate."

"And his parents?"

"His mother gave him some religious mumbo jumbo, and his dad went along with it. They also told him not to tell his story to anyone else."

"What did you tell him?"

"I told him I'd open an investigation."

"The Reverend Wayne is at least partially responsible for my being district attorney. Nobody can get elected to anything in this town without his approval. When we first moved here seven years ago, Vicki and I joined his church. When I ran for district attorney four years ago, after David Helms retired, I ran unopposed because I had his endorsement."

Benewski's eyes narrowed; the concern on his face was easy to read.

"Don't worry," Devore said, "not everybody's corrupt. Open an investigation, both of the possible murder and rape and of the police department's reaction to Joe Tolleson's story. The first issue will be the identity of the dead girl. If there's been a crime committed, Joe Tolleson and Silas Wayne are to be regarded as equally suspect, so conduct your investigation accordingly. Silas Wayne knows every person worth knowing in Hidden Falls. Be discrete. There's something unusual about his way with people. You'll have to live here a while before you understand the kind of power he has. It's an old fashioned term, but you could say that he's venerated. Let me know what you find."

"Okay."

He walked to the door. As he turned the handle, Devore said, "remember, be discrete."

*   *   *

That night, Joe had a disturbing dream. He was in a low place, a canyon whose walls were darkness. Before him was a ladder ascending to a high platform that was barely a speck in the sky. The platform was next to a set of railroad tracks. The tracks formed the horizontal top of a "T" with the ladder and stretched in either direction to distant points on the horizon where the parallel rails met. There was red-orange glow on the right horizon. It was dark in the bottom of the canyon, but it grew lighter as he climbed the ladder.

As he progressed upward, the glow to his right came closer. It was a train, drawn by an old fashioned coal-fired locomotive. After climbing the ladder for what seemed a long time, he reached the platform and waited for the locomotive.

The locomotive pulled up to the platform and he could see Silas Wayne standing in the engineer's compartment at the head of the train. The minister was dressed in a flowing, hooded black robe, which, like a black hole, seemed to suck in the light generated by the coal burner. The robe was drawn closed at the waist by a white rope belt. Around the minister's neck was a golden chain with an ivory cross pendant.

The train stopped at the platform, and Silas looked expectantly towards him. Joe averted his eyes, looking at the passenger car behind the locomotive. In two of the windows he saw the floating faces of his mother and father. They looked at him with the same expectancy as Silas. He looked back towards Silas. Two red hot coals replaced the minister's eyes. Their laser-like beams penetrated the back of his eyes. He held Silas's gaze for a long time. Finally, the train pulled away from the platform. As the train went by, he saw many disembodied faces. Some he knew, some he did not. He saw Sergeant Ruprecht. He watched the train until its red-orange glow met with the point on the left horizon where the two rails seemed to merge into one.

He awoke, gasping and sweating. After a long while his anxiety subsided and he fell back asleep.

CHAPTER 6

▼

DISAPPEARANCE

The next morning Gary Benewski entered the anteroom of his and Mike Devore's offices. Gail Smathers was already at her desk, typing. Smathers was in her mid-thirties, a pretty brunette with blue eyes and a quick smile. She was pleasant and hard working. She had emigrated from Great Britain with her family when she was sixteen, but she retained her British accent, reserve, and sense of humor. She was married to an accountant and they had two children.

"Good morning, Gail. Would you call the three junior high schools and the high school and get the names of all the female students who were absent from school Monday and today? When you get the names, try to find out if there are any whose whereabouts are unknown."

"Certainly, Gary." It had taken two weeks of good natured insistence by Benewski before his secretary would call him by his first name. "Mr. Devore had a question for you." Devore did not insist that she call him by his first name.

"Thanks." He walked into his office, put his overcoat and coat on a stand in the corner and sat at his large, gray, government-issue desk. He buzzed Devore.

"What do you need, Mike?"

"I was thinking about this Tolleson case last night. How did Joe Tolleson get into the church?"

"He picked the lock on the main church door. His father owns a hardware store and he taught himself how to pick locks."

"That's odd. Why would he do that?"

"You would know better than I. He didn't tell me why he learned to pick locks. Sometimes these bright ones are a little strange."

"And what's that got to do with me?"

"Oh, nothing, nothing at all. Have you taken off your coat yet?"

"Talk to you later, smart ass."

A short time later, Gail buzzed, "Gary, the schools will have the names you requested later this morning."

"Thanks. I don't know the name of the principal at the high school, but would you call him for me? Identify yourself and then put him through to me."

A minute later, Gail buzzed again, "Gary, I have the principal, Art Mendolson, on the line."

"Thanks. Good morning, Mr. Mendolson. I'm Gary Benewski, the assistant district attorney. I'm calling to ask about one of your students, Joe Tolleson."

"I'm surprised someone from the district attorney's office would be asking about him." Mendolson paused, evidently awaiting some explanation.

After an awkward silence, Benewski asked, "how long have you known Joe Tolleson?"

"Since he was a small child. He skipped the first grade. Two years ago he entered Hidden Falls High School at the age of fourteen. This is his senior year. He has the highest grade point average in his class, he's fluent in German and French, he loves computers, and he plays the violin and piano. He's applying to most of the prestigious colleges and he'll have no trouble getting accepted. I don't see him much around the high school anymore. Most of his classes now are at the branch college of the state university."

"Has Tolleson ever got into any kind of trouble or presented a disciplinary problem?"

"No, not at all. Joe goes his own way; he's a loner. There was only one incident I can tell you about, in his sophomore year, and he wasn't at fault."

"Uh huh."

"We have a large lobby with benches where the kids congregate during breaks. Joe was walking through there one day. He was reading a book and not watching where he was going. He walked by a bench where Scott Maguire was sitting. Maguire was a senior and the star running back on the football team. He was sitting with his girlfriend and a couple of his friends. Just to get a laugh, he stuck out his foot and tripped Joe. Even though Joe is small for his age, he doesn't usually get picked on."

"What did he do?"

"He stood up, then he turned around, towards where Maguire and his friends were laughing. He said, 'Aren't you Scott Maguire?'

"Maguire said, 'Yeah, that's me.'

"Then Joe said, 'You scored three touchdowns last week against Rushton Valley.'

"Maguire said, 'Yeah, I did. What about it?'

"Joe said, 'Enjoy the limelight, asshole, because that's going to be the high point of your whole life. Everything is downhill from here. You won't even make it out of Hidden Falls.'

"Well, at first everybody was too stunned to say anything, but then Maguire's girlfriend started laughing at him. He was furious. He picked up Joe, slammed him against the wall and gave him a black eye and bloody nose. Joe was lucky that Coach Gowan walked through the lobby. He pulled Maguire off before Joe really got hurt. You know, the funny thing is, Joe was right; Maguire hasn't made it out of Hidden Falls. He's working as a short order cook over at Brigg's Diner."

"Wow, that's quite a story," Benewski said, remembering some of the self-absorbed brats with whom he had played football. "Do you ever talk with Joe's teachers about him?"

"Anybody as bright as Joe is going to be talked about. He intimidates a lot of teachers, but Barbara Martel, the math teacher, raves about him. In junior high school, Joe was on a structured program in math where he worked at his own pace. By the time he reached high school he was eligible to take calculus 1B, which is normally a senior level course. After two weeks of the fall semester Barbara ran into the teacher's lounge, and she could barely contain herself. I've never seen her so excited. She said she couldn't figure Joe out at first, because he sat in back of the class, not looking at her while she lectured and never taking notes. Are you familiar with the fundamental theorem of integral calculus?"

"It's been a long time since I took a math class."

"Well, it's the foundation of integral calculus, and it's difficult to understand. Most students don't get it until their second or third calculus class. Barbara was lecturing and she looked at Joe. He appeared to be oblivious, leaning back in his chair with his eyes closed. She asked him about the fundamental theorem.

"Without saying anything, Joe walked to the front of the room. He did a proof of the theorem on the blackboard, explaining each step as he went along. Barbara said she had never seen that particular proof of the theorem, but it was correct and easier to understand than hers. When Joe finished, he returned to his seat without saying another word.

"Let me tell you another story about Joe," said the principal, apparently warming to his subject. "One day I visited Henry Blake's American history class. He was lecturing on the Constitution. You're a lawyer, so I'm sure you know a lot about the Constitution."

"More than I know about calculus."

"Well, at one point in his lecture Blake said that the Constitution was primarily concerned with the protection of political, not economic, rights. Joe raised his hand and said 'you're wrong.' Henry invited Joe to elaborate. For ten minutes Joe talked about the Constitution. His voice was steady and he didn't use notes. He had done his research. He talked about the unamended Constitution's prohibition of a direct tax, pointing out that the Revolutionary War had started over a matter of taxation. He mentioned the commerce clause, the contract clause and the 'takings' clause. He argued that the prosperous merchants and farmers who wrote the Constitution were concerned with both economic and political liberty. He concluded that it was impossible to separate the two. It was a powerful argument. I have to give Henry credit. He probably didn't like being upstaged by his pupil, but all he said was 'I stand corrected.'"

"That says something about the teacher. When was the last time you actually talked to Joe?"

"About two months ago, just after the fall term started. We make it a point to have the guidance counselor, Christy Jastrow, or me, talk with every senior about their plans for the future. I talked to Joe. He said he wanted to study music and either computer science or physics and he already knew where he was going to apply to college. Like I said, he's going to have his choice of schools and his father can afford to send him anywhere. There was one interesting moment, though. I asked him what he liked to do."

"What did he say?"

"He said, 'I like to think. I like original ideas, especially mine. I get excited when I think of something I've never thought of before. It feels like my mind is on fire. Sometimes I stay up all night, thinking about new things.' I've never heard a student say anything like that.

"Then I asked him what he didn't like. He's stoic, so it's hard to tell, but I think he got a little wistful. He said, 'Most of the time when I've thought of something new, I want to talk about it with somebody else. I can't seem to do that, I've tried. The other kids think I'm weird, and some of the teachers do, too.' Now I'm not particularly creative—"

"Neither am I, maybe that's why we both work for the government."

"That's funny." Mendolson said, not laughing. "Not being particularly creative, it's hard for us to understand how difficult it can be to be brighter and more original than everybody else. I hope Joe finds college more stimulating."

"Yes, it sounds like he needs a lot of challenges. Thank you for your time, Mr. Mendolson, and please keep this conversation confidential."

"Of course. Good-bye, Mr. Benewski."

"Good-bye."

Benewski leaned back in his chair. Beneath Joe's intimidating brilliance there was vulnerability—he attributed to others his own benign motives. He walked through a crowded lobby with his nose in his book, trusting that no one would annoy him. He corrected his teacher in a spirit of dispassionate intellectual discourse. And then last Friday perhaps everything changed—the lamb discovered the wolf.

His secretary buzzed.

"Gary, the schools have returned my calls. There are six female students who were absent yesterday and today."

"Okay, call their homes and see if there are any who can't be accounted for. Also, would you bring in the Tolleson file?"

"Certainly."

Smathers buzzed again a few minutes later. "Gary, I can't find the Tolleson file. Shouldn't it be between the Robinson and the Townsend files?"

Like most attorneys, Benewski was compulsively organized. "Yes, it should be. I put it there last night."

"I'll look again."

Smathers walked in a moment later. "Here's the Tolleson file. It was between the Quincy and Randall files."

"Thanks. I'm going to the bakery for a doughnut. Do you want anything?"

"Just a coffee, thanks."

When Benewski returned Smathers said, "Gary, there's one girl who's been missing since last Friday. I called Nancy Walton about her daughter, Marsha. When I identified myself as being with the district attorney's office, her first words were 'what's Marsha got herself into now?' I asked her why her daughter was absent from school Monday and today. She said that Marsha had run away Friday. Then she got very sarcastic and said, 'I'm surprised the district attorney's office would call me about it. She's run away twice before and I reported it to the police, but they never do anything about it. This time I didn't bother.'"

"Call her back and tell her I'd like to see her. Get her address and set up a time for me to talk with her."

An hour later, Benewski pulled his car up to the Walton residence, in the poor section of town. A partially uprooted, unpainted picket fence surrounded a front yard of weeds. A ten-year-old Chevy sat in the dirt driveway. On the weather-beaten wood porch a broken swinging loveseat creaked on rusty hinges. The one story, clapboard house was coated in peeling white paint. He knocked on the front door and peered in the kitchen window. A layer of grime made the dark interior seem even darker. A light went on in a distant part of the house.

After a few moments the front door opened. "Hello, handsome, what can I do for you?"

"Mrs. Walton?"

"Yes."

"I'm Gary Benewski, from the district attorney's office."

"Come in."

Nancy Walton's voice had the huskiness of too many cocktails and cigarettes. She was in her late thirties. Despite the cocktails, cigarettes, and other self-destructive efforts, she was still attractive. Her original hair color was indeterminable beneath a blonde tint with platinum high-lights. A pretty face was unnecessarily hidden by bright make-up and she wore a cynical expression that mocked evil and good without distinction. Hard blue eyes, encir-cled by crimson rims, destroyed the intended effect of heavy mascara and eye shadow. Her purple sweater, black skirt, hosiery and high heels were cheap, but showed off her well proportioned figure. She led him through the kitchen, where Benewski noticed several half empty liquor bottles on the counter. He declined her offer of coffee. The poorly lit living room smelled of dust and tobacco. Benewski sat on a Naugahyde recliner and she sat across a chipped, wooden coffee table on a hide-a-bed sofa. She crossed her legs and lit a cigarette. Her nail polish matched the redness of her lipstick and eyes.

"Mrs. Walton—"

"Call me Nancy."

"Nancy, you told my secretary, Gail Smathers, that you haven't seen your daughter since last Thursday. You believe that she's run away?"

"That's right. Marsha's not a bad girl, but she's pretty and she's running with a fast crowd. She'll be fifteen next

February and she's in her last year at the junior high school. When she pays attention she does well in school, but she's got a mouth on her and she can be a first class bitch. I can't imagine where she gets it from." Walton rolled her eyes. "Anyway, she's been getting into trouble. Last year, she got sent home from school for a day after mouthing off to one of her teachers. About six months ago she left for the first time. She was gone for two days before she came back. She wouldn't say a word about where she went or what she had done. She left again two months ago, right around Labor Day. She was gone for four days."

"You must have been worried. Did you call the police?"

"I went down to the station, but those guys are jerks. They make you feel like a criminal and I don't need the leers. They took reports, but didn't do anything else. I'm worried about Marsha, but she's come back before and she'll come back again. She's tough, and I've taught her a thing or two about taking care of herself. Why are you here? Are you the district attorney or a truant officer?"

"I'm an assistant district attorney, and Marsha's disappearance may be connected with a matter under investigation by our office. I'd like to say more, but I can't. I have just a couple of other questions."

Her eyes narrowed—her suspicion was evident. "What else do you want to know?"

He sipped his coffee and then set the cup down on the table. "Do you know Joe Tolleson?"

"Is that the Tolleson of Tolleson Hardware and all those car dealerships? I can't say I've had the pleasure of meeting the man. We must travel in different social circles."

"That's Jack Tolleson, Joe's father. Joe is a senior at the high school. Is it possible that Marsha knows him?"

"Marsha knows some older boys, but I don't remember her saying anything about a Joe Tolleson. I don't know the names of all the boys in her life, though."

"Do either you or Marsha know Silas Wayne?"

"The preacher? Sure I know Reverend Wayne. He's the only guy I know who's not a bastard. Eight years ago, my ex-husband, Ronnie, walked out on us, just before Christmas. Marsha's little sister, Janice, was four months old and that son of a bitch left me without a dime. Silas heard about it and he gave me some money until I got back on my feet. He also brought Marsha and Janice Christmas presents. He checks up on us every two or three months. Silas is great; he doesn't care what side of the tracks you live on. I go to his church once in awhile." She ran her hand through her platinum-blonde hair.

"So Marsha knows him as well?"

"Yeah, but she doesn't like him and she won't go to church. I asked Silas to talk to her when she started getting into trouble. He's helped out some mixed-up kids. They sat here and talked for half an hour. Silas didn't say much before he left, so I asked Marsha how it went. You know what that girl said? She said: 'Mom, most of the guys you know are losers, but at least they know they're losers, they're not pretending to be something better. That guy's a loser pretending he's a saint.' That made me so mad, I slapped her across the mouth. That seemed almost…What's that ten dollar word? It starts with a 'b'."

"Blasphemous?"

"Yeah, blasphemous. Silas has been so good to us through the years; I just couldn't stand her smart-alecky mouth. That was about a month ago, and I haven't seen him since then. Why are you asking me about Silas?"

Benewski had to disclose something to assuage Nancy Walton's mounting suspicion. "Are you absolutely certain that Marsha has run away? I don't want to alarm you, but it's possible she was abducted."

He heard a quaver in her voice. "Yeah, I'm sure."

"How can you be so positive?"

There was a long silence. She sighed and he could tell she was fighting tears. She extinguished her cigarette and lit another.

"Listen, I do the best I can for my girls. I'm a waitress down at the Starlight Lounge. Usually I work the happy hour and dinner shift, and then I come home. But a girl's got to live a little, so sometimes I stay down there and have a few drinks and go dancing. Once in a while I meet somebody and bring him home. Marsha hates it when I do that; she thinks they're all trash. The first two times she ran away were after I had brought guys home. Then last Thursday, I met a new one, Phil. I thought he was going to be different; he seemed so nice. He came over for a nightcap.

"We were here on the couch when Marsha walked in on us. She didn't say anything, but I could tell she was furious. She walked out of the house. I told Phil he had to leave and I went looking for her, but I couldn't find her. I came back and fell asleep. I heard her the next morning, getting ready for school, but I was still tired, so I didn't get up. I don't know if she came back home from school before she left, but she wasn't here Friday night when I got home from work. I sure hope she's coming back."

Nancy's voice broke on the last sentence and she quietly sobbed. Benewski guessed that she had omitted a few details, but at this point, it didn't matter, he had what he needed. His face assumed an expression of concern and he said, "I'm sure she'll be back, and I'll do everything I can to find her. Could I ask a couple of favors?"

Nancy sniffed, picked up a Kleenex from a box on the coffee table and blew her nose. "What do you want?"

"I know your experience with the police hasn't been good, but would you file another missing person report, and make sure they give you a copy. Please don't say anything to them, or anybody else, about our conversation."

"Yeah, I can do that. What else?"

"Could I borrow a photograph of Marsha? I'll return it when our investigation is finished."

"There's one in my room." She rose from the couch and went to the back of the house.

She returned a few moments later with a photograph, which Benewski examined. Her daughter was a pretty girl, with long blond hair, intelligent blue eyes and a winning smile.

"Thank you very much."

"You're welcome. Will you let me know if you find out anything?"

"Sure. Here's my card, with my office phone number. Call me if you think of anything else."

They rose and walked towards the front door. She opened the door and Benewski could see she wanted to say something. She hesitated, and then said, "Mr. Benewski, I didn't mean what I said earlier, about all men being bastards."

"Don't worry about it. Take care, I'll let you know how things are going."

Benewski returned to his office. His secretary said, "Joe Tolleson called. He left his number and said to call back, but if either of his parents answered the phone, to please hang up and try again, later."

"Okay. Would you call the school back and find out if Marsha Walton was absent Friday?"

"Certainly."

Benewski sat at his desk and dialed Joe's number. Joe answered.

"Thanks for calling back, Mr. Benewski. Sergeant Ruprecht saw me leaving your office yesterday. He was coming out of the men's room across the hall. He didn't say anything, but I could tell he was upset."

"Okay, Joe. Thanks for telling me that, it might be important."

There was a long silence. Benewski guessed that Joe wanted him to volunteer something about the progress of the investigation. Benewski said nothing.

"Good-bye, Mr. Benewski."

"Good-bye."

Later in the day, Benewski wrote up notes of his conversation with Nancy Walton. As he was putting the notes in the Tolleson file, he remembered that it had been misfiled that morning. Perhaps it was misfiled because Albert Ruprecht had been looking at it last night. Ruprecht knew that Joe had talked to someone in the district attorney's office. Through the police department he probably had access to either a set of building keys or lock picking tools. If Ruprecht were coming in at night, Benewski would have to be careful about what he left in the Tolleson file. He wondered if he should say anything to Devore, but decided against it. However, he devised a way to verify his suspicions. He put the notes of his conversation with Nancy Walton and the picture of Marsha Walton in his briefcase. With a glue stick he lightly glued two tiny spots of the Tolleson file folder together. He walked into the anteroom.

"Gail, where did you say you found the Tolleson file this morning?"

"It was between the Quincy and Randall files."

"I'm going to put it back between those files. Don't open the file or move it before you go home tonight."

"May I ask why?"

"Somebody may be going through our files at night, and I want to find out for sure."

"Who could be going through our files?"

"I don't know, but leave the file as it is now."

"Certainly. By the way, Marsha Walton wasn't absent from school Friday."

"Thanks. Good night, Gail."

"Good night."

CHAPTER 7

THE MAYOR

"Reverend Wayne?"

"Yes."

"This is Doctor Erickson, in the emergency room. Mayor Matlock had a heart attack earlier this evening, while he was eating dinner. We tried to revive him, but he didn't make it. Sarah and the kids are in the waiting room. We haven't told them yet. You were close to the mayor, and I thought you'd want to know. I'm sorry, sir."

There was a long silence before Silas spoke. "Thank you, Doctor Erickson. Is anybody there now with Sarah and the children?"

"Bruce and Darcy Linden brought them to the hospital and they're in the waiting room."

"Okay, as long as somebody's there when you tell them. They won't stay very long at the hospital. I'll meet them at their house."

"I'm sure they'll appreciate that, sir. Again, I'm sorry."

"Thanks for the call. Good night."

"Good night."

Doctor Erickson hung up the phone and turned towards the operating table where the mayor of Hidden Falls, Chester Matlock, lay dead. A sheet covered the body and its outline reminded Erickson of a small pup tent. Matlock weighed over two hundred and seventy five pounds and the sheet bulged at the enormous mound of his belly. His heart attack came as no surprise to the emergency room personnel. A nurse was wheeling a monitor away from the table and Doctor Harris, Erickson's partner in the emergency room, was removing his rubber gloves.

"Did you get a hold of the Reverend Wayne?" Harris asked. Both doctors were in their mid-thirties. They enjoyed a warm friendship and shared the same black sense of humor, which they regarded as a necessity for their job.

"Yes, he said he'd go over to the house. I guess it's time to tell the family."

"One," Harris said, smacking his right fist into his open palm. Erickson simultaneously made a similar motion. "Two." Both men repeated the motion. "Three." Harris left his hand in the shape of a fist. Erickson formed his fingers into scissors. "Stone takes scissors," Harris said. "Sorry, buddy."

Doctor Erickson walked out from the emergency room into the waiting room, his face a mask of calm sympathy. Mayor Matlock's family—his wife, Sarah, and their two children, fourteen-year-old Cindy and nine-year-old Clinton, were huddled in a tight cluster. Darcy Linden had her arm around Cindy's shoulder. Bruce Linden was pacing back and forth. Erickson said nothing to Sarah, Cindy and Clinton Matlock as they rushed towards him. When Sarah Matlock reached him, he clasped her hands, looked into her eyes, and slowly shook his head. She realized that her husband was dead and she put her arms around her children. They struggled to support themselves and each other as they erupted into tears. Erickson looked over the pathetic group and saw Bruce Linden walking down the hall to the pay phone.

Back at the parsonage, Silas Wayne pondered the news of the mayor's death. He would go to the Matlock residence and console the grieving family, but there was no use letting a good pork chop and salad go to waste. He sat at his kitchen table and finished his meal.

For Silas, Chester Matlock's life had been an exercise in string pulling. Chester's father, Jeff, had owned the town's only hardware store. When he died, Chester inherited it. Chester was inept—he couldn't run a lemonade stand, much less a hardware store. Within a year, the hardware store's ordering system was snarled, the accounting and billing were hopelessly tangled, and suppliers were threatening to cut off trade credit.

Fortunately for Chester, Silas devised a solution for his business difficulties. He convinced up and coming businessman Jack Tolleson to pay a fair price for the store. To get Chester to sell, he persuaded him to run for mayor. Chester was initially reluctant, knowing that most of the electorate considered him a buffoon, but he dimly realized that with the minister's endorsement and behind the scenes influence, he would win the election. Silas prevailed upon the town council to increase the salary of the ceremonial position so that Chester would have enough to support his family. Chester won the election, running unopposed, and Jack Tolleson quickly restored the hardware store to profitability.

Chester had been the mayor for sixteen years. His most demanding duty was riding in the front car in the annual homecoming parade, and he spent most of his time on the job "sounding out his constituents." This meant that he could be found almost every afternoon at either Seaver's Grill or the Taproom. There was no objection to the waste of money that was Chester's salary. Nobody would challenge an arrangement that had the Reverend Wayne's blessing. He won reelection three times, in each election running unopposed.

The Reverend Wayne finished his dinner, put his plate in the dishwasher and washed his hands. The new mayor would be Harvey Roach, currently the chairman of the town council, and Roach was just as much in his pocket as Chester had been. Matlock had to pin his name on his shirt every day; he was too dim-witted to be of much value to the minister. Roach, on the other hand, was intelligent. Silas would make sure the mayor's duties and powers were expanded beyond the ceremonial. He felt a happy satisfaction as he left the parsonage and drove to the Matlock residence.

He had to park a block away from the house because so many people had already arrived. It always amazed him how quickly bad news raced through a small town. Entering the modest house, he stood in the entryway and surveyed the living room, packed with people. Somebody had fixed coffee and pastries, and most of the people were standing in various clusters, quietly talking, eating and sipping coffee. In one corner of the room a large group of people surrounding a couch where the family was huddled. He heard Sarah Matlock's steady sobbing and intermittent wails from Cindy and Clinton. He waited for the assembled friends and well wishers to notice his arrival.

When they did, they parted and he approached the family. He hugged Sarah while she cried without restraint. He reached out to the two children and took their outstretched hands in his own. He spoke in a tone reserved for eulogies.

"Chester was a fine man, a good husband and father. Clinton and Cindy, I know this is hard to understand, but now he's with God. It's always difficult for those of us left behind to comprehend God's plan, but we have to accept that it is God's plan."

One of the onlookers, a middle-aged woman, turned to her husband and whispered, "he always says the right thing, in the right way, at the right time."

The minister embraced the entire family as they wept and said nothing more for a long time. Eventually, the middle-aged woman's husband turned to her and whispered, "he also knows when it's the right time not to say anything."

Silas sat with the family for several hours, occasionally murmuring consolations as Sarah greeted a steady stream of friends. After a while the children were given a mild sedative and Sarah led them to their bedrooms. When she returned, he whispered to her, "may I talk to you briefly in the kitchen?" They walked to the kitchen, where they were alone.

"Silas," Sarah said, hesitantly, her eyes brimming with new tears, "I've tried not to think about this, but when Chester was having his heart attack, I kept telling myself it was my fault. For dinner tonight he had four slices of ham, three helpings of mashed potatoes and two of creamed corn, and three rolls. He slathered everything with butter and covered the plate with gravy. The way he ate...I feel like I killed him." She wailed.

Guilty as charged—Sarah's huge meals were legendary.

"Sarah, you can't blame yourself. Chester was going to eat, whether you fed him or not. He went out for big breakfasts and lunches almost every day. But he came home every night for dinner. That's the important thing— that he ate with his family. Try to remember the pleasure your meals gave him. Nothing you could have done would have stopped him from eating." He took her in his arms. He could not tell if she found his words reassuring, but gradually her sobbing subsided. When she stopped, he freed himself from her embrace and looked into her wet, red-rimmed eyes.

"I'll do anything you need me to do for the funeral arrangements," he said, taking her hands. "You're in shock, but I'd like to ease your mind about one thing. I don't know if Chester told you, but about three years ago the town council paid for a life insurance policy for him. The council has also been making contributions to a vested pension plan. It won't be easy street for you and the children, but money shouldn't be an immediate concern."

"Silas, I...I don't know what to say. Thank you."

"There's no need to thank me." He walked over to a counter, took a pot of coffee from the coffee maker, poured two cups of coffee and handed one to her. "Let's go sit down."

They walked back into the living room and sat next to each other on the couch. Sarah talked quietly with her friends. Silas said little. After a while, Sarah stood and excused herself, saying she was going to bed. She took a sedative. Her friends hugged her and wished her well. She sobbed as Silas embraced her and whispered soothing words in her ear. Her closest friend, Amy Sheehan, escorted her to her bedroom. Silas left after receiving assurances from the group in the living room that they would stay with the family through the night.

CHAPTER 8

▼

VIGILS

Benewski noticed the flags at half-mast as he entered the town hall Wednesday morning. He had not met Chester Matlock, but he knew the mayor had been the butt of some sort of Hidden Falls' joke. Lowering the flags was a mockery—they should have been lowered at Seaver's Grill. Inside the town hall, nobody seemed particularly distressed or shocked by the death of the mayor. Gail Smathers did not mention it when he greeted her.

Benewski looked in the filing cabinet. The Tolleson file was where it had been left, misfiled between the Quincy and Randall files. However, it had been opened; the sides of the file were no longer glued together. Someone had come in last night and checked up on the Tolleson investigation. He buzzed Mike Devore.

Five minutes later, he sat in the chair before the district attorney's desk. Devore was wearing another impeccably tailored suit—navy blue with narrow pinstripes. Benewski had neither the inclination nor the income to buy expensive suits, but he felt rumpled around his boss. He told Devore about his suspicion that Albert Ruprecht had gone through his files the previous two nights. Devore sat silently for several moments, thinking.

"It will," he said, "complicate matters if Ruprecht knows that we're investigating Silas Wayne. I wonder if he's told Silas anything?"

"When Joe told me about his session with the police, he said Ruprecht seemed hostile towards him. Does Ruprecht attend Silas's church?"

"Every Sunday. You're going to have to be careful about what you put in that file. Keep booby trapping it every night so you know if someone's looked through it. Have you made any progress in the investigation?"

Benewski told Devore about his visit with Nancy Walton the previous day, concluding that regardless of what Mrs. Walton thought had happened to her daughter, if Joe Tolleson had seen a corpse dangling at the church, it was Marsha Walton.

"Why are you so certain?" Devore asked.

"Because Marsha went to school last Friday. Why would she go to school if she were going to run away? She's not exactly a model student."

"Good point. Have you brought that up with Nancy Walton?"

"No, I didn't think about it until after I had talked with her. I'm not going to say anything until I have something more definite. She's already worried."

"Okay."

Benewski left Devore's office.

About an hour later Devore called and asked him to return to his office. He detected a trace of excitement in Devore's voice. When he sat down, he could see Devore was in the throes of a brainstorm. He recognized the look that was a mixture of agitation, impatience and delight with his own cleverness. As if to put a brake on himself, Devore took off his glasses and removed a folded cloth from his coat pocket. He unfolded the cloth and carefully cleaned his glasses, inspecting each lens. He put on his glasses, refolded the cloth and put it back in his pocket.

"Gary, somebody is going through your files. Why don't we try to turn that to our advantage? We have no case until we find the body. Let's assume that Ruprecht talks to Silas, so Silas has known everything since the night Tolleson told his story to the police. What's he done with the body? Since he knows we're investigating him, if he didn't dispose of the body the weekend after the murder, he might still be hiding it somewhere. Right now he's in a perfect position, because as long as the body doesn't show up, Marsha Walton is a runaway and her disappearance is accounted for. If her body turns up, he's the prime suspect because of Tolleson's story. So he has to be certain that the body is never recovered. It's not that easy to eliminate a body. If you throw it in a river or lake, or bury it, you run the risk that it will eventually be discovered and identified. You can chop it up and the pieces are easier to dispose of, but that's a grisly process. If Silas has a good hiding place for the body, he may be waiting until the heat dies down before he ultimately disposes of it."

"That makes sense, but how do we use it?"

"Silas doesn't know that we know that he knows about our investigation."

"Try saying that three times fast."

A smile appeared, then vanished, from Devore's face. "If we could put something in that file tonight that would make Silas apprehensive that we know where the body is, it might force his hand."

"What's your plan?"

Devore rose from his chair and paced behind his desk. "Have Gail type up the top part of a search warrant—the specification of the crime and the suspect's name, and most importantly, the name of the suspected victim. Silas doesn't know that we might know who the victim is. Leave out the particulars of the location of the search."

"That will make the warrant less credible."

"Probably, but if we specify a location and Silas has hid the body somewhere else, he'll figure that we're bluffing and he may even realize that we know about Ruprecht's nocturnal visits. We'll have blown our cover and we can't run that risk. Put tomorrow's date on the search warrant and put it in the file before you go home tonight. Maybe Ruprecht will come in tonight and report back to Silas that we've made out a search warrant for the body of Marsha Walton. You'd better be right about the identity of the victim, because that's what will give our warrant credibility. If he thinks that we know where the body is, he may panic and try to move or dispose of the body tonight."

"Are we going to conduct a stakeout tonight over at the parsonage?"

"You'll be staking out at the parsonage. I'll be watching Tolleson's house."

"Why?"

Devore quit pacing and sat down. He leaned towards Benewski as he talked, his hands folded on his desk. "Remember what I said—we have to assume that both Joe Tolleson and Silas are suspects. For all we know, it could be Tolleson coming in and checking our files late at night. He picks locks. He could have invented his story about Albert Ruprecht seeing him coming out of your office. Perhaps it's more plausible to suspect that Ruprecht is going through the files, but if we charge Silas and go to trial, our investigation will be closely reviewed. We must proceed impartially and at this point we can't eliminate Tolleson as a suspect. For whatever reason, Tolleson might be trying to frame Silas. While you're watching Silas tonight, I'll be watching Tolleson. We're going to have to watch them from public areas, places where they have no expectation of privacy, because we can't get a warrant for these stakeouts. That's no problem at the parsonage; you can watch the whole house from behind the bushes and trees next to the church parking lot without being seen. I've been to the Tollesons'; they live at the end of a cul-de-sac. I can park at the other end of the street and watch their house."

"We'll take our cell phones so we can communicate. Maybe Gail should watch the office tonight."

"From where? There's no place she can safely hide in either one of our offices without running the risk of discovery. She can't position herself in the hall—she would be seen—or in the men's room across the hall, for obvious reasons."

"You're right about that. What time do you want to start?"

"The building closes at nine and either Ruprecht or Tolleson will probably wait an hour or two before he comes to the office. Just to be safe, let's get some dinner and meet back here at eight."

"But I'll miss 'Who Wants To Be A Millionaire?'"

"That's quite a loss. Do you really watch that?"

"Once in a while. Margie and the kids watch it all the time."

"I've only seen it once. It seemed pretty easy. Returning to the matter at hand, tear yourself away from Regis and come down here. Then we'll drive to our stakeout locations. Make sure you bring coffee and something to eat, it may be a long night."

"Okay, see you at eight."

*   *   *

They met that night at Benewski's office. They both had cell phones and binoculars.

"Smathers checked this afternoon; Marsha Walton is still missing," Benewski said.

Devore nodded. "When you get out to the parsonage, call me about every two hours. If Silas gets in his car and goes somewhere, try to follow him, but don't let him see you. Call me and stay on the line."

Benewski drove his old Ford out to the church at the north end of town. The only place to park with a view of the parsonage was in the empty church parking lot. From there, his car would be visible to Silas from the parsonage. He drove past the church and parked his car a quarter of a mile away, behind some bushes where it could not be seen from the road. He walked back to the church, listening to his boots crunching gravel. He carried a bag for his candy bars, fruit, portable phone, binoculars and thermos full of coffee. When he reached the church parking lot he stopped and reconnoitered.

The church was to his right. Behind and to the right of the church extended an annex for Sunday school classrooms. The parking lot in front and to the left of the church was large and well lit. At the end of the parking lot, a narrow driveway ran back about fifteen yards to the parsonage, Wayne's residence. The parsonage was a two-story Victorian cottage. Benewski guessed it had two or three bedrooms. Tall oak trees framed the house with a small lawn surrounded by a white picket fence. To the right of the driveway was a stand-alone garage.

A copse of bushes to the left of the parking lot provided the best vantage point for watching the house. He walked around the parking lot to the bushes and found a clear spot in a dark area with an unobstructed view of the parsonage. He leaned against a tree, poured a cup of coffee, called Devore and told him he was in place. He surveyed the parsonage through his binoculars. The only light shone through a curtained window on the top floor of the house, on the left hand side. The light came from either Silas's bedroom or study.

After an hour of watching the house, Benewski's attention wandered. He shifted his binoculars to the right, towards the church. By the light of the half moon he saw the outline of the towering steeple at the front of the church. A vaulted black slate roof extended back into the darkness. Down the left side a row of elongated stained glass windows stood high above gray granite masonry. The light from the moon above and the parking lot lights below gave the church a sinister aspect. It was incongruous for a town the size of Hidden Falls to have such a monumental edifice. Benewski had read a chamber of commerce brochure on the town's history, and the story of the church, just before he moved.

Hidden Falls was situated five miles below the confluence of a small river, known as the East Fork, into a much larger river, the West Fork. It was named for a spectacular waterfall in a box canyon on the West Fork, three miles above the confluence. In the late 1800's, Jeremiah Redlin had discovered a lode of mineral ores about two miles upriver from the box canyon. Hidden Falls was a small trading post at the time, but it grew quickly with the success of Redlin's mining operation. The railroad built a spur line and Hidden Falls became a boomtown.

Redlin was a devout man who did not want to see Hidden Falls go the same sinful way as other mining towns. The town needed a church and he would build one scaled to what he hoped the town would become, not what it was. There were whispers that atonement might also have been a motive—his wife had died under mysterious circumstances. He journeyed to Europe to gather ideas. No particular cathedral served as a model, but when Redlin returned he knew he wanted the trappings of Europe's finest, especially an enormous nave and transept configuration in the shape of a cross to impress upon worshippers their humble insignificance. It took seven years to build the church and he spent most of his fortune. He died shortly after completing his life's work, his soul presumably at peace. Unfortunately, Redlin's mineral lode died shortly after he did, and Hidden Falls never became a metropolis.

Nevertheless, his church became Hidden Falls' symbolic center; the passage of Hidden Falls' lives marked by the rituals performed at its altar—birth and baptisms, coming of age and confirmations, marriage and weddings, death and funerals. Benewski knew that when Joe had told his story to the police, Marsh and Ruprecht would have found the site of the alleged crimes as upsetting as the actual crimes. A body of a young girl dangling from the rafter above the choir loft, silhouetted against the stained-glass cross, would desecrate the town shrine.

Benewski's attention shifted back to the parsonage. A light came on from the bottom floor, on the right side of the house. With his binoculars he could see through the window, which had no curtains. Silas was in the kitchen—Benewski saw a sink and a refrigerator. The minister walked by the window. The light stayed on for about a minute. Several moments later a shadow moved behind the curtain on the top floor room; Silas had gone back upstairs. Benewski called Devore.

"Anything over there, Mike?"

"Nothing so far. There's a light on downstairs and I can see Jack Tolleson sitting on a couch—he's watching TV. There's a light on upstairs, probably from Joe's bedroom. Once in a while the kitchen light goes on, and I caught a glimpse of Alice Tolleson. If anything is going to happen here, it will happen after they all go to bed. How about you?"

"Nothing yet. Silas has been in a room on the top floor. He got up and went to the kitchen for a moment, but then he went back to that room. Have you been in the parsonage?"

"Just once. The room on the left side of the top floor is his study and the one on the right is his bedroom. There was a phone in the kitchen, so he might have got a call from Ruprecht. Then again, he probably has a phone in his study."

"I don't think he took a call in the kitchen; he wasn't there very long."

"Okay, keep watching and call me again."

"Sure."

At about 11:30 the kitchen light went on again. This time it stayed on for almost ten minutes. Benewski tensed when Silas opened the front door and stepped onto the porch. He walked down the porch stairs and towards the garage. Benewski debated calling Devore. However, Silas walked past the garage and continued towards the rear of the church. Benewski saw a faint glow coming from the stained glass windows along the side of the church; Silas had turned on a light. The light stayed on for about a minute and he emerged from the church and walked back towards the parsonage. Through his binoculars, Benewski could see he was holding a book in his left hand. To Benewski's disappointment, Silas returned to his house, turned off the kitchen light and went back to his study.

Benewski checked in with Devore. Devore said all the lights were off in the Tolleson house and the family had gone to bed. Shortly after this brief conversation, the light went off in Silas's study and went on in the bedroom next to the study. This light stayed on for about half an hour and then went off. Silas was calling it a night.

Devore and Benewski stayed at their posts until day-break the next morning. The plan had not worked; their efforts had been rewarded with a sleepless night. Benewski was frustrated. The plan had been a long shot, but it was all they had. Now he was up against a wall with no idea how to pursue the investigation. He went home and showered and shaved. Margie fixed him scrambled eggs for breakfast, and then he returned to the office. When he arrived, his frustration increased. The tiny spot on the Tolleson file he had glued was again unstuck—the file had been opened the previous night.

CHAPTER 9

▼

THE SWORD

"Gary, Joe Tolleson's on the line," Gail Smathers said, over the intercom.

"Thanks, Gail, put him on."

"Hello, Mr. Benewski, I was wondering how your investigation is going."

Should he dismiss Joe with a statement that he couldn't say anything about an ongoing investigation? He'd be revealing information to a suspect. However, he heard the anxiety in Joe's voice and felt sympathetic. Joe had shown a lot of courage talking to him, especially after the reactions of the police and his parents. There was nothing improper about Joe wanting to know about the progress of the investigation. Benewski had to remember Devore's admonitions. However, if he didn't say too much, he could justify talking to Joe with the rationale that disclosure to a suspect can diminish his apprehension and lower his guard. He chose his words carefully.

"Joe, we think that Silas may know that he's being investigated."

"Through Albert Ruprecht?"

There was a painfully long silence. Benewski's message was clear—he would tell Joe what he could, but Joe was not to ask questions.

"As you probably realize, the key to this investigation is finding the body you saw in the church. We think we know the identity of the victim. Two nights ago, Wednesday, we tried to make Silas think that we knew where the body was. We staked out the parsonage, hoping he would panic and lead us to the corpse. Unfortunately, he never left his house, except once when he walked over to the church to pick up a book. However, like I said, we think we know the identity of the victim, so we've made some progress. I wish I could say more, but I can't. I know it's hard, but try not to worry. We won't let this one get away."

"Thank you, Mr. Benewski. Have a nice weekend." Joe hung up the phone in the kitchen. He didn't know much more than before he called, but he felt better. Benewski's understanding of his situation encouraged him. Benewski had kept saying "we" this and "we" that. Who else was involved with the investigation? He went to the refrigerator and poured a glass of milk.

He walked into the living room, sat on a couch and drank the milk. Surrendering to an overpowering need, he fell asleep. An hour later, the voices of his parents in the kitchen awoke him.

"The wedding is at seven o'clock, so you have time to shower and shave."

"Okay. I can understand them not wanting to get married on the same day as a funeral, but why didn't they postpone the ceremony, instead of moving it up like this?"

"They couldn't postpone it without messing up the arrangements for their honeymoon in Europe."

"Oh. Weren't there a lot of people at the mortuary? I didn't know Chester had so many friends. Ned Stiles did a great job. Our illustrious mayor looks better dead than alive. Maybe because he hasn't had a drink in three days."

"Jack, that's terrible."

"How about that coffin? What a crate! I heard Chester was pushing three hundred when he died. No wonder he had a heart attack. What time's the funeral tomorrow?"

"10:30."

"I wonder why Sarah wants me to be a pallbearer. I didn't overpay that much for the hardware store. I'll have to go to the mortuary early."

"No, you don't. Ned said Sarah asked him to take the coffin to the church after the public viewing this afternoon. You just have to carry Chester out, after the service."

"I hope there's eight of us. Look at the time, we'd better get ready."

The kitchen door swung open and they stepped into the living room. Alice saw Joe on the couch and stopped. They were both aware of an uneasy tension, the same uneasy tension that had beset the family all week.

"Joe," she said, hesitantly, "you're invited to Dave and Dorothy's wedding tonight out at Dave's ranch. Would you like to go?"

Joe stared at his mother, taking perverse satisfaction in
her obvious discomfort.

"No."

"Okay. You'll have to fend for yourself for dinner.
There's some stew and tuna fish in the refrigerator or you
can have bacon and eggs. Leave us a note if you go out."

"Sure." Joe rolled over, facing the back of the couch,
cutting off further conversation.

Alice and Jack walked up to their bedroom—a spacious
room with rosewood drawers lining the walls and matching nightstands on either side of a king size bed. There
were two walk-in closets and a big-screen television in the
corner. Through a large window opposite the bed, Jack
could see both sides of the street below. The streetlights
had just come on. Alice pulled the curtain over the window and turned towards him.

"I'm worried about him, too, Alice."

"He's never like this. He hasn't taken an afternoon nap
since he was a baby. Every morning he comes down to
breakfast and his eyes are puffy and red. He's not sleeping,
and he doesn't eat. I don't know what really happened last
week, but something has got into him, and we've got to
find out what it is."

"Do you think he saw a girl hanging from the rafters in
the old church?"

She threw him a cautionary glance. "No. But I think
this story, and the way he's been acting all week, are a cry
for help."

"What do you mean?"

"From day one, when he was a baby, Joe was different.
Even you could see that. So alert, so curious, so self-contained.
There's always been something special about Joe, but—"

"He's special all right, and we've never pushed him."

"No we haven't, and that's part of the problem. Not that we didn't push him, but maybe we haven't paid enough attention to him." She hesitated. "We've always thought he liked being by himself, that he's not interested in other people, but maybe we're wrong. You said we should let him go his own way."

"Well, he's always seemed happy."

Alice moved to a chest of drawers, folded a sweater, and laid it on top of the chest. "We should have made him make some friends and join in with the other kids. Just because everything seems perfect doesn't mean that it is. I'll bet Joe wants friends and I'll bet he wants something more from us. We've been too low key about his accomplishments. He needs recognition, just like everyone else. We're not stupid, but we're not as smart as he is. Just because you're smart doesn't mean you don't get lonely. Maybe you get even lonelier, because it's hard to find people like you. I think that after years of keeping it inside, he wants some attention."

Jack walked over to Alice and, standing behind her, placed his hands on her shoulders. "You may be right, dear, but I think trying to change him while he was growing up would have been easier said than done. He's too damn stubborn—when he doesn't want to do something he doesn't do it."

Alice turned towards her husband and shrugged, letting a long silence acknowledge the truth of his words. "Well, at least you two talk and spend time together."

"Yeah, I talk with him, sort of. It's amazing how quickly he picks up on the details of business, but when he goes off on those weird tangents, he loses me and he knows it."

"Maybe we both have to try harder. Tomorrow morning, we're all going to have a long talk. We've got to find out what's really bothering him."

"Okay, but we've got to get moving. I'll jump in the shower."

When Joe's parents came downstairs forty-five minutes later, Joe was asleep. They did not wake him; hunger pangs half an hour later did. He dragged himself into the kitchen and rooted through the refrigerator. It was the first time all week that he had felt hungry and he decided on leftover stew and bacon and eggs. He ladled the stew into a pot, cracked three eggs into a bowl, laid several bacon strips in a pan, and put the pot and pan on the stove.

Could he learn to live with his parents? Would the pain and anger from their refusal to believe him ever go away? He had long looked forward to leaving Hidden Falls, but now that desire overwhelmed him. He had to leave this dead end little town and his parents and get involved with college life. The night of the incident, his mother had questioned his perception. He smiled his ironic smile. It had been a rough week, but his perceptions—and his sanity—were intact. He wouldn't be destroyed.

He sprinkled salt and pepper on the eggs. Something his mother said earlier bothered him. Something about the funeral. Why was the undertaker, Ned Stiles, taking Chester Matlock's coffin to the old church today? He had only been to two funerals, and in both they had brought the coffin into the church at the beginning of the service. Matlock was the town clown, but shouldn't the mayor's funeral be in the traditional manner? The hearse should arrive at the church and the pallbearers should carry in the coffin. Why did Sarah Matlock ask Stiles to take the coffin to the church early?

And then a sword cut a knot. Who had consoled and advised grieving Sarah Matlock? Who planted the idea with her that the coffin should be delivered to the church the day before the funeral? Who left his house only once the night he had been set up and staked out, to walk over to the church? Who knew every nook and cranny of that church and would know of a good hiding place for the body? Who knew that if the body was disposed of permanently, there would be no case against him? And who knew that if two bodies were hidden in Chester Matlock's coffin, instead of one, and the coffin was then buried, there was virtually no chance that the second body would ever be recovered? Joe dropped his spoon in the stew.

Silas was going to put the young girl's body in Chester's coffin that night. He had hid the body somewhere in the church. Benewski's set up and stakeout had worked to the extent that it made Silas apprehensive that the whereabouts of the body were no longer secret. The night of the stakeout, Silas may not have checked on the body when he went to the church, but perhaps he had an arrangement, like the piece of paper in the door in old gangster movies, that let him know if his hiding place had been disturbed. The stakeout hadn't worked because Silas knew that nobody had found the hiding place. Now he planned to put the victim's body in the coffin with Chester Matlock's. Joe's father had said the coffin was a crate, so two bodies would undoubtedly fit. How ingenious.

Joe paced in front of the stove as the odor of burning bacon filled the kitchen. He had to go to the church, before Silas returned from the wedding. Finally noticing smoke, he turned off the stove and ran upstairs to his room. He grabbed his car keys, a flashlight, his coat and his father's lock picking tools. He had to call Gary Benewski. He dialed information. An automated voice gave him Benewski's home phone number, which he dialed and let ring twelve times with no answer. How could the guy not have an answering machine? He raced to his car, started it and gunned the engine. Fighting himself, he kept his speed down as he drove on Main Street through town out to the old church. He couldn't risk an encounter with Hidden Fall's ticket-happy traffic cops. He drove past the old church and parked his car behind some bushes by the side of the road. His cell phone was not in its customary place in the glove compartment. He suddenly remembered he had left it in his locker at school. There was nothing he could do about it now; he didn't have time to get it. Dismayed, he walked the quarter of a mile back to the church parking lot. Although he was not cold, the sight of the old church made him shiver and he put on his coat.

CHAPTER 10

▼

REVELATION

Life—a battle against fear. Fear of darkness, fear of light; fear of wrong and fear of right. Fear a different drum, fear the crowd; fear the humble and fear the proud. Fear to fail, fear to succeed; fear the one who fills your need. Chimeras you fear the most—the unknown shadow and the Holy Ghost. A young boy looks in an old man's eyes, and boldly asks him why he is wise. Does he fear the thunder or the passing years? There's an answer for you my son; wisdom dims all fears save one. Not the thunder or the passing year, what I know is a fear of fear.

Joe walked through the parking lot. The church loomed before him, the tangible embodiment of his fears. The moon, partially hidden by a thin layer of clouds, illuminated the church's imposing outline and steeple. Somewhere inside was the corpse. If he didn't find it before Silas returned and Silas found him, he was dead. He ran his tongue over the dry stickiness in his mouth. Something constricted in his chest and at the base of his throat. He walked up the stairs and into the shadow of the church.

Hindered by both darkness and nerves, it took him several minutes to pick the door lock. He had trouble remembering the right pattern from the previous week. His hands shook and once he dropped his lock pick. Finally the bar dropped and he swung the heavy bronze door open. It was dark inside. He switched on his flashlight and walked through the vestibule.

The nave was garishly lit in an irregular patchwork of colors by the moon shining through the stained-glass. He stood at the end of an aisle. At the other end a closed casket rested on a portable stand. A blue light, in the distorted shape of the stained-glass cross, extended over the chancel, across the casket, and into the empty pews. He walked up the aisle, drawn by the casket. Reaching it, he ran his hand down one side. He found two latches, unclasped them, pushed open the lid and stared at the face of Mayor Matlock. The skin was waxy, with a cosmetic sheen. The mayor lay on a surface of beige, crushed velveteen and his hands were folded over his mountainous belly. Despite his bulk, there was room in the coffin for another body. Joe closed the lid and clasped the latches.

He walked away from the coffin towards the door to the left of the chancel. A semicircular passageway extended from the right side of the door, behind the chancel to the other side of the nave. To the left of the door hung four seven-foot high tapestries depicting Biblical scenes. The bottoms of the tapestries were a foot and a half from the floor. He got on his hands and knees and directed the flashlight beam along the bottom of the wall, looking for a crack that would indicate a hidden door. He slowly walked through the semicircular passageway, shining his light on both sides. Halfway around the semicircle, directly behind the altar, was a plainly visible door on the right hand side of the passageway. The unlocked door opened into a small vestry. He shined his light along the opposite wall where robes hung from a clothing rod. To his right were shelves for candle holders, communion chalices and other ceremonial artifacts. He walked across the room and opened a narrow door. A tall, paneled screen stood between the vestry on the one side and the altar and the pulpit on the other. He closed the door, returned to the other door and left the vestry.

He slowly walked through the semicircular passageway to the other side of the nave, examining the walls. There were four more biblical tapestries and again he got on his hands and knees and directed the flashlight beam along the bottom of the wall. He stood and shined his flashlight on the tapestry at the far right. Jesus sat with a child on his lap. The caption below the scene read: "Let the children come to me." Joe lifted the bottom fringe of the tapestry. Six inches above the bottom of the tapestry ran a three-foot long, horizontal crack. He shined his light to the left along the crack. It ran into a vertical crack.

He quit raising the tapestry. He ran his light along the left edge of the tapestry. He stepped closer to it, carefully examining the edge. About four feet up, two hairs were glued to the tapestry and to the wall—Silas's indicator. Raising the tapestry further would break the hairs. He slowly raised the tapestry and followed the vertical crack with his flashlight beam. The hairs snapped and six inches later there was a small, curved metal handle, recessed into the wall. He pulled it. A door momentarily caught and then opened.

A blast of cold air escaped from below. The breath of death. He could see a narrow landing and steps leading downward. He stepped to the landing and shined his light to the bottom of the flight of rough hewn stairs. He descended, counting twelve stairs. At the bottom were two narrow, perpendicular tunnels, about eight feet high, carved out of the bedrock. One tunnel led directly from the stairs and one tunnel went to the right, back under the pews. Catacombs. Somewhere far away water dripped. He shined his light along the cobweb covered ceiling of the tunnel in front of him and shivered. Spiders.

He felt and heard the grit under his feet as he walked down the tunnel leading from the stairs. Coming to an opening on his right, he shined his light on a small empty room. Further down the tunnel he felt a draft from the right. It was another tunnel; the flashlight beam did not reveal its length. Past this tunnel was a wooden door on the right side. He heard a motorized hum from behind the door, which was padlocked shut. The padlock clasp and lock were identical to ones sold in his father's hardware store. Their metallic luster indicated they were new. He took out a lock pick, sprung the lock and opened the wooden door.

To his left was the source of the hum, a gasoline-powered portable generator. An electric cord ran from the generator to the ceiling and an uncovered light bulb. Another cord connected to an ice machine. He rolled the circular switch on the cord leading to the light bulb.

The yellow light revealed a macabre crypt. On a table in the center of the room was a large metal tub filled with ice. Two legs, wrapped in plastic, rested on top of the ice. He advanced to the tub and scooped away ice with his hands. The girl's body was enshrouded in transparent plastic wrapping. An incision had been made down the length of her chest and stomach and her interior organs had been removed. He had to look away from the girl's vacant eyes. The body was strangely translucent—her blood had been drained. Another metal tub, smaller than the one on the table, sat in the corner, covered by a sheet of plywood. He went to it and pulled off the cover.

The foul stench of her blood made him retch; he replaced the wooden cover. On a shelf on the back wall were three large jars, the type used for home pickling, which smelled of alcohol and contained various organs. Beside the jars were several knives, a two foot long pipe, a box of surgical gloves, a wrench and a can of metal sealant. He picked up the pipe.

He placed his flashlight and the pipe on the table with the corpse. He gathered the girl in his arms, feeling her cold, rigid lifelessness through her plastic shroud and his thin jacket. Raped, hung, eviscerated, and drained—she was no more than fifteen years old. He picked up the pipe in one hand and his flashlight in the other. Sliding the pipe under the body, he opened the wooden door. He left the door cracked for the light and started down the long, narrow tunnel.

He struggled under the girl's weight, eighty to ninety pounds. Eighty to ninety pounds without blood and organs. Despite the subterranean cold, he was warm. Beads of sweat dribbled down his neck and back and under his arms. He felt a draft from the tunnel that he had shined his light down earlier. He kept his beam fixed on the stairs at the end of the tunnel. There was a feathery wisp of pressure on his left shoulder. He shuddered—cobwebs or spiders. Or a hand! The grip tightened, pulling him backwards. A wraith stepped in front of him. He could see a flashlight in the wraith's left hand. His right hand went to his jacket pocket and removed a revolver. He switched his flashlight on and aimed the beam at Joe's eyes. Joe moved his flashlight beam to Silas's face. Silas smiled.

"Joe and Marsha, what a surprise. I always thought you two would make a cute couple."

Joe opened his mouth to shout, to scream, to make some sort of noise. All that emerged was a guttural garble.

"Cat got your tongue? Sometimes it's hard to know just what to say, isn't it?"

His heart beat all over his body—blood pulsed through his arms and legs, throbbed at the base of his neck, pounded behind his eyes and ears. His hyper sensitized nerves felt as if individual atoms and molecules brushed against individual skin cells. He heard the faintest sounds (the water dripping) and saw the smallest things (a tiny patch of stubble at the end of Silas's chin). Each moment seemed infinite.

"Joe, would you kindly drop your flashlight and step back?"

It was a long interval between when he released the flashlight and when he heard the lens and bulb shatter. He stepped away from Silas.

"'I am the light and the way," Silas said. "Did you know Marsha Walton before her untimely demise?"

He shook his head, unable to speak.

"Why do you think he said 'Let the children come to me'? Children can be so bothersome, especially when they believe their elders' hypocrisies about telling the truth. I tried to show Miss Walton the light and the way, and how did she respond? 'Reverend Wayne, you're full of shit.' I couldn't decide if she was a heretic or a witch. Fortunately, it didn't matter; God renders his justice to both."

Slow your breathing, he told himself. Try to complete one thought before you jump to another. Try to listen to this demented soliloquy. Try to think of a way out.

"I am an agent of God's justice. I debased her chastity and extinguished her love of her own life. You should have seen her struggle when she realized I was going to rape her—she was magnificent. Your nymph, your delicate flower, had the strength of a cornered animal. Somewhere in my church, perhaps directly above our heads, I tamed this feral bitch. Her screams echoed off the altar."

Silas paused, waving his gun absently towards the body. "The church ignores so many screams. When she saw her noose in the choir loft, I could barely get it around her neck. She took a long time to die, Joseph. Like those trick candles, her light wouldn't go out. That's when you came in."

He was seeing the rarest of phenomena—a soul revealing itself. A soul that knew no fear because it knew that its listener would soon be dead. Think of something!

"And now you've again discovered my handiwork. I've prepared her for burial and you're taking her away. But you can't, she belongs to God. Her lifeblood's been drained. Poor Alice."

"Why did you say 'poor Alice?'"

"You don't know, do you?" Silas's face, but not his body, seemed to move towards him. "Alice isn't a heretic, more's the pity her son is. Your mother loves me, Joseph."

"My mother loved you?"

"I didn't use the past tense. Do you think men really worship the contradictory babbling of a messianic mystic who lived two thousand years ago? Men worship what your mother has, her beauty, her grace—and what she once had—her glorious independence." Silas was rocking slightly on his heels, seemingly entranced with his own words. "Alice was every women's envy and every man's downfall. Paradoxically, I destroyed your mother by mastering my desire for her. The torture of denial was trivial compared to what the torture of submission would have been. If I had surrendered, I would have been a prisoner of my own lust—craving ownership of a woman who couldn't be owned. If you give a woman what she thinks she wants, she won't want you. By saying no to myself, I imprisoned her—she submitted to me."

"You had sex with my mother?"

"I never had sex with your mother." An enigmatic smile. "But I fucked her. Have you ever wondered how a goddess ends up with a mediocrity? Your mother's talent and ambition matched her beauty. I made her choose between me and her dreams. She chose me, but then I was gone and so were her dreams. With no birds in hand and your father waiting in the bush, she allowed herself to succumb to his pedestrian charms. I blessed the marriage. She's stayed with him for you and for me. I admire her martyrdom."

He would kill the Very Reverend Silas Wayne. Only one course of action had any chance of success. Silas's attention was shifting from Joe to his own confession. He inched towards Silas. He waited, watching him, but no longer concentrating on his words. He slid his hand under the corpse and grabbed the pipe. Silas continued his private benediction, talking about the girl he had killed and the woman he had destroyed. A flicker of the light from the room behind Joe momentarily distracted him. Now! Joe stepped towards him and dumped Marsha Walton's body into his arms.

A shot fired wildly into the floor; the corpse threw off Silas's aim. His flashlight fell to the floor and Joe heard the sound of breaking glass. Joe ducked down the tunnel to his left, carrying the pipe. Cobwebs brushed against his face as he raced away from Silas. Another shot—the bullet hit the wall to his right. He lowered himself into a running crouch to present a smaller target. His head was the first thing to hit the wall at the end of the tunnel. The next shot hit the wall just above him. He slumped to the floor, waves of pain pulsing from his head through his spinal cord to his legs and feet. He did not pass out, but he was nauseated and his dry heaves would have been wet ones if he had eaten any dinner. He crawled on the floor. It appeared that another tunnel, parallel to the main tunnel leading from the stairs, ran to both his left and right. Crawling to his right, out of the line of fire, he pulled himself up and sat against the wall. His nausea subsided and he regained his ability to think.

Silas had a revolver. Three shots had been fired, which meant that he had three shots left, unless he was carrying extra bullets. He didn't know if either of his two shots down the tunnel had hit Joe and he had no way of finding out, since his flashlight was broken. He could come after

Joe, but now with both their flashlights inoperative, sound became as important as sight. The noise he would make walking on the gritty tunnel floors would alert Joe to any advance. Joe rubbed his head with his hand. The swelling knot was distressing, but his situation was not hopeless.

Silas couldn't let him escape. Joe had no influence with the police, but Benewski would come back to the church when Joe told him what had happened. It would be difficult for Silas to hide the body and dispose of the evidence in his makeshift mortuary before Joe and Benewski returned. Silas had to try to apprehend him and although he had a gun, he was at a disadvantage—Joe could hear him coming and could run the opposite direction. He quietly crept down the tunnel to verify that it connected with the tunnel to the right of the stairs, which it did. It wouldn't matter from which direction Silas made his attack, he would be leaving an escape route open. If Silas committed too far along the square, Joe could go the other way, return to the stairs and escape. Joe crept back to the corner opposite the corner at the bottom of the stairs.

Joe had the advantage of time. Silas had to kill him, and put Marsha Walton's body in Chester Matlock's coffin, before tomorrow's funeral service. Joe could wait all night, if necessary. Silas could place the girl's body in the coffin at any time and still watch the hidden door. However, Silas had to kill him before the funeral service or Joe would emerge during the service to reveal Silas's subterranean secrets. Silas would have to come after him. Joe had to stay awake and be patient, but he could wait until Silas moved.

There were two problems with his plan. Even if he made it to the stairs before Silas, his advantage would be temporary. Silas would chase him back to his car and he did not know if he was faster than Silas. Also, the minister had a gun and could shoot him from behind. Even if he escaped, he would be leaving the body—the key piece of evidence—with Silas at the church. He needed another plan.

When Silas came after Joe, the minister would be alert to the possibility of escape, but perhaps not to the possibility of ambush. Joe devised a plan—a desperate, dangerous plan.

Hours passed. Joe urinated, the flow to the floor a rainstorm in the subterranean silence. He was hungry, not having eaten since lunch. Occasionally he heard distant shuffling sounds—Silas moving around. His eyes adjusted to the dim light and he saw the outline of his own hands and feet. He was closer to the water leak—a regular drip, six seconds between drips. Sometimes he stood and sometimes he sat. His head ached where he had run into the wall and his thin jacket offered no protection from the underground chill.

How could mom have fallen in love with Silas Wayne? Couldn't she see he was a fraud? Was she still in love with him? Was that why she had refused to believe his story? Had they had sex? Were they still having sex? Why was it easier to imagine her having sex with Silas than with dad? He winced. Think of something else, think of your plan.

When Silas comes, keep your eyes fixed on the target. Keep a loose grip on the pipe so your arm muscles stay relaxed. Let your wrists roll, as if you're swinging a baseball bat. Think of a karate master breaking a board—hit through the target to an imaginary spot on the other side.

He heard the crunch of steps on grit; Silas was moving down the main tunnel. The door of the crypt opened; Silas was putting Marsha's body back on the ice. He didn't close the door, leaving it open for the light. That would help him, but it would also help Joe. Slow, heavy footsteps advanced down the tunnel. Joe stood and peeked around the corner. He saw Silas's silhouette. Silas advanced and then paused, listening. Joe took deep breaths. Carefully he stepped away from the corner, to give himself more room to swing at Silas. Silas's footsteps were getting closer; Joe detected the irregularity of a slight limp. The crunch of the minister's heavy tread grew louder; he was almost to the corner.

Joe had his eyes trained upward to see Silas's head, but the first thing he saw was the gun. Wait! Silas's head came into view and he turned to the left, away from Joe. Swing! His wrists rolled and he connected with a spot he never took his eyes off of above and behind Silas's right ear. He heard a crack and Silas's knees buckled. He'd hit a home run, broken the board! Wobbling, Silas turned towards him. The gun was pointing at him. Swing again! He didn't make quite the same contact, but he hit Silas's forehead, which split open. Blood streamed down his face as he slumped to the ground, unconscious.

Joe panted, exhilarated. He kneeled and pried the revolver from Silas's hand. He fingered the trigger and moved the gun to Silas's temple. He looked into Silas's glazed eyes and at the blood pouring from his forehead. He pressed the trigger. He would kill him. Kill him!

His hand wavered. He heard music. The first notes of the final movement of Rachmaninoff's Third Piano Concerto. The percussive piano, the exuberant flourishes of the horns. This was what you lived for—the intensity, the inventive brilliance, the drama of Rachmaninoff's Third Piano Concerto. Kill an unconscious man and you'll answer for it. Try extricating yourself from the web of the Hidden Falls' legal process. There goes Rachmaninoff's Third Piano Concerto. There goes your life. Your life. The price of vengeance was too high.

"If I pull the trigger you win, you miserable son of a bitch," he said, removing the gun from Silas's temple and placing it in his jacket pocket. He stood and walked to the main tunnel and the crypt. Get Marsha Walton's body. Don't take the chance that Silas awakens and does something with the body before you return with Benewski and the police.

Silas had put the girl back on the ice. Joe gathered her in his arms and walked to the door. If you turn off the light you won't be able to see, but neither will Silas when he revives. He turned off the light and walked through the darkness of the main tunnel. Struggling with the girl's weight, he climbed the twelve stairs. The light of early dawn surprised him when he pushed open the door behind the tapestry; he thought it would still be night. He glanced at the coffin, walked down an aisle, through the vestibule, out the front doors and into the parking lot.

Walk faster, even though your arms, back and legs are tiring under the girl's weight. Walk faster, you're halfway across the lot. He heard the heavy creak of the church doors opening. Damn. Don't look back, you know it's Silas. Don't take the gun from your pocket and fire wildly across the parking lot. Forget the ache in your arms and shoulders and carry the girl as fast as you can, the car is only a couple of hundred yards away. He heard the labored plod of Silas coming down the stairs. Don't look back, he can't be moving that well after the way you hit him. You're out of the parking lot and to the road. Be careful running on the gravel, it's slippery. Silas screamed, in a high pitched wail, from the parking lot.

"Joseph…Joseph."

Don't look back, you're almost to the car. What will you do when you get there? Your keys are in your left front pants pocket. Pin the girl against the car with your body and take the keys out of your pocket with your left hand. Unlock and open the front door and dump the girl in the passenger seat. Start the car; don't flood the engine. Slowly pull away from the parking area or the tires will slip on the gravel and loose dirt. He heard irregular footsteps—Silas had reached the road. Running fast. Don't look back, here's the car.

He pinned the girl against the car with his body, took his keys out of his left front pocket with his left hand, unlocked and opened the door and dumped the girl in the passenger seat. Don't look back! He heard Silas panting as he closed the door. He didn't flood the engine and his car started on the first try—made in Japan! Silas thumped against the door and fiddled with the door handle as the car started to move. Don't look to your left, just accelerate.

The tires spun and then caught. Silas could not maintain his grip and fell away. Joe reached the road and turned towards Hidden Falls. To his left was the church and the morning sun peeking over the steeple. He saw Silas in the rear view mirror, getting smaller and smaller.

Chapter 11

Confrontation

"Honey, get the phone."

"Who the hell is calling this early?"

Gary Benewski and his wife, Margie, had been asleep, not yet awakened by the morning sunlight poking through the curtains of their bedroom window. He rolled over and picked up the phone receiver on the nightstand by his bed.

"Hello."

"Mr. Benewski?"

"Yes."

"It's Joe Tolleson." He could hear the effort Joe was making to control his voice. "I found the body. After I talked to you yesterday I figured out that Silas hid it in the church. He was going to put it in Mayor Matlock's coffin. There's a secret door behind a tapestry at the church and the body was in a room underneath the church. Silas tried to kill me, but I got away. The body is in my car. I want to come to your house. I don't want to go to the police."

Why had he drunk so many beers last night? Benewski tried to think, with little success. The mental fog was not so thick that it prevented the landing and takeoff of all thought, but it sure required the use of navigational instruments. He needed a cup of coffee in the worst way.

"Where are you?"

"In the parking lot at Prater's Exxon, at the pay phone."

"Where's Silas?"

"At the church."

"Go to the police station. I'll be there as soon as I can. Just get to the police station. You woke me up, so it'll take a few minutes to get dressed, but I'll be there. Unfortunately, they might arrest you."

"Arrest me! Why?"

"Because you have the body."

"And if I'm arrested?"

"I'll make sure they arrest Silas Wayne as well. Once the arrests are made, the police are out of the picture. Further prosecution of the case will be done by the district attorney's office."

"Will you be handling that?"

"Yes."

There was a long silence.

"After all this and I might be arrested. Damn! All right, I'll go to the police station. Can I wait for you in the parking lot?"

"No, find the officer on duty and tell him that you have the body in your car. I don't know what his reaction will be, but say as little as possible. If you're arrested, don't say anything at all. I'll see you at the police station."

"Okay."

Benewski hung up the phone. If Joe had the body it was a huge break in the case. But there was something troubling about what Joe had said, something about figuring out where the body was after he had talked with Benewski yesterday.

At Prater's Exxon, Joe returned to his car. He had laid Marsha Walton's body across the back seat. He drove the short distance to the town hall and parked his car by the rear entrance of the police department. He looked through the glass door and almost turned around. Sergeant Ruprecht was the officer on duty. He opened the door and approached Ruprecht's desk. Ruprecht was reading a magazine for physical fitness enthusiasts, but he saw Joe coming.

"What do you want?"

"The body that I told you about the last time I was here is in my car in the parking lot. Silas Wayne murdered and raped the girl. He's at the church and should be arrested. That's all I have to say."

"Nick," Ruprecht said, motioning to a nearby policeman, "watch the kid while I check out his car."

He hurried out to the parking lot and spotted Joe's blue Toyota with its license plate holder that read "Tolleson's Toyota." He peered through the back window. Unlike his counterparts in larger cities, he had seen few bodies. He could see that the body had been mutilated. He shook his head and whispered, "Holy Mother of Christ."

He ran back into the police station. "Nick, get a couple of guys and take the body out of the back of the Toyota in the parking lot." He went to his desk, opened the top drawer and pulled out a large key ring. He flipped through several keys and then held up a key. "Take the body down to the lab in the basement. Here's the key."

Nick took the key ring and went to find someone to help him with his grisly task. Ruprecht turned to Joe and said, "you stay here." Joe nodded. Ruprecht went to his desk and dialed the phone. He reached Chief Marsh at home and told him what had happened. Joe sat in a chair against the wall and waited. Ruprecht said, "I'll see you in a few minutes, Chief."

Nick and two other policemen came back about ten minutes later, chattering about the body. Chief Marsh arrived and began questioning Ruprecht and the policemen. He turned towards Joe.

"Arrest the kid."

"Chief, shouldn't we bring Silas in?" Ruprecht rarely questioned his chief, and never in front of other policemen.

"No. Why should we do that? We've got the suspect and we've got exhibit A. I won't arrest Silas Wayne."

"You will arrest Silas Wayne," boomed a voice from across the room.

Chief Marsh turned towards the speaker. Gary Benewski stood in the doorway.

"Who the hell are you, telling me how to do my job?"

"I'm Gary Benewski, the assistant district attorney, and believe me, I'm quite interested in how you've done your job."

Marsh directed his most intimidating stare at Benewski. He stepped towards him, but pulled up short. The ex-football player had two inches and twenty-five pounds on the chief. Benewski returned Marsh's stare.

"If you don't arrest Silas Wayne, you can answer to a judge why you ignored Mr. Tolleson's account of a possible rape and murder a week ago last Friday. The judge will also want to know why your department ignored a missing person's report filed by the probable victim's mother, Nancy Walton. I would say, Chief Marsh, that it's time you started doing your job."

There was a long silence. Marsh pointed at Ruprecht. "You and Nick drive out to the church and bring in Silas." Marsh turned back towards Benewski. "We're still going to arrest the kid."

"That's your prerogative."

Marsh turned to one of the remaining policemen, "Mark, are there any empty cells or do the DUI's have them all?"

"I think there's a couple."

"Okay, do the paperwork and put Mr. Tolleson in one of them."

"Yes sir."

It was the moment Joe had feared. The scene seemed strangely unreal; he felt as if he were watching himself in a movie. He saw himself stand and walk with the policeman to the booking desk. He heard himself answer a series of questions as the policeman filled out forms. After one question he withdrew a gun from his pocket and slid it across the desk to the policeman. Then he remembered something that seemed both important and unimportant. He heard himself ask the policeman if he could call his father. He saw the policeman push a phone across the desk.

"Joe, where are you? You're mother and I have been worried sick. We were about to call the police."

"I'm at the police station. I found the body of the girl; it was under the church. I'm being arrested and so is Silas Wayne. I'll tell you the whole story when you get here."

"You found the body and you've been arrested? Why are they arresting you?"

"Because I have the body and Chief Marsh doesn't believe my story. Dad, I can't say too much because there's a policeman here."

"Okay, we'll be there shortly. We haven't slept all night, so it won't take us long to get ready." There was an awkward pause. "Son, you must be scared and confused, but we'll work this thing out. We're not going to let anybody railroad you. We love you."

"Thanks, Dad," Joe said, his voice shaky. He hung up the phone. The policeman read the Miranda warning and led him to the elevator, which they silently rode to the basement. Two heavy security doors opened and he was led to an empty cell in the corner. It was an old fashioned jail with bars. There were eight cells and only the one next to his was empty. Most of the other prisoners were asleep, but one unkempt man in his late thirties or early forties cast a brief, disinterested glance at him and then turned away. Joe crinkled his nose as the policeman shut his cell door; he smelled vomit and urine.

The only item in the cell was a narrow metal cot with a thin mattress and pillow.

Thirty minutes later Ruprecht and Silas came through the security doors. Silas had a large bandage on his forehead. They did not speak or look at him. Ruprecht opened the door of the cell next to his and Silas entered. Rubbing his head, Silas sat on the bunk against the back wall. He turned away from Joe.

Shortly after Silas's arrival, the policeman named Nick came to Joe's cell. He unlocked the door and told him that his parents had arrived. He led him to the jail's visitors' room.

He and his parents sat on opposite sides of a thick, wire-embedded window, which partitioned the room. He was the only prisoner in the room. A policeman was visible through a small window in the prisoners' door. Light yellow walls, a scuffed black and white tiled floor and an absence of furnishings or decoration, other than a row of armless chairs upholstered in green vinyl, accentuated the room's depressing purpose. A hole covered by a metal grate, similar to those found in banks, allowed for conversation with his parents. His mother sobbed, occasionally replacing her Kleenex. His father wore the stunned, uncomprehending look of a survivor of a natural disaster.

"Joe," his father said, "are you all right? One of the policemen said you had a gun."

"Yes, I'm fine, but I'm very tired and hungry. When we're done, could you go get me some breakfast? I think Brigg's Diner is open."

"Sure, we'll do that." His father cast an anxious glance towards his mother. She did not look at him and continued to sob. "Joe, the policeman said that Silas was messed up when they arrested him. He had a big gash on his forehead and a large knot on the back of his head. What happened?"

He recounted the events of the previous night, omitting what Silas had said about his mother. Occasionally he looked at her; she was oblivious. Sometimes she would slightly cock her head when he mentioned Silas. He felt dazed and lightheaded—he needed food and sleep.

After he finished his story, his mother seemed to become aware of her surroundings. She surveyed the room. In a weak voice, muffled by her Kleenex she said, "Joe...Joe, you're in jail." She sobbed. "Joe, did you..." she sobbed and sniffled, "...did you kill that girl?"

She had not listened to his story. She thought he could murder and rape. He glanced towards his father, who was visibly anxious. Then he turned toward her. He felt like he had when he held the gun to Silas's head. This time he would not check his violent impulse; he intended to wound.

"No, mother," he said, keeping his voice icily precise, "I didn't kill Marsha Walton, and you wouldn't ask that question if you were not in love with Silas Wayne."

She wailed and slid down into her chair, wailing. The blood drained from his father's face as he moved his lips, unable to make a sound. Joe stood and walked out of the visitors' room. He closed the prisoners' door and began to shake, uncontrollably. The policeman helped him to his cell.

In the visitors' room, Alice and Jack sat for a long time, Alice crying, Jack silent. Finally, Jack turned towards his wife and spoke, his voice cold.

"What really happened between you and Silas Wayne?"

His wife would not answer. He waited almost ten minutes, but she continued to cry.

"Come on," he said, standing, "let's go home."

They said nothing to each other as they left the visitors' room and walked to their car. He did not touch her. She sobbed as they drove home. He forgot to stop at Brigg's Diner for Joe's food. When they arrived at their house, she went to the kitchen and placed a large crystal tumbler, a bucket of ice and a bottle of scotch on a silver tray. She carried the tray to the master bedroom and flipped the door lock. She did not leave the bedroom for the rest of the day.

CHAPTER 12

▼

THE ACCUSED

"Joseph, Bertrand Russell once said: 'there is not one word in the Gospels in praise of intelligence.'"

It was Saturday afternoon, and this was the first time either of the prisoners had spoken to the other. Earlier, a policeman had brought them a lunch of hamburgers and French fries. Chief Marsh had come by to tell them that since the magistrate judge was out of town for the weekend, they would have to wait in jail until Monday for their first judicial proceeding.

There were eight cells, barred cages, in the jail, four on one side of a walkway and four on the other. A guard sat at one end of the walkway, to monitor the prisoners and escort them to the shower and restroom. Joe lay on his cot in a corner cell. Silas was in the adjacent cell. Prisoners lying on their cots occupied the other cells. They paid no attention to Joe or Silas. Joe tried to doze. He heard Silas's comment, but did not respond.

"I know you hear me, Joseph." Silas's voice was low, almost a whisper. He apparently did not want to be heard by the other prisoners. He paced from one end of his small cell to the other, clasping his hands behind his back. "There's a locked door most people try to open. On the other side is everybody else. People want to open that door, not because they want to know those on the other side, but because they want those on the other side to know them. Not just to know, but to listen, to pay attention, to accept and ulti-mately, to love them. Unfortunately, the harder they try to open the door, the more impenetrable it becomes.

"There isn't one in a thousand who will understand what I'm about to say, but I think you will. The key to the door is thought—the thought that the door doesn't bar you from the world, but rather bars the world from you. You open the door by stepping away from it. You can have as much or as little of the world as you desire when you don't need its attention, acceptance, or love. Life becomes your choice, not theirs. When you close the door, those on the other side will attempt to break through your barrier. They'll call you arrogant or indifferent, but you'll open the door only for those you want to let in, regardless of how loudly they pound."

Silas paused, seemingly awaiting a response. Joe sat up on his bunk and watched the minister, who returned his stare. Both their faces were impassive, revealing nothing. He was fascinated by Silas's words—refractions, if not reflections, of his own thoughts. However, he remained silent. There was no use acknowledging and thereby encouraging Silas. Wouldn't it be interesting if the rest of the town could hear what their icon really thought? Could he ask Benewski for a tape recorder? No, Silas was too smart—he would clam up if Joe left his cell for any length of time. Silas continued pacing across his cell with his hands clasped behind his back. It seemed to help him concentrate. He resumed his meditations.

"There's only one authentic key to the door, Mr. Lockpick, but there are many counterfeits. Religion is one. Faith in unproven propositions will open the door. Once opened, what's on the other side? A God who hears all prayers; who judges, but ultimately accepts; whose love is unlimited and unconditional. It's exactly what those who never step away from the door want to hear. No thought necessary. Thought is work, and requires being alone with one's own mind. No wonder the Bible doesn't have anything nice to say about intelligence.

"Better to replace all that painful philosophical speculation with myths and the conventional wisdom. Never mind that the resultant hodgepodge of bromides, snippets from self-help manuals and who knows what else is rife with contradictions. They won't discover them if they keep their talismans tucked away, never considered or questioned. They stay on the path marked 'settled routine,' ignoring their own desperate insecurity. There are the standard duties—earning a living and raising a family—and the standard amusements to divert their attention. Your eyes are getting wide, Joseph; you know I'm right. Unfortunately, they haven't really opened the door. So they flock to people like me, offering counterfeit keys, and they hate people like you, who have the key and keep the door locked against them. That's why you shouldn't be congratulating yourself yet. The game isn't over between us, it's just begun."

The man was a gargoyle, but Joe couldn't dismiss what he said. How could he know what he knew, yet be what he was? Joe turned away. He had to consider Silas without being distracted by Silas. The minister did not resume his sermon.

In another part of the town hall—the district attorney's office—Mike Devore and Gary Benewski were engaged in a tense conversation. Benewski explained that Joe and Silas had been arrested as suspects in the murder and possible rape of Marsha Walton. He told Devore that Joe claimed he had found the body underneath the church and had been discovered by Silas Wayne, who had tried to kill him.

"How did Joe Tolleson know that the body was underneath the church?" Devore asked.

Benewski shifted in his seat. "I talked with Joe this morning, before he brought the body to the police station. He said that he had figured out that the body was underneath the church after he talked to me yesterday afternoon."

"You talked to Joe Tolleson yesterday?"

"Yes, I did. He called me at the office. He wanted to know about our investigation. I didn't say much, but I did tell him that we had staked out the parsonage Wednesday night, trying to get Silas to reveal the location of the body. I told him that the only time Silas came out of his house was when he went over to the church to pick up a book. It's possible that Joe deduced from that information that the body was still in the church. When I talked to him this morning, he said that Silas planned to hide the body in

Mayor Matlock's coffin. I'm not sure if Silas told him that while they were under the church or if he figured it out beforehand. I understand that Matlock's coffin was brought to the church Friday afternoon, and that's not the way things are usually done."

"Do you see the problems with what you did, talking to Joe Tolleson yesterday?"

Benewski heard anger in Devore's voice, and the district attorney's eyes were drilling him with the kind of glare normally reserved for hostile witnesses on cross-examination. He again shifted in his chair. "As a rule," he said, feeling like a child made to answer an obvious question, "the district attorney's office shouldn't disclose information about an ongoing investigation to someone who is a potential suspect in that investigation."

"That's correct. Everything we do on this case will be scrutinized. If Joe Tolleson used information that you supplied him to uncover the girl's body, and that comes out during the trial, it'll be considered a procedural irregularity and we'll take a lot of heat for it. However, there's another problem that may be much more serious, a procedural issue."

"Of course," Benewski said, hitting his forehead with his open palm. Suddenly he understood his anxiety that morning when Joe had told him how he had deduced the location of the body. Although he had been too excited to recognize the issue at the time, it had registered somewhere in his subconscious.

Devore shook his head. "That's right. Wayne's attorney will spot it, too." Devore took off his glasses and carefully performed his glasses cleaning ritual. When he spoke, his voice had recovered its even modulation. "Continue to treat both Joe Tolleson and Silas Wayne as suspects in the murder of Marsha Walton. The magistrate judge is Homer Watkins. See if he can come down to the town hall and conduct the first appearance for both suspects."

"Watkins is on a hunting trip and won't be back until Monday."

"That's unfortunate. Then we have no choice, the suspects will have to be held over the weekend. Has Silas made any kind of statement?"

"No."

"Has the coroner had a chance to look at the body yet?"

"He was present when Nancy Walton identified her daughter, but I don't think he's done any kind of detailed examination."

"Were you there when Mrs. Walton made the identification?"

"Yes, she fell apart. I had to carry her out of the lab. She came down to the station with a couple of friends and they took her home. The poor woman."

"It tears you up, doesn't it? I was there once when a father had to identify his son. I can't think of anything worse. The man just cried and cried." Devore paused. "Have two complaints ready for Monday morning. Doctor Pace probably won't do an autopsy until Monday, but have him examine the body to determine if the girl was raped. That way we won't have to amend the complaint and add a rape charge. This is an unusual case in that we have probable cause for two suspects, but only one committed the crimes. Ask the judge for identical bails for both suspects, pending further investigation. We'll know a lot more after the autopsy and the investigation of the crime scene."

"Chief Marsh has already agreed not to conduct any part of the investigation at the church if I'm not present." Benewski smiled. "I think he'll be very cooperative from now on. He wouldn't allow Mayor Matlock's funeral to be performed at the church, so they're moving it to Bloomstown. Should we ask him to allow services to be held in the church tomorrow?"

"Yes, I think this town is going to need a church service tomorrow. Have Marsh cordon off the area around the secret door and don't let anybody go up to the choir loft. I've never been to the church when Silas wasn't there to conduct the services. We'll have to bring in the Reverend Ellison from Bloomstown."

*   *   *

Sunday morning, the Reverend James Ellison surveyed the largest congregation he had ever addressed. He was in his late thirties, but his thin build, long, wispy brown hair, circular wire framed glasses and insubstantial mustache gave him the look of a graduate student. Light streaming through the stained-glass windows fell on the congregation in irregular colors and patterns. The people of Hidden Falls had squeezed into every pew and were standing in the aisles and at the rear of the old church. He knew why they had come. They needed to tell each other what they were doing and how they reacted when they heard the news. They needed to share their shock, their horror and their grief. They needed to ask each other questions for which there were not yet answers. And they needed to see the scene of the crimes—the choir loft and the secret door behind yellow tape. The Reverend Ellison felt the heat of tension rising from the packed congregation. He was about to raise his hands to quiet them for his opening prayer when the murmuring suddenly died.

Alice and Jack Tolleson had entered the church and were walking down the middle aisle. Jack held Alice on his arm, supporting her. Her face was drained of color and occasionally she rubbed her eyes and temples. They walked to the middle of the church and an open space appeared next to the aisle. They sat down.

The Reverend Ellison had prepared a sermon, but set it aside. They did not need a sermon today. He did not know the Tollesons, but considered himself a close friend of Silas Wayne's. He limited himself to several prayers and a brief, impromptu comment. His words were punctuated by sobs from throughout the church. He closed with a prayer.

"Almighty God, regardless of how this tragedy is resolved, please keep forgiveness in the hearts of your children. Let us not condemn, for it is your place to judge. Let us offer our solace and support to those who must bear this burden, as you support us as we bear our burdens. Amen."

"Amazing grace, how sweet the sound, that saved a wretch like me…"

The gelatinous voice of Nora Grimes, a massively overweight woman who dispensed advice to anyone she could trap, arose from the back of the church. Her first wobbly notes would have died a solitary death if Madge Holmby and Dora Nederham, two heavyset friends, had not come to the rescue, joining her in the old standard. Cowed by that look which says: don't ask questions, their husbands joined the chorus of the obese. Others scrambled for their hymnbooks and the unknown words after the famous first lines. The initial embarrassed hesitation gave way to a community moment as many voices became one, reverberating off the old church's stone walls. By the last verse, many had linked hands and they could not restrain their tears as the final notes echoed throughout the church. The congregation had congealed.

The throng respectfully waited for Alice and Jack Tolleson to depart. As the couple started down the aisle, Alice saw her close friend, Sandra Mayes, and motioned for her. The threesome walked out of the church and stepped into the muted autumn sunlight. A cold breeze blew dead leaves across the parking lot. Alice leaned over and whispered into Sandra's ear. Sandra shook her head in response to Alice's question. No, the family of the girl who was killed was not at the church that morning.

The threesome stood on the church steps as the congregation left the church. Some of Jack and Alice's friends hesitantly approached them, but Jack noticed that others stayed away. Those that spoke to them offered only tepid sympathy and support. The congregation that had just sung "Amazing Grace" with such fervor believed his son had committed the crimes. He took his wife by the arm. They separated from Sandra Mayes and walked down the church steps and across the parking lot to their Cadillac. When Jack closed the door, Alice surrendered to the tears she had been fighting all morning. She put her head on his shoulder and cried as they drove back to their house. It was going to be a long Sunday.

*　　　　　*　　　　　*

It was a long Sunday for the two prisoners. They did not speak to each other all day. That evening they ate a dinner of gristly roast beef, overcooked broccoli, white bread and margarine, and lime Jell-O with fake whipped cream. Silas finished his milk, set down his tin cup and wiped his mouth with a paper napkin. He turned to Joe and began pacing across his cell. Joe sat on his cot, watching the preacher.

"Do you know, Joseph," Silas said, his voice again low, "that today was the first time I've missed a service since I became the minister at the church? Twenty-four years. I wonder how the flock did without their shepherd.

"I like talking to you, Joseph, even if you don't say anything. When I was your age, I spent a lot of time reading. I was trying to understand a world that didn't seem to understand or care about me. It didn't take me long to realize that life is about power. History is the story of one group struggling to control another; what we do in our own small way is merely a microcosm of this larger struggle. There's nothing particularly original about that, but I think another insight I've had is more astute."

Silas stroked his chin thoughtfully. "Rulers come and go, control shifts, but one group has a power that lasts beyond their lifetimes. Nobody worships Alexander or Caesar or Napoleon, but people worship the great religious figures—Jesus, Mohammed, Buddha. At the core of religion are precepts that have an enduring appeal. These ideas can be used to control other people."

"Why do you want to control other people, especially if they're as stupid and pathetic as you make them out to be? It sounds like they do a fine job of messing up their lives without your help."

Silas stopped pacing for a moment, and then resumed. "The best that this pitiful world has to offer is power. One can be the puppet or the puppeteer." He held his hands up and moved his fingers, manipulating imaginary strings. "Pull the right strings and most people will voluntarily dance; the fate of the rest is inconsequential." He clasped his hands behind his back. "Create confusion and anxiety—get people to work at cross-purposes with themselves. Desire, interest and joy are wrong; duty, sacrifice and guilt are right. Zero yourself out of existence. Of course you're unhappy, but have faith; life is short and eternal happiness is yours when you're dead. Still confused? Listen to me, I'll tell you what to do. I wish I could take credit for these ideas, but they've been around a long time and others have used them more effectively than I. It still amazes me, though, how many people mistake pure poison for the milk of human kindness."

"But the girl hanging in the church—she didn't want you pulling her string—so you slipped it around her neck. You talk a good game, but if you couldn't handle her rejection, you sure haven't opened any doors." Joe stood up from his cot. "What do you get out of running other peoples' lives? You dime-a-dozen dictators, you 'people who need people,' always hate the idea that somebody can get along without you. Why? Why is everything about power? What's wrong with people living their own lives, getting what they want through production and exchange?"

"It's nonsense," Silas said, his voice rising as he waved his hand. "That's the morality of the marketplace—a Chamber of Commerce plaque hanging on a wall in your father's hardware store. Those of us who understand, who are meant to pull the strings, have nothing but contempt for the kind of ideas that guide a mediocrity like your father."

"You never answer my questions, Mr. Self-anointed string puller. Say what you want about my father, but he doesn't rape and murder customers who don't buy his product. Have you ever done an honest day's work in your life? A lot of people sneer at businessmen like my father, but I've noticed that most of them somehow wind up on the payroll. I know how much my father puts in the plate every week; he's been paying your salary for years."

There was a lengthy silence. Both prisoners sat on their cots, engulfed in the dimming light. Silas was never challenged—he preached, not debated. His ideas had developed in a vacuum that Joe had unsealed. Having lost a duel with his weapon of choice—words—he was unarmed, speechless. The silence lasted several hours.

Joe asked to be escorted by the guard to the bathroom. When he returned he took off his shoes and lay on his cot, ready to sleep. The cot's mattress was narrow, lumpy and smelled of disinfectant. He was not optimistic about getting a good night's sleep. Silas lay on his cot. The minister spoke, but for the first time he raised his voice enough for the other prisoners to hear. Several turned their heads towards him.

"You've never been in love, have you, Joseph? Wait until someone falls in love with you, then you'll know hatred. What are you proudest of? Your curiosity? Your creativity? Your integrity? Your independence? Your ability to think? I pity the first fool who falls for you. She'll love the freckles on your nose, or your blue eyes, or your mop of blonde hair, or your bright prospects or something equally irrelevant. In fact, she'll think you're perfect;

except that sometimes you're preoccupied by your own thoughts and don't listen to her gossip, and sometimes you make ironic jokes about acquaintances that neither she nor they understand, and sometimes you don't seem to care about what everyone knows is important—family, stability, security and society. But she'll know that once she ensnares you, she'll change all that. When you see this wretched creature in what is supposedly the highest state of human experience, you'll develop your own contempt for humanity."

"Silas, I'm real sorry you've been disappointed in love. I'll probably kiss a few frogs before I find my princess, but there are three or four billion women on this planet. I think I'll run into one who appreciates the real me."

"Don't mock me, you blasphemous brat. People don't want or deserve your world, and that's not the world we're moving towards. Life isn't as simple as your theories."

"You're right; it's usually simpler. Good night."

*   *   *

Joe and Silas were awake when Chief Marsh entered the cellblock early the next morning, followed by a policeman holding a tray with their breakfasts. The prisoners had done their best to clean up, taking showers and combing their hair. Silas had tried to shave with a disposable razor that one of the guards gave him, but there was no mirror in the bathroom and nicks were visible on his chin and neck. Chief Marsh's imposing bulk seemed to fill the walkway between the cells. All the prisoners watched him. He brusquely addressed Silas and Joe.

"After breakfast, you'll be brought to your first judicial appearance, before Magistrate Judge Homer Watkins. Reverend Wayne, you'll appear first, and then you, Tolleson. Harvey Roach has made arrangements for your attorney and bail, Reverend Wayne. You'll be represented by Preston Catledge.

"Tolleson, your father has made similar arrangements for you. I believe your attorney will be Ned Burroughs. I don't know how the district attorney's office plans to proceed. You'll find out more in court."

Chief Marsh turned and walked out of the cellblock. The policeman handed both prisoners their breakfast, but neither one ate. They did not speak. Sergeant Ruprecht came to escort Silas to his first appearance. As Ruprecht shut the door to Silas's cell, Silas turned towards Joe.

"I suppose your father will post your bail. Enjoy your freedom, it will be brief."

"You'll never be free, Silas—your personality is your prison."

Silas turned and walked away. Ruprecht shot a malicious glance at Joe, and then followed Silas.

Joe did not have long to wait for his judicial appearance. The policeman named Nick escorted him to the courtroom. His father and two men he did not know greeted him. His father introduced the men, Ned Burroughs and Matthew Hoskins, and told him that they would be his attorneys. Burroughs was a distinguished looking man, of medium height and a solid build with dark brown hair streaked with gray. He was in his late forties or early fifties. His black-rimmed glasses magnified his alert blue-gray eyes. He wore an expensive tailored black suit. Hoskins about fifteen years younger than Burroughs. He was tall and lanky, with blond hair above an angular face and darting green eyes. His rumpled blue suit was off the rack.

"Joe," Burroughs said, "this proceeding is merely to inform you of the charges against you and set your bail. Just listen to the judge and answer his questions. He may ask you for bodily samples. You don't have the right to refuse those samples, so I'd advise consenting to his request. If you get confused by anything, you can always speak to Matt or me."

Joe nodded. He understood what was about to happen, but he was still anxious. He walked with his attorneys to the front of the courtroom and sat at the wooden defendant's table. Gary Benewski and Mike Devore sat at a similar table on the other side of the courtroom. Magistrate Judge Homer Watkins sat at the imposing wooden bench. He was a short, fat man in his mid-fifties. He had small, porcine eyes and a fringe of brown hair on the sides and back of his balding head. He turned towards the defendant's table.

"Mr. Joseph Samuel Tolleson?"

"Yes."

"You have been named in a complaint by the district attorney's office charging you with the rape and first degree murder of a victim tentatively identified as Marsha Walton. You have the right to remain silent and anything you say in court or to the police may be used against you at trial. You have a right to counsel, or if you are indigent, counsel will be provided for you. Do you understand the charges and your rights?"

"Yes."

"Bail for your release has been set at $100,000. Your father has posted a ten percent bond for your appearance at all further judicial proceedings. This bail is subject to revision pending further investigation by the police and district attorney's office. Charges may be dropped or further ones may be added depending on the results of these investigations. The district attorney's office has requested that hair, blood and tissue samples be taken from your body as part of their investigation. Will you submit these samples?"

"Yes."

"You will be taken to the police lab after this hearing. The preliminary hearing for this case will be conducted after the completion of the autopsy and the investigation at the scene of the suspected crime, and when the results of the bodily sample analyses are available, upon the motion of the district attorney. After you submit the required samples you are free under the bond posted by your father. Do not leave Hidden Falls without the court's permission. That is all."

Magistrate Judge Watkins banged his gavel and Joe turned to his lawyers.

"Joe," Hoskins said, "the samples are just like blood tests when a person is arrested for a DUI. The Supreme Court has ruled that you don't have a Constitutional right to refuse them. Silas Wayne has agreed to submit samples. They'll be matched against evidence found at the church and on the body of Marsha Walton. The district attorney might also ask for a DNA analysis."

"Okay." A policeman motioned for him and they walked out of the courtroom to the elevator, which they rode to the police laboratory in the basement. A pretty black woman in a white lab coat introduced herself as Sheila Bartlett. She pricked his finger for blood samples, cut several locks of hair from his head, scraped the inside of his mouth with a toothpick and smeared the skin tissue on glass slides. As Joe left the lab, she smiled and wished him good luck.

The policeman returned with Joe to the courtroom, where his father was waiting for him. As they left the town hall, a small crowd of people standing on the steps greeted them. His father put his arm around him and escorted him through the crowd. Cameras clicked and two reporters from the *Hidden Falls Herald*, holding notebooks and pens, approached them.

"We have nothing to say. Please allow us to leave. Thank you." His father voice was flat. The reporters let them proceed down the steps to their car. His father opened his door and Joe sat down. There was something comforting about the plush leather seats and the power of the big, black Cadillac. As it pulled away from the curbside space in front of the town hall, he turned to his father.

"Thanks, Dad. I wasn't sure what was going to happen after Saturday."

"We'll talk about that later. I asked the attorney who handles my business affairs, Don Hamlin, for the name of a good criminal lawyer and he recommended Ned Burroughs. Matthew Hoskins is Burroughs' associate. I talked briefly with Gary Benewski from the district attorney's office. I guess you know him. He said that the investigation and autopsy shouldn't take more than a couple of weeks, but that it might be a month before they get back the results from the analysis of your samples. They're going to do DNA tests. He didn't come right out and say it, but I think he believes that they'll be able to drop the charges against you when they have all that."

"What about you, Dad, what do you believe?"

"Son, I know you didn't rape and murder that girl. I went along with your mother, but I should have believed you when you told us what happened. I was in a daze all weekend thinking about Silas…and your mother."

"Where's mom? I thought she'd be with you."

"She's at home. When I left she was asleep. She's not handling this very well. We went to church yesterday. That was a mistake, but she wanted to go. When we got home she went straight to our bedroom and locked the door. I haven't seen her since."

"Is she sick?"

"No, it's very strange, she's drinking."

"She's never done that before."

"No, she hasn't. I don't know if she'll be up when we get home. I hope she snaps out of it." His father turned towards him. "How do you feel? Do you even want to go home?"

"I want some breakfast. I took a shower this morning at the jail, but I feel like I need another one. I need to sleep. I hope mom's going to be okay. I'd like to talk with you more, but at this point, I'm numb. Let's just go home and I'll crawl into bed."

"Sure."

They drove to their house and his father fixed his breakfast. After he ate he went upstairs to his room and sat on his bed. He heard his father calling his mother's friend, Sandra Mayes, from a telephone in the hall. His father explained that he had to go to his Buick dealership and do some paperwork. He asked her to come over and stay until his mother awakened. That was the last thing Joe heard before he fell asleep, still in his clothes.

CHAPTER 13

▼

THE FUNERAL

Gary Benewski and Mike Devore sat in a pew behind a small crowd of mourners at Marsha Walton's funeral service. They heard a loud sob from the front pew, where Nancy Walton and her daughter, Janice, sat. Benewski winced as he recalled his last conversation with Nancy Walton. He had learned that she wanted Silas Wayne to perform the funeral and had gone to her house to try to dissuade her. He sat at her shabby kitchen table. She fixed a pot of coffee. The smell filled the air when she poured the steaming liquid into Benewski's cup. She walked to the counter, pulled the cap from a bottle of whiskey, poured some into her cup and then poured her coffee. He declined her offers of whiskey, milk and sugar.

"Nancy," he said, "are you sure this is what you want to do? The Reverend Wayne may be responsible for Marsha's—"

"I know, I know. I mean I know that you're charging him. But I know Silas. Silas loves our little family, he's the only one who's always been there for me and the girls." She started to cry and reached across the table for a Kleenex. "The kind of man he is…there's just no way he could do what you've accused him of. It's got to be that kid—Tolleson." She sipped her coffee.

"Nancy, at this point in our investigation, I would say the evidence points towards Silas."

"I don't give a damn about your evidence. Where was Tolleson and his rich daddy when we needed help? They don't give a shit about us; they don't even know we're alive. What kind of person do you think I am? Do you think I'm going to turn my back on Silas now, when he needs all the support he can get? That's a lot of people's idea of friendship; I see it all the time. Sure, I'll be your friend—until you need a friend. Well, I've got more loyalty than that; I stick with my friends when the chips are down, just like Silas did for us. Now, Mr. Benewski, I'm going to have to ask you to leave, before I get madder than I already am. You go back to your investigation, you'll see. Silas didn't murder my daughter."

She was adamant; there was nothing Benewski could do. He turned towards her as he left her house, trying to think of something appropriate to say. She stood in the doorway, hands on her hips, feet apart, stance defiant. Her lower lip quivered and an occasional tear rolled down her cheek. He felt sympathy for this proud woman.

"Call me anytime, Nancy."

Another loud sob brought his attention back to the service. Silas Wayne was eulogizing Marsha Walton.

"I knew Marsha Walton."

A Biblical double entendre? He glanced at Devore, who did not take his eyes off the minister. Silas continued.

"Yes, I knew and loved Marsha, although she did not like me. Marsha was a fine and beautiful girl, with head-strong ways and a quick tongue. It is of no consequence that she had not fully accepted the Lord's plan for her life when her life ended. Some of his servants who are closest to him initially reject his truth. Like the father of the prodigal son, the Lord never stops loving his children."

How could he eulogize the girl he had raped and murdered? Benewski stared at Silas, trying to catch his eye.

Silas was conscious of Benewski and Devore's scrutiny. He had glanced at the men from the district attorney's office as they had entered the church, but tried not to look in their direction during the service. He did not make eye contact with Benewski or Devore, sitting behind the other mourners, or with Nancy or Janice Walton in the front row.

He concluded his eulogy and congratulated himself as the organ began to play. He had wanted to refuse Nancy Walton's request to perform Marsha's funeral service, but there had been no plausible way to do so. Most of the funeral service was rote, but the eulogy had been difficult, requiring all of his concentration. He looked around the church. Weak light rays filtered through the stained-glass windows. Candles were lit, but their light barely penetrated the haze that enshrouded the proceedings. He glanced towards the choir loft and could just make out the organist. Chief Marsh had allowed her into the choir loft, but not a choir, since the investigation at the church was not yet finished. Silas wiped sweat from above his upper lip, and looked down at his hand written notes. He flipped through the pages he had completed and put them to one side of his pulpit. Sometimes drafts blew through the cavernous church. He placed a paperweight with the symbol of a fish on top of the pages.

Iesous Christos, Theou Uios, Soter, was Greek for Jesus Christ, Son of God, Savior. The acronym for this phrase was *ICHTHUS*, the Greek word for "fish." The sign of the fish was how persecuted Christians in ancient Rome had signaled their religion to each other. He glanced at Marsha Walton's casket.

Kill her! He clinched his teeth against his own fury. Kill her! His grip tightened on the sides of the pulpit. Women were fish—flashing, letting you catch a glimpse of their slippery beauty, then flashing again. If you caught them, you had to hold them and squeeze them until they died, or they flashed away. And when you killed them, you cut them and cleaned them and froze them. Women were fish, and women were the devil.

He was nothing to them. His mind, his pride, his self-control, and his righteousness—these he had offered, as a dog on its back begs to be scratched. He got a dagger through the belly. Remember Reverend Ames, his teacher. Never a word of praise from that old fool. One smile from Alice, and she had the key to his kingdom. Women have the key to the kingdom, and men can't own it, can't steal it, and can't control it. They can only destroy it. The fish in the coffin said he was full of shit. He had destroyed her, before she destroyed him. And now he'd never let them know—he'd slip away like a flashing fish. He had his lie, and he had something he hadn't counted on, something that he'd turn to his advantage. He would elude their net.

When had the organ music stopped? He looked out at the pews. The mourners looked back at him, expectantly. His flock. His sheep. The shepherd was their invention, a myth for those seeking salvation from themselves. The wolf was real—the predator hunting its prey. A lupine smile momentarily played across his lips, before he remembered where he was. He said, "that concludes our memorial service for Marsha. Nancy and Janice, know that our thoughts and prayers will be with you in the coming weeks and months. We will now proceed to the Whispering Pines cemetery for the grave side service."

Four pallbearers carried the coffin down the aisle. Behind them were Nancy and Janice Walton, both dressed in long black dresses, with no veils. Nancy Walton was no longer crying and she carried herself with dignified grace. Benewski and Devore filed in behind the mourners as they walked down the aisle and out of the church. They were both dressed in heavy overcoats. They were greeted by the kind of weather associated with funerals. A chill wind blew across the parking lot and gray clouds blanketed the sky—harbingers of snow and winter. Devore slipped on a pair of leather gloves from his overcoat pocket. Benewski and Devore got in Benewski's old Ford and they drove out of the parking lot.

"Silas is a good actor," Benewski said, glancing sideways towards Devore.

Devore did not respond.

"Did you notice that he never looked at us? You told me that Silas Wayne is an accomplished public speaker, so he should make eye contact with his entire audience. I think that he deliberately didn't look at us. Another thing. It was cold and drafty in the church, but he wiped sweat off his upper lip twice and once off his forehead. Also, there was that long pause after the organ music, like he was preoccupied. Now maybe he's just unsettled by all of this, but then again, maybe he's trying to hide something."

"If he is, he's got a tough road."

"How many murder cases have you prosecuted?"

"Just a couple—you don't see a lot of murders in a small town."

"I've had about a dozen. There's nothing more difficult for a murderer than trying to maintain his innocence when he's actually guilty. Because of his emotional state at the time of the crime, his memory of what actually occurred is usually clouded. That makes it harder to stitch together a plausible lie. I guess it's one for the psychologists as to whether or not they have a subconscious desire to be caught, but I know on a conscious level they're terrified of conviction." Benewski disliked the pedantry he heard in his own voice.

"I think," Devore said, "that what may be even harder than keeping the truth from everyone else is keeping the truth from themselves. Both the murderers I convicted will go to their graves without admitting their guilt. Watch out for that pothole on the other side of this intersection." Devore pointed.

The Whispering Pines cemetery was on the opposite end of town from the old church. The small funeral procession was making its way down Main Street. A policeman in the intersection waved Benewski's car through a red light. Benewski noticed a few people on the sidewalk, looking at the hearse a block ahead.

"The murderers that I've dealt with have been a mass of contradictions," Benewski said. "Deep down inside, they hate themselves. I haven't seen enough of Silas Wayne to say for certain, but assuming he did it, we'll eventually see his self-loathing. Although even with his slip-ups today, he's been pretty slick so far. He's got brass balls, performing the funeral for the girl he's murdered in front of the her mother and sister. You've got to wonder what kind of lies he tells himself." He looked at Devore, but there was no clue on the district attorney's face as to what he was thinking. He pressed on, ignoring a feeling that he was digging himself into a hole.

"Perhaps he has some sort of delusion of moral superiority. You ever read *Crime and Punishment*?" He immediately wished he had not asked the question—it sounded stupidly condescending.

"Raskolnikov's Napoleonic complex. Of course, you're assuming Silas is guilty, which you can't assume. Maybe Silas isn't so slick, maybe he didn't actually do it."

Benewski nodded. Before he could make a case against Silas, he would have to convince his boss. He turned his car into the Whispering Pines cemetery and parked at the end of a short line of cars parked behind the hearse. The two men got out of the car. The hearse was parked in front of a newly dug grave. The four pallbearers carried the coffin from the hearse and placed it on a dark red pad behind the grave. A small group composed of Marsha's mother and sister, a few friends and the pallbearers stood in front of the grave. Benewski and Devore walked to the group and stood behind them. Silas was behind the coffin. He opened a Bible. The wind blowing through nearby trees and rustling dead leaves made it difficult to hear his voice as he read verses.

Silas spoke for several minutes and then closed the Bible. He walked over to Nancy and Janice Walton and embraced them. After consoling them and greeting the other mourners, he walked to his car, where he sat for several minutes before leaving the cemetery.

The mourners quickly dispersed. Nobody wanted to stay outside; the wind was picking up and it was growing colder. Benewski and Devore walked to the car, got in and hastily closed the doors. As they pulled away, Benewski looked back towards the gravesite. One of Nancy Walton's friends stood by a car parked at the curb. Janice Walton was standing next to her mother, who was kneeling at the end of her other daughter's coffin. Nancy Walton's head rested on the coffin and her arms were outstretched as if she were trying to embrace it. Spasmodic upheavals racked her body as she cried without restraint.

CHAPTER 14

▼

THE DOUBLE HELIX

Joe sat in a classroom at the local branch college of the state university. Christmas break was three days away. He was not looking forward to the break; it would give him unwanted free time. His mind needed to be occupied, to think about something besides Marsha Walton, Silas Wayne, DNA tests and judicial proceedings. He no longer slept—his insomnia was only occasionally interrupted by a light doze. He no longer tasted what he ate, although he forced himself to mechanically swallow food to keep up his strength. He no longer read the *Hidden Falls Herald*. Not one in a hundred people in Hidden Falls believed that Silas Wayne had raped and murdered Marsha Walton, and the local paper reflected the popular belief. The police and the office of the district attorney were not releasing details about their investigations, so there were no facts available to counter the prevailing prejudice. He no longer had contact with the people of Hidden Falls. They had always let him go his own way; now he was completely shunned. Customers at the hardware store avoided him, waiting until another clerk was available. He no longer talked with his fellow students at the high school and the branch college.

The only person who would talk with him was his father. Joe knew that his father was alarmed by the dark circles under his eyes, the way his clothes drooped on his thinning body and his isolation within Hidden Falls. The previous evening, he had been sitting at the dining room table, absently staring into space. His father had entered the room and rested his hand on Joe's shoulder.

"Joe, what did Silas tell you under the church about your mother and me?"

Joe looked at his father. He wanted to tell him the truth, but he did not know where to begin. He was encouraged by the quiet gravity of his father's expression.

"He said that mom loved him, but that he had controlled his desire for her so that he could destroy her. He said that she was beautiful and talented and ambitious, but that he made her choose between her dreams and him. She chose him, and he rejected her. He said that you were her second choice. He said more, but I don't remember it all and that's the upshot of what he said."

His father was enraged about everything that had happened. His anger was ever present, palpable though seldom expressed. Now Joe could see the muscles in his father's face tightening as he pulled a chair from the dining room table and sat down.

"That's about what I imagined he said. I see you moping around and your mother drunk all the time and I think, Silas Wayne, you son of a bitch, you're guilty of a lot more than murder and rape. He's taken the life out of you and ruined my marriage. I can't even talk to her anymore, Joe—you hear the fights. I live in the guest room of my own house and most nights I don't feel like coming home from work. Hating is a waste of time, but I hate Silas Wayne. I had my repo man go out to the parsonage and repossess the Buick I donated to him. I could have done it, but I didn't trust myself if I happened to see him. I'll never set foot in that church again, at least not until he's gone."

"I know, Dad. I try not to think about it. I have to force myself to listen to the teachers, to study, to do anything. I'm glad I've got college applications to fill out and you've got some things for me to do over Christmas break. Otherwise I'd go nuts with all the free time."

Joe was grateful that his father now believed his story and that he wanted Silas convicted. The ordeal was taking its toll, but it would have been far higher without his father's support. He just wished he could sleep. If he could sleep, everything else might take care of itself. Physically, his insomnia seemed to have little effect, but it hampered his concentration. Now, sitting in the classroom, he forced himself to listen to Mr. Hale's lecture on the properties of light. The lecture was interrupted by a knock on the classroom door. Mr. Hale opened the door a crack. After talking briefly with someone outside the door, he left the room.

He returned a short time later with Gary Benewski. Both the teacher and the assistant district attorney motioned for Joe. He stood and walked to the front of the class. He heard the other students murmuring behind him.

"Joe, would you come with me?" Benewski said.

They left the classroom and met two uniformed police-man in the hall. Joe looked inquisitively at Benewski.

"We've received the results of the DNA tests. DNA from foreign pubic hair found in Marsha Walton's pubic hair, as well as from skin under her fingernails and from sperm within her vaginal cavity is identical, meaning it all came from one source. Furthermore, the DNA corre-sponds to the DNA submitted in your blood, hair and tis-sue samples. You're under arrest for the rape and murder of Marsha Walton."

Joe felt his legs buckle at the knees and suddenly he could not see; everything was black. Benewski reached out and grabbed his elbow to support him. He heard Benewski say something about continuing the investiga-tion and he was conscious of an amplified pulsing sensa-tion in the veins at his neck and temple. Benewski motioned to one of the policeman to put his handcuffs back on his belt.

The DNA test results had arrived that morning. Benewski had gone to Devore's office and informed the district attorney, who seemed relieved that the tests implicated Joe rather than Silas Wayne. Benewski stood in the doorway of Devore's office and Devore sat behind his desk.

"There must have been a mistake," Benewski said.

"Your reaching, Gary." Devore waved his hand, dis-missing the idea. "Draft a motion to drop all charges against Wayne and draft another to arrest Tolleson."

"We should raise Joe's bail."

"There isn't going to be any bail. When people find out about the test results, they're going to be furious. It's bad enough that he'll be charged with Marsha Walton's rape and murder, but he also tried to frame Silas. We'll keep him in jail for his own protection. There's also the risk that he might try to leave Hidden Falls. Draft a motion for preventative detention."

Benewski had to plead for several minutes before Devore allowed him to go with the police to the branch college for Joe's arrest. He had left Devore's office feeling confused and angry and walked back to his own office. He placed his head on his desk for several minutes. Then he called information, got the number for Tolleson Toyota, called Jack Tolleson and told him the news. There was a long silence on the line.

"I can't believe it, there has to be some sort of mix-up."

"That's what I said, too, Mr. Tolleson. However, Joe's going to be charged."

"Are you going to the branch college to arrest him?"

"Yes."

"May I come with you?"

"No." After Devore's reluctance to let him attend Joe's arrest, Benewski knew that the district attorney would never permit Mr. Tolleson to be there.

"Okay, I'll see you at the town hall with our lawyers."

Now Benewski supported Joe as they walked through the halls of the branch college with the two policemen. Joe's face was drained of color and the look in his eyes suggested a cornered animal—wild, dazed confusion. Confusion was replaced by comprehending anguish when they walked out of the building and he saw the police car parked at the curb. The policemen allowed Benewski to sit in the back seat with Joe.

Joe's father, Ned Burroughs and Matthew Hoskins were waiting for them when they arrived at the police station. Jack hugged his son, but they did not speak. Joe and the two attorneys went into a conference room and Joe saw his own reflection in the highly polished veneer of the circular conference table. Ned Burroughs was the first to speak.

"Joe, at your initial appearance, Magistrate Judge Watkins delayed the preliminary hearing until the completion of the autopsy, the investigation and the DNA analysis. The preliminary hearing will be the next step in this process. That's a quasi-adversarial hearing where the district attorney will present witnesses and evidence to persuade the magistrate judge that there is sufficient probable cause for the district attorney to file an indictment with the general trial court."

Joe was stunned by the attorney's matter-of-fact tone. "How can this be happening?" he stammered. "I didn't do anything, there's been a mistake."

"I know you want to talk and explain your position, but at this point don't say anything to us. Definitely don't talk without one of us present to the police, the district attorney's office or anybody else. There will be plenty of opportunity for you to tell us your story, but after we've done our own investigation. Your arrest is an unexpected development."

Joe slumped in his chair. The two attorneys began discussing legal strategies, taking no further notice of their client.

"Ned, we can challenge the admissibility of the DNA tests," Hoskins said. "It's a controversial area of the law. Nobody questions their use on a theoretical level—the chances of two individuals having the same DNA are infinitesimal. However, there have been cases, like O. J.'s, where the tests have been successfully challenged because of faulty testing procedures or because of unclear results."

"Yes, look into that. Get copies of the report from the testing lab. Also get copies of the autopsy and the police report on the investigation. We'll be going before Judge Watkins soon. The district attorney will probably move for preventative detention. We should oppose the motion as a matter of form, but given the circumstances of this case, I think the district attorney will prevail. Joe, what that means is that you won't be granted bail; you'll be spending some more time in jail."

Joe nodded listlessly without speaking.

"I'm also going to check into Joe's medical and psychological history," Hoskins said. "We might have to lay the groundwork for a diminished capacity or an insanity defense."

Burroughs scowled at his young associate. He turned to Joe, whose eyes had widened at the mention of an insanity defense.

"Joe, we don't think you're insane. As your attorneys, we have to consider worst case scenarios. I apologize for Matt, sometimes he thinks, and speaks, too quickly for his own good. We have a lot of work to do before we can decide what your plea will be."

"Sorry, Joe," Hoskins said.

There was a knock on the door. A policeman opened it and told them that they were to go to the courtroom for an appearance before Magistrate Judge Watkins. They silently proceeded to the courtroom. The hearing was almost a replay of Joe's initial appearance. This time, however, Joe was not asked to submit samples and bail was denied. After the brief proceedings were finished, a policeman came to take Joe to the jail. Before he was led away, his father came up to him. They both had tears in their eyes.

"This is all wrong, Joe, there's been a mistake. We'll get to the bottom of this—I'll do everything I can. Is there anything I can get for you?"

"A pillow, Dad…a pillow," he mumbled. "The one in the jail isn't any good."

"Okay, Joe," Jack Tolleson's face contorted with rage as he fiercely embraced his son. "Goddamn it, if it's the last thing I do, I'll get that son of a bitch. We'll get you out of here."

They separated and a policeman led Joe to the jail in the basement, where he was put in the same cell he had been in before. He sat on his cot, slumped with his back to the corner of the small cell. He watched the guard shut the cell door and then he did not move for a long time. His face never changed expression as he stared at the wall of the cell opposite his. Suddenly he jumped up and began pacing back and forth.

"Insane…" he screamed, stopping his pacing. He heard his own voice bounce off the jail walls.

"Insane…" he again screamed. It had been his impression when he entered the jail that the cells were deserted, but now he noticed an old man in the cell next to his, lying on the cot and watching him. The grizzled figure wore a tattered overcoat, oversize pants so stained that their original color could no longer be ascertained, fingerless gloves and heavy work boots. His weathered, seamed face was covered by white and gray whiskers. He had been watching Joe since Joe's arrival, but now, as Joe screamed, his face never changed expression. Joe recognized both stupidity and curiosity in the way the old man looked at him. He rarely blinked, but when he did, it seemed as if he actually thought about the process, tightly squeezing his eyelids shut.

The old man was Mason Mingus, a drunken derelict. Somewhere in his harsh life he had encountered a virus whose untreated progression had rendered him deaf. Mingus refused the help of the Hidden Falls' social agencies, instead performing odd jobs for sympathetic residents in exchange for food or money. In good weather he slept in doorways or on park benches and in the winter he was allowed to sleep in a jail cell if there were one empty.

"What are you in for, Mason, drunk and disorderly? Joe nodded several times. "I see. I've been charged with insanity." Joe's eyes widened and he grinned demonically, Jack Nicholson style. "Two months ago one of my teachers said I was a genius. Now I'm insane. I guess it really is a thin line. I saw the man who has this town by the balls with the girl he raped and strangled. I was insane enough to think that if I told people they would do something about it. I risked my life to prove what I saw, and now I'm the one charged because I'm insane." Joe's lowered his voice to a stage whisper. "There's something wrong here, Mason."

Joe's took a couple of steps toward Mingus. The old man did not move. He continued to look at Joe in his stupidly curious way.

"You can't hear a word I say, can you? Beethoven was deaf, and Edison was partially deaf. It didn't seem to hurt them. Maybe that's why there's that thin line—some geniuses can't tune out the world's noise and it pushes them over the other side. Being deaf might not be such a bad thing—maybe there's a tradeoff. The world doesn't listen to you; you don't listen to it. Like the world's listening to me, anyway. I can clear my mind and hear music—my own music. I once got up in the middle of the night and wrote out the first movement of a symphony. I can do differential equations in my head and I can think in three languages. But it's all a product of insanity. Right now, I'd be better off if I were like you—I wouldn't...I wouldn't have heard that noise in the choir loft." Joe's voice wavered.

Mingus shifted his position on the cot and then stood, weaving unsteadily. He reached his hand towards his crotch and Joe thought he was going to scratch his genitals. Instead, he reached into his pants and pulled out a half-full pint of whiskey. He unscrewed the top and took a long pull. He extended the open bottle towards Joe, who reached through the bars and took it.

"It looks like Hidden Falls' finest didn't do a very good job of frisking you, Mason. Somebody once said that he drank to make other people more interesting." Joe took a small sip from the bottle, feeling the hot liquor move down his throat. He took a bigger drink and set the bottle on his cot. "Most people are looking for someone to listen, even though they don't have much to say. If they met Einstein on the street, they'd tell him their problems. The more you have to say the less anybody listens. Have you ever talked with somebody and then can't remember a thing you talked about after the conversation? No, of course not, you're deaf. Maybe when you drink people do get more interesting. Maybe you hear them lying to themselves. There's a big lie that everybody knows about, Mason, but nobody admits. I'm not quite sure what it is, but if you make people confront it, you get a hell of a reaction. That's why I'm here—Silas uses that lie."

Joe stopped talking and stared at Mingus for several moments. Mingus returned the stare with no indication of what he was thinking. He blinked his eyes tightly several times. Then, he probed his left nostril with his right index finger, withdrew his finger, inspected it and wiped it on his pants.

"Picking your nose, farting, belching, scratching your balls—those are the kinds of things that might keep you off the Hidden Falls' Social Register. Not that you should listen to me about what it takes to be a social success in Hidden Falls. Clearly your career has outshone mine. Have you even been charged with anything, or are you just sleeping off a drunk? I'm a dangerous, insane, felon, arrested for rape and first degree murder. My real crime is getting too close to that lie. The Social Register has something to do with that lie."

He picked up the bottle of whiskey and put it to his lips, pretending to drink. Mingus nodded, signaling that Joe could drink again from his bottle. Joe took two long drinks and handed the bottle back to Mingus. He could feel the alcohol starting to dull the anger, confusion and fear churning in his stomach.

"Yes, Mason, if you've heard it once you've heard it a thousand times—we all want to be liked. We want to be liked more than we want to be honest, more than we want to do the right thing, more than we want to find out the truth about sinners masquerading as saints. I want to thank you for your hospitality, Mr. Mingus. I think some of it's going to my head and I need to lie down." Joe lay on his cot, cursed the thin pillow and eventually fell into an uneasy sleep.

Around Hidden Falls after the arrest there was a chorus of "I told you so's." Within an hour, everyone knew about Joe's reincarceration and Silas Wayne's "exoneration." A sense of triumphant vindication, tinged with unstated relief, swept the town. At both the high school and the branch college, students and teachers talked about the crimes of the disturbed whiz kid. Only a few of Joe's teachers expressed skepticism about his guilt. In a deserted classroom, Barbara Martell, the mathematics teacher, sat at a desk and cried.

At The Cut Above beauty salon, cosmetologists and customers chattered about the newest development.

"You knew there was just no way that Silas did it," said Molly Richards, a member of the church choir. She was the only one present who was unaware that her husband, tired of her insipidity, was having an affair with a woman in his office.

"There's usually something weird about really smart people," commented Nora Needham, a beautician who had recently been certified after her third attempt on the state cosmetology test.

"I feel so bad for Alice and Jack," said Maggie Finstermacher. She worked with Alice on several church committees. Her husband had once owned a warehouse, but sold it to Jack Tolleson and now worked for him.

"My heart goes out to them, but you know, something always seemed too perfect about the Tollesons. Alice has looks that the rest of us would kill for, Jack's loaded and the kid's a genius. I don't think God lets anybody have it all, you find a skeleton or two in every closet," commented Dolores Maywood, a close friend of Alice and Jack Tolleson.

At Brigg's Diner, Scott Maguire, ex-star running back of the Hidden Falls high school football team, flipped a hamburger patty on the grill and listened to two customers at the counter talk about Silas Wayne and Joe Tolleson. He smiled slyly when he thought about Tolleson behind bars. The twerp had it coming to him.

Jack Tolleson had left the police station and gone home to tell Alice the news. She had been drinking, but she was sober enough to understand what had happened. Jack closely studied her reaction after he told her. Her eyes were directed at his, but their glassy opacity indicated that she had withdrawn into her own thoughts. After several minutes of silence, she stood up, walked out of the living room and into the kitchen. Jack heard her pour her drink into the sink and run the water. She returned to the living room.

"I'm going to take a shower," she said.

"It's good to see you're so concerned about our son," he said, as she started up the stairs.

"Your son," she said, slurring the "s." She climbed the stairs.

At the Starlight Lounge, Nancy Walton was in a small storeroom behind the bar, which the cocktail waitresses derisively called "the employees' lounge." She had just punched the time clock and was sitting on a crate, replacing the flat shoes she wore to work with the high-heeled pumps she was required to wear on the job. Another waitress, Sally Adams, walked into the employees lounge. Her shift was ending.

"Nancy, did you hear the news?"

"What news?"

"They arrested that kid—Tolleson, and dropped the charges against Silas."

Nancy was too stunned to speak for several moments. "Oh my God…" she stammered, "thank God." She cried and hugged Sally Adams for a long time.

In a trailer at the Cline's Grove Mobile Home Park, about two miles outside Hidden Falls, Edna Mayhew listened to the news on the radio. The elderly widow sat in her cluttered living room in a threadbare easy chair. A tray with a microwaved dinner of baby peas, pressed turkey and stuffing with authentic home-style gravy rested on her lap. She listened to the lead story about Joe Tolleson and the Reverend Wayne. At one point she put her dinner on the floor, waved away her cat, Patches, and picked up a tablet and pen. She made the notation "Gary Benewski— assistant district attorney" on the tablet and then rescued her tray from Patches.

She finished her dinner and went into the kitchen to throw away the tray. She walked with some difficulty, but she did not like to use her cane. Walking back to the living room, she picked up a picture from the top of the television set and looked at it. In the foreground, she stood with three other elderly women. Standing behind the group was the Reverend Silas Wayne in his ministerial robe. She said, "Silas, I don't know how you did it," and placed the picture back on the television set.

*   *   *

Joe lay on his cot during his first night back in jail, fighting a headache by reviewing his biochemistry and visualizing the model of DNA. An atom—a negatively charged electron or electrons revolving around a positively charged nucleus consisting of one or more protons and neutrons. An element—the basic unit of matter, composed of one or more identical atoms, which can't be changed except through sub-atomic disintegration. A compound—a combination of at least two atoms from at least two different elements. A molecule—the smallest particle of either an element or a compound that can exist in a free state and retain the properties of the element or compound. The molecules of elements consist of one atom or two or more identical atoms; those of compounds consist of two or more different atoms. Adenine, thymine, guanine and cytosine—four molecules, composed of different combinations of the elements carbon, nitrogen, hydrogen and oxygen (except adenine, which has no oxygen). Deoxyribonucleic acid (DNA)—a molecule composed of a core of adenine-thymine and guanine-cytosine base pairs joined to two sugar-phosphate molecular strands spiraling around each other. The basic genetic material within the chromosomes of the cell nucleus, DNA transmits the hereditary pattern for every living organism.

The double helix structure of the molecule, first discovered by James Watson and Francis Crick in 1953, was a ladder spiraling around itself. The parallel rails of the ladder were the sugar-phosphate molecular strands. The rungs of the ladder were either the adenine-thymine or guanine-cytosine base pairs. The spiraling parallel of the sugar-phosphate strands and the infinite permutations of the thousands of base pairs were the code of life, determining both what an organism would be and its characteristics. A beautiful paradox—the complex simplicity of the double helix.

He did not know the forensic history of DNA testing, but he understood its theoretical basis. Within a species, most of the DNA of any organism is identical to the DNA of any other organism within that species, since the organisms within a species have more similarities than differences. However, there are small segments of the DNA sequence that are unique to an organism and which account for the unique characteristics of that organism. These unique segments can be analyzed with sophisticated chemical techniques that operate on the molecular level. Theoretically, it is possible to develop a DNA profile for any person based on those base pair combinations within the DNA molecule that are unique to that person.

Wasn't it ironic that he fully understood and appreciated the theoretical underpinnings of the applied science petard of DNA testing upon which he was being hoisted? What would happen if identical twins were suspected in a crime, since their DNA would be identical? For that matter, what would happen if two suspects were related? It might be difficult to distinguish DNA profiles, since they would have more genetic similarities than two unrelated individuals. He bolted upright in his cot, then jumped up and began pacing back and forth across his cell, like an animal in its cage at a zoo. He would pace most of the night, grappling with a disturbing question that chased away any hope of sleep.

CHAPTER 15

▼

AFG-2073

Benewski rose from his chair as Gail Smathers opened the door for Mrs. Edna Mayhew. Thin, frail, she used a sturdy wooden cane and walked slowly with a slight stoop, her flowered cotton dress hanging loosely about her. The wisps of her gray hair dropped to her ears and neck. A pair of horn-rimmed bifocals rested on the bridge of her long, thin nose. Her green eyes suggested both maturity and youth. The crinkled wrinkles at their corners and their calm, steady gaze bespoke the wisdom of age, but the alert way she surveyed his office was youthful. She sat and smoothed her dress.

"I'm Gary Benewski, Mrs. Mayhew," he said, as he sat in his chair behind his desk. "I'm pleased to make your acquaintance. What can I do for you?"

"Pleased to make your acquaintance, sir."

He could tell that she was not well from her voice, which had an unhealthy rattle as air was drawn through a diseased respiratory system. He guessed that she was suffering from lung cancer or emphysema.

"I've lived in Hidden Falls for over fifty years. This was my husband, Ralph's, hometown. We came here after he got out of the army. Ralph was a butcher at Darwin's Market. He retired ten years ago. Three years later he died of a stroke. You know, we all have to go sometime, but knowing that doesn't make it any easier when your husband goes. When he died, all I wanted was to join him. I thought he was the lucky one, leaving this earth first.

"Ralph and I went to the old church—Silas Wayne's church. It wasn't Silas's church when we got here; Reverend Ames was the preacher. After Ralph died, going to church was the only time I would stick my head out of my hole. My son, Oscar, lives in town and he and his wife, Wilma, did all my shopping. Eventually, I got so depressed that I even stopped going to church."

He stifled his urge to interrupt the elderly woman with questions. It would be disrespectful. She would get to the point in her own way.

"That's when Silas started coming over to my house. I live in a trailer out at Cline's Grove. For a while Silas was visiting almost every day. At first I wouldn't say much, but Silas kept encouraging me to talk. That poor man; I must have talked his ears off. He drew me out of my shell. I went back to church. Silas suggested I join the women's prayer group. I refused, but he kept after me. I finally joined and rediscovered some old friends. See, here's a picture of me and my friends in the prayer group. That's Silas in back of us."

She took a picture out of her large brown handbag and handed it to him. He examined the picture of her, three other women and Silas Wayne and nodded his head without saying anything.

"About two years ago Silas suggested that I become an aide for one of the Sunday school classes. He said it would do me good to be around children. I didn't want to do it; you lose your patience with children as you get older. Silas just kept insisting, like he does, and I became the aide for Mrs. Brody's Sunday school class. Silas was right again; I enjoy it. I'm not going to be able to do it very much longer, though, on account of my illness."

With the reference to her illness she stopped to catch her breath. It was as painful for him to listen to her wheeze through her story as it was for her to tell it. He hoped she would finish soon. After several minutes she resumed.

"One of the things I do is help set up the refreshments for the Sunday school classes after the classes are over. We have refreshments in the recreation room annex next to the church. The Sunday after the girl was killed, before they discovered the room underneath the church, I noticed that the ice machine in the kitchen next to the recreation room was gone. I asked Silas about it. He told me it was broken, so he had taken it in to be repaired."

He moved forward in his chair; she was about to make her point.

"I didn't think any more about it until a week later, when I read in the Herald that one of the things they found in the room under the church was an ice machine. I don't know if that was the same ice machine that was in the kitchen, but if it was, something doesn't add up."

She paused to catch her breath and then continued.

"If it was the same one, why wasn't Silas surprised when I told him it was missing, and why did he tell me he had taken it in for repairs? If Silas really did take the ice machine in for repairs, you could check that out with whatever repair shop he claimed he took it to. If that ice machine is the same one that was in the kitchen, then Silas may have been lying when he told me he had taken it in for repairs. And if Silas is lying, maybe he's got something to hide."

Her voice broke on her last sentence and she removed a Kleenex from her handbag to wipe her eyes.

"Why did you wait this long before you said anything?"

"Well, I'm sorry, Mr. Benewski, but I thought the truth would come out and there would be no need for me to say anything. But now they've arrested that poor boy and Silas is free. I'm not long for this world—my cigarettes caught up with me. I can't stay silent about my suspicions and keep a clear conscience. You're still young, but when you get older you'll understand. When you know you're going to die, you want to make sure everything's squared up. Maybe the ice machine under the church is a different ice machine than the one in the kitchen. If it is and Silas's story checks out, I'll be happier for it. But if Silas was lying and the Tolleson boy is convicted of Silas's crimes…well, I can't die with that on my conscience."

"Mrs. Mayhew, I'm not mad that you didn't come forward sooner. It takes a lot of courage to say anything against Silas Wayne. I'm just glad you came forward. Of course we'll check out your story. I assume you would be willing to testify, under oath, to what you told me."

"I certainly will. You know, in seventy-eight years you pick up a thing or two. One thing I know is that only fools pay attention to what people say about other people. Now everybody you talk to says that Joe Tolleson is some sort of disturbed genius. I wish I had a dime for every person that I've heard called a genius, but this kid does well in school, he does all sorts of interesting things and holds down a part time job. He's got a promising future and all the potential in the world. That doesn't seem to me like the kind of kid who would rape and murder a young girl."

"Is there anything else, Mrs. Mayhew?"

She looked around his office, not focusing on any one thing. He saw that she was making an effort to compose herself. Finally, she spoke, in a voice more labored than before.

"One other thing I've learned is that there's usually something wrong with a person everybody likes. When someone is too good to be true; it's too good to be true. Now I admire Silas, but I've always wondered about him a little, too. I don't think he's a perfect saint, and one of the reasons I don't think so is because that's what he wants everybody to think. When I was talking to him a lot, somehow he'd let it slip that he had helped so-and-so, or that he had donated money or given his time to this or that organization. I'll be very sad if it turns out Silas did it, but knowing what I do about people, I won't be surprised."

Why were old people ignored? Like most of the elderly, Edna Mayhew wanted to talk, even if it pained her ailing lungs, and like most of the elderly, she had nobody who wanted to listen. Lifetimes of experience and observation ignored. Why were those with the most to say afforded the least opportunity to speak?

"Mrs. Mayhew, is there anything else? I'll check out everything you've told me. Thank you for coming in."

"Thank you, Mr. Benewski. I hope you get to the bottom of all this. I've said everything I need to say."

"Here's my card with my phone number. Please call me if you think of anything else."

He stood and handed her his card. He opened the door for her and volunteered his secretary if she needed a ride back to her house. She assured him that her son would pick her up. Returning to his desk, he opened a file folder drawer and withdrew a thick file labeled "Marsha Walton Investigation." From the file he pulled out a long sheet of paper, a checklist of items of evidence. He had not said anything to Edna Mayhew, but a notation on his checklist indicated that the serial number on the ice machine matched the serial number on a receipt found in Silas's files. The ice machine was purchased three years ago and there was a handwritten notation—"Recreation Room"—on the receipt. Mrs. Mayhew was right; something didn't "add up."

He reviewed the rest of the checklist. According to Jasper Wooters, the caretaker hired by the church for the parsonage, the two tubs—for Marsha Walton's corpse and her blood—came from Silas's garage. Wooters also confirmed that the portable generator came from a hutch under Silas's back porch. A church deacon, Thadeus Franklin, recalled that the deacons had authorized Silas's request for a portable generator several years ago, in case the power went out at the parsonage. The generator's serial number matched the serial number on a receipt in Silas's files. The table on which the tub with Marsha Walton's body had rested was identical to tables in the Sunday school classrooms and the recreation room annex. Silas had volunteered no information about any of the items found under the church.

He moved down the checklist, to a number of items that had red stars next to them. The stars indicated that he had been unable to trace the origins of the items. The transparent plastic sheet—Marsha Walton's shroud—was a type commonly used to cover large pieces of furniture during shipping, but there were no identifying markings. The lock and clasp on the door of the room were of the same brand, but they had no serial numbers and were sold at four different stores in the area, including Tolleson's Hardware. The key to the lock had not been found. The jars that had contained Marsha Walton's internal organs were the type commonly used for pickling or preserving fruits and vegetables. The knives used to eviscerate Marsha Walton were top quality and appeared to be new. Like the lock and clasp, they were sold in several local stores, including Tolleson's Hardware. They did not match any knives found at either the parsonage or the Tolleson's house. The two electrical cords, for the ice machine and the light bulb, were also untraceable.

The last two starred items were the rubbing alcohol in the jars that the organs had been stored in and the box of surgical rubber gloves. He had asked Gail Smathers to call every drug and discount store within thirty miles of Hidden Falls to determine if any of them had sold, sometime after Marsha Walton's death, a large number of bottles of alcohol and a box of surgical gloves. He buzzed his secretary.

"Gail, would you call the stores again about the alcohol and gloves? Why are they taking so long?"

"I called them three days ago; there are only two that haven't responded. Perhaps it takes a long time to go through all the cash register tapes. None of the stores that have checked their tapes have found anything. The two stores that haven't responded are both part of national chains and send their tapes back to their main headquarters. I'll call the store managers again."

"Thanks."

"Ned Burroughs called. Joe Tolleson wants to talk to you. He says he thought of something that might help you with the investigation. Burroughs says he has no problem with what Tolleson wants to tell you. If you consent to a meeting, Burroughs will be with him."

"Sure, I'll meet with them. Try to set something up in about half an hour."

"Okay."

He returned to his list. He had drawn a heavy black line to separate items found in the room under the church from other items that were important to the investigation. Below the line were three items that had question marks beside them—Marsha Walton's clothes, the plastic sheet that was placed under her body and the rope used to hang her. None of these items had been found. The next notation was for a Smith and Wesson, .38 caliber revolver. A note indicated that the registered owner of the gun was Silas Wayne, three bullets and three shell casings had been found in the gun and three fired bullets had been found in the tunnels under the church. The metal pipe was next on the list. The last two items were a red flashlight and a yellow flashlight, with a note that both were broken.

He put away the list and reread the autopsy report. Nothing new there—Marsha Walton was still raped and the cause of death was still strangulation and she was still dead. But something didn't "add up." The ice machine that Silas said was in for repairs was found in the subterranean room. It was possible that Joe had taken the generator and the two tubs from the parsonage, but it didn't seem likely. How would he have known to look in the garage for the tubs and under the back porch for the generator? Benewski picked up the lab report on the DNA tests. This was the key—something was wrong with the tests. Joe Tolleson didn't rape and murder Marsha Walton.

Smathers buzzed him when it was time to meet with Joe Tolleson and Ned Burroughs. They met in a conference room next to the jail's visitors' room. Two policemen escorted Joe and then stood guard outside the door. Joe, Benewski, and Joe's attorneys, Ned Burroughs and Matthew Hoskins, sat around a circular table. Joe appeared distraught and exhilarated at the same time. His eyes were puffy, and Benewski guessed he had not slept the previous night. When he spoke, Benewski heard excitement in his voice.

"Mr. Benewski, I thought of something last night. When I was under the church with Silas, he told me that my mother was in love with him. I asked him if he had ever had sex with my mother, and he said, 'I never had sex with your mother, Joseph, but I fucked her.' When he said that, I thought that he meant that he had never had sex with my mom, but that he had 'fucked' her by destroying her dreams. Maybe I misinterpreted him. What if he meant that he had never had sex with her in the sense that sex was an expression of love, but that he had had sex with her to express his contempt for her? If he actually did have sex with her, he might be my father. If so, maybe it threw off the DNA tests—there might be similarities in our DNA."

Wow! It would explain a lot if Silas and Alice Tolleson had once been in love, especially if there was still something between them. Poor Joe—that would be why his mother didn't believe his story. His concern about the test results seemed plausible. He would have to talk with somebody in the pathologist's office and find out the methodology of the tests.

"You must feel like Luke Skywalker after Darth Vader told him he was his father. Is there anything else you want to say?"

Joe smiled weakly at the joke and then looked at Ned Burroughs, who shook his head. "That's all I have to say."

Benewski returned to his office. He told Smathers to call Alice Tolleson and ask if he could meet her at her house that afternoon. He also asked her to call the police lab and set up a meeting with the people responsible for the DNA tests. He left his office with the DNA test report and rode the elevator to the laboratory in the basement.

A black woman who introduced herself as Sheila Bartlett opened the door to the police lab. Her loose lab jacket did not hide her taut, well-proportioned body. She smiled—the contrast of her teeth to her skin seemed to illuminate the angular beauty of her face—and asked him to wait for a moment. He noticed the lightness of her step—a dancer's or an athlete's—as she walked to Doctor Pace's office, a glass walled enclosure in the corner of the lab. She returned to escort him to the office.

Doctor Pace rose and the two men shook hands. Doctor Pace sat in his chair behind a desk neatly stacked with copies of journals entitled Forensic Pathology and

American Pathologist. He was a short, wiry man whose evasive, nervous eyes were the unnatural blue produced by tinted contact lenses. His dark brown hair was carefully slicked over from one side of his head to the other in a vain attempt to hide a bald spot. Brown whiskers with small flecks of gray were closely cropped in a thin mustache and goatee. He drummed his fingers on his desk. He motioned for Sheila Bartlett to sit in a chair beside the desk. Benewski sat in a chair facing them.

"Mr. Benewski, I'm Doctor Randolph Pace, what can I do for you?"

"Pleased to meet you, Doctor Pace." Benewski placed his copy of the lab report on the desk. "I have some questions about the lab report on the DNA tests in the Marsha Walton case. I was hoping you could answer them."

"We'll certainly try." A perfunctory smile momentarily crossed Pace's face.

"Exactly how were these tests conducted?"

"Sheila can tell you about the basic procedures for the test."

Bartlett reviewed the sampling procedures for the two suspects. "Once I had their samples, I put the hair samples in small plastic bags, the blood samples in glass vials and the tissue samples on glass slides. I gave each suspect a code number and taped labels with the code number to each sample. Then I put both groups of samples in separate plastic, resealable pouches and wrote the code number on the outside of the pouch. Can I see that report?"

He handed her the lab report.

"Yes, here it is. Joe Tolleson's code number was AFG-2073 and Silas Wayne's was BPP-4522. I also wrote down those code numbers in my lab log book. After I was done with the samples I addressed an express mail box, to send all the samples to the lab in Tyler City that does the actual DNA analysis." She handed the report back to him.

"Is there any way the labels could have got mixed up?"

"I don't think so. Even if I made a mistake labeling one of the samples, it would have shown up when the DNA tests were performed. That sample would have been inconsistent with the suspect's other samples, and consistent with two out of three of the other suspect's samples."

"I've been working with Sheila for six years, Mr. Benewski," Pace said. "She doesn't make mistakes."

The lab assistant smiled, embarrassed.

"Were the suspects present when you labeled their samples?"   .

"Yes."

"Did you take the package to the express mail office or did they pick it up?"

"The express mail office won't pick up packages. I didn't take the package to their office, though; Doctor Pace did. I was pressed for time because I had to pick up my daughter from school for a dentist's appointment. I left the pouches with the samples from Joe Tolleson and Silas Wayne on the counter. Doctor Pace told me that he would stop by the morgue at the hospital to pick up the foreign samples found on Marsha Walton's body and the samples from Marsha Walton's body. He put together the package and dropped it at the express mail office on his way home."

"Did anybody else have access to the laboratory?"

"No," Pace said. "I was here for the rest of the day after Sheila left the samples in the express mail package on the counter. Nobody else came into the lab."

"So there were four sets of samples that went in the express mail package?"

"Yes," Bartlett responded.

"You dropped the package off at the express mail office, Doctor Pace?"

"Yes, I did."

"Would you find the receipt and send it up to my office?"

"Certainly."

"So after the package was mailed, it was out of your hands until the report came back from Tyler City?"

"That's correct."

"There's a great deal of technical explanation in the report from the Tyler City lab that I don't understand, but the upshot of the report is that DNA from the foreign samples taken from Marsha Walton's body match the DNA from the sample encoded AFG-2073."

"That's correct," Pace said.

"Now is there any possibility that there could have been an error in the tests? I know that the use of DNA tests has been challenged in court."

"Well, Mr. Benewski, assuming competent administration of the DNA tests, there are two basic grounds for challenging their admissibility. The first instance is when the samples are old or of poor quality. I don't think that will be an issue in this particular case. The foreign samples that were found on the body of Marsha Walton were of excellent quality. We found three foreign pubic hairs in her pubic hair. There was foreign skin tissue under her fingernails. Also, because the body was on ice, the semen sample we extracted from her vaginal cavity was in good condition—there was little decomposition. The quality of these foreign samples allowed for an accurate analysis of the DNA segments. I talked to one of the technicians in Tyler City, and the DNA segment images, which are called autoradiographs, were clear." Pace paused and contemplatively stroked his goatee before continuing.

"Defendants have been able to successfully challenge autoradiographs when they were blurred due to the decomposition of the subject samples. In this case, the autoradiographs of the foreign samples taken from Marsha Walton's body were clearly identical to each other and to the autoradiographs taken from the sample labeled AFG-2073, Joe Tolleson's sample. If Mr. Tolleson's lawyers challenge the DNA tests, I will testify in court that the tests were accurate."

"What's been the other ground for challenging DNA tests?"

"There have been a few cases where defendants have claimed that their genetic relationship to another party precludes the use of DNA tests. There was a case where a defendant was convicted on the basis of a DNA test in which the prosecution experts were allowed to tell the jury that there was a 96 million to 1 probability that the DNA in the sample was that of somebody other than the defendant. It turns out the defendant came from a small village where there was extensive intermarriage. Everyone was related to everyone else, and the probability quoted to the jury should have been much lower. In fact, the tests probably shouldn't have been used at all, since at one point in the case one of the defendant's relatives was considered a suspect."

"That's terrible. What happened to the defendant?"

"He's probably still on Death Row, or he's been executed."

"That's disturbing. Is there any possibility in this case that the DNA tests could be challenged on the grounds that the suspects were related?"

"What do you mean?"

"This has to remain in strictest confidence, but there's a possibility that Silas Wayne may be Joe Tolleson's father."

"That's unlikely."

"Why?"

"Because the DNA analysis reveals that the DNA from the two suspects' samples was quite different. If the two suspects were related, there probably would be more similarities in their DNA profiles. There is actually more similarity between Tolleson's and Marsha Walton's profiles than between Tolleson's and Wayne's profiles. That information is contained in the part of the report you said you found difficult to understand. It's not dispositive, but I don't think Silas Wayne is Joe Tolleson's father. You look disappointed, Mr. Benewski."

"Not at all, Doctor Pace. At this point, I don't have any other questions, but if I do, I'll give you a call. I thank you, and Ms. Bartlett, for your time."

Benewski left the coroner's office and went for lunch at Brigg's Diner. He sat at the counter and ordered. Notwithstanding what he had told Doctor Pace, he was disappointed that Silas Wayne was not Joe Tolleson's father.

Juries afforded too much respect to scientific evidence. Faced with conflicting testimony and evidence, they grasped at anything with the aura of scientific certainty. He had to challenge the DNA tests; they didn't comport with the rest of the evidence. He had been at similar impasses in other cases. The key was persistence. He had

to keep working every loose strand; eventually the knot
would unravel.

Waldo Brigg, the owner of Brigg's Diner, had an effective marketing technique. Hamburgers and cheeseburgers
came with grilled onions and bacon. Brigg would grill
onions and bacon even before the lunch hour crowd came
in, so that the smell wafted out of the diner, enticing people throughout Hidden Fall's small commercial district.
Benewski devoured a cheeseburger with these irresistible
trimmings and glanced at his watch. It was 1:45, he had a
2:00 meeting with Alice Tolleson. Although it was well
past the lunch hour the diner, with its six counter stools
and seven tables, was still packed. He dipped his last
French fry in catsup and ate it, then wiped the grease from
his chin with a napkin, put money on the counter and left
the diner.

He drove to the Tollesons' house, which was at the end
of a tree lined cul-de-sac in the nicest part of Hidden Falls.
Jack Tolleson had built a typically suburban, two story
wood framed house, painted white with brown trim.
There was a large picture window on the bottom floor and
three sets of windows on the second floor. A variety of
deciduous trees, their branches stripped of leaves, covered
a large front lawn. Flower bushes, bare from the winter
cold, extended down both sides of the house. It was a
comfortable house, but it lacked the ostentation that
would have indicated that its owner was a multimillion-
aire. He parked his car in the spacious driveway, next to an
almost new, red Cadillac. Alice Tolleson greeted him at the
door shortly after he rang the bell.

He was shocked by her appearance. Mike Devore had
told him that she was beautiful, but today she was far from

it. Even the expert application of cosmetics could not hide the puffy redness of her eyes and the swelling of her face. She was at least thirty pounds overweight and it showed not just in her face, but in her uncovered hands and forearms and the tight fit of her simple, but expensive, green dress. She returned his shocked expression, which he was unable to hide, with a smile that seemed both wry and wise.

"Mr. Benewski?"

"Yes. Please call me Gary."

"Certainly, Gary, please come in. Why don't we sit in the living room. Can I get you anything?"

"No, thanks."

They walked to the living room and he sat on a beige leather couch. She sat facing him on the opposite couch.

"I think I know why you want to talk to me, Gary."

"Why, Mrs. Tolleson?"

"Please, it's Alice. I believe you're here to ask me if there is any possibility that the Reverend Silas Wayne is Joe's father, since that might affect the DNA tests."

He stared at her. Was she naturally direct or had she been emboldened by a cocktail or two? The rumor around Hidden Falls was that she was drinking heavily.

"Well, Alice, you're right, that's why I'm here. Is there any possibility that Silas Wayne is Joe's father?"

"No, unless you believe that Silas is capable of immaculate conception. Some people probably do. I have never had sexual relations with Silas Wayne."

"Are you aware that your son says that Silas Wayne told him, that night under the church, that you were once in love with him?"

"I didn't say I didn't want to have sexual relations with Silas. I did, but he wouldn't. I never wanted anything so much in my life, but I assure you now, and I would testify in court, that I never made love to Silas Wayne."

Was she still in love with Silas Wayne? It wasn't germane to this phase of his investigation, it would have been unprofessional to ask. He had what he needed, it was time to go. "Alice, thank you for—"

"No, Mr. Benewski, there's no doubt that Jack Tolleson is Joe Tolleson's father. What I've always wondered is if I'm Joe Tolleson's mother."

"Huh?"

"It's those eyes, those deep blue eyes set in brilliant white. The first time they brought him to me, after the surgery, those eyes looked up at me. And do you know what I thought? I thought, he's judging me. Even then it seemed that those eyes never blinked, never missed a thing. There was no affection, no love, no need; just appraisal, analysis and judgment. What a mother is supposed to feel for a son; I wanted so much to feel for him. After he was about two years old, do you know that the only time I could hold him was when he was asleep? I wanted to teach him, to watch him grow. Once he started to talk, which was very early on, he'd say 'what?' or 'how?' or 'why?' and then not another word. Those eyes would just look at me, waiting for an answer. I'd answer and then another question, another answer and another question, until I either ran out of patience or answers. Then he was gone, reading or taking something apart or playing his piano.

"I remember one day when he was eight years old. I went into his room and he was sitting at his little desk, reading an encyclopedia. He looked at me and said, 'Mom, do we have seasons because the tilt of the earth on its axis varies or because the distance from the earth to sun varies as the earth orbits the sun?'

"I never bluffed when I didn't know the answer. I told him I didn't know. Then I felt something, I think it was fear, because I realized that not only didn't I know the answer, I didn't really understand the question. I got annoyed, and I suggested that he go outside to play. He said, 'I'd rather read, Mom,' and turned back to his encyclopedia. I stood looking at him a long time, but he never turned around.

"How does a mother love a mind, Gary? What does a mother give to a mind? I've always wanted to ask Silas if it was possible that this child wasn't mine, that he was sent to me from some other place. To tell you the truth, I wouldn't know if he came from heaven or hell. Everybody used to congratulate me for my brilliant son, but I've never even felt like he was mine."

What could he say to that? There was an awkward silence and he finally rose from the couch. She followed him to the door. There was one question he had to ask.

"Either your son or Silas Wayne raped and murdered Marsha Walton. Who do you think did it?"

She was silent. She looked at him, but nothing registered on her face to indicate that she had heard the question.

"I'm sorry, Alice, you must have tortured yourself for days trying to answer that question."

"No, I've tortured myself for days trying to avoid that question. I'm sure you'll figure it out, though. I'm going to have a scotch. Good day."

He returned to his office. Gail Smathers had some new information. She had called the two drug stores that had not reviewed their register tapes. The store manager at the Buy-Rite Drug Store in Bloomstown said that on the Saturday following Marsha Walton's murder the store had sold nine bottles of alcohol and a box of rubber gloves in one transaction. The sale had occurred sometime between 10:00 and 11:00 that morning. Also, Sheila Bartlett had called from the coroner's office and said that Doctor Pace could not find the express mail receipt for the package of DNA samples. Benewski asked Smathers to call Tolleson's hardware so that he could talk to the person responsible for employee records. He also asked her to call the express mail company and verify when the DNA sample package had been mailed.

A short time later, Smathers buzzed him to tell him that Dina Marston, of Tolleson's Hardware, was on the phone.

"Ms. Marston?"

"Mrs. Marston."

"Excuse me. I'm Gary Benewski. Mrs. Marston, are you in charge of time clock records?"

"Yes I am."

"Do you have the record available for Saturday, November the ninth of last year?"

"Hold on." He could hear her shuffling papers. "Here it is."

"What is your record for Joe Tolleson?"

"He worked eight hours that day, and the only time he clocked out was at 12:30 for his lunch break. He clocked back in at 1:17 and clocked out for the day at 5:12."

"Could he have left without clocking out?"

"I don't think so, Mr. Benewski. Mr. Tolleson is very strict about that. He's fired people for clocking other people in, or for leaving without clocking out, and he doesn't play favorites with his son."

"I see. Thank you very much, Mrs. Marston."

"You're welcome."

He hung up the phone. A loose strand was starting to unravel. The only purchase of rubber gloves and a large amount of rubbing alcohol was made in a town thirty miles away from Hidden Falls at a time when Joe Tolleson had a solid alibi. The drug store purchase might not be admissible courtroom evidence, since there was no way to tie it conclusively to the room under the church, but prosecutors didn't have to rely solely on courtroom-worthy evidence when developing their cases. The drug store purchases were like Silas's lie to Edna Mayhew—something else that didn't "add up." His thoughts were interrupted by Smathers, who knocked on his door and walked in before he could say anything.

"Gary, there's something strange here. I called the express mail company to verify that Doctor Pace mailed the DNA samples on the afternoon of the day the samples were taken. The clerk had no record of a package being received from the coroner's office that Monday afternoon. I asked him to make sure, and he read off every package that came in that Monday. Just to be thorough, I asked him to check the next day's records. Guess what? The package was mailed that next day. It was the first package mailed, at 8:02 Tuesday morning. I asked him if it was possible that the package was mailed the previous day and the record was not entered until the next day. He said that would be impossible, since the record was automatically entered in the computer when a mailing label was issued for the package."

"Gail, without telling him why I want to see him, call Doctor Pace and tell him I need to talk with him immediately."

Doctor Pace arrived in Benewski's office about five minutes later. He was visibly annoyed, emitting an exasperated sigh as he sat in the chair in front of his desk.

"Doctor Pace, you said you mailed the package containing the DNA samples. The samples were taken that Monday morning. When did you mail the samples?"

Pace's eyes narrowed, but he looked directly at him. "I mailed the samples that afternoon."

"The express mail company's records indicate that no package was received that afternoon, but that a package was received early the next morning from the coroner's office."

Pace was one of those small people who couldn't admit a mistake. Or a lie. There was a long moment of silence; the tension was palpable. Pace shifted his position in his seat.

"Come to think of it, I didn't mail that package until the following morning. That's right. Sometimes I can be a bit absent-minded. Sheila asked me to mail the package that afternoon, but I forgot about it until I was almost home. By then, I didn't have enough time to go by the morgue at the hospital and then back here to pick up the two samples before the express mail office closed. So the next morning I went by the morgue to get the two sets of Marsha Walton samples. Then I picked up the samples here at the police lab and went to the express mail office and mailed the package. I completely forgot about that."

Benewski did not need an admission from Pace that he had lied; they both knew he had. There was no need to press the issue, but Benewski wanted to establish one point.

"So Joe Tolleson's and Silas Wayne's samples were left in the police lab overnight?"

"That's correct."

"Doctor Pace, thank you for your time."

He did not escort the coroner to the door. He buzzed Smathers and told her he needed to talk to Mike Devore as soon as possible. She buzzed back a few minutes later and told him Devore could see him immediately.

He made a trip to the restroom across the hall before he went to Devore's office. He needed to mentally outline what he was going to say to the district attorney. He walked into Devore's office and sat down, noting with a trace of annoyance that Devore had taken off his glasses and was beginning his glasses cleaning ritual.

"Mike," he said, trying to sound coldly rational, "there are serious inconsistencies in the case against Joe Tolleson." He talked to the district attorney in the same way he talked to a judge when making a motion. He pointed out the conflict between what Silas told Edna Mayhew and the discovery of the ice machine in the underground room. He argued that Joe could not have purchased the alcohol and surgical rubber gloves that were used in the grisly operations in that room. He concluded with the observation that the one piece of evidence that supported Silas—the DNA test—was of questionable validity since the samples were left in the police lab overnight and they knew that Albert Ruprecht had access to keys for the entire building. Ruprecht could have gone into the lab that night and switched the labels on the samples. He ended his argument. Now it was time for the closing statement and request for relief from Judge Devore.

"In light of all this, I think we have to make a motion to the court to redo the DNA tests under the court's supervision. Attorneys from our office, as well as Joe Tolleson and Silas Wayne's attorneys should be present when the samples are taken and delivered to the express mail office. We should move that Joe Tolleson's bail be reinstated until we receive the results of the new tests. I think we should also move to take blood tests for Jack, Joe and Alice Tolleson and Silas Wayne, to establish Joe Tolleson's paternity once and for all."

"We can't do it. We're going to look like idiots, asking for new DNA tests. Nobody is going to believe that a member of the Hidden Falls police department tampered with evidentiary samples. What would happen if we got new DNA tests and the results were identical to the first tests? We'd be crucified."

You chickenshit bastard, Benewski screamed to himself. It was Tyler City all over again. In Tyler City, he had prosecuted an explosive case all the way up the political ladder—to the mayor's office—despite warnings from his boss, the district attorney, to back off. He had got his convictions and the mayor resigned, but after the publicity died down, he had been "laid off." The official explanation was budget cutbacks, but he had been the only one let go. Now the man who had saved him after that fiasco, giving him a job, was going to walk away from this case. He would protest, or threaten to resign, or do something dramatic.

He looked down at Devore's desk for several moments. No, he told himself. He tightly clenched his hands and bit his lower lip. No. Think, before you open your mouth. Think, and take a deep breath, it may be the only way to save this case. Think, and take another deep breath, it may be the only way to save your friend. Think, because this speech is going to have to be your best. When he finally spoke, it was in a measured, controlled tone.

"Mike, remember when we were in law school. You used to speak in epigrams back then. You said once 'you don't play the game, it plays you.' That one stuck in my mind. I went into criminal law because I found it interesting. You saw it as a springboard for your political ambitions. You know you can't save the world, but you want to make a difference somewhere. There's nothing dishonorable about that. But now you have the same choice every politician has at some point in his career. We can ignore these evidentiary conflicts and accept the original DNA test, but it wouldn't be right. We can tell ourselves that we didn't act out of personal cowardice, but rather for some higher principle—the greater good. We've been hearing that one from politicians since who knows when. It was charming when we heard it from Roosevelt and the Kennedys and Clinton. Johnson and Nixon weren't charming, so with them a lie's a lie.

"We used to mock liberal guilt. Sin is a matter of individual choice, we agreed, not a social failure. Guilt is a person's subjective reaction to his own moral shortcomings. A long time ago the guilty purchased indulgences; now politicians purchase their indulgences with other people's money. Maybe you can get elected as mayor of Hidden Falls—there's an opening." His voice grew stronger, angrier. "Just remember when you're expiating your guilt, spending other people's money and tallying your deeds for the greater good, that you sent a kid who had the balls to tell the truth to the penitentiary, or maybe the electric chair." He lowered his voice. "Remember Joe Tolleson when you're the mayor. Perhaps when you cut the ribbon to dedicate the Silas Wayne Home For Wayward Girls."

The district attorney stared at the assistant district attorney for a long time. Benewski noted with satisfaction that he had not put his glasses back on. Devore's face was virtually frozen, only small twitches and minute movements of his eyes signaled his agonized deliberations with himself. Benewski was running a risk; he had broken his vow not to question a decision about how to prosecute a case. However, he was running less of a risk than his friend. When Devore finally spoke, it was in a flat tone of resignation.

"You never hit anybody that hard on the football field. Have Gail type up the motion and bring it over to my office." He smiled weakly—polished glass was shattering. "I'm going to call Vicki and tell her to start getting quotes from the moving companies."

Benewski granted his friend the dignity of not showing his relief. He said, in the best matter-of-fact tone that he could muster, "It will take a while to get the motion typed. You don't have to hang around, it's almost 6:30. You can sign the motion in the morning."

"No, I'll wait. I want to review the motion. Besides, you don't want to give me a chance to change my mind."

It took Benewski almost three hours to draft the motion and another hour to amend it after Devore reviewed it. Without directly saying so, he had to cast suspicion on the Hidden Falls police department. Thus, he had to detail every step of his investigation. He referred to the initial hostility of Chief Marsh and Sergeant Ruprecht to Joe's story, to Sergeant Ruprecht's knowledge that Joe had talked to the assistant district attorney and to the apparent nighttime break-ins in his office. He then argued that because security in the town hall may have been compromised, there was a possibility that the DNA samples left in the police lab overnight were subject to tampering. He did not actually accuse anyone on the police force of entering the lab and altering the samples, but Magistrate Judge Watkins was fairly astute. Benewski was confident he would read between the lines.

The redrafted motion was eleven pages. Mike Devore signed it at 10:30 and then walked with Smathers and Benewski to Brigg's Diner for a late dinner. Benewski had his second cheeseburger that day, covered with grilled onions and bacon. Devore and Smathers had the same thing and all three devoured their food, not speaking. They washed it all down with beer, which diminished the tension that had propelled them for the last few hours. After finishing their cheeseburgers they talked, but not about the case—there was a risk of being overheard.

"Did Fred sign up for basketball this year?" Devore asked, referring to Benewski's twelve-year-old son.

"Yeah, but he had to change his position from guard to a forward. He's grown five inches since last year."

"How tall is he?" asked Smathers.

"Five ten. What about Jenny, Mike?"

"She's the starting point guard. Even with practices every afternoon, she comes home and goes down to the school to play with the older boys. She's better than most of them. Vicki can't get her off the court. Next year she'll play on the high school team. After that, who knows? Maybe she can get a scholarship for women's basketball."

"She's that good?"

"She's that good." Devore seldom talked about his personal life, but he had a soft spot for his only child.

They ordered banana cream pie and coffee and continued to talk about Benewski's two boys, Smathers' two girls, and Devore's daughter. When they finished the pie and coffee, they were the only customers still in the diner. Waldo Brigg was counting the day's cash receipts as they left.

There were times in his college football career that Benewski was so exhausted there was nothing he could do but sleep. What he felt when he lay his head on his pillow that night was similar to that feeling, but not identical. His body was tense, not bruised and sore like after a hard practice or a game. He had to will himself to relax, to release the tension. It was his mind and spirit that were exhausted; he needed to recover from the day's stress. He could not stop thinking about the case. Finally, he listened to Margie, who had been talking about the kids for some time and who, in his preoccupation, he had been ignoring. He was asleep in less than a minute.

*   *   *

Magistrate Judge Watkins granted the district attorney's motion. He ordered bail reinstated for Joe Tolleson. The charges of murder and rape were reinstated against Silas Wayne, but he was allowed to post the same bail. Both defendants were ordered to resubmit hair, blood, and tissue samples for DNA analysis. This time a court bailiff, Gary Benewski, Matthew Hoskins and Silas Wayne's lawyer, Preston Catledge, were present at the police lab when Sheila Bartlett withdrew blood, scraped tissue and obtained hair samples from Tolleson and Wayne. This coterie rode in the same van to the express mail office, they watched as the package was placed in the bin and they all received copies of the express mail receipt. The laboratory in Tyler City had retained the four sets of original samples, including the samples from Marsha Walton's body and the foreign samples found on her body, so it only had to redo the DNA tests on the samples from Tolleson and Wayne.

Devore was right about the uproar in Hidden Falls. The tension that had disappeared with the results of the first DNA tests resurfaced with greater intensity. In the incessant conversations about the case, there was a general sense of outraged disbelief directed against the office of the district attorney. Devore ordered Benewski not to talk about the case and reporters who inquired were given copies of the district attorney's motion. Elsewhere, their questions were met with silence. Silas Wayne said nothing. Joe Tolleson said nothing.

CHAPTER 16

▼

THE OFFER

Snowy winter wind rattled the windows and glass doors at Tolleson Toyota. It was nine o'clock at night. Jack Tolleson sat at the desk in his office, trying to concentrate on closing the books on another profitable year. He listened to the wind, hearing two strains: a low murmur—monks chanting a requiem mass; and a high pitched wail—a mother mourning her lost child. His pencil lead snapped. It was no use; he could not stop thinking about the last two weeks.

When Joe was a child, the family would wake up early on Christmas, anticipating the day's gifts and festivities. This recent Christmas morning, Joe and Jack were awaked before sunrise by Alice retching in the bathroom. She was sick the entire Christmas day, moving between her bed and the bathroom. Jack prepared dinner, attempting to preserve a semblance of Yule spirit, but gloom settled over the dining room as he and Joe chewed their overcooked turkey. He excused himself and went upstairs to check on Alice. She was passed out on the bed. He stood for a long time, an unmoving silhouette in the master bedroom window, trying to understand his pain. An occasional tear leaked from the corner of his eye. He loved her, but he could not reach her, could not help her fight her anguished confusion, and could not release her from her alcoholic prison. She needed professional help.

Nobody could stop her drinking. She had thrown a bottle at Sandra Mayes when her friend told her she had a problem. Sandra overlooked the incident and continued to come and sit with Alice. Her children were grown and she did not work, but it was still an imposition. Once she arrived in the morning, Joe and Jack escaped to one of the dealerships or the hardware store. They went to restaurants for dinner and Jack returned to work—the end of the year was always busy. Joe filled out college applications at home.

His life was a hellish nightmare. Adding to his humiliation, Hidden Falls learned there was a question regarding Joe's paternity. The Herald obtained a copy of the district attorney's motion and reported that there was a possibility that he was not Joe's father (while not mentioning that Silas was the other candidate). Two days after Christmas, Sheila Bartlett came to Tolleson Toyota and drew his blood sample. Then she went to his house and drew his wife's sample.

His nerves were raw. He felt like a soldier tiptoeing through a battleground after a cease fire, unsure of the illusion of peace. The insignificant and trivial became important while the important went unnoticed—he did not trust his own perceptions. His friends' expressions of sympathy seemed to carry an undertone of malicious delight. He felt the cuckold's sense of laughter behind his back. He and Alice had always attended several New Year's Eve parties. This year they received fewer invitations. He told himself he was being overly sensitive and that it was a moot point, since the invitations they received were declined. But their once unassailable social position within Hidden Falls was eroding, grains washing from a sand bar in a swift stream.

He knew he was Joe's father, but he was still relieved when Gary Benewski called him two days after New Year's Day with confirmation. Benewski explained that blood tests could never conclusively prove that two persons were related, but could prove that two persons were not related. While the blood tests did not definitively establish his paternity, they did prove that Silas Wayne was not Joe's father. He asked Benewski to make sure the *Herald* got the news.

A loud pounding on the front door of the dealership interrupted his painful rumination. He walked through the showroom and pushed open the door against the howling winds and a growing snow drift. Harvey Roach, a member of the Hidden Falls town council and the acting mayor, stood in the doorway. Roach owned the largest real estate agency in Hidden Falls and had been a fixture within the town for as long as Jack could remember. He was president of the chamber of commerce and a deacon at Silas Wayne's church. He wore a thick woolen coat, a fur-lined cap with earflaps and rubber boots.

"Good evening, Jack, mind if I come in?"

"No."

"I need to talk to you."

"Let's go into my office."

Inside, Roach took off his heavy coat and hung it on a stand in the corner. A tall man with a slight paunch, he looked as if he had just stepped off the pages of an Eddie Bauer catalogue. He wore a brown flannel shirt with a duck emblem on the pocket and light green khaki pants. His face was deeply tanned, although it was the middle of winter. He sat in a chair facing Jack's desk, removed his hat and gloves and set them in his lap. Every silver hair remained in place. A quick, ingratiating smile revealed capped teeth. He pulled up the right sleeve on his shirt, flashing the inevitable Rolex. He wore a gold wedding band, inlaid with a large diamond, on his left hand. His fingernails were manicured.

"Winter's finally arrived, hasn't it? It's not fit for man or beast tonight."

"No, it's not. We won't be able to get half the cars started tomorrow."

"Do you mind if I fire up my pipe?"

"No."

Roach took out a pouch from his shirt pocket and removed a pipe from it. He carefully filled the pipe with tobacco, tamped it and lit it. After several puffs he was enveloped in a wreath of smoke.

"You're probably wondering why I would come out to talk to you on a night like this."

"The thought crossed my mind."

"Jack, this Marsha Walton business has upset a lot of people. At this point, the whole affair is in limbo. There's one set of tests that implicates Joe and we're waiting for the second set of tests. Those tests might also implicate

Joe, or they might not. Joe has his story, and although the Reverend Wayne hasn't said anything yet, we know he has his. If you're a betting man, it's almost impossible to handicap this thing if it's allowed to run it's full course. However, there are a lot of people who would be happier if this race were never run."

"What do you mean?"

"We don't know how the second set of tests will come back. Whether it points to Silas or your boy, though, a trial is going to be difficult for Hidden Falls. Many people would prefer that were no trial, of either Joe or Silas."

"How can there be no trial? The district attorney is involved and there's been all sorts of publicity."

"If Joe stands trial, the main witness would be Silas. If Silas stands trial, the main witness would be Joe. What if both witnesses suddenly became unwilling to testify? Mike Devore couldn't make his case. Presented with a *fait accompli*, he'd have no choice. He's no fool; he wouldn't make trouble over a lost cause. He'd drop the case for insufficient and conflicting evidence. The newspapers would squawk for a few weeks and then they'd be on to the next story."

"Why would Silas Wayne agree not to testify?"

"For a couple of reasons, Jack. Silas isn't a vengeful man. Joe's got a hell of a future before him; his life would be ruined if he went to prison. Silas wants a chance to help him, to redeem him. Also, he knows a trial would tear the town apart. Of course, if Silas were to agree not to testify, Joe would have to make a similar pledge on Silas's behalf."

"This is the worst kind of horseshit. Silas put you up to this, didn't he? Things are moving against him, and he's trying to cut a deal to save his ass."

A twinge of anger passed over Roach's face, but he held his temper. There was a moment of silence and he took a deep, audible breath. He flashed a fake smile, removed his pipe from his mouth and pointed the bit towards Jack.

"Let's say you know what you're talking about, which you don't. There are several things you should consider, Jack. Bill Simes and Mac Barnes, on the town council, are both lawyers and they've read the district attorney's motion. Your son claims that the day he supposedly discovered the body under the church, he talked to the assistant district attorney, Benewski. The Fourth Amendment requires search warrants. Bill and Mac say there's a serious question as to whether the body and everything else Joe supposedly found under the church could be admitted as evidence. He used information from the district attorney's office, but he didn't have a search warrant. There's no case without that evidence, even if Joe testifies. Ask Ned Burroughs if you don't believe me."

Jack put his hands on his desk and slowly clenched and unclenched his fists. Roach appeared not to notice.

"Here's something else to think about. I know you believe Silas is guilty and your son is innocent. However, one DNA test points the other way. What if Joe is guilty or there's another 'mistake' on the second DNA test? You have a chance right now to make sure there's no trial. Do you want to play chicken with your son's life?"

"So you're saying that we could shut the whole thing down and pretend nothing happened?"

"Jack, you have to believe me, most people in town would like to do just that. I have their support. Right or wrong, they would be very angry if Joe testified against Silas Wayne."

Jack sat in stunned silence. The desolate wind howling outside his window matched something howling inside his soul.

"What…what about Marsha Walton's mother? Doesn't she care about finding out who killed her daughter?"

"Nancy Walton knows who killed her daughter, and it isn't the man she asked to perform her daughter's funeral service. She's a no account bar slut. However, if you're worried about her, it's my understanding that she wants to leave Hidden Falls. The town council is prepared to offer her relocation assistance. You're welcome to contribute."

"You mean I can help buy her off."

"Call it what you will. You're a businessman, and you should be thinking about this like a businessman. You have very little to gain by seeing this through, and a lot to lose."

"What do you mean by that?"

Roach eyes wandered around Jack's office. They stopped at the computer behind his desk, the painting on the wall and the open door to the well appointed bathroom next to the office. He turned in his chair and surveyed the showroom floor, where four new Toyotas were parked.

"Jack, I remember how hard you worked to set up this dealership. You needed a zoning variance and boy, did you 'lobby' for it. Gifts like zoning variances, building permits, environmental clearances and so on are never really permanent; they can be taken back. You also have several lucrative sole source contracts with our procurement office that we might have to review. These are things the town council can do, legally and officially. Above and beyond that, it may be difficult to protect you from certain elements that don't observe the law. If you want to take this thing all the way, you'd better make sure your insurance is paid up."

Jack shook his head in disbelief.

"It's not just business. Alice is taking this pretty hard. Nobody's seen her for weeks and people say she's drinking. How's she going to hold up if there's a trial? I saw Sylvia Thornton, the teacher, the other day. She says Joe looks like a ghost; he's lost a lot of weight. I think it would be in his best interest not to have a trial."

"You don't know my son if you think he would agree to forget about this. He almost got himself killed that night under the church. Besides, there are a lot of people in this town who think he raped and murdered Marsha Walton. He may not give a damn what anybody thinks about him, but something like this could follow him for the rest of his life."

"Yes, I know he's got his story and his reputation. Think about one thing, though, Jack. When I was growing up, when my father said to do something, it was done—no questions asked. I've raised my children the same way. Maybe you're raising Joe differently, after all, nobody makes him go to church. It seems to me, though, that if you tell him to not to testify, he won't testify. He's going to have his choice among several prestigious institutions to continue his education, and when he goes, he'll leave all this behind. However, those colleges aren't cheap. I know Joe's worked, but I don't think he's saved that kind of money. It really would be to his benefit if he would agree not to testify. You're proud of your son, but there are a lot of people in this town who don't share that feeling. I'd hate to see Joe become a victim of his own unpopularity. His reputation and future would be impaired more by testifying than not testifying."

Jack folded his hands on his lap. He didn't know what to say. A lot of thought had gone into this smooth-talking bastard's proposal. It reflected a shrewd assessment of the relevant considerations, risks and potential outcomes. Roach was a snake, but there was an internal logic to this proposition that made it impossible for him to reject out of hand. What would be Joe's reaction if he accepted this clandestine offer? He shuddered.

"I need to check a few things and consider what you've said." Petitioning for a stay of execution.

"Sure, but you can only have a couple of days."

"A couple of days?"

"If you decide to accept our proposal, we need to withdraw the second set of samples from the lab in Tyler City before they have the results."

"If I accept your offer we're both guilty of obstruction of justice."

"This conversation never happened, Jack. A number of people would be willing to provide me with an alibi." Roach's mirthless smile revealed all of his perfect teeth. He stood and said, "get back to me soon."

Jack showed Roach to the door. Roach insisted on shaking his hand. After he left Jack walked back to his desk. He sat for a long time, his head resting on his hands. He left the dealership in an agonized quandary.

He used the entire two days to make his decision. His employees noticed his preoccupation, unaware of the debate raging within him. Ned Burroughs verified what Roach had said about the evidence found under the church. There was a Constitutional issue, but like so many legal issues its outcome was unclear—he could not say how a judge would rule. If the evidence were inadmissible, the district attorney would have no case against Wayne. After the phone conversation with Burroughs, Jack stared out the showroom window at his Buick dealership for over an hour.

He loved his son, he believed his son, and he wanted Silas brought to justice. A trial would devastate Alice, but if Silas was convicted, it might be worth that price. However, the damn Constitutional issue complicated everything. Roach had "support" for his proposal, and his implied threats were no bluff. If he rejected Roach's offer, his bravery would be worse than useless if the evidence were ruled inadmissible. He might lose everything, including his wife, and have nothing to show for it.

Another consideration was his son's welfare. Joe was an idealist—he would want to press ahead with the case against Silas. If he didn't testify, many people in Hidden Falls would believe he had committed the crimes. However, he would be leaving Hidden Falls and hopefully, what the people in town thought wouldn't be a hindrance to him. Besides, what if somebody had managed to rig the second DNA test? Joe would face charges and a trial in the hostile environment of Hidden Falls. He was smart and mature, but he was still only sixteen. There were times when the parents knew what was best for even a smart, mature child.

On the afternoon of the second day, Jack made up his mind. He marshaled his arguments for his conversation with his son, even drafting an outline of what he would say. It seemed more unquestionably logical after he had set his reasons down on paper. There were many times in his career when he had made the best of bad situations. This would be one of them. He was in for a rough spell with his son, but eventually Joe would understand that he was acting in their best interests. He drove from the Toyota dealership to the hardware store. He told Joe that he would grill a couple of steaks so they could eat at home that night.

As had become her habit, Alice ate a light dinner by herself in the master bedroom. Joe and Jack ate in the dining room, and then cleared the table. Jack told Joe that he needed to talk with him. They sat facing each other across the dining room table. Jack's voice had a brittle edge. His presentation was not smooth; he repeated several of his arguments. Joe did not make it any easier. He folded his hands across his stomach and rested his elbows on the arms of his chair. Occasionally his eyes would narrow, but they never stopped looking at him. It was hard for Jack to look his son in the eye. For about ten minutes he presented his case. Then he was not saying anything new, only prolonging Joe's response. He stopped talking and there was a long silence.

Jack succumbed to the tension of the silence. "Well, Joe, what do you think? I know it'll be difficult, but would you agree not to testify against Silas?" He hated the insecurity in his voice.

"No."

There was another lengthy silence. He was defeated, but he tried again.

"I thought you might say that, but I'm not sure you're thinking this through. I want to see Silas in prison as much as you do, but he won't stand trial if the evidence is inadmissible. We could risk everything for nothing. After that first set of DNA tests, aren't you nervous about the second set? In a perfect world, Silas spends the rest of his life in prison, but this isn't a perfect world. A lot could go wrong. Think about it, this isn't that bad a deal."

"No."

"Why?"

"Dad, that first DNA test was screwed up because Albert Ruprecht screwed it up. On the second test, Mr. Benewski watched every step. I trust Mr. Benewski, and I didn't rape and murder that girl. Silas Wayne did. Like you say, he should be in prison for the rest of his life. I don't know enough about the Fourth Amendment to make a judgment about the evidence, but I'm willing to run that risk as well. Silas Wayne should be convicted and locked up."

"Son, I wish things were that black and white. Unfortunately, you're going to find, as you get older, that things are often gray."

"Marsha Walton was forced to have sex with Silas Wayne. She saw her noose hanging from the rafters. She dangled from that rope until she died. I saw her body hanging in the old church. Silas Wayne told me that he raped and murdered her. What's gray about any of that? Isn't gray just a combination of black and white that most people are either too lazy or too corrupt to sort out?"

Jack rubbed his face with his hand. "Look around you, kid. Look at this house; look at everything you have. I've busted my ass all my life for this. Now you want me to throw this all away so you can go tilting at windmills."

"Is that it? Do our principles have a profit and loss statement? We only follow our conscience when it's to our commercial advantage. Is that what you taught me?"

"No, damn it, it's not, but this isn't just about you. You're asking me to risk everything, to have faith in the law and the courts. Let me tell you something, and believe me, I know. The law is elastic; a law that seems to say one thing can be made to say the exact opposite. And there are a lot of judges for sale. That's the real world, Joe. Do I like it? No. Have I made my bargains with it? Yes. Do you think any of this has been easy on me? I haven't slept with my wife for two months; she's an alcoholic. Look at us, our family. You're being pretty damn selfish about all this."

"That's the first thing you've said tonight that I agree with." His voice became very quiet, almost a whisper. "Mom's not going to start loving you if you abandon your principles and everything you stand for."

The dagger pierced all the way through his abdomen—the same sensation he had felt in the prison waiting room. Joe had once again implied what he was afraid to admit to himself—that Alice didn't love him. For several moments he could not breathe. A heavy weight seemed to crush his chest.

"That's a low blow. I always thought you cared about your family...your parents. Maybe I was wrong about you. Maybe I'll remember this when it's time to start signing checks for tuition next year."

Joe's eyes widened as they bored in on his father. He rose from his chair and placed both of his hands on the table.

"You can keep your goddamn money, Dad, because I'm going to testify against Silas Wayne." His words sounded like multiple gunshots in a regular cadence, each word separately stressed. He walked towards the front door.

"Where are you going?"

"Out."

"Joe, remember one thing. Life isn't always as simple as your black and white ideals."

Joe turned and smiled at his father. Jack would always remember that smile; it held both pained recognition and ageless irony.

"You're right, it's usually simpler. Good night."

Joe picked up his coat, gloves and hat from a stand by the front door and opened the door. A gust of snow greeted him. He climbed into his Toyota and backed out of the driveway. He had no idea where he was going. Not far, he was too upset to drive the icy road. He wanted to be alone. The parking lot at the Hidden Falls, eight miles out of town, would be deserted this time of night, in the middle of winter.

He drove to the lot and parked under a snow covered tree. His was the only car there. He left the engine on to run the car's heater and radio. The mournful third movement of Brahms' Third Symphony came from the radio. He put the car seat back and stared at the car's ceiling.

One day, when he was twelve years old, he sat by himself during recess, on a bench in the schoolyard, reading a book about Roman history. A classmate, Frank Stokes, approached him from across the schoolyard. Frank was a good natured boy who told stories and jokes and was popular with most of the other children. He had plenty of friends, but as he later disclosed, he regarded Joe as a challenge.

"You know," he said, smiling, as Joe looked up from his book, "if you're only going to talk with people who are as smart as you, you're never going to have any friends."

"The nice thing about reading is that the writer thinks about what he wants to say. A lot of times when people talk, they don't think."

Frank's forehead crinkled. "You're right. What are you reading?"

"A book about the Romans. Do you like history?"

"Yes."

After a few minutes of conversation, Joe realized he liked Frank. A friendship began and they became inseparable. Frank's sharp wit sprang from his restless intelligence. He was the only person who could consistently make Joe laugh. They engaged in surprisingly sophisticated conversations.

One summer day, Frank approached Joe as he lay in a hammock under a big tree on the Tolleson's front lawn.

"Hey, Joe, want to go swimming with Dean and Mark and some of the other guys?"

"I don't know." He did not like group activities. "Are you going to the pool?"

"The pool's for old ladies. We're going to the river."

The boys were going to a deep hole, created by a large sand bar, on the West Fork about two miles downstream from town. The hole was desirable because it was dangerous; several children had drowned. If anybody else had asked, he would have declined. However, this was Frank.

"Sure, let's go."

They met up with a group of boys at the swimming hole. Frank took off all of his clothes and the other boys followed. After a moment's hesitation, Joe also stripped. The boys jumped into the hole and frolicked for a while.

"Hey," a boy named Mark shouted, "let's see who can swim out to the buoy and back the fastest."

A buoy marked the separation point between the hole and the fast current of the West Fork. Mark was appealing to the boys' natural competitiveness. The element of danger—swimming so close to the main channel—increased the proposed contest's allure. The boys shouted their assent and Dean Grimes, who had a watch with a second hand, was appointed official timekeeper.

Joe was still trying to decide if he should swim to the buoy when the other boys shouted that it was his turn. He was a good swimmer. He couldn't embarrass himself in front of Frank and his friends. He swam away from the bank, toward the buoy. For a long time he could not tell how far he had progressed, then the buoy loomed before him. He felt a stronger undertow and when he reached the buoy he stopped for a moment to rest. As he swam back to the bank, he wondered if his time would be competitive with the other boys.

He approached the bank. The boys had disappeared. When he was about ten yards away, they stepped from behind a stand of trees. Unfortunately, they were now dressed and accompanied by a group of girls. He stopped swimming and started treading water, far enough from the bank so the girls could not see his naked body. The group laughed uncontrollably. Frank stepped out from the group and held up Joe's clothes.

Joe tread water for several minutes. The group kept laughing. There was only one thing to do. He swam to the bank and approached Frank. He did not try to hide his nudity. The laughter died. He stared at Frank for several moments and then took his clothes from him. He dressed, although he was dripping wet. Then he walked away from the group. He had gone about two hundred yards when Frank ran up to him.

"I'm sorry, Joe, we were just playing a joke on you. I guess it's not that funny."

"Go back to your friends, Frank."

He walked away from Frank that day. Now, remembering the long forgotten incident, tears trickled out of the corners of his eyes. He felt the same pain of betrayal, but now the sensation was many orders of magnitude more intense. His father, who had been on his side, had gone the other way. The tears flowed freely. He grabbed some Kleenex from a box on the passenger seat. It might cost him his future, it might cost his father his businesses, it might destroy the Tollesons and it might be for nothing, but he couldn't refuse to testify against Silas Wayne. If he didn't testify, he would see Marsha Walton hanging in the choir loft for the rest of his life. He had to do what he had to do.

*   *   *

Silas Wayne was shoveling the late January snow from the driveway in front of the parsonage when the police car entered the church parking lot. The car drove across the parking lot, towards the parsonage. The driver, Sergeant Albert Ruprecht, thoughtfully stopped before he reached the end of the driveway, which was not shoveled. Ruprecht and Chief Marsh got out of the car and walked towards Silas.

There were no pleasantries; they all knew what was going to happen.

"The tests came back, Reverend Wayne," said Chief Marsh. "This time they implicate you. You're under arrest for the rape and murder of Marsha Walton. Please come with us."

Silas nodded, but said nothing. Ruprecht opened the back door on the passenger side for him. They drove in silence to the town hall. Ruprecht showed Silas to his cell in the basement jail. Later that day, the original complaint was reinstated against Silas Wayne. Two days later, the preliminary hearing was conducted and Silas was arraigned. He pled not guilty. The trial date was set for May the twelfth.

The day Silas was arraigned, Joe Tolleson, a prospective witness, gave the office of the district attorney written notice of a change in his address; he had moved into an apartment building near the high school. The notice also stated that he was no longer employed part-time at Tolleson's Hardware Store and was seeking other employment.

CHAPTER 17

▼

THE FOURTH AMENDMENT

The right of the people to be secure in their persons, houses, papers, and effects, against unreasonable searches and seizures, shall not be violated, and no Warrants shall issue, but upon probable cause, supported by Oath or affirmation, and particularly describing the place to be searched, and the persons or things to be seized. The Fourth Amendment.

Gary Benewski was looking down at his notes, so the first thing he saw were her shoes—black leather pumps with inch-high heels. Translucent, black nylon sheen highlighted her slender ankles and well-defined calves. Her skirt hung just below her knees, leaving the rest of her long legs to his imagination. She wore a tailored black suit and a silk, cream-colored blouse. When he was in law school, female students had been advised to neuter themselves sartorially—boxy, padded jackets, utilitarian blouses, and long, straight skirts. She couldn't have hid her rounded hips, narrow waist, prominent breasts and perfectly proportioned curves under a burlap bag. Her stance conveyed the confidence of a great athlete. She slowly surveyed the courtroom, her strikingly beautiful face impassive. Brunette hair, matching her dark eyes, fell in elaborate curls to her shoulders. She had a high forehead, angular nose, high cheekbones and sensuous lips, slightly pursed. Her light makeup was an unessential highlight. She wore diamond stud earrings. He guessed she was in her mid-thirties.

Benewski looked away; if she was conscious of his examination she did not show it. He glanced at Mike Devore and watched him perform a similar once over.

"So that's Rachel Strassberg," Devore said.

Gary smiled. "I'd say the point spread just shifted a couple of points against the home team. No wonder they brought her in."

They were interrupted by the sheriff.

"The Merton County district court will now reconvene for its afternoon session. All rise."

Judge Daniel Longworth entered the courtroom from his chamber and sat in his chair behind the bench. Although his cropped hair was gray, his alert blue eyes belied his age, which was mid-sixties. He was known as a tough, but fair, judge with no tolerance for lawyers' contretemps. Good lawyers respected him; incompetent lawyers had a rough time. His stern face rarely changed expression.

He looked out over the courtroom, an old fashioned affair with a high ceiling and windows, a small gallery area, wooden benches and narrow aisles. In front of the rail separating the gallery from the participants, to his right at the defendant's table, sat Silas Wayne, Preston Catledge and a woman he did not know, Rachel Strassberg, from New York. He bore no animus towards out of town lawyers—they were often better than the locals. Mike Devore and Gary Benewski sat to his left, at the prosecution table. A few spectators, mostly from the press, sat in the gallery. This was a pretrial motion; the real crowd would not show up until the trial began—if it began. The court clerk announced the case—State versus Silas Wayne—and he addressed the courtroom.

"Today, the court will hear arguments and consider a pretrial motion by the defense to exclude certain evidence. The basis for the motion by the defense is that the search, which produced the evidence, violates the defendant's Fourth Amendment rights. The defendant is represented by Mr. Preston Catledge and Ms. Rachel Strassberg. The state will be represented by Mr. Michael Devore and Mr. Gary Benewski, from the office of the Merton County district attorney. Who will argue this motion for the defense?"

"I will, your Honor," replied Strassberg, standing.

"Very well, and who will argue for the prosecution?"

"I will, your Honor."

"Thank you, Mr. Devore. Ms. Strassberg, you may begin your argument."

"Thank you, your Honor. The facts upon which our motion is based are not at issue. In a deposition taken in discovery, the prosecution's main witness, Joseph Tolleson, describes a conversation he had with the assistant district attorney, Mr. Benewski, on the afternoon of the day of his alleged discovery of the body of Marsha Walton and other evidence under the church. Mr. Benewski's account of the conversation in the prosecution's motion to reinstate charges against the defendant, in an affidavit, and in testimony in the pretrial hearing is substantially the same as Tolleson's. Mr. Benewski conveyed information, which Tolleson claims allowed him to deduce that the body was hidden under the church.

"Tolleson, as a private actor, could not procure a search warrant before he broke into the church. He claimed that once he deduced the location of the body, time was of the essence because it was the defendant's plan to hide the body in the casket of Mayor Chester Matlock, who was to be buried the following morning. He tried to call the assistant district attorney, but Mr. Benewski could not be reached. Then he broke into the church and claims that after an extensive search, he found the body and other evidence. He claims that he was confronted by the defendant and removed the body from the church after an all night stand-off with the defendant."

Strassberg paused and shuffled through papers on the defense table, moving several to the top of her pile and then looking up at the judge.

"It's our contention that when a private individual uses information from a governmental agency—in this case the office of the Merton County District Attorney—to search for evidence, that private individual becomes subject to the same Fourth Amendment prohibitions that apply to the government. Mr. Benewski would have had to obtain a search warrant to search the church. This Fourth Amendment duty cannot be negated by the transfer of information to a private party.

"The United States Supreme Court, in *Burdeau v. Mcdowell*, ruled that the Fourth Amendment 'was intended as a restraint upon the activities of sovereign authority, and was not intended to be a limitation upon other than governmental agencies.' However, a search conducted by a private party is considered a governmental search when it was ordered or requested by a government official, when it was a joint endeavor of a private person and government official, or when a government official was standing by, giving tacit approval.

"It's not possible to ascertain what the assistant district attorney's intentions were when he told Joe Tolleson what he had seen on the night he observed the defendant, but it's clear that Tolleson wouldn't have deduced the location of the body without Mr. Benewski's information. Furthermore, the district attorney's office benefited from Tolleson's alleged discovery under the church—there would be no case without it."

Strassberg gestured slowly and deliberately, in a way that reinforced her argument.

"In *Knoll Associates, Inc. v. Federal Trade Commission,* the United States Second Circuit Court of Appeals held that if a private person makes a search for the purpose of aiding the government and the government uses the evidence obtained, the taint of the unlawful search is transferred to the government so as to make that use unlawful. The Supreme Court ruled in *Weeks v. United States* that the federal government is prohibited from using evidence obtained in an unlawful search and that rule was applied to the states in *Mapp v. Ohio.*"

She reviewed applicable state rulings. She argued that the state's supreme court had a more expansive interpretation of search and seizure protections than the United States Supreme Court. She concluded her argument.

"On the basis of these rulings, the defense moves that all evidence found under the church be ruled inadmissible as the product of an unlawful search that violated the Fourth Amendment rights of the defendant. Thank you." She remained standing for several moments, as if to emphasize her request.

Mike Devore had often argued with nonlawyers who accused lawyers of making simple matters needlessly complex and obscuring the relevant in a fog of irrelevant detail. Conceding that the generalization applied to some incompetent lawyers, he would maintain that the essence of legal reasoning and argument was to separate the important from the unimportant and to distill a complicated analysis into a straightforward oral or written presentation. He admired Strassberg's argument—it was a concise, easy to follow summary of the main points of the defense's motion. Her delivery was flawlessly unstressed, and there was a subtle persuasiveness in the controlled, confident tone of her voice. He had polished his glasses while she spoke. Now he slipped them on and rose to present the prosecution's counterargument.

"Your Honor, Joe Tolleson's discovery of Marsha Walton's body and the other evidence found under the church wasn't the product of an unlawful search. The defense has cited, both in its motion and in Ms. Strassberg's oral argument, the case of *Burdeau v. McDowell*. Unfortunately, in citing *Burdeau*, the defense ignores the Court's underlying rationale. The rule of *Weeks v. United States*—that the product of unlawful searches must be excluded as inadmissible evidence—is meant to deter the government from unlawful searches. The Court in *Burdeau* emphasized this deterrence function. Although a search by a private party can, in some circumstances, be considered a governmental search, such cases are limited to instances in which application of the exclusionary rule would serve to deter the governmental agency. In this case, application of the exclusionary rule would serve no such deterrent purpose.

"As Ms. Strassberg has noted, it's impossible to know Mr. Benewski's intent when he talked with Mr. Tolleson. However, it strains credulity to suggest that he had already deduced the location of the body and meant to use Mr. Tolleson as a proxy to circumvent the requirement of procuring a search warrant, especially when one considers the trouble Mr. Tolleson endured to bring the body out from under the church after he found it. If Mr. Benewski had deduced the location of the body, he could have procured a search warrant. His initial interview with Mr. Tolleson, his surveillance of the defendant, and the fact that Mayor Matlock's coffin was to be placed in the church the night before his funeral would have constituted probable cause. Mr. Benewski didn't seek a search warrant because he didn't know the location of Marsha Walton's body. The *Weeks* exclusionary rule has no deterrent value when applied to an official who has no knowledge of the location of the evidence in question."

Judge Longworth leaned forward in his chair. Devore raised his voice slightly.

"Ms. Strassberg cites the ruling of the Second Circuit Court of Appeals in *Knoll Associates, Inc. v. Federal Trade Commission*. However, neither the Supreme Court nor the other ten Circuit Courts of Appeals, including our own, has adopted this ruling. It hasn't been adopted by our state supreme court. To say that a warrantless search by a private person becomes unlawful if the private person intended to aid the government when the government subsequently uses the evidence obtained ignores the deterrence function of the exclusionary rule. The government must exercise some control over the private party's intent. If the government has no control over the intent of the private party, the private party cannot be deterred by application of the exclusionary rule. For this reason, the *Knoll* ruling has been ignored by other courts."

Devore glanced towards the defense table. Strassberg was watching him, her face impassive.

"However, even if this court accepts the defense's interpretation of the relevant law, the evidence found under the church is admissible. The Supreme Court, in *Katz v. United States*, ruled that the Fourth Amendment 'protects people, not places. What a person knowingly exposes to the public, even in his own home or office, is not a subject of Fourth Amendment protection.' According to *Katz*, what a person 'seeks to preserve as private, even in an area accessible to the public, may be constitutionally protected.' Justice Harlan's concurring opinion defined what has become the commonly accepted test for what constitutes a justifiable expectation of privacy. He said that 'there is a twofold requirement, first that a person have exhibited an actual expectation of privacy and, second, that the expectation be one that society is prepared to recognize as "reasonable".'"

Devore paused and took a sip of water from a glass on the table. He adjusted his glasses and looked directly at Judge Longworth, not referring to his notes.

"Your Honor, although the defendant demonstrated a subjective expectation of privacy when he hid the evidence below the church, this is not an expectation that society should recognize as reasonable. The church where the defendant worked was held open to members of the public. Furthermore, unlike a person's home or business, the minister of a church does not have a property interest in a church, the church is owned by the members of the congregation. This doesn't mean that ministers have no place they can consider private. Although the congregation usually also owns the minister's residence, the minister has a more justifiable expectation of privacy there than in the church where he works."

Devore discussed the relevant points of state law. He argued that the state supreme court's interpretation of Fourth Amendment guarantees was no more expansive than that of the United States Supreme Court.

"Your Honor, Mr. Tolleson's search beneath the church did not breach the defendant's justifiable expectation of privacy. Mr. Tolleson was not under the control of Mr. Benewski, and Mr. Benewski did not know that the evidence could be found under the church. Application of the exclusionary rule would have no deterrent value. The defense motion should be denied and the evidence should be ruled admissible. Thank you." He bowed his head slightly towards Judge Longworth and then sat down.

Judge Longworth cleared his throat. "Thank you, Mr. Devore. Ms. Strassberg, you didn't talk about the defendant's expectation of privacy in your argument, although it's discussed in the defense motion. Is there anything you would like to say about that issue?"

"Thank you, your Honor," Strassberg said, standing. She flipped through the papers on the table, withdrawing several from the bottom of the stack. "The prosecution apparently believes that an individual's expectations of privacy are only reasonable in areas or buildings where that individual has a property interest. In *Mancusi v. Deforte*, the Supreme Court recognized that offices, stores, businesses and other commercial premises are Constitutionally protected, not because of a person's property interest in such places, but rather because people justifiably consider at least some areas in such places as private. If the property interest were determinative, then only the owners of a business, not the employees or the customers, would have a justifiable expectation of privacy at that business.

"The Supreme Court has never made such a distinction, and has ruled that employees, customers and others may have a reasonable expectation of privacy in areas of a business that are not generally open to the public. A church is not a business, but it is where a minister works. Although the defendant's church was held open to the public, it was only held open at certain times, for certain events. At the time Mr. Tolleson conducted his search; the church was locked. Furthermore, the evidence in this case was found below the church, in an area that perhaps only the defendant knew even existed. The defendant's expectation that this area of his workplace was private is certainly reasonable. There's one other consideration. The Constitution contains safeguards to protect religion from governmental intrusion. In light of the First Amendment's separation of church and state and protection of religious freedom, the Fourth Amendment should be more expansively interpreted with regard to church premises. An expectation of privacy is more justified in this area than in any other. Thank you, your Honor."

"Thank you, Ms. Strassberg. Mr. Devore?"

"Thank you, your Honor," Devore said, standing and walking out from behind the prosecution table. He did not refer to his notes. "A businessman or an employee may have a reasonable expectation of privacy in certain areas of his workplace. Such areas are those that are generally recognized as repositories of private or confidential material—an office, a desk or a locker. While the defendant thought that the hidden tunnels and small rooms under the church were his secret, is that expectation one that, in the words of Justice Harlan, 'society is prepared to recognize as reasonable?' Secret, subterranean hideaways are often used to hide illegal activities and the evidence of such activities.

"Yes, the Constitution does demonstrate a special solicitude for religious activities and the separation of church and state. However, that solicitude should only extend to those activities within the church that are colorably part of the church's religious function. Rape and murder are not religious activities; they are crimes. Crimes deserve no special Constitutional protection, and neither does the hiding place for their evidence. Thank you, your Honor."

Judge Longworth looked towards the prosecution table and then the defendant's table. "Thank you, Mr. Devore and Ms. Strassberg. This court is adjourned until nine o'clock tomorrow morning. I will reread your motions tonight, consider your oral arguments, and announce my ruling tomorrow. The jury pool has been selected and both sides should be prepared for *voir dire*, in case I deny the defense motion. Good day."

The bailiff led Silas Wayne out of the courtroom, to the jail. The attorneys stood and prepared to leave. Preston Catledge introduced Rachel Strassberg to Mike Devore and Gary Benewski. After brief pleasantries the prosecution attorneys left the courtroom. Rachel Strassberg packed her oversize legal briefcase and Catledge waited for her.

"Mr. Catledge, I ate at the hotel restaurant last night. I'm hoping there's someplace better to eat in town. Do you have any recommendations?"

"Please, it's Preston. I was just going to invite you over to the house tonight. There are some things we need to discuss about the case. We could plot strategy and then sit down for one of Marian's dinners. You're on the road all the time, I'll bet you haven't had a home cooked meal in months."

"I don't want to inconvenience your wife."

"Don't worry about that. Marian's been hoping for a chance to meet you. Our daughter, Lisa, is in law school in California. It's four now, come by at around six-thirty. Here's the directions to our house from your hotel."

He drew a map for her. They walked out of the courtroom. She had only met him at the airport yesterday afternoon (although she had communicated with him by phone, overnight mail and Fax machine for months), but she had already noticed his courtly chivalry—an ingrained, automatic feature of his character. He walked with her to her rented car, held the door open and told her to call if she had any difficulty finding his house.

CHAPTER 18

▼

RACHEL STRASSBERG

Rachel Strassberg drove to her hotel to relax for a couple of hours. She had sandwiched this case between a trial in Florida and an appellate argument in New York next month. If there was a trial she was well prepared. Mr. Catledge (she would address him by his first name but she could not think of him by his first name—Preston seemed too informal for the dignified gentleman) had done a superb job with the pretrial discovery and the preliminary motions. She had read the depositions and had almost memorized Joe Tolleson's. Mr. Catledge had provided profiles of the members of the jury pool and Judge Longworth. She had talked with Silas Wayne for several hours the previous evening. They could win this case.

She always took advantage of her infrequent opportunities to exercise. Ignoring the leers of two middle-aged men by the hotel pool, she swam for half an hour, returned to her room, showered, and took a nap.

She arrived at the Catledge residence at 6:30. Preston Catledge answered the doorbell, invited her in and introduced her to his wife. Marian Catledge shared her husband's dignified propriety and many of his physical characteristics. Like him, she was tall and thin and had streaks of graying hair. They both wore horn-rimmed glasses. Strassberg glanced at first the husband and then the wife. Their lined faces were intelligent and impassive—knowing much, disclosing little.

"Preston," Mrs. Catledge said, "you need some time to discuss your case. I was going to put the chicken in the oven now. That would give you about an hour, will that be enough?"

"I think so, if it isn't we can talk after dinner."

"Good. You'll be in the study?"

"Yes."

They entered Catledge's study. Strassberg, expecting musty volumes and the lingering aroma of fine cigars, was surprised by the spacious, well ventilated room. Against the right wall was a large, modern desk with a computer terminal and a small bookcase filled with legal reference books. An abstract painting hung above the desk. To the left was a bar with three bar stools. In the middle of the room two black leather sofas faced each other, with a rectangular glass coffee table in between. Floor-to-ceiling windows, running the length of the back wall, framed a spectacular view of the West Fork River valley. A red, orange and purple sunset illuminated the mammoth rock formations and stately pines and glinted off the surface of the river. She sank into one of the sofas.

"How do you get any work done? I couldn't keep away from the window."

Catledge walked over to the bar. "We've been in this house for 24 years and I love the view. We remodeled about seven years ago. A great place to think, but not always the best place to work. Can I get you a drink?"

"Mineral water with a lime, please."

He fixed her drink and bourbon over ice for himself and sat on the sofa opposite her.

"How did we do today?" he asked.

"Fine, but we're not going to win. From what you told me, Judge Longworth has a conservative interpretation of Constitutional rights. Devore gave him enough to hang his hat on. We made our record for the appeal, and that's all we can do. Even if our judge had a different Constitutional perspective, I've sure he wants to see a trial. This case is probably the most interesting one he's had in years."

"We don't get a lot of murders, and you're right about Judge Longworth." Catledge stood and walked behind his desk, picked up his briefcase and returned to the sofa. "Assuming we're going to trial, how are we going to win?"

They reviewed their case and tried to anticipate the prosecution's. An hour had gone by when Mrs. Catledge entered the study, told them that dinner would soon be ready and left. Catledge rose from the sofa.

"My son, Bart, will be joining us for dinner. He'll be going to college in a couple of years. He's a good kid, but let me warn you, he's at that age where he knows everything, and what he doesn't know isn't worth knowing."

She smiled. "Before we go to dinner, can I ask you a couple of questions?"

"Sure."

"Coming to a small town like Hidden Falls seemed incongruous, although my specialty has taken me to some strange places. Now that I'm here, I'm even more surprised you decided to hire me. How did you make your choice?"

"I've done some criminal law work, but a small town attorney has to be a generalist. I recognized the Constitutional question, but Silas needed someone who argues such issues all the time, especially if there's an appeal. I suggested it to Silas. He said I should look for someone on the way up, but who hadn't quite made it to the top yet. He said that trial lawyers live off their egos and once they make it, they become too full of themselves and lose their drive. Of course he's right, but that's pretty astute for a layman. I did my homework. You've got a great record, but you're only well known among lawyers, you're not a celebrity yet. I got the impression that you prefer it that way."

"I do. The Reverend Wayne didn't object to my sex or my religion?"

Catledge took a long drink, returned to the table and set his glass on it. "Frankly, I thought he might, but he surprised me. He didn't care about your religion and he thought having a female attorney would help neutralize some of the jury's natural sympathy for the victim. I was thinking the same thing. Why did you take the case?"

"Because of the Constitutional issue. An increasing number of governmental functions within the criminal justice system, including the provision of the security and incarceration, are being turned over to the private sector. In this case, a big portion of the prosecution's investigation was performed by Mr. Tolleson. If private parties perform these functions, they should be subject to the same Constitutional constraints that apply to the government. Aside from the Constitutional issue, I'm intrigued by the facts of the case itself. This will be more interesting than, say, your run of the mill drug trial.

"One more question. You've been pretty vague about who's paying for this. I'm not cheap; paying clients subsidize my pro bono work. Unless he's got a TV ministry or a trust fund, our client can't afford me. Who's picking up the tab?"

Catledge paced in front of the large window, drink in hand. "Silas has a lot of friends in Hidden Falls; people he's helped through the years, who admire his ministry. He's in trouble and they want to help. When Silas was arrested after the second set of DNA tests came back, a group approached me, including a man who's now the mayor, Harvey Roach. I was given a blank check—they're underwriting every expense."

She said nothing, but the crinkle in her forehead suggested she found the idea of the town's mayor helping fund Wayne's defense either perplexing or perturbing.

Catledge changed the subject. "I'm glad you were able to fit this case in. I was surprised when we met yesterday. You're different from what I thought you would be."

"What were you expecting?"

Catledge smiled. "An ugly zealot."

"Looks like it's time to eat."

Marian Catledge was standing in the doorway. They walked into the dining room, whose large windows featured another view of the valley. Bart Catledge was slouched in his seat at the end of a long table. He was lanky, like his parents, had a thin face, dark blond hair, restless blue eyes, a mouth full of braces and a face full of acne. They joined him at the table. Mrs. Catledge served a salad, asparagus with hollandaise sauce, baked chicken, rolls, and potatoes au gratin. Strassberg, who normally ate restaurant salads or low-cal plates, surprised herself by asking for second helpings. The home cooked food and the Catledges' proud conversation about their four children and three grandchildren allowed her to relax as she recognized a rare sensation—trusting the basic decency of the people around her. The country was filled with people like Mr. and Mrs. Catledge, she reflected, but criminal lawyers don't see them very often.

Only the behavior of the Catledges' son marred the meal.

"Bart," Strassberg said, passing him a basket of rolls, "what's Joe Tolleson like? Are you two in the same grade?"

"No," Bart responded, not looking up, "he's a senior and I'm a junior. He's strange; I never talk to him. Nobody ever talks to him."

"Is he smart?"

"Yeah, a regular genius."

"How come nobody talks to him?"

"Don't know."

And so it went. She changed the subject, asking him about his future plans. His answers were noncommittal, never more than a few words. He occasionally interrupted the conversation with sarcastic snippets and disparaging comments. His parents did not approve, but it was apparent he was challenging them.

"Rachel, do you travel a lot?" asked Mrs. Catledge.

"Yes, I do. I—"

"So you've gotten criminals off on technicalities all over the country," Bart said, smirking.

Strassberg's smile had all the brilliance and absence of warmth of the sun on a clear winter day. "How old are you?"

"Sixteen."

"When my father was your age, two men in black uniforms, from the government, came to the tenement where his family had been consigned. The government had already taken my grandfather's business and his house, and they were about to take his son. The men in black told my father to report the next morning to the train station, with no explanation. My father was to be taken to a forced labor camp. Where my father came from, the government didn't need to observe that Fourth Amendment technicality requiring an arrest warrant and probable cause. Even if they had wanted to resist the government, my father and grandfather had no means to do so. There was no Second Amendment technicality barring the government from outlawing the possession of firearms, and it had done so.

"My father's family went to the train station and watched as my father was loaded, with thousands of other young men, into one of a long line of cattle cars. There was no charge made against my father, no bail, no presentation of evidence before an impartial judge or jury; there was no trail or any of those other due process technicalities we have in this country by virtue of the Fifth and Sixth Amendments. Nevertheless, he spent the next three years in a succession of forced labor camps, with inadequate food and water and no medical care. The government was not hindered by that Eighth Amendment technicality against cruel and unusual punishment."

She paused, but her eyes never left Bart's. He was petrified.

"Why did they take my father? What was his crime? He was a Jew. There was no First Amendment technicality guaranteeing freedom of religion. My father was ultimately sent to Auschwitz. The rest of his family died at different slave labor camps. My father survived, but no one should have to endure what he endured. Do you know what kept him alive?"

Bart shook his head.

"He would lie awake at night and think about a country where the government had to observe technicalities. Freedom is precious, but fragile. As soon as the war was over, he came to the country that tries to make its government play by the rules."

There was a long silence. Bart was palpably embarrassed. Finally, he opened his mouth, trying to form words. "The Nazis…" he stammered.

"Yes, the Nazis, the National Socialist Workers Party of the Third Reich. Those technicalities are the difference between our form of government and the Nazis. The Constitution is a dead letter if criminals aren't occasionally set free, represented by lawyers like me who make sure the government observes the technicalities."

Preston Catledge and his wife exchanged a connubial glance that conveyed an entire conversation. She pulled away from the table.

"Preston, let's have coffee and dessert in the study. Bart, would you care to join us?"

"No thanks, Mom. I've got to get going on my homework." He retreated from the dining room.

"I've never seen him so anxious to study," Mrs. Catledge said. "Rachel, would you like coffee or desert?"

"I'll have coffee, but I'd better pass on dessert. I've already eaten too much."

"That's a decision you may want to reconsider," Mr. Catledge said. "Marian's apple pie is sensational, especially with vanilla ice cream. It's worth the extra hour in the gym."

"You're twisting my arm, bring on the pie."

They went to the study and settled into the black leather sofas. Mrs. Catledge brought in coffee and three plates with hot apple pie and quickly melting ice cream.

"I hope I wasn't too hard on Bart," Strassberg said.

"You weren't too hard on Bart; he had it coming," Mr. Catledge said. "Perhaps he'll start thinking before he opens his mouth." He smiled. "I feel sorry for the witnesses you're going to cross-examine."

"Your father survived Auschwitz," Mrs. Catledge said. "He must be an extraordinary person."

"He was, he died several years ago." Her voice had an emotional edge. It was difficult to talk about her father. The Catledges, sitting on the opposite sofa, stared at her intently, expecting her to continue.

"He built a garment contractor in New York, and he did it the right way. No kickbacks, no sweetheart contracts, no corruption of any kind. He wasn't always the low bid, but he always delivered as promised on the contracts he got. He did it while raising my brother and me by himself—my mother died when I was six."

"Did he have anything to do with your career choice?" Mrs. Catledge asked, as she refilled their coffee. "Were you interested in the law at an early age?"

"We would discuss current events and politics during dinner every night. My father knew what he believed in, but he was more interested in making us defend our positions. He used the Socratic method, question after question—he could have been a law school professor. I enjoyed the give and take. I think that's what got me interested in the law. I told a friend once that after twenty years of my father, law school seemed easy."

"It must have been," Mr. Catledge said. "You were first in your class."

"I loved what I was doing. After my first moot court argument I was hooked, I wanted to be a courtroom attorney."

"Did your father have anything to do with your interest in civil liberties?" Mrs. Catledge asked.

"I was twelve when my father first told David and me about Auschwitz. You can imagine the impact. Auschwitz turned my father into a political philosopher. He distrusted the whole idea of government. One night a man came to dinner, a fundraiser for Israel. My father listened to him without saying a word. When the man got the point of actually asking for money, my father said, 'I know what's going on in Israel. Taxes are high, the government owns most of the industry, the unions run the country and the kibbutzim have collectivized farming. I left one socialist paradise and I'm not going to underwrite another. Please leave and don't come back.' Father would acknowledge that government was a necessary evil, but he believed its powers must be carefully delineated and limited. What I do with civil liberties is consistent with that belief."

"You miss him," Mrs. Catledge said.

A wistful, sad shadow passed over Strassberg's beautiful face. "Very much. He never remarried after my mother died. I once asked him why. He said, 'it's not difficult to find somebody who will share your disappoints and sorrows—there's always a shoulder to cry on—but your mother was the only woman I've known who could share my happiness.' After everything he'd been through, he was still a happy man. And a great one, an honorable businessman who never wavered in his beliefs. "

The conversation trailed off as they finished their ice cream and coffee. Strassberg glanced at a clock on the wall.

"It's getting late; I should go. This may be our last chance for a good night's sleep until the trial's over. Marian and Preston, thank you for the wonderful dinner, it was the best I've had in months."

They walked to the entry hall and exchanged pleasantries for another fifteen minutes before Strassberg left. After she closed the door, Marian Catledge said, "it's a shame Lisa couldn't have been here tonight, she would have enjoyed meeting Rachel. Such an austere, lonely woman."

*   *   *

The next morning, Judge Longworth announced that the defense's motion to exclude all evidence found underneath the church was denied. Jury selection began after the announcement.

CHAPTER 19

▼

ALONE

A $100,000 contract down the drain. Jack Tolleson had supplied the town government of Hidden Falls its vehicles, and the servicing for those vehicles, for eighteen years. Yesterday, he received word from Mayor Roach that the contract would not be renewed. He did not make much money on the vehicles—Hidden Falls received fleet prices, but the service contract was lucrative. Losing the contract was the latest in a series of setbacks. He had been denied a zoning variance for an expansion of his Buick dealership. The town of Hidden Falls had condemned a twenty-foot strip of land in front of a hotel he owned, to make room for a street widening project. He was contesting the condemnation, but if he lost he would have to spend thousands of dollars to reconstruct the parking lot in front of the hotel. His was the only property in Hidden Falls condemned for the project. As recently as six months ago, there were no plans to expand the street, but it had been proposed and approved with lightning speed by the usually torpid Hidden Falls town council.

He sat in his study on a Sunday evening, staring at a computer spreadsheet, hoping revenues would add up to a bigger number than expenses. A business downturn exacerbated his problems. People were not buying as many cars and profits were off at his other businesses. He was not yet losing money, but he would be if the present trend continued.

"Hi, Dad."

He swiveled in his chair and saw Joe standing in the doorway, holding a suit bag. He had seen his son on only a few occasions since Joe had moved out of the house.

"I needed to pick up my suits and shirts for my testimony. I won't be here long."

Jack did not say anything for several moments. Joe could still change his mind. Preston Catledge had pulled out all the stops for Silas's defense, bringing in a hotshot female lawyer from New York. Bert Weathin, the TV preacher, was going to testify as a character witness for Silas. His headstrong son was going down in a losing cause and he was paying the price. He felt a frustrated anger, tinged with another emotion he refused to acknowledge— pride in his son's obstinacy. It was no use hoping; Joe wouldn't change course.

"Okay, Joe. If you don't mind, your mother and I may watch your testimony tomorrow. I don't know if Alice can make it through a full day in court, but she wants to try. You might look in on her before you go, she's in the bedroom."

"I don't mind. Mr. Devore said my testimony should last a couple of days. I'm the first witness. If you're coming, get there early; the courtroom will be crowded."

"We'll get there early." Jack hesitated. "Good luck, Joe."

"Thanks, Dad."

Joe walked down the hall towards his parents' bedroom. He was debating with himself whether he should say something to his mother when he heard her voice.

"Is this all there is, Joe?"

He entered the bedroom and hung his suit bag on the open door. She was lying on the bed, propped up on a stack of pillows. The television was on, but the sound was muted. Used Kleenex overflowed a wastebasket next to the bed. On the stand by the bed sat an ice bucket, a bottle of scotch and a crystal glass. The seal on the scotch was unbroken, the ice in the bucket had melted and the glass was unused. He walked toward the bed.

"What do you mean, Mom?"

"Is this all there is? Is there a before or an after? Is there magic, mystery and miracles, or are we prisoners of reality—working, reproducing, socializing, sleeping, eating, and drinking...drinking, to forget we're imprisoned? Life is an hourglass and we each have only so many grains of sand. If they're right, when all the sand is at the bottom, the hourglass is turned over and the sand never runs out. Life becomes a choice whether eternity will be ecstasy or torture, a choice you make by how little you live for yourself."

Her eyes widened. Was she delirious? She looked in his direction, but she was looking past him, at her own private vision. "But what if they're wrong and Joe's right, what if there is no eternal hourglass and the choice is between ecstasy or torture the first and only time the sand runs?

Then each grain is precious and you race against the falling sand by following your dreams, by making your happiness the object of your life. There are no grains to spare for homecoming queen contests or church bazaars or Silas Wayne or men you don't love. Why torture yourself, living for everybody else, if the sand only runs once? Let Silas worry about his soul, and Joe worry about his, and everybody else about theirs, and I'll worry about mine." Her eyes refocused on her son. "We're the lucky ones, you and I; we dream. Dreams are the most precious grains, Joe. You've chosen ecstasy and you may find it, but they'll torture you. Don't trade your dreams for their bargain—a job you hate, a wife you don't love, friends you don't admire, platitudes you don't believe, activities that kill your time and mind and a thousand other compromises that add up to a wasted life. If we're all prisoners of reality then I haven't made the best of my time. You will. Don't throw it away betting that the hourglass will be turned over when the sand runs out." She reached out to him and clutched his hand. "This may be all there is, Joe."

"I think so, Mom."

She sank back into the bed and turned away from him. He could not tell if she was crying. He waited a long time, but she did not turn back. He walked away from the bed, took his suit bag from the door and walked out of the room. He met his father in the hall.

"She's in bad shape, isn't she, Joe?" His father frowned. "I don't think she'd be like that if you hadn't done what you've done."

"I'd be like that if I hadn't done what I've done."

He walked away from his father, down the stairs and out the front door. He stood on the porch for several moments without moving, burning with anger. He realized something was brushing against his leg. It was the neighbors' cat, Amanda.

He bent over and scratched the purring creature's head. He heard the loud crack of a high-powered rifle and the impact of the bullet in the door above his head at the same time. He dropped his suit bag and fell to the porch. Amanda scrambled away. There was another shot and the bullet hit the wooden frame of the porch below Joe. He frantically reached upward, trying to find the doorknob. Just as he grasped it, there was another shot that barely missed him to the left. He turned the knob, pushed the door open and rolled into the entry hall in a continuous motion. A fourth shot hit the mirror that hung on the wall at the end of the entryway. Joe heard the tinkle of glass and then the squeal of tires as a car sped away.

His father came flying down the stairs, threw his arms around him, picked him up and pulled him away from the entryway, into the living room. He pulled him to the floor, behind the couch. They were both panting.

"Are you okay?"

"Yeah, I wasn't hit."

"Joe…Joe," it was his mother from the top of the stairs. Her voice, panicked, was much higher than usual.

"Joe?"

"He's okay, Alice," his father shouted. "We're in the living room. Stay upstairs until we're sure they're gone."

His father told Joe to stay down, behind the couch. He crawled to the entryway, avoiding the broken glass of the mirror, and closed the front door. He crawled back to the living room and motioned for Joe to follow him. They crawled away from the couch and scrambled up the stairs to Alice. She sobbed as she hugged her son.

"Dad, we should call Mr. Benewski. His number is 5762788."

His father went to his study while his mother clung to him, stroking his hair. He felt uncomfortable. After several moments his father returned.

"Benewski will be here shortly, he's bringing the police."

Joe stood, freeing himself from his mother's embrace.

"Joe," his father said, "this is real life, not the movies. In real life the hero doesn't always ride off into the sunset. These people are playing for keeps; you could have been killed. Don't say anything now, but think about one thing. What are you risking your life for?"

Jack and Joe sat down at the top of the stairs and an awkward silence ensued. After a few minutes they heard the scream of sirens. Jack and Joe walked down the stairs, followed by Alice, unconscious of her nightgown and unkempt appearance. When Jack opened the front door they saw four patrol cars and several civilian vehicles coming up the cul-de-sac. The cars screeched to a stop and uniformed policemen jumped out and ran towards them, followed by Benewski. In the street a crowd of onlookers was already forming.

"What happened?" Benewski yelled.

Joe waited for Benewski to cross the lawn before answering.

"Somebody tried to shoot me. There were three or four shots. I think they came from the other end of the street." He swung the open door closed and motioned at a bullet hole about five feet up, in the center of the door. "This is where the first shot hit. I was lucky. If I hadn't bent down to pet the neighbors' cat, I would have been hit. Then I think there were one or two more shots. You can see one hit here, to the left of the door. I got the door open and as I was going into the house there was another shot." Joe reopened the door. "There at the end of the entry hall—it hit the mirror."

Benewski turned to one of the policemen. "Officer, see what you can do about cordoning off the entire street. Pretty soon this is going to be a mob scene. There may be evidence around the area where the sniper was and it could be destroyed. Have a couple of your men come with me; I think it's best if we take this inside." He motioned to Jack and Joe, who were standing on the porch, and they went into the house, followed by two policemen.

Alice was still standing at the bottom of the stairs. When she saw the policemen, she went back upstairs without saying anything. Benewski gingerly stepped through the broken glass to the mirror and inspected it for several moments. The group then walked into the living room and Benewski, Jack and Joe sat on the couch. The policemen stood by the doorway.

"Mr. Tolleson," Benewski said, "in a few minutes the police detectives will arrive. They'll need to conduct an investigation." He looked at his wristwatch. "It's four-fifteen now and they'll be here for several hours. I'm going to recommend that Joe be put under twenty-four-hour police protection. I know Joe isn't living here, but tonight he might want to consider staying at home."

Joe looked at Benewski and then his father. He remembered what his father had said at the top of the stairs. His father could be extraordinarily persuasive. Joe was weak, drained of energy. Did he have the strength to resist a night of his father's subtle importuning? Many motives came disguised as love, but the hardest to detect or resist was that of control. His father would say that he was only thinking of what was best for his son. He would talk of risks and rewards, best and worst case scenarios, and limited upsides and unlimited downsides. By the end of the evening it would seem like the rational move, playing the percentages, and Joe would agree that he shouldn't testify in the morning.

"I'll go back to my apartment. Mr. Benewski, would you give me a ride? Maybe one of the police officers can bring my car after the street is cleared."

Benewski and his father exchanged a long glance. Joe stood and walked to the doorway. One of the policemen had brought in his suit bag. He picked it up and turned around, towards where Benewski and his father were still sitting.

"I'm ready to go," he said.

They walked out to the entryway. Jack grabbed Joe's arm and hugged him with a fierce protectiveness. Joe stepped away.

"Are you going to say good-bye to your mother?"

"No."

"We'll see you in court tomorrow."

Joe and Benewski walked to Benewski's old Chevy. Before he got into the car, Joe took a key ring from his pocket, removed the key to his Toyota, gave it to a policeman and asked him to bring his car to his apartment. Then he got in the car with Benewski. They drove through Hidden Falls to Joe's apartment, saying nothing. Joe felt a numbing shock spreading out over his body. A police car with two policemen followed them. They pulled up to Joe's apartment building.

As Joe opened the car door, Benewski said, "Joe, what happened today might have changed your mind about testifying. Think it over; you may decide that it isn't worth the risk. Nobody could blame you if that's your decision. Call me later tonight, let me know if you still want to testify."

Joe stepped out of the car. "I'll give you a call."

He went to his apartment, followed by the two policemen. He told them they did not have to come into his apartment. They reluctantly agreed to stand guard outside his door, but one of them warned him not to go near any windows. Once inside his apartment, he turned on the television and collapsed into a large easy chair. He needed to think, but was too shocked to do so. Watching television was the easiest way not to think.

It took a detective show and an insipid comedy, starring jiggling breasts and long female legs, before the numbness began to fade. It vanished when the news came on and he saw himself on videotape, standing on the porch at his house. He hadn't noticed the cameras, but now he watched himself walk to Benewski's car with Benewski as a TV reporter described the incident. There were close-ups of three bullet holes, but evidently Joe's father wouldn't allow the cameras into the house to show the world the broken mirror. The news program returned to the studio.

"The prosecution's lead witness, Joe Tolleson, was badly shaken by the incident, according to Gary Benewski, from the office of the district attorney," the woman announced from the television. "However, he will be under police protection for the duration of the trial, if he testifies. Now here's Mark Garcia with a feature on the dangers of liposuction."

Joe turned off the television and went into his small kitchen, which was not separated from the living room in his studio apartment. Foraging through the refrigerator, he found sliced roast beef, cheese, bread and mustard. He opened a can of soup and let it heat up while he made a sandwich. He took the soup and sandwich, a bag of potato chips and a soda and sat at his small table.

He kept returning to his father's question—what was he risking his life for? Someone had fired four shots at him, had tried to end his life. How would he benefit by testifying against Silas Wayne? Marsha Walton would still be dead. Nobody, not even Mr. Benewski, would blame him if he decided not to testify. Mike Devore had told him that his testimony would not assure a conviction. They had won on the Constitutional issue, but that ruling could be overturned on appeal. Devore said that Silas's attorney, the woman from New York, had won many such rulings on appeal. Joe finished his meal and washed the dishes. He was hated in his hometown, estranged from his parents, pursuing what ultimately might be a failed quest for justice. Why not quit while he still had his life and his future? If he didn't testify, many people in Hidden Falls would think he committed the crimes, but they might think that even if he did testify. Did he really care what they thought? He finished his meal, washed the dishes and sat in his easy chair.

Over and over he asked: what was he risking his life for? Sometime late that night, the sword cut the knot. He was alone, and that is the state of human existence. One can have a spouse, a family, and friends, but one is still one.

Sensations, emotions and thoughts are communicated, but never shared; they are sensed, felt and thought by the individual. Others hide from themselves that they are alone, hoping to belong. They make friends, take lovers, have children; they join clubs, corporations, governments and churches. But they die as alone as the day they were born.

Few accept being alone and fewer still discover its glory—acceptance of that first truth leads to other truths. Belonging requires a lie—the surrender of self. Surrender to those who surrender to you. It was the big lie he had mentioned to Mason Mingus, the one they all knew but never admitted. Everyone wants to open Silas's door, everyone wants to belong. Afraid of being alone, they join the crowd, checking their minds and souls at that unopened door. Faith is the token received in exchange; what's checked is seldom reclaimed. Faith—their belief in belonging—doesn't negate being alone; it negates the faithful. A seamless web, they all believe because they all believe.

He would rend the web. If he testified, he'd be alone with the truth. If he didn't testify, he'd be alone with his silence. Could he remain silent? Life parallels philosophy, and the search for truth was a first principle. Silence was not the truth. If he didn't testify, his life would be at cross-purposes with his philosophy. Parallel lines don't intersect. A ladder with crossed rails can't be climbed. Trains won't progress down twisted tracks. The life code of the double helix would be destroyed were its parallel strands to intersect. A refusal to testify, to tell the truth, would be his destruction. When people believe that there are higher values than the truth, or that truth doesn't

exist, they sign their own death warrants. He had to tell
the truth for himself and for the people of Hidden Falls,
so they could protect themselves from Silas Wayne.
Hidden Falls could reject his truth, but he would do
what his conscience required.

Someone had fired four shots at him, had tried to end
his life. He smiled—he was stepping back from Silas's
door. There is strength in being alone, in living by no one's
standards but one's own. He called Benewski.

"Hello."

"Mr. Benewski, I'll see you in court tomorrow."

CHAPTER 20

▼

WITNESS

"The State calls Joseph Samuel Tolleson," Gary Benewski announced.

It was Monday morning and Joe was the first witness for the prosecution. In the preceding two weeks, the pre-trial motions had been argued and the jury selected. Mike Devore and Preston Catledge had made brief opening statements to the jury. The small courtroom was sticky and hot from the sun shining through the high windows and the body heat of the densely packed gallery. Joe sat directly behind the prosecution's table. He walked to the front of the courtroom. He wore a dark gray suit, white shirt, red tie and black wing tip shoes. His normally unruly mop of blonde hair was neatly combed, and he appeared composed as he scanned the courtroom. The court clerk stood, approached him and held out a Bible. Joe placed his hand on the Bible.

"Do you swear that the evidence you are about to give is the truth, the whole truth and nothing but the truth, so help you God?"

"I do."

"Please be seated."

Gary Benewski rose and walked towards the witness box. He seemed to fill the front of the courtroom. He wore a dark blue suit, a silk tie with an abstract pattern, a tailored white shirt, and expensive shoes—Devore had told him that the rumpled look would be unacceptable for the trial. Devore had also granted his request to examine Joe; the witness would be more comfortable with him.

"What is your name?"

"Joseph Samuel Tolleson."

"What is your occupation?"

"I'm a student at Hidden Falls High School and at the state branch college."

"You will graduate from the high school next month?"

"Yes."

"How old are you?"

"Sixteen."

"Are you graduating early?"

"Yes, I was advanced a grade when I was ten."

"What is your class rank and grade average?"

"I'm first in my class with a straight A average."

"Do you plan to attend college?"

"Yes, in the fall, to study music and either computer science or physics."

"What is your current address?"

"Two twelve Pine Avenue, Apartment 304, in Hidden Falls."

"Do you live with your parents?"

"No."

"Why?"

"Objection," Preston Catledge said.

"On what grounds?" Judge Longworth asked.

"Relevancy."

"Mr. Benewski?"

"The motivation of the witness will undoubtedly be put in issue by the defense. His separation from his parents bears on his sincerity and the sacrifices he has made to testify."

"Objection overruled."

"You may answer the question, Joe," Benewski said.

Joe looked at the gallery and saw his father and mother. His father's face was grim.

"My father didn't want me to testify and he threatened to not pay for my college education. I moved out five months ago and quit my part-time job at his hardware store."

"Have you found any other part-time job?"

"No."

"How do you pay your apartment rent and living expenses?"

"I've worked part time during the school year and full time in the summer for the last three years. I'm paying expenses out of my savings."

"Joe, where were you in the late afternoon, November the eighth of last year?"

"I was at the First Christian church."

"Where is that church?"

"On the main highway, about two miles outside of town."

"Would you please tell us what happened that afternoon at the church?"

Joe told of picking the lock on the old church's front
door and wandering around the nave until he heard the
creaking noise from the tenebrous choir loft. There were
gasps from the gallery and the jury when he described the
scene in the choir loft—the hanging body of the young
girl silhouetted against the stained-glass cross. He
recounted his confrontation with Wayne and his subsequent escape.

"The man who confronted you in the choir loft, is he
in this courtroom?" Benewski asked.

"Yes."

"Please point to that man."

Joe pointed towards the defendant's table. Silas Wayne
sat at the end of the table, next to Preston Catledge. He
stared straight ahead as Joe made his identification.

"Let the record show that the witness pointed at the
defendant, Silas Wayne. After you jumped from the choir
loft, did you run from the church?"

"Not immediately; my legs hurt too much."

"Did the defendant say anything to you?"

"Yes, he did."

"Objection," Rachel Strassberg said, "this will be
hearsay of the defendant and the prosecution has proffered
no independent corroborating evidence."

"Your Honor, the defendant will have the opportunity
to tell his version of events, and we certainly will produce
independent evidence."

"Overruled, the witness may continue."

"He said, 'only those who forsake their lives for my
sake will know life everlasting. Welcome to hell, young

Joseph, you're about to find out why I'm the Very Reverend Silas Wayne.'"

"Those were his exact words?"

"I think so."

"What happened after he said that to you?"

Joe described how he had run from the church into town to the police station and the reactions of Ruprecht and Marsh. He was calm and his voice was steady. He tried to keep his eyes fixed on Benewski, but sometimes his gaze wandered around the courtroom. He occasionally looked towards the defendant's table. Rachel Strassberg never changed her position. She sat back in her chair with her hands resting on the table. Her eyes bore in on him—they didn't seem to blink. He made a point of neither staring back nor looking away too quickly. He would not be intimidated, but he could not help noticing her beauty.

She saw him glance once at her crossed legs under the table. Her greatest strength as a trial attorney was her concentration—she shut everything from her mind and listened to testimony with her full attention. Although she never took notes, she could recite long stretches of testimony verbatim. She detected the slight voice quavers, tiny inconsistencies and wandering eyes that often signaled that a witness was shading the truth or lying.

Aside from his momentary distraction, she was not picking up any of those signals from Joe. There was an even, unstressed quality to his voice as he testified about the reaction of the Hidden Falls Police Department and then his parents to his story. Only an intelligent, self-confident witness with a credible story, thoroughly prepared by his attorney, could make the difficult task of testifying in public appear easy.

Joe's testimony progressed slowly. Benewski asked him many questions to clarify details. Joe testified for two hours and reached the point in his story where he deduced that Wayne was going to hide the body in Mayor Matlock's casket. When Joe mentioned his phone conversation with Benewski, the assistant district attorney introduced into evidence his own testimony at the preliminary hearing and an affidavit containing his account of the conversation, which was virtually identical to Joe's. Benewski questioned Joe about the conversation, and then led him through each step of his thought process as he had prepared dinner on the night of his inspiration about the location of the body.

"Mr. Benewski," Judge Longworth said, "I'm going to have to interrupt you, it's time for lunch recess."

The courtroom quickly emptied. Joe went for lunch with Benewski and Devore at Brigg's Diner, followed by two policemen acting as Joe's bodyguards. The diner was noisy, crowded, and filled with Brigg's trademark aroma of grilled onions and bacon. They sat at a table with a sign that read: "Reserved for Mr. Benewski and Mr. Devore." The policemen stood unobtrusively next to the wall. Benewski and Joe ordered cheeseburgers, and Devore had a tuna salad sandwich. Their lunches were quickly brought to them.

"I think the time we spent preparing for this really paid off, Joe," Devore said. "You did a great job."

"Thanks," Joe said, taking a bite from his cheeseburger.

"There's Catledge and Strassberg," Benewski said, pointing across the diner. "Waldo is reserving two tables for the attorneys for the duration of the trial. Look at that line in front. The afternoon session will have started by the time some of those people get fed."

They reviewed Joe's testimony as they ate their lunches. After they finished, both attorneys ordered coffee, which a waitress quickly brought them. They drank their coffee and Benewski ordered two cups to go, explaining to Joe that the two attorneys were averaging three hours of sleep a night and needed all the help they could get. Several reporters accosted them as they left the diner. They said nothing to the reporters, but a photographer snapped Joe's picture. There was a large crowd waiting for them at the courthouse and Joe saw two television cameras. Benewski, the ex-football player, ran interference through the throng and the policemen brought up the rear. Devore said "no comment" to reporters' questions.

Joe's testimony picked up where he had left off before lunch. He told about driving through town and past the church and then parking his car to the side of the road.

"Then I walked back towards the church, across the church parking lot and up to the main church door. I hesitated for several moments."

"Why?"

"Because I was afraid. I had just remembered that I had left my cell phone at school. I didn't know when Mr. Wayne would return from the wedding and if he found me looking around the church he would kill me. The church was gloomy in the moonlight and I was going in there to look for the girl's body. I knew that the mayor's coffin would be sitting out front. It took me a while to get up enough courage to open the door."

"Did you open the door the same way you had previously, by picking the lock?"

"Yes."

"Once in the church, what did you do?"

Joe recounted what had happened inside the church. The gallery grew still. Benewski asked few questions, letting Joe tell his story. There were few objections—Judge Longworth would not have tolerated defense objections that were merely attempts to break the flow of the story. The only noise besides Joe's voice was the light tapping of the court reporter and an occasional sob from the back of the courtroom, especially when the name of Marsha Walton was mentioned.

The sobs came from Nancy Walton, sitting in the last row. She had fought a battle with herself. She was a subpoenaed witness and would have to testify, but she had not planned to attend the rest of Silas's trial. However, morbid curiosity had compelled her. Her sobbing became wailing when Joe told of finding Marsha's body.

Joe described his confrontation with Wayne underneath the church. Benewski introduced into evidence a diagram representing the subterranean stairs, tunnels and rooms.

"Did the defendant say anything to you after he confronted you?" Benewski asked.

"He told me that Marsha Walton once told him that he was 'full of shit'."

There was a loud wail from the back of the courtroom.

"Objection," Strassberg said, "this is hearsay."

"The statement is not introduced to prove what Marsha Walton said," Benewski responded.

"Overruled."

"Please continue, Joe," Benewski said.

"Like I said, he told me that Marsha Walton once told him that he was 'full of shit.' He called her a 'heretic' and a 'witch.' He told me how he had raped her in the church."

"Objection, this is a hearsay admission with no independent corroboration," Strassberg said.

"Defendant will have an opportunity to tell his version of events and we will produce such corroboration."

"Overruled, please continue."

"He said that she had struggled and screamed, but that nobody heard her screams. He said she struggled and screamed even more when she saw the rope in the choir loft, and that he could barely get the rope around her neck. He said something about a trick candle, and how her light didn't go out for a long time. He said that's when I discovered him, and that I had discovered him again."

The wailing from the back of the courtroom reached a new intensity and Nancy Walton left the courtroom.

"He said he had prepared her for burial and had drained her lifeblood. Then he said 'poor Alice.'"

Joe looked at his mother. He did not speak for several moments.

"Why did he say 'poor Alice?'" Benewski prompted, moving closer to Joe.

"That's what I asked him. He told me that my mother loved him."

"Your mother's name is Alice?"

"Yes. He said she was beautiful and men worshipped her. He said he had destroyed her by not submitting to her and by making her submit to him. I asked him if he had ever had sex with her."

There was another long pause.

"How did he answer?" Benewski again prompted.

"Can I have a glass of water?" Joe's eyes glistened.

Benewski walked back to the defense table and poured a glass of water from a pitcher. Joe took a long drink.

"Thank you. He said 'I never had sex with your mother, Joseph, but I fucked her.'" The gallery murmured. Joe looked again at his mother. Her face was tightly expressionless, but her eyes had closed and her head was slowly nodding.

"He said that she had talent and ambition and that he had destroyed her dreams. He called my father a 'mediocrity' and said that she did not really love him. He said he had always admired her martyrdom. Then I lost track of what he was saying because I was thinking about how to escape."

"Had you ever heard anything before this time about your mother and Mr. Wayne?"

"No."

Joe then told of stepping towards Wayne and dumping Marsha Walton's corpse in his arms, of being shot at three times and of running down the tunnel. He described the all-night standoff and how he devised his ambush strategy. The gallery again grew hushed as he told about hitting Wayne twice with the pipe, knocking him out, picking up Wayne's gun and pointing it at his head.

"Did you want to kill the defendant?" Benewski asked.

"Yes."

"Why didn't you pull the trigger?"

"I heard music."

"You heard music?"

"Yes, I heard the opening of the third movement of Rachmaninoff's Third Piano Concerto. It's my favorite music. I guess it sounds weird, but the music was coming from inside my head. It was very clear. That's what stopped me. I said something to him and then I walked away."

"He couldn't hear you though, because he was unconscious."

"Objection, counsel is leading the witness," Catledge said.

"Sustained."

"Could he hear you?"

"No, because he was unconscious."

There were titters from the gallery.

"Do you remember what you said to him?"

Joe stared at Wayne at the defense table. Wayne returned his stare. "I said, 'if I pull the trigger you win, you miserable son of a bitch.' Then I put the gun in my pocket and walked through the tunnel to get Marsha Walton's body." Joe finished his story about the events of that night, concluding with the chase back to his car.

Benewski surveyed the courtroom. The jury and the spectators were enthralled; Joe's testimony was having an impact. The dramatic moments—when he told of finding Marsha Walton's corpse, when he talked about his mother and Wayne and later, when he looked at Wayne and described how he spared the ministers' life—were creating emotional support and perhaps countering his image as a remote whiz kid.

Benewski questioned Joe, clarifying the details of his story, until Judge Longworth adjourned court. The spectators filed out of the courtroom, the previous hush giving way to a cacophony of excited chatter. Joe sat in the witness box and watched his parents walk together up the middle aisle. His father had his arm around his mother's shoulders.

He watched his parents and Rachel Strassberg watched him. As draining as the day's ordeal had been, he retained a look of calm, albeit tired, composure. His eyes closed as he folded his hands in his lap. The high-ceilinged courtroom had a slightly musty smell and the diffused, somber lighting that was characteristic of rooms—courtrooms, legislative chambers, law libraries—whose function was the law. However, the sun had moved into a position such that a ray of light came through a high window to the left and illuminated his face in a curious manner, as if the light came from a source within. It reminded her of the luminosity created by the artist Vermeer. She looked at him until he revived. As he stood, he became conscious that she was looking at him and returned her stare. She walked with Preston Catledge out of the courtroom.

*   *   *

Joe resumed his testimony the following morning. He told of driving back into Hidden Falls, stopping at Prater's Exxon and calling the assistant district attorney at his house. Benewski's questions emphasized that Joe had acted on his instructions to go to the police station, impressing upon the jury that the information he gave to Joe the night of Joe's discovery was an inadvertent mistake, and that he had respected the prerogatives of the Hidden Falls Police Department.

Joe's testimony proceeded to his arrest and incarceration in the Hidden Falls jail.

"Now Joe, you said that the defendant was placed in the cell next to yours. Your cells were the traditional barred arrangements?"

"Yes."

"So you and the defendant could speak to each other?"

"Yes."

"Did you in fact have any conversation with him?"

"Yes."

"And could you tell us what was said?"

"Objection," Strassberg said, standing. "Unless what the witness says bears directly on our client's alleged actions with regard to his alleged crimes, the probative value will be outweighed by its prejudicial effect. We ask your Honor to instruct counsel to rephrase to question so that the witness testifies only about those parts of the conversation which bear on the defendant's alleged criminal activities."

"Your Honor," Benewski replied, "the defense will be calling a number of character witnesses on behalf of the defendant. They will try to portray the defendant as a modern saint. I think anything that reveals the defendant's philosophy, and his attitudes towards people, is relevant information about his character and motives. Besides, Ms. Strassberg seems to be assuming that the conversations, if disclosed, would put her client in a bad light."

"Your Honor, I assume that Mr. Benewski would not wish to get these alleged conversations into evidence if he thought they would make my client look good. Thus, assuming the alleged conversations do not cast the defendant in a favorable light, their effect will merely be cumulative to the witness's testimony as to what the defendant allegedly said and did in the choir loft and under the church."

"The objection is sustained. Mr. Benewski, you will rephrase your question so that the witness's answer is confined to what the defendant might have revealed about the circumstances of the crimes."

Benewski looked back towards the prosecution table. Devore was scowling.

"Joe, let's return to something we touched on yesterday. You said you are no longer living at home, with your parents. When did you move out?"

"January of this year."

"Now you said your father didn't want you to testify. Did you have a conversation with him about your testimony?"

"Yes."

"When was that conversation?"

"January seventh of this year."

"Did your father initiate the conversation?"

"Yes."

"What did he say?"

"Objection," Preston Catledge said, standing. "This will all be hearsay."

"Your Honor," Benewski replied, "the witness's father will be called as a witness and be available for cross-examination by the defense. Furthermore, we're not offering this conversation to assert the truth of what was said, but rather to show the witness's sincerity by demonstrating some of the obstacles he's overcome to testify."

"Objection overruled."

"You may answer the question, Joe."

"My father said that he had a conversation with Mr. Harvey Roach. Mr. Roach offered him—"

"Objection," Catledge yelled. "This is a hearsay within a hearsay. Mr. Roach is not on the list of prosecution witnesses, so he is unavailable for cross-examination."

Devore had taken Mayor Harvey Roach's deposition and he had denied having the conversation with Jack Tolleson. He had produced the names of six people, including two members of the Hidden Falls Town Council, who would vouch for his whereabouts on the night of the conversation with Tolleson. It would have been pointless to call him as a witness.

"Your Honor," Benewski said, "we can't convey the substance of the witness's conversation with his father without reference to his father's conversation with Mr. Roach."

"The objection is sustained. Mr. Benewski, you will ask your questions without reference to any alleged conversations between the witness's father and Harvey Roach, and the witness will answer accordingly."

"Joe," Benewski said, "without getting into the particulars of your conversation with your father, would it be fair to say that your father asked you not to testify against the defendant, Silas Wayne?"

"Yes."

"And how did you respond to his request?"

"I refused."

"What did your father do when you refused?"

"He said something to the effect that he would remember my refusal when it came time to start signing checks for college."

"How did you respond?"

"I told him to keep his money, I was going to testify against Mr. Wayne. Then I left the house and took a drive."

"Did you have any further discussions with your father about your testimony before you moved out of your house?"

"No."

"When did you move out of your parents' house?"

"The following weekend."

"And did you also quit your job at your father's hardware store?"

"Yes, at the same time."

"I have no further questions."

"It's almost noon," Judge Longworth said, "let's break for lunch and then we'll proceed to cross-examination."

Joe ate a subdued lunch with Devore and Benewski at Briggs' Diner. Devore was upset.

"You could have got the jailhouse conversations into evidence, Gary," Devore said. "You got cute with the comment about the assumption that they would make Wayne look bad, and Strassberg pounced. We didn't think we'd get Roach's offer in, but you gave her an opening on those conversations."

"Yeah, that last crack was stupid. Strassberg doesn't miss a trick."

"She sure doesn't." Devore turned to Joe. "Joe, you did great with the direct examination, but cross-examination is going to be a lot tougher. I'm assuming Strassberg will do it, and she's a tiger. She'll do everything she can to challenge your credibility. Just keep telling the truth. Answer her questions the way she asks them and don't elaborate. Don't get cute—we've seen what she does with that—and if you can't remember something, say so. It will get tedious—she'll ask the same questions over and over. Don't get frustrated, that's when you'll make mistakes. We'll try to help you out with objections. Don't worry if the answers to some of her questions put you in a bad light. The most important thing we want to establish with the jury is that you're telling the truth. It's odd, but sometimes it builds credibility if you admit to things that make you look bad."

Joe felt like a golfer who leads after three rounds of a four round tournament. Although he had done well, the real challenge was still ahead of him.

CHAPTER 21

▼

CROSS-EXAMINATION

Benewski, Devore, Joe and the ever-present pair of policemen left the diner and returned to the courthouse, fighting their way through the crowd on the courthouse steps. Benewski wished Joe good luck as he returned to the witness stand. Everyone rose for Judge Longworth's entrance. He addressed the courtroom.

"We will begin defense counsel's cross-examination of the witness. Who will be conducting the cross-examination?"

Strassberg stood. "I will, your honor."

"Very well, proceed."

"Thank you." She stepped from behind the defense table and walked towards the witness box. She wore a light gray suit with a white silk blouse, a burgundy scarf and gray leather pumps with low heels.

"Mr. Tolleson, how did you enter into the old church?"

"I picked the lock on the front door."

"Were you aware that picking that lock was a crime?"

"Yes."

"But you nevertheless picked the lock?"

"Yes."

"You used tools that belonged to your father. Was your father aware that you were using his tools in this fashion?"

"No."

"Did you pick other locks?"

"I did a few times when I was younger."

"How much younger?"

"Three or four years ago."

"Could any of these other lock pickings be characterized as crimes?"

"Yes."

"Why did you stop?"

"There are two standard types of internal mechanisms in locks—wafers and pins. Once I had done a few of each I didn't bother with it any more, because I knew how to do it. I stuck with the church front door, though, because it had an old style lock that I couldn't figure out."

"How many times did you attempt to pick the church door lock before the day in question?"

"Four or five."

"And when did you make these other attempts?"

"I would say it was over the last two or three years."

"And the other times you tried to pick this church door lock, you were unable to do so?"

"Yes."

"But on that day you were able to pick the lock?"

"Yes."

"And just coincidentally, that was the day that you claim you saw a body hanging from the rafter in the church?"

"Yes."

"The other times that you picked locks, did you enter the buildings where you had picked the locks?"

"No, not usually, I just wanted to pick the locks."

"But this time you entered the church, stepped into the vestibule and then walked into the nave. Why did you do that?"

"I'm not sure. I think I just wanted to look around, I hadn't been in the church for a while." Joe saw Devore wince; he had given extraneous information.

"How long had it been since you were in the church?"

"Objection, what is the relevancy of when the witness might have been in church?" Devore asked.

"Your Honor," she responded, "we intend to show that the witness had a preexisting animus towards both our client and religion. This question bears on that issue."

"Overruled."

"Please answer the question."

"It had been four years since I had been in the church."

"So you were in the church, in the nave, and you heard a noise. What kind of noise did you hear?"

"I heard a creaking noise. I thought it sounded like timber shifting under some sort of strain."

"Where was the noise coming from?"

"It sounded like it was coming from the choir loft."

"But you couldn't be sure?"

"No."

"Why?"

"It was too dark. It was late in the day and the only light came from outside, through the stained-glass windows."

"So it was too dark to see clearly?"

"It was too dark to see the choir loft from where I was standing in the aisle, looking up at it."

Devore and Benewski exchanged a knowing glance.

"Have you discussed your testimony with anybody?"

"Yes, Mr. Devore and Mr. Benewski."

"Were your conversations extensive?"

"Yes."

"Thank you. Returning to your testimony, you walked back into the vestibule. That's when you decided to go up to the choir loft?"

"Yes, I was curious about the noise."

"The stairway door to the choir loft is in the vestibule?"

"Yes, to the left as you enter the church."

"You walked up those steps and turned on a light?"

"Yes."

"Then you walked down the hall to the choir loft door and opened the door, where you saw a girl's body hanging by a rope from one of the wooden ceiling rafters?"

"Yes."

"What was the position of the body?"

"It was about four feet off the ground, and it was twisting around. It was also moving back and forth a little."

"I thought it was dark. How could you see the body?"

"It was highlighted against the stained-glass cross, and there was still some light coming in through the stained-glass windows. Also, as I said, I had turned on the light in the hall outside the choir loft."

"What was your reaction to seeing the body?"

"I was horrified."

"But instead of running out of the church, you walked down to inspect this hanging corpse?"

"Yes, because—"

"Please, when I ask a 'yes' or 'no' question, just give me a 'yes' or a 'no' answer. You walked down to look at the body. Did you ever actually touch the body?"

"No."

"How close would you say you got to the body?"

"Maybe three feet away from it."

"Now you said on direct examination that you thought that the girl might have been raped because you saw 'something glistening from the inside of her thighs.' Are you aware that when someone is strangled, their sphincter muscle, which controls bowel movement, relaxes and the body voids its waste?"

"I was not aware of that then. I am now."

"Yet you said earlier that there was a horrible smell and that there was a plastic sheet beneath the body?"

"Yes."

"So is it possible that the glistening you saw could have been voided waste, rather than semen?"

"I don't think so. Semen looks different than...than voided waste."

"But since you never touched the body, and since you only saw it from three feet away, and since you didn't have the best light, can you be certain that what you saw was semen?"

"No."

"Was it at this point that the door to the choir loft closed behind you?"

"Yes."

"And you said that the person who shut the door came towards you?" She took a step towards Joe. He was distracted by the scent of her perfume. It was the light, airy fragrance of a solitary flower, not the olfactory cacophony of an entire bouquet.

"Uh, yes."

"And as this person came towards you, you backed down the choir loft stairs, away from this person, correct?"

"Yes."

"Until you backed into the railing at the bottom of the choir loft?"

"Yes."

"How close was this person when you jumped out of the choir loft?"

"He was about three or four feet away."

"It was twilight or early evening?"

"Yes."

"And the person had closed the door to the loft, so there was no light from the light in the hall outside the loft?"

"Yes."

"You said that some light was coming in through the stained-glass cross, but if your back was to the railing, then that light was to your back as well?"

"Yes."

"So there was very little light?"

"Uh, yes."

"And when this person was three or four feet away, you jumped over the rail as this person lunged at you?"

"Yes."

"How did you jump over the rail? Did you do a backwards somersault or what?"

"I rolled to my left, over the railing."

"And like a cat, you happened to land on your feet in an aisle instead of on one of the pews?"

"Yes."

"How far above the church floor is the choir loft?"

"Maybe fifteen or twenty feet."

"And what is the floor of the church made of?"

"Some sort of stone."

"Didn't your fall hurt your legs and feet?"

"Yes."

"But you still managed to run out of the church and approximately two miles back into town, to the police station?"

"Yes."

"The first person you encountered at the police station was Sergeant Ruprecht, and he took you into the office of Chief Marsh. You told them your story, and you say they didn't believe you and refused to take any action?"

"Yes."

"Why do you think they didn't believe you?"

"I don't know why they didn't believe me, but whether they believed me or not, they should have driven out to the church."

"Mr. Tolleson, do you think that what you said about the defendant to Chief Marsh and Sergeant Ruprecht was defamatory?"

"Objection," Devore sprang to his feet. "The question asks the witness to make a legal conclusion and the witness is not a legal expert."

"I think," Strassberg replied, "that the valedictorian of Hidden Falls High School knows the general meaning of the word 'defamatory,' even if he doesn't know all its legal connotations. However, I'll withdraw the question. Mr. Tolleson, can you give me a definition of the word 'defamatory'?"

"A defamatory statement would be one that injured the reputation of someone."

"Thank you, Mr. Tolleson, a law school professor couldn't have said it better." Strassberg smiled. Her smiles were diamonds, made more brilliant by their scarcity. "Do you think your statements to Chief Marsh and Sergeant Ruprecht, if believed, would have injured the defendant's reputation?"

"Yes."

"Chief Marsh told you not to make further statements about what you claimed to have seen in the church, statements which you agree would have injured the defendant's reputation if believed. He also told you that if you did, he would arrest you for trespassing and breaking and entering. Do you dispute the notion that you either trespassed on church property, or that you broke into and entered the church?"

"No."

"Later, when you brought Marsha Walton's body to the police station, you were incarcerated for the weekend. When you were arrested, didn't you also have a gun?"

"Yes."

Devore almost held his breath as Strassberg continued her cross-examination, feeling like a father watching his son negotiate dangerous rapids in a kayak. She probed every weak spot in Tolleson's story, every implausible element. She had lost her gambit when she asked him why Marsh and Ruprecht didn't believe his story, but had recovered by making the witness accept her characterization of their actions. Books and movies did a poor job of portraying the subtle process of impeaching a witness. Unlike bad drama, witnesses seldom broke down in court.

Rather, a skillful cross-examination revealed the inevitable flaws, inconsistencies and memory lapses that occurred in any story. The attorney inculcated a growing, cumulative doubt in the minds of the jurors. Devore's anxiety increased as Strassberg grilled Joe on his deductive process as he stood in the kitchen.

"So Mr. Benewski told you that he had staked out the parsonage and church the previous Wednesday evening, but that the defendant never left his house except for one brief trip to the church?"

"Yes, well I mean he said more—"

"Please, yes or no will suffice. You overheard your parents talking about Mayor Matlock's funeral and how the coffin was to be moved to the church that evening?"

"Yes."

"And from those two shreds of information you were able to determine that the Reverend Wayne had hidden the body in the church and planned to dispose of it in Mayor Matlock's coffin?"

"Yes, well I figured—"

"Please, all we need are 'yes' and 'no' answers to 'yes' and 'no' questions. So you reached your conclusion and you tried to call Mr. Benewski, correct?"

"Yes."

"But nobody was home and there was no answering machine?"

"Yes."

"You drove to the church?"

"Yes."

"You're standing in front of the church. You have a hunch that Marsha Walton's body is in the church. You know that the person you say killed her will return at any time. He must enter the church to get the body and put it in the mayor's coffin. You're thinking that if he returns he will kill you. Nevertheless, you enter the church, because of your hunch?"

"Yes."

"You walked into the nave. Mayor Matlock's coffin was before the altar. You looked in his coffin, to make sure that the body wasn't already there?"

"Yes."

"You actually opened the coffin?"

"Yes."

"After that ghoulish experience, you started on the left hand wall, looking for some sort of secret hideaway, and you proceeded back around behind the chancel to the right hand side of the church. How many tapestries hung on the two sides of the church, to the sides of the altar?"

"Eight."

"Did you look under any of the other tapestries before you looked under the tapestry that hid the secret door?"

"No."

"And why did you look under that particular tapestry?"

"I was frustrated, and on the spur of the moment, I picked up the bottom of the tapestry."

"In other words, like your initial entry into the church on the day you claimed to have first seen the body, you didn't have any definable reason for what you did, you just did it?"

"That's right."

"And lucky for you, there was a crack running parallel to the floor and you had discovered a secret door?"

"Yes."

Strassberg paced back and forth in front of the defense table. "You're a lucky fellow, Joe. You fall fifteen feet from a choir loft to a stone floor, but you land in an aisle and don't hurt yourself. You overhear your parents talking about a funeral and you figure out a grand scheme to hide a body. And now, you happen to raise a tapestry and find a hidden door. Earlier you said there was a strand of hair stuck on the wall and to the tapestry. You found the secret door, and you're excited, but not so excited that you didn't take the time to inspect along the surface of the rug for hairs?"

"That's right. I thought that—"

"So now you've found the door—"

"Objection," Devore said. "Ms. Strassberg should give the witness a chance to finish his answers."

"Sustained. The witness may finish his answer."

"I thought that Mr. Wayne would probably leave some sort of marker to let him know if anybody else went through the secret door."

Strassberg shifted her questioning to the details of Joe's discovery of the body. She spent little time on Joe's initial confrontation with Silas, not wanting a replay of Joe's testimony about what Silas had said under the church. She also asked few questions about Joe's ambush of Silas, not wanting to give him an opportunity to remind the jury of his courage and resourcefulness. She dwelled on one point.

"You had a gun pointed at the defendant's head and you wanted to kill him. Yet, you didn't because you heard music, is that correct?"

"Yes."

"And what was the music you heard?"

"Rachmaninoff's Third Piano Concerto."

"The third movement?

"Yes."

"Of course. Where was this music coming from?"

"From inside my head."

"I see. Do you often hear music coming from inside your head?"

"Sometimes. Sometimes it's music I've heard before, and sometimes it's something new. That's how I get ideas for compositions."

"You hear music in your head. Now why would that lead you to withdraw the gun from the defendant's head?"

"Something about the music made me realize that I had a lot to live for. If I killed Mr. Wayne, it would have ruined my whole life."

"Sounds like a religious experience."

He did not take the bait, remaining silent.

"You retrieved the body and left the church, carrying the body. The defendant chased you to your car. The body slowed you down, but you had a head start and the defendant didn't catch you. How far was he from you when you reached your car?"

"He was about twenty or thirty yards away."

"But another lucky break for you, he didn't catch up to you until you were pulling away in your car?"

"That's right."

"You didn't fumble the keys or have any trouble getting the car started?"

"No."

"But you were frightened?"

"Yes."

She paused and walked back to the defense table. After examining some papers she turned back towards Joe.

"Mr. Tolleson, when did you first meet the defendant?"
Judge Longworth interjected before Joe answered.

"Ms. Strassberg and Mr. Tolleson, it's almost five. Let's call it a day. Court is adjourned until tomorrow at nine."

The sheriff gaveled the courtroom to its feet as the judge stood and exited to his chamber. The jury went to the jury room and the spectators and reporters filed out of the courtroom. A bailiff took Silas to his cell. Strassberg returned to the defense table and chatted with Preston Catledge, making plans to meet him at his office after a two-hour break for dinner. Benewski and Devore approached the witness stand.

"I'll bet you're glad to call it a day," Benewski said, smiling.

"That was tougher than I thought it was going to be. How do you think I did?"

"You did fine," Devore said. "She was good and she scored a few points, but that's going to happen. She didn't put any major dents in your testimony." He looked at his watch. "If you were a little older I'd buy you a drink. You want to get a milkshake or a soda?"

"Sure."

They walked up the aisle, accompanied by Joe's police escort. They were the last to leave the courtroom.

*   *   *

Preston Catledge had made his law office a symbol of his successful legal career. As befitted the senior partner of the preeminent law firm in Hidden Falls, he had a corner office on the top floor of the best of the town's few office buildings. A maroon leather chair sat behind a handcrafted antique desk—a desk from whose aged and burnished mahogany emanated a patina of understated, but unassailable, influence and privilege. Behind the desk an antique credenza's rolled cover hid state-of-the-art computer and communication systems. In front of the desk sat two black leather chairs. To the left and right of the desk, along the wall, were two cabinets, in the same style as the credenza. On one cabinet stood an abstract sculpture of polished jade. Floor-to-ceiling bookcases along the opposite wall contained Catledge's legal library. In the center of the room was a circular mahogany table with four office chairs. The night after Joe's first day of cross-examination, Rachel Strassberg and Preston Catledge sat at this table, arguing. Catledge's associate, Mark Dougherty, listened to the argument, but said nothing.

"Preston," Strassberg said, "he was a much better witness than I thought he was going to be. I hit all the implausible elements of his story, and I'm certainly going to stress the many coincidences and fortunate turns of events in my closing argument, but I haven't found inconsistencies. He's told the same story to the police, his parents, the district attorney's office and now in court. He knows when I'm homing in on the weak spots, but he doesn't back off. He believes his story and he's been well prepared. He's also a quick study—he senses when I'm trying to trip him up and he's avoided the traps. You know he's making a good impression on the jury. We should get him off the stand."

"I'm not saying that he hasn't been a strong witness," Catledge responded. "What I'm saying is that we haven't played to our strength yet. Four years ago he refused to be confirmed as a member of the church. It's clear that he hates our client, but I think we can show that he hated him before all this happened. We have to show that he was motivated by something other than a passion for justice. We have to at least partially negate his testimony the past two days. The only way to do so is to make this thing look like a vendetta."

"Okay," she said, standing up, moving behind her chair, and placing her hands on the top of the chair back. "Let's come at this from a different angle. Let's say, hypothetically, that Joe Tolleson is either telling the truth or at least believes he's telling the truth. There are such witnesses. They know their story, they have the motivation to tell what they know and are sharp enough to remember the details. Wigmore said cross-examination is 'the greatest legal engine ever invented for the discovery of truth.' However, sometimes, it doesn't work as planned—relentless questions and traps sometimes reinforce a truthful witness's credibility with the jury.

"We don't know how Tolleson will respond to our questions about his religious beliefs, but assume the best case from our standpoint. Say he admits that he doesn't believe one word of the Bible and that he's hated Silas Wayne since the first time he met him. If he handles those admissions in the same way he handled some of the weak spots in his story today, we'll be hurting ourselves with the jury. They'll say to themselves: 'if this witness will admit that kind of thing about himself, we can probably trust him on the other things he says.' Let's call it a day and go on to the next witness."

Catledge stared at his co-counsel for a long time before he spoke. "I think it's fair to say that a lot of sophisticates on the coasts underestimate the importance of religion to people in the heartland. Church, the Bible, and regular religious observances are the core of our community. Around here, religious fundamentalism isn't some fringe political movement; it's a way of life. If we can show the jury that Joe Tolleson doesn't believe the same things as they do, they'll doubt him on other issues as well. His honesty will work against him. He might admit to things that more experienced, mature souls wouldn't admit to, even if they honestly believed them. He's smart, but at sixteen, he's still a boy."

"Joe Tolleson is as much a man as anybody in that courtroom," she said, shocking herself and the other two lawyers with her vehemence. They regarded her with suspicious curiosity. Her voice softened, "I mean, he's handled himself like a man so far."

"Rachel, I hate to pull rank here, but we should stick with the original game plan. If you want, I'll continue the cross-examination."

Strassberg's chuckle was mirthless.

"Why are you laughing?"

"There's a certain irony here. I'm going to act like some modern Torquemada, grilling a witness about his religious beliefs."

"I said I'd do the cross-examination."

"No, if that's what we're going to do, then I should do it. The Reverend Wayne is entitled to the best execution of our strategy, whether I think it's the right strategy or not. It'll raise questions and hurt his case if we suddenly switch cross-examiners."

Across town, in a tiny studio apartment, the cross-examinee lay on his bed, his hands folded behind his head, staring into the darkness. He could still smell the scent of his interrogator's perfume. When he closed his eyes he saw legs, curves, and intelligent, dark eyes. It was to be a long, hard night.

*   *   *

Strassberg opened her cross-examination the next morning by repeating her question from the previous afternoon.

"Mr. Tolleson, when did you first meet the defendant?"

"I was four years old. I met him after a church service when he greeted the congregation."

"Did you have any particular feeling towards him then?"

"No."

"Did you attend church services after that?"

"Yes."

"Did you want to attend those services?"

"No."

"Why did you attend?"

"My parents made me."

"Did the Reverend Wayne ask you to attend confirmation classes when you were twelve?"

"Yes."

"Did you agree to attend?"

"No."

"Why?"

"I didn't like Mr. Wayne, and I didn't believe in his religion."

"You didn't believe in his particular doctrines, or you don't believe in the Christian religion generally?"

"Objection," Devore said. "What is the relevance of Mr. Tolleson's beliefs to the issue of the guilt or innocence of the defendant?"

"Ms. Strassberg?" Judge Longworth asked.

"Mr. Tolleson's religious beliefs, or the lack of such beliefs, are part and parcel of his hostility towards Reverend Wayne. This hostility existed long before the alleged incident in the church and thus, bears upon the witness's motivation and credibility."

"Overruled. Mr. Tolleson, please answer the question."

"I don't believe in the Christian religion generally."

"Did the Reverend Wayne try to change your mind?"

"Yes, he came over for dinner one night."

"What happened?"

"He asked me what parts of Christian doctrine I didn't believe. I said, 'all of it' and walked out of the room. I didn't talk to him again that night."

"When did you develop your antipathy towards the Reverend Wayne?"

"I can't pinpoint the exact time, it was a gradual thing."

"Now you said that you don't believe in the Christian religion. Without getting into specific doctrines, do you think that there is a higher purpose in life than serving one's own self-interest?"

"No."

"So there is no other person or group whose interests you would place before your own?"

"No. Whose interests should I place before mine?"

Strassberg barely suppressed a smile. The question captured centuries of philosophical speculation. "Please, just answer the question that I ask. Is it true that you spoke out at a student council meeting last year at Hidden Falls High

School against a proposal requiring all students to engage in community service work, and threatened not to fulfill the requirement if it was instituted?"

"Yes. I think coerced community service is wrong."

"Would you say that your opposition was one of the reasons that the requirement was not instituted?"

"No, I don't have that much influence."

"Is it true that you didn't attend the First Christian church for four years after you refused confirmation?"

"Yes."

"Would it be an accurate characterization of your feelings before the first alleged incident at the church to say that you disliked the Reverend Wayne and that you didn't believe in the tenets of the Christian faith?"

"Yes."

"Would it also be fair to say that you made no particular effort to hide these feelings from the people of Hidden Falls?"

"Yes."

"So that your feelings could have been known by both members of the police department and your parents?"

"Objection," Devore said. "The question asks the witness to speculate about matters of which he has no first hand knowledge."

"Your Honor, I will amend the question. Mr. Tolleson, did you at any time make either members of the Hidden Falls Police Department or your parents aware of your feelings about the Reverend Wayne and religion?"

"Only my parents. I told them how I felt."

"Let's return to your beliefs. Do you feel that there is any power which transcends human thought and understanding?"

"No, I don't think there's any power greater than the reasoning and creative powers of the human mind." Joe smiled. "Not my mind...or yours."

"The witness has been repeatedly instructed to answer only the questions that are asked. I have no further questions."

"Mr. Benewski, do you have any questions on redirect examination?"

Benewski stood, moved away from the prosecution table and took several steps towards Joe. "Yes, your Honor, thank you. Since we're talking about your motivations, let me ask you something Joe. Neither the police nor your parents acted on your account of Marsha Walton's body hanging in the church, and they told you not to pursue the matter. When you finally figured out how the defendant intended to dispose of her body, you risked your life to uncover that crucial evidence. Now you're living by yourself, you've quit your part-time job and you'll have to fund your own education because your father didn't want you to testify. Why have you risked so much, why have you gone to this trouble?"

Joe paused for several moments to gather his thoughts. When he spoke, his voice was steady and clear. Many of the spectators and some of the jurors leaned forward and the courtroom grew still, hushed.

"I've done what I've done because nothing, except life itself, is more important than the truth. I had to tell the truth. None of us is safe if we allow people like Mr. Wayne to live in society—if he's not in prison he could do what he did to someone else. If I ignored what I saw, my silence would be on my conscience for the rest of my life. To me, not testifying would be the same as lying, and I would be a coward."

"Is it true that the day before you began your testimony here, someone fired four shots at you as you were leaving your parents' house?"

"Objection," Strassberg shouted, "no showing of relevance."

"Sustained. Mr. Benewski, you know better than that. The question shall be stricken from the record. The jury will ignore the question."

"I have no further questions then, your Honor." Benewski winked at Devore as he returned to the prosecution table.

At the defense table, Preston Catledge turned to Rachel Strassberg and whispered, "you were right." She nodded.

"No further questions your Honor."

"The witness may step down."

CHAPTER 22

▼

THE PROSECUTION

"The State calls Nancy Walton," announced Mike Devore, standing. His short hair was combed back, each individual hair in position. From the padded shoulders to the cuffs of his pants, resting on gleaming black leather shoes without breaking the crease, his expensive blue suit hung perfectly on his slender frame. He wore a crisp white shirt with a red and blue striped tie.

Nancy Walton walked from the back of the courtroom to the witness stand. She wore the only conservative outfit she owned—a black suit, pink blouse and flat, black shoes. The oath was administered and Devore began questioning her. After she stated her address and occupation, she recounted what happened the night before her daughter's disappearance. She had drunk cocktails and danced with a man named Phil Bassett after her shift at the Starlight Lounge and then they had gone to her house. They were engaged in "amorous activities" on the living room couch when Marsha walked into the room. Furious, her daughter left the house. Her mother searched for her, but unable to find her, returned to the house and passed out.

"Did Marsha come back to the house?" Devore asked.

"She must have. I heard her getting ready for school the next morning."

"Did you see her then?"

"No."

"Why not?"

She hesitated. Her right heel moved up and down without tapping the floor. "I was a little hung over, and I didn't feel like getting out of bed. I guess I was also afraid to see her, because I knew she'd still be angry."

"She didn't return from school that afternoon?"

"No."

"Had Marsha run away before?"

"Yes."

"How many times?"

"Twice."

"Do you know why she ran away?"

The up and down motion of Walton's heel stopped, but she shifted in her chair. "She was mad at me for bringing men home. She didn't like that. She said it was low class."

"So she had run away twice on the days following nights when you had brought men to your house?"

"Yes."

"Had you ever communicated that fact to Silas Wayne?"

"Yes, after the second time she ran away."

"You didn't see Marsha that Friday morning. Was the confrontation the previous night the last time you saw your daughter alive?"

She nodded, fighting her tears.

"Please, we have to have an audible answer."

"I didn't see her again," she whispered.

"I know this is difficult for you. Now, the two previous times when Nancy ran away, did you notify the police?"

"Yes."

"Did you file a report with the police after the third disappearance?"

"Yes, Mr. Benewski told me to file the report."

"And when was that?"

"The Tuesday after the Friday when she disappeared."

"And until you talked with Mr. Benewski, you definitely thought that your daughter had again run away?"

"Yes."

Devore picked up a piece of paper from the prosecution table. He showed it to the witness.

"Is this your copy of the report you filed?"

"Yes."

Devore introduced the report into evidence, after showing it to the defense attorneys and the jury.

"What was the police response to this report?"

"Objection," Strassberg said, "the witness doesn't have first hand knowledge of the police response to the report."

"Sustained."

"Mrs. Walton, did you ever receive any communication from the police about this report after it was filed?"

"No."

"Mrs. Walton, how long have you known the defendant?"

"About ten years."

"Do you attend the First Christian Church?"

"Yes."

"Did Marsha know Silas Wayne?"

"Yes."

"Did Marsha attend the First Christian Church?"

"Not unless I made her. We went to Christmas Eve services."

"Was Marsha confirmed as a member of that church?"

"No, she wouldn't go to the classes."

"Did Silas Wayne ever say anything to you about that?"

"No."

"Did Silas Wayne have a conversation with Marsha after the second time she ran away?"

"Yes, I asked him to talk with her. I knew that he had helped some kids who had problems."

"Is that when you told Silas Wayne that Marsha had run away twice after you had brought men to your house?"

"Yes."

"Did Marsha say anything to you about her conversation with Silas Wayne?"

"Yes."

"What did she say?"

"Objection," Strassberg said, "hearsay."

"Obviously," Devore responded, "the declarant, Marsha Walton, is unavailable, and the answer is being introduced to demonstrate her feelings towards the defendant, not to establish facts about the character of the defendant."

"Overruled, please answer the question."

For the first time in her testimony, Nancy Walton looked towards Silas Wayne. His face was an unchanging mask. He sat erectly in his chair, hands folded in his lap. He had intently watched Joe Tolleson's and now, Nancy Walton's testimony, never losing his composure. He rarely spoke to Catledge, who sat next to him, but they occasionally wrote notes to each other. He returned Nancy

Walton's gaze without changing expression. She turned her head and her right heel moved up and down.

"Marsha said something like, 'Mom, most of the guys you know are losers, but at least they know they're losers, they're not pretending to be anything better. This guy's a loser pretending he's a saint.'"

"Is that all she said about that conversation?"

"Ah…yes."

"Do you think it's possible during Marsha's conversation with the defendant that she said something to him to the effect that he was 'full of shit?'"

"Objection," Strassberg said, "the question requires a speculative answer outside the witness's first hand knowledge."

"Sustained."

"Did Silas Wayne ever say anything to you about this conversation with Marsha?"

"No."

"Did your daughter know Joe Tolleson?"

"I can't say, for sure. I don't think so."

"Do you recall her ever mentioning Joe Tolleson's name?"

"No."

"Thank you, I have no further questions. Your witness."

Preston Catledge stood, but did not approach the witness stand. "Mrs. Walton, who performed your daughter's funeral?"

"The Reverend Wayne."

"Thank you. I have no further questions."

Nancy Walton stepped down from the stand and left the courtroom to smoke a cigarette on the courthouse steps. A throng of spectators for the lunch recess soon joined her.

Reporters quickly surrounded Joe as he emerged from the courtroom, separating him from his two police body-guards. He tried to ignore them, as he had since the trial began, but now there was no Gary Benewski to run interference. The mob momentarily parted and he glanced at Nancy Walton, standing alone, smoking. They caught each other's eyes before a reporter stepped between them. Followed by the reporters, he walked to his car without saying a word and then drove to the local outlet of a fast food chain. The reporters stayed at the courthouse.

To avoid stares inside the hamburger stand, he ate his lunch in his car. He had felt surprisingly exhilarated answering Rachel Strassberg's questions that morning. His mother had once told him to avoid controversial subjects like religion and politics in polite company. He remembered her queer look and the ensuing silence when he asked her what polite people talked about. Unfortunately, he found most people felt as his mother did. Conversations about interesting (controversial) topics were rare, treasured luxuries. He would have preferred to discuss his views with Ms. Strassberg in a different venue than a courtroom, but he had still enjoyed his session on the witness stand.

After lunch, he drove to the high school. Now that his testimony was over, he felt an anticlimactic letdown. He ignored the curious stares of the other students as he walked through the halls with his police escorts. He found it difficult to concentrate on his physics teachers' lecture—his mind was still in the courtroom—but he forced himself to listen. Finals were in three weeks.

Back at the courtroom, Mike Devore called the prosecution's next witness, Lou Santori. A short, handsome man in his early thirties stood and walked to the witness stand. He had black hair, a full black moustache, brown eyes and a swarthy complexion. His brown suit did not hide his muscular physique.

"State your name, address and occupation."

"Lou Santori, 57 Maple Lane here in Hidden Falls, and I'm a bartender at the Starlight Lounge."

"What is your usual shift at the Starlight Lounge?"

"I work from three o'clock until midnight."

"Did the defendant, Silas Wayne, ever come into the Starlight Lounge?"

"A few times, maybe five or six."

"Were you surprised that he came into the bar?"

"The first time, yes. He came in one afternoon. He didn't order anything alcoholic, though, he never did. He had a soda. I think he was just looking for some conversation. We talked for a while, then he went to the pool table. He played a game, but he wasn't very good." Santori glanced at the defendant, who stared back at him.

"Did you ever have a conversation with Mr. Wayne about your fellow employee, Nancy Walton?"

"Yes, I talked with him twice about her."

"What was said during those conversations?"

"He said that he was a friend of Nancy's and that he worried about her working in a bar. He asked me if she was happy working at the Starlight and if she ever got in trouble with the customers. The second time we talked about her, he asked me if she ever went home with men she met at the bar."

"Objection," Strassberg said. "Nancy Walton's personal life is not an issue in this case, and the defense will stipulate that it will not be made an issue."

"Your Honor, if Mr. Santori may complete his answer, the relevancy to the issues in this case should be apparent even to Ms. Strassberg. We are certainly not trying to make an issue of our own witness's personal life."

"Overruled, please continue your answer."

"The Reverend Wayne asked me if Nancy ever went home with men she met. I said that I didn't know where she went, but that she had left the bar several times with men. He said he wasn't spying on Nancy, but that he was concerned. He gave me his card with his phone number and asked me to call him when she left the bar with a man. He said I could call him the night it happened or the following morning."

"To the best of your recollection, when was this conversation with Mr. Wayne?"

"About two months before Marsha disappeared."

Devore went to the prosecution table and picked up a business card. "Is this the card, with his phone number, that Mr. Wayne gave to you?" He handed the card to the witness.

"Yes it is," he said, handing the card back to Devore.

Devore gave the defense attorneys and the jury a chance to inspect the card and entered it in evidence.

"Mrs. Walton has testified that the night before her daughter's disappearance, she left the bar with a man named Phil Bassett. Did you call Mr. Wayne to tell him that she had left the bar with a man?"

"It was late when she left so I called the following morning. I reached him at the parsonage. He didn't say much, he just thanked me and hung up."

Murmurs ran through the gallery. Judge Longworth banged his gavel.

"Mr. Santori," Devore said as he handed the witness several sheets of paper, "is this the original copy of your phone bill for last November?"

"Yes, it is."

After showing defense counsel and the jury the bill, Devore entered it in evidence and then handed it back to the witness.

"Does item twelve on that bill indicate that a call was placed from your house to the local phone number 5769491 at 10:09 A.M. on the day of Marsha Walton's disappearance, November the eighth?"

"Yes, it does."

"And is that the same number as the number on the card Mr. Wayne gave to you?"

"Yes, it is."

"And that's the number Mr. Wayne indicated was the number for the parsonage?"

"Yes, it is."

"Thank you, Mr. Santori, I have no further questions."

"Mr. Santori," Strassberg said, standing, "you testified that you told the Reverend Wayne that Nancy Walton left the bar with a man. Did you know that man?"

"No."

"Did you know his name?"

"No."

"Did you know if they were going somewhere together?"

"Well, they looked like they were getting pretty friendly, so I assumed they were going somewhere together."

"But you didn't know?"

"No."

"He might have been walking her to her car?"

"Yes."

"And you say that you didn't call the Reverend Wayne until the following morning?"

"That's right."

"And all you said was that Nancy Walton had walked out of the bar with a man the previous evening?"

"That's right."

"I have no further questions."

"The State calls Sally Kennedy," Devore announced.

A young girl walked to the stand. She resembled Marsha Walton, with the same long blond hair and bright blue eyes. Her voice quavered as the oath was administered and Devore asked her to state her name, address and occupation.

"Thank you, Sally. How old are you?"

"Fifteen."

"And you were good friends with Marsha Walton?"

"Yes."

"You usually walked home from school together?"

"Yes."

"On the afternoon of November the eighth of last year, did you walk home with Marsha Walton?"

"Yes, we walked as far as my house. Marsha's house is another mile up the road."

"Have you walked from your house to Marsha's house?"

"Yes, many times."

"Could you describe the road from your house to hers?"

"Until you get to where she lived, where there's some houses, there's not much around. You walk through some trees and down a hill and then up a hill. There's a lot of trees on both sides of the road and there aren't any houses or businesses around there. When you come up the hill it's about a quarter of a mile to Marsha's house, and that's the first time you see houses or anything."

"Are there a lot of cars on that stretch of road?"

"No."

"And as far as you know, when you stopped at your house the afternoon of the eighth, Marsha planned to proceed to her own house by walking along that road?"

"Yes, that's right."

"Did Marsha say anything about planning to run away?"

"Objection," Strassberg said, "hearsay."

"Sustained."

"I have no further questions, your Honor."

Rachel Strassberg advanced towards the witness stand.

"Sally, on the afternoon of the eighth, you assume Marsha was walking to her house after she left you at your house because that's what she usually did?"

"Yes."

"Did you see anybody else on the road that day?"

"No."

"Thank you, Sally. I have no further questions."

The next prosecution witness was Chief Frank Marsh of the Hidden Falls Police Department. After Marsh was sworn in, he testified that Joe Tolleson had told him and Sergeant Ruprecht a story that matched, in all particulars, his testimony during the trial. Marsh also admitted that he had told Joe not to repeat his story, and had threatened to arrest him for trespass and breaking and entering if he did.

"Why didn't you investigate Mr. Tolleson's story?" Devore asked. "Why didn't you at least drive out to the church?"

Marsh shifted slightly in his chair. "It just didn't seem possible that the kid could be telling the truth. He's a fairly odd duck, and he's talking about the Reverend Wayne.

The police department has had some political troubles the last few years—with the recession and tax shortfalls our funding has been cut. If we investigated Reverend Wayne, we'd be making things harder on the department. We'd take a lot of heat for that investigation."

"So the primary reason you didn't investigate Joe Tolleson's complaint was because of political considerations?"

"No, the primary reason was the Reverend's reputation."

"But political considerations were important?"

"Yes, but—"

"How long have you known Mr. Wayne?"

"Over twenty years."

"Do you attend services at the First Christian church?"

"Yes."

"When Joe Tolleson told you the story the night of November the eighth, did you know him?"

"No, I had never met him."

"So your estimation of him as a 'fairly odd duck' was based on what other people had said about him?"

"Yes."

"The following Tuesday, did Nancy Walton file with your department a missing person report for her daughter, Marsha?"

"Yes, she did."

"What was the response of your department to that report?"

"Because Miss Walton had previously run away, we treated the case as another attempt to run away. There's a nationwide database that tracks runaways and we listed our report with that database. We didn't do anything else. We used to have a man who worked on these types of problems, but when our funding was cut I had to lay him off. With our limited resources, we have to concentrate our efforts on more serious matters."

Devore took several steps towards the witness, so that he was very close to him. "Chief Marsh, we're all sorry your funding was cut. However, you had a report from Joe Tolleson that he had seen the body of a girl, whose general description matched that of Marsha Walton, hanging from the rafter of Silas Wayne's church, and also an indication that this girl might have been raped. What is a more serious matter to the Hidden Falls Police Department than murder and rape?"

Marsh's face reddened. "Well, nobody made the connection between what Tolleson had said and the missing person report. Neither myself nor Sergeant Ruprecht were personally aware of the missing person report and we were the only ones who knew about Tolleson's story."

"So Tolleson's story never even circulated within the department?"

"Uh…that's correct."

"And Nancy Walton's missing person report never circulated within the department—at least it never came to your or Sergeant Ruprecht's attention?"

"Uh…that's correct."

"I see." Devore stepped back from the witness stand. "Now when Mr. Tolleson came to the police station a week later, the following Saturday morning, with Marsha Walton's body in the back seat of his car, were you at the police station?"

"No, I was at home. Sergeant Ruprecht called me and I went down to the station."

"What did you do when you got to the station?"

"I ordered the arrest of Joe Tolleson and the Reverend Wayne."

"You ordered the arrest of Wayne at the same time as you ordered the arrest of Tolleson?"

"Yes."

"Didn't you order the arrest of Mr. Wayne after a confrontation with Mr. Benewski?"

"I really don't remember the exact sequence of events. I know I was initially reluctant to arrest the Reverend Wayne, but I eventually ordered Albert Ruprecht and a patrolman to go to the church and make the arrest."

"Was there a confrontation with Mr. Benewski?"

"I wouldn't call it a confrontation. I do remember that he felt that the Reverend Wayne should be arrested."

"I have no further questions." Devore returned to the prosecution's table.

"Marsh wiggled out of a tight spot," Benewski whispered. "I should have developed the point about the confrontation during Joe's testimony." Devore nodded.

"Our first character witness," Strassberg whispered to Catledge. She stood and advanced towards Marsh.

"Chief Marsh, what was it about the Reverend Wayne that made you initially reluctant to pursue Joe Tolleson's story, and later reluctant to arrest him?"

"Well, as I said, I've known the Reverend Wayne for over twenty years. I've never met a gentler, more charitable man. He's been involved in every civic activity in this town. When we get emergency cases, accidents and such, it's standard procedure to call him. I've seen him at the hospital emergency room many times, consoling victims and their families. When my mother got sick a few years ago, he visited her every day until she died. I just didn't believe that Si…the Reverend Wayne could do what that kid said he had done. I still don't."

"When Joe Tolleson brought Marsha Walton's body to the police station, why did you arrest him?"

"We had probable cause to arrest him. He had the corpse of a young girl and a revolver as well."

"And you did order the arrest of the Reverend Wayne?"

"Yes."

"And you've fully cooperated with the district attorney's office in the subsequent investigation of this matter?"

"Yes."

"I have no further questions."

"The State calls Sergeant Albert Ruprecht," Devore said.

The oath was administered to Ruprecht. He verified Tolleson and Marsh's testimony about Joe's story and about what had transpired the Saturday morning a week later, when Joe brought in the corpse.

"Now," Devore said, "you saw Joe Tolleson when he told you and Chief Marsh his story that Friday night. You also saw him a week and a day later, that Saturday morning when he brought in Marsha Walton's body. Did you see him at any time between those two times?"

Ruprecht's eyes narrowed. "Yes, I did."

"When was that?"

"I saw him coming out of the district attorney's office. I believe it was the following Monday, in the afternoon."

"So you knew that Joe Tolleson had talked with someone in the district attorney's office?"

"Yes, I did."

"Did you communicate that information to anyone else?"

"No."

"You told nobody else, not even Chief Marsh?"

"No."

"No further questions." Devore returned to the prosecution's table and leaned towards Benewski. "We got what we wanted—he's on record saying that he told nobody he saw Joe Tolleson leaving our office."

"Why is he up there?" Strassberg whispered to Catledge.

"I'm not sure. They may have been trying to develop something against him if they take him to trial. Do you want to ask him anything?"

She shook her head.

"No questions, your Honor," Catledge said.

Judge Longworth adjourned court for the day.

$$*\qquad\qquad*\qquad\qquad*$$

Joe heard the Hidden Falls from the parking lot—the ceaseless spill amplified by the box canyon a half-mile away. The asphalt path grew slippery from the spray as he walked toward the falls, and the low din became a thundering roar. He rounded a rocky outcropping. Thousands of gallons of water poured off a sheer ledge in the narrow box canyon, dropped over 200 feet, pounded into a pile of granite boulders, then fell away, becoming the West Fork River again.

Joe stepped up to the fence on the viewing platform, placing his hands on a rail. A light on the platform and the churning phosphorescence of the falling water provided illumination. It was two o'clock in the morning and he had been unable to sleep.

He had done all he could, but now that his testimony was over he felt as helpless as flotsam borne over the falls. People, as individuals, were generally as harmless as drops of water, but the crowd could be as terrifying and destructive as the falling, churning mass. The dark chapters in human history were stories of torrential irrationality, given expression and illusory legitimacy by a mob. Man owed his progress to solitary reason and creativity, but how many had, through the years, been swept away? The difference between those that survived and those that didn't—was it as arbitrary as which drops became spray? He closed his eyes, still seeing the phosphorescence and feeling the misty wetness on his face. A consoling thought—falling water and mobs dispersed, spent by their own fury.

When he opened his eyes, Rachel Strassberg stood next to him, wearing a sweat suit and tennis shoes, her presence remarkably unremarkable.

"I only saw one car in the parking lot," she said, loudly over the crash of the falls. "You must have given the policemen the slip."

"I did. Why are you here?"

"I was too tired to sleep and needed to clear my head. I decided to see the town's namesake."

"I enjoyed your cross-examination today. I—"

"For your sake as well as mine, don't talk about the trial."

He said nothing. They stood watching the falls, intensely conscious of each other. Then she turned toward him and he stepped towards her; they were very close. He smelled the solitary flower of her perfume and was conscious of his own breathing—slow and shallow, as if drawing air might shatter the fragile moment. A primal force rose within him. He looked into her dark eyes. Her gaze was both an invitation and a warning.

"Have you ever been with a woman, Joe?"

"No." He took her hand.

"For my sake as well as yours, don't do what we both want you to do."

"You wouldn't stay on the case?"

"No."

"There would be a mistrial?"

"Yes."

"You might be subject to some sort of sanctions?"

"Yes."

"I would have to do this all over again?"

"Yes."

"When?"

"When it's over, including the appeals."

He withdrew his hand. "Let's go."

They walked in silence back to the parking lot. He escorted her to her car.

"Do you ever get lonely?" she said, as he opened her car door.

"Only when I'm with people."

She held his eyes a long time. The essentials were understood; the details would be filled in later. She shut the door and drove out of the parking lot. He returned to his apartment and did not sleep.

*   *   *

She had defended worse, Strassberg told herself as she entered the courtroom the next day. She unloaded her bulky briefcase, arranging her materials on the defense table. The bailiff brought in Silas Wayne from a side door. What was behind the expressionless mask? He gave her his customary brief nod and settled into his seat next to Catledge. He would not be a client with whom she chose to spend time. Some of her drug dealer clients were more accessible. Not likeable, but at least approachable.

"All rise," the sheriff intoned.

Judge Longworth entered the courtroom from his chamber and sat in his chair.

"The Merton County district court is now in session, Judge Daniel Longworth presiding. The case is the State versus Silas Wayne."

"The State calls Jack Tolleson," Devore announced.

Joe's father was sworn in and took his seat on the stand. He verified that Joe had told him and Alice his story.

"What was your reaction to your son's story?" Devore asked.

"I didn't know what to think."

"Did you believe your son?"

"No, but not in the sense that I thought he was lying."

"Then in what sense did you not believe him?"

"I thought it was more like he had made a mistake—that he had been in the church and had been spooked by the place."

"Is your son honest?"

"To a fault. He has a hard time even being tactful."

Devore reviewed the events on the afternoon of the day Joe discovered Marsha Walton's body. Tolleson told of the conversation with his wife regarding Mayor Matlock's coffin being taken to the church that evening, instead of the next day, before the funeral service. Devore shifted to another topic.

"In mid-January, did you have a conversation with Joe, a conversation in which you tried to convince him not to testify against the defendant?"

"Yes."

"Did you refer to a conversation you had with Mr. Harvey Roach?"

"Yes."

"And what was said in that conversation?"

"Objection," Strassberg said. "We objected to the introduction of this conversation as hearsay earlier and the objection was sustained. The conversation is still hearsay and the prosecution is still unwilling or unable to get Mr. Roach to corroborate the details of this alleged conversation."

"Sustained."

"Mr. Tolleson, without reference to your conversation with Mr. Roach, would you say that you argued with your son that night, trying to get him not to testify?"

"Yes."

"Were you worried about the reaction of certain people in Hidden Falls if Joe testified?"

"Yes."

"Did you convey that concern to Joe?"

"Yes."

"Did your son agree not to testify?"

"No."

"Did you also try to pressure him into not testifying by threatening to withhold funding for his college education?"

There was a long silence. "Yes."

"Was it your idea that he move out and quit his job?"

"No, it was his."

"I have no further questions. Your witness."

Strassberg stood and advanced toward the witness stand.

"Mr. Tolleson, you said that you didn't believe your son's story when he first told it to you and your wife. You said that you thought he might have been 'spooked' by the old church. Is there another reason you didn't believe your son?"

"I don't know what you mean."

"Mr. Tolleson, who performed your wedding? Whose church have you been attending and financially supporting for over twenty years?"

"Silas Wayne's."

"What was your opinion of the character of Mr. Wayne?"

"I thought he was a decent man, sincere in his religious beliefs."

"Did you think he could do what your son said he had done?"

"No."

"Thank you, Mr. Tolleson. I have no further questions."

"I have just one question on redirect," Devore said, not rising from his chair. "You didn't think then, when Joe told you what he had seen, that Mr. Wayne could have done what your son said he had done. Do you feel that way now?"

"No."

"Thank you, Mr. Tolleson."

Tolleson walked back to the gallery and sat next to his wife. She squeezed his hand.

"The State calls Detective Sergeant Peter Baerwald," Devore said.

Baerwald was the detective with the Hidden Falls Police Department who had conducted the investigation at the church and parsonage after Joe Tolleson had brought in Marsha Walton's body. He was of medium height, with light brown hair neatly combed away from his pronounced forehead. His eyes—pinpoint pupils in small green irises anchored in a sea of white—gave an impression of unusual concentration. A smile would have been foreign to his severe, Teutonic face.

After he was sworn in and his credentials established, Devore led him through the steps of his investigation at the crime scene and his description of the evidence. It was a necessarily tedious process. They began with the investigation of the choir loft. There had been extensive dusting for fingerprints, but the detective had been unable to lift a clear set of fingerprints that matched either Joe Tolleson's or Silas Wayne's—there were too many other prints on the choir loft benches and railing. However, he had found minute dried flecks of a brownish material in the carpet of one of the aisles. The material could be human fecal matter, but it was impossible to make a definite determination. The detective had also examined all of the rafters above the choir loft, but had found no signs that would indicate where a rope might have hung.

The questioning proceeded to Baerwald's investigation under the church. After Devore introduced into evidence objects found in the room where Marsha Walton's body had been hidden, Baerwald described his findings for each item. The table that the tub of ice rested on was of an identical make to tables in the church recreation room. The serial numbers on the ice machine and portable generator matched the serial numbers found on receipts in Mr. Wayne's files. There were gasps when the detective described the three jars containing Marsha Walton's organs and the tub with her drained blood. Macabre fascination permeated the courtroom when he elaborated on which organs were in which jars and the volume and type of blood in the tub—even Judge Longworth leaned forward. Baerwald had been unable to determine the origins of the light bulb and circular switch, the two electric cords, the surgical gloves, the knives, the wrench, the can of metal sealant, the door lock and clasp, and the jars and alcohol.

Moving from the room where Marsha Walton's body had been hidden to the subterranean tunnels, Baerwald described his findings as Devore introduced items into evidence. Using the prosecution's diagram, he pinpointed the locations of the three bullets that had been found. Ballistics tests confirmed that the bullets came from a .38 caliber Smith and Wesson revolver registered to Silas Wayne and found on the person of Joe Tolleson when he turned the body over to the police. Both Wayne and Tolleson's fingerprints were on the revolver. At an intersection of two of the tunnels, Baerwald had found two broken flashlights. At another intersection of tunnels, he had discovered and analyzed bloodstains from the floor. The blood type matched Silas Wayne's. Near the stains was a pipe with Tolleson's fingerprints. About ten feet down one of these tunnels, on the floor and wall, was a urine stain. Several spectators chuckled, recalling Joe's testimony about urinating while he had waited for Wayne.

Baerwald's testimony concluded with his investigation of the church's premises. Tire track impressions from the area where Joe Tolleson, and earlier Gary Benewski, had parked their cars matched the treads of their cars. Furthermore, it appeared from the impressions that matched Tolleson's car's tires' that Tolleson's car had sped away, because the tracks had been partially destroyed by what were probably spinning tires. There were also three sets of footprints in the area that matched those of Wayne, Tolleson and Benewski. Baerwald's testimony took almost five hours, not counting the interruption for lunch. It was after four o'clock when he finished.

Strassberg frowned as she rose to cross-examine the detective. She glanced at the jury. They were bored with Baerwald's lengthy testimony and it was obvious they were looking forward to adjournment. Tedium blanketed the small, poorly ventilated courtroom. Sweat was visible on some foreheads and some of the spectators were asleep. She had hoped that direct examination would take all afternoon; she wanted to do her cross-examination in the morning, when the jury was well rested and attentive. Her cross-examination would be the defense's first attempt to develop its theory of the case, a theory that would correspond to Silas Wayne's testimony. Generally, she carefully questioned investigators—more than once it had led to exculpatory revelations. She decided that to regain the jury's attention, she would delay detailed questioning until the morning and merely touch on points that supported the defense's main contentions.

"Detective Baerwald, you said that you found small flecks of a brownish substance in the carpet of the choir loft. You are unable to say what that substance is, correct?"

"That's correct."

"It could have been mud or dirt?"

"Yes."

"You can't say how long that substance had been there?"

"Correct."

"You were also unable to find any evidence, from your examination of the rafters above the choir loft, that a rope had been placed around those rafters. Is that correct?"

"Yes."

"You have mentioned numerous items, found at the church, that you have examined. Did you find and examine a rope?"

"No."

"Did you find and examine articles of clothing?"

"No."

"Did you find and examine a plastic sheet?"

"Only the clear plastic sheet wrapped around the victim's body. However, Mr. Tolleson has said that there was another plastic sheet, under the girl's body when she was hanging from the rafter. That sheet, according to Mr. Tolleson, was smaller and was white, like a garbage bag. It hasn't been found."

"Now you said that you were unable to determine the origin of a number of items from the room under the church. Did you check with various stores in the area to see if they sold the type of items in question?"

"Yes."

"Did you check with Tolleson's Hardware?"

"Objection," Devore said, rising to his feet. "We were barred by a pretrial ruling from introducing evidence from the Buy Rite drugstore in Bloomstown about the possible origins of several evidentiary items found in the room under the church. Similar reasoning should bar Ms. Strassberg's speculative questioning about the origins of these items of evidence."

"Your Honor, this question is being asked to help establish a contention that someone other than the defendant was responsible for the death of Marsha Walton. Part of that contention is that someone other than the defendant had the means to commit these crimes."

"Ms. Strassberg," Judge Longworth said, "you are arguing against the arguments you made when you responded
to the prosecution's pretrial motion. You can't have it both
ways. Consistency dictates that the motion be sustained."

"Detective Baerwald, did you find any knives or jars
like those found in the room under the church in the
parsonage?"

"No."

"And the light bulb in that room was of a different type
than the light bulbs in the parsonage, correct?"

"That's correct."

"And the only fingerprints you found in that room were
Joe Tolleson's?"

"Yes."

"And you can't say who fired the revolver three times?"

"No."

"Both Tolleson's and Wayne's fingerprints were on the
gun?"

"Yes."

She glanced at the clock on the wall at the rear of the
court and then the jury box. The members of the jury
appeared more interested than when she began.

Judge Longworth noticed her looking at the clock.
"Let's call it a day. Court will reconvene at nine o'clock
tomorrow morning."

Driving back to her hotel, Strassberg reviewed the day's
courtroom proceedings. Baerwald's dry, precise style had not
held the attention of the jury, but she had noticed that her
client leaned forward in his chair throughout the detective's
testimony. He would want to make sure that his testimony
matched the physical evidence. Her cross-examination the
following day would provide further assistance.

That night, Joe called Gary Benewski.

"Joe," Benewski said, "I was surprised you weren't in court today to hear your father's testimony.

"What did he say?" Joe asked, without explaining his reluctance to hear his father's public admissions.

Benewski told Joe about his father's testimony. He also gave him a summary of Detective Baerwald's testimony and cross-examination. He was about to hang up, telling Joe that he had to get back to work, when he remembered something.

"Joe, on redirect examination, Mike asked your father if he still believed that Silas Wayne couldn't do what he's accused of doing. Your father said that he didn't."

"I know. It makes what he's done that much worse. What happens tomorrow?"

"Strassberg will cross-examine Baerwald."

"I won't come back to court until Silas testifies. I shouldn't miss any more school, but I want to hear him testify."

"Okay, Joe, we'll see you then. Keep in touch."

"Thanks."

Rachel Strassberg's cross-examination of Detective Baerwald the following morning established several points. There was no physical evidence that proved either that the defendant had been in the choir loft on the evening of November the eighth or that the body of a young girl had hung from a rafter there. Detective Baerwald found no glue or tape residues on the tapestry covering the secret door to the church underground. The only fingerprints found in Marsha Walton's crypt were Tolleson's, which were on the tub containing Marsha Walton's body, the wood cover over the tub containing her blood and on the lock and clasp on the door to the room.

Somebody's prints were on the circular light switch, but they were smeared and indistinct. Both Tolleson's and Wayne's fingerprints were on the plastic wrapping that served as the victim's shroud. The evidence was consistent with either Tolleson or Wayne firing the revolver.

Strassberg did not try to lead the detective into any particular conclusions about what might have happened under the church. Rather, she wanted to demonstrate to the jury that the detective's investigation and the physical evidence would support more than one interpretation. Silas Wayne would supply am alternative interpretation. As she concluded her questioning and returned to the defense table, she saw her client again leaning forward in his chair.

The next witness was Jasper Wooters, an elderly man who tended the grounds at the parsonage once every two weeks. He was sworn in and stated his name, address and occupation.

Devore held up the State's evidentiary exhibits eleven and twelve, the two large metal tubs that had held Marsha Walton's body and her blood.

"Mr. Wooters, were there two tubs, similar to these two tubs, in Silas Wayne's garage?"

Wooters pondered the tubs. "Yep, those look like them."

Devore pointed to prosecution exhibit ten, the gasoline powered generator that provided the electricity for the light bulb and ice machine in the room under the church.

"Mr. Wooters, is this generator like the one underneath the back porch at the parsonage?"

Wooters pondered the generator. "Yep, looks to be the same one."

"Mr. Wooters, would you know Joe Tolleson if you saw him?"

"Yep."

"Have you ever seen Joe Tolleson on the premises of the church or parsonage?"

"Nope."

"Thank you, no further questions."

"Mr. Wooters," Catledge said, rising, "can you say with one hundred percent certainty that the two tubs are the same ones that were in the Reverend Wayne's garage?"

"Not a hundred percent, but they sure look like them."

"And can you say with one hundred percent certainty that the generator was the same one that was under the porch?"

"Not a hundred percent."

"Mr. Wooters, if an ice machine was broken in the church recreation room, would you be responsible for fixing it?"

"Yep."

"Thank you, no further questions."

"Your Honor," Devore said, "our next 'witness' is the videotaped deposition of Edna Mayhew. At the time of her deposition she had been diagnosed with a terminal illness and it appeared that she would be unavailable as a witness for this trial. Mrs. Mayhew unfortunately passed away about two months ago. Pursuant to an agreement with defense counsel, we would like to show the videotape of her deposition. We'll need to set up the television monitor and turn the lights off."

Benewski wheeled in a television monitor and the lights were turned off. The videotape played and the courtroom saw Edna Mayhew sitting upright in a hospital bed, tubes running from her body to various bottles. She was surrounded by a court clerk, a court reporter, Mike Devore and Preston Catledge. Responding to Devore's questions, she wheezingly recalled her relationship with Silas Wayne and how he had reinvolved her with church activities after her husband died. After much huffing and puffing and several interruptions to breathe from an oxygen mask, she recounted Silas's response when she told him about the missing ice machine in the kitchen of the church recreation room. It was the Sunday after Joe Tolleson had seen Marsha Walton's body hanging in the church, and Silas had said that the machine was in for repairs. Murmurs came from the darkened courtroom. This was the same ice machine that Detective Baerwald had said was in the room under the church. The spectators were asking themselves the same question Edna Mayhew had asked—why would the minister say the machine was in for repairs?

Preston Catledge's cross-examination had been gentle and brief. Dying witnesses are usually considered honest witnesses and he had not wanted to appear to be badgering the sick old woman. He made a few attempts to establish that her memory was suspect, but she clearly recalled both her conversation with Silas Wayne and the time that the conversation occurred. His cross-examination ended.

After the lights came on and the television monitor was wheeled out of the courtroom, Devore announced the next witness—Sarah Matlock, wife of the late Mayor Chester Matlock. She was sworn in and stated her name, address and occupation.

"Mrs. Matlock," Devore said, "on Tuesday evening, November the twelfth of last year, your husband died. The funeral was scheduled for the following Saturday morning. However, his casket was moved to the First Christian

Church the Friday afternoon before the service. Why was that done?"

"The day after Chester died, I had a conversation with Reverend Wayne. The casket was open Friday afternoon, at the mortuary, so people could pay their last respects. Silas and I were talking and it came up that it might be appropriate, since Chester was a religious man, that he spend his last night at the church, rather than the mortuary. I've never liked mortuaries, I guess nobody really does, and it just seemed like a good idea. I had Ned, that's Ned Stiles, the mortician, take the casket over to the church after the mortuary closed that afternoon."

"You said that the idea to do this 'came up' in a conversation with Mr. Wayne. Whose idea was it?"

"I really don't remember. It was a very trying time for me and I can't remember all the things that happened then."

"But the idea did come up in a conversation with Mr. Wayne?"

"Yes."

"So Silas Wayne knew that your husband's casket would be in the church the night before the service?"

"Yes."

"Your husband was a very large man, was he not?"

"Yes, he weighed about two hundred and seventy pounds."

"And he had a large coffin?"

"Yes, Ned said he gave Chester the largest model he had."

"Thank you, Mrs. Matlock, I have no further questions."

Strassberg's limited cross-examination established the point that Mrs. Matlock did not recall whose idea it was to move the coffin to the church the night before the funeral. After she stepped down, Judge Longworth adjourned court for the lunch recess.

The attorneys made their customary trek to Brigg's Diner, planned strategy while they ate, and then returned for the afternoon session. Devore and Benewski had two scientific expert witnesses and what they called their "grand finale" witness and then they would rest their case.

Their first expert witness was Doctor Pace, who had performed Marsha Walton's autopsy and had gathered the samples for the DNA tests. Pace painstakingly described the condition of Walton's body. The prosecution attorneys had realized that Pace would not be a likeable witness. They had spent hours preparing him for his testimony, trying to tone down his bristling officiousness. Although he occasionally slipped in an unnecessary polysyllabic word or lapsed into medical jargon, he was reasonably effective in describing the results of his autopsy. The cause of death was strangulation and marks consistent with rope marks had been found on the victim's neck. There was an eleven-inch laceration from the victim's sternum to a spot two inches below the naval and most of the internal organs had been removed. Semen was found in the victim's vaginal cavity. There were a number of contusions and abrasions on the victim's face and body, consistent with a struggle with her murderer.

Pace then described the procedures for the DNA tests, and how the samples were sent to the testing facility in Tyler City. The foreign samples taken from the victim's body were consistent with the samples coded for Silas Wayne and not for samples coded for Joe Tolleson. Devore introduced Pace's autopsy report and several grisly photographs of Marsha Walton's body (which the members of the jury inspected) into evidence and concluded his questioning.

Strassberg began her cross-examination.

"Doctor Pace, how many times were the DNA tests conducted?"

"Objection," Devore shouted, springing to his feet. "Your Honor, may counsel approach the bench?"

"Yes."

Devore and Strassberg approached the judge. Devore spoke in a low voice, out of earshot of the jury and the spectators.

"Your Honor, recall your pretrial ruling that no mention would be made of the results of the first set of DNA tests, because security was breached in their administration."

"Ms. Strassberg?"

"Your Honor, I have no intention of mentioning the results of the first DNA tests. However, I do want to establish that there were irregularities in that first set of tests, and that such irregularities cast doubt on the ability and competence of Doctor Pace to perform such tests."

"The objection is overruled. Ms. Strassberg, you may ask your question, but if any mention is made of the results of that first test, you will be subject to sanctions."

Devore walked back to the prosecution table, seething.

"Doctor Pace," Strassberg repeated, "how many times were the DNA tests conducted?"

Pace looked at Judge Longworth, who nodded. "Please answer the question, Doctor Pace."

"The DNA tests were administered twice."

"And is that because there were errors in the administration of the first test?"

"Yes."

"What were those errors?"

If hostile looks could make someone vanish, Strassberg would have disappeared. She waited, impervious to Pace's antagonism. After a strained silence, he answered her question, his words like drops wrung from a not very damp washcloth. "I forgot to mail the samples to the DNA testing facility the day the samples were gathered. They were left on a counter in the lab overnight, which compromised security, and by implication, the integrity of the samples."

"Thank you, Doctor Pace." Strassberg closely questioned the doctor about the details of his autopsy report; in the same way she had questioned Detective Baerwald. It was obvious that he resented her questions, but she was unable to force any other damaging admissions. She concluded her cross-examination, hoping that the doctor's defensiveness had rubbed the jury the wrong way.

The prosecution's other scientific witness was Doctor Ruben Alvarez, a consultant to the state's DNA testing facility. Tall and thin, the unstressed dignity of his posture and carriage projected self-confidence. The touches of gray at his temples indicated that he was in his late forties or early fifties and accentuated his dark, angular handsomeness. He responded to the oath in a low, powerful voice that filled the courtroom. His words were precisely enunciated, with the even modulation of an aristocratic British accent. He wore an expertly tailored blue suit.

"Please state your name, occupation and professional credentials."

"My name is Ruben Alvarez, and I am a research microbiologist. I grew up and received my early schooling in Barcelona, Spain. I took my undergraduate training in biology at Oxford, and both my masters and doctorate at Harvard. My specialization is genetics and for the past ten years I have been involved with the development of DNA identification technologies. I have published sixteen articles on that subject, taught classes at the state university and am a consultant to the state's DNA testing facility in Tyler City."

In response to Devore's questions, Alvarez launched into a description of the theoretical basis of DNA testing and how DNA tests were conducted. Alvarez had familiarized himself with the testing procedures and results for the samples taken from Marsha Walton's body. DNA was chemically removed from the semen taken from the vaginal cavity, from the foreign hair taken from the pubic hair, and from the skin tissue removed from beneath the fingernails. In each case the DNA was broken into fragments and chemically processed so that it could be analyzed through the use of a radioactive tag. The radioactive tag allowed radiation-sensitive film to record the pattern of each DNA fragment. The record of a DNA fragment pattern, called an autoradiograph, looked something like a bar code found on grocery labels. Doctor Alvarez summarized the DNA testing procedures, doing an excellent job of making this technical subject accessible to the jury.

"Doctor Alvarez, can you tell us the results of the DNA testing procedure in this case?" Devore asked.

"Analysis of the autoradiographs indicates that the three foreign samples taken from the body of the victim are from the same person. These autoradiographs correspond to those derived from hair, tissue and blood samples taken from the defendant, Mr. Wayne."

"And can you give an approximation as to the probability that the autoradiographs could correspond to one another, but that the DNA extracted from the samples taken from Marsha Walton's body was not the same DNA that was extracted from the samples taken from the defendant?"

"Objection," said Strassberg, standing. "Assigning such a probability would convey a misleading precision to the use of this evidence. It is a matter of scientific debate as to the probability of one set of DNA matching another. The witness's answer to the question will be necessarily speculative and the potential to prejudice the jury far outweighs the scientific value of the witness's estimate."

"Your Honor, in this state there is no prohibition on the use of probability estimates. Allowing the estimate doesn't preclude the defense from challenging the estimate with their own experts."

"Overruled."

"The defense attorney has made a good point," Alvarez said. "There is no way to assign an exact probability that one person's DNA autoradiographs will be identical to someone else's. However, when DNA is analyzed, it is broken into fragments. Assume there is a probability of ten percent, or one in ten, that two fragments will match. Now assume that there is a probability of ten percent that a second pair of fragments will match. The mathematics of probability is such that the probability of both sets of fragments matching will be multiplicative, or in plain English, the probability will be one in one hundred, the product of multiplying the two probabilities. Similarly, if we continue to assume that the probability of another segment match is one in ten, the probability that three sets of segments will match is one in one thousand, or one in ten times ten times ten."

Strassberg looked towards the jury box. Mathematics anxiety was clearly etched on the faces of several jurors.

"The probabilities that are assigned to the various fragment matches are based on population studies, conducted by the Federal Bureau of Investigation, of several thousand people's blood samples. In this case, there were five matches between the DNA fragments of the samples taken from the victim's body and the fragments of the samples taken from the defendant. It is common practice to assign a range of probabilities to any one fragment match. I always use the lowest number in the range. Thus erring on the side of conservatism, I would say that the probability of the DNA fragments from the victim's samples coming from someone other than the defendant is about one in two hundred and fifty million. Using probabilities at the high end of the ranges would result in a much lower probability."

"Two hundred and fifty million is a little less than the population of the United States, is it not?"

"Yes, it is."

"Thank you, Doctor Alvarez, I have no further questions."

Strassberg advanced towards the witness. "Doctor Alvarez, you said that you were a consultant to the state's DNA testing facility in Tyler City that conducted these tests."

"That's correct."

"Are you paid by that facility for your services?"

"Yes, I am."

"And when you testify as an expert representing the facility, are you paid for your services?"

"Yes."

"How many times have you testified as an expert representing the testing facility?"

"Around twenty times."

"And have you vouched for the accuracy of the test results of the facility that pays you in each of those twenty cases?"

"Yes, I have."

"Now you said that the DNA fragments taken from the victim's body matched those taken from the defendant. Did you know the identity of the person who gave the samples when you performed the analysis?"

"No, I did not."

"So you were only subsequently informed that the samples were taken from the defendant?"

"That's correct."

"Isn't it also correct that you had to perform this analysis not once, but twice, in the present case?"

"Yes, but—"

"Thank you Doctor Alvarez. Isn't it also true that you were asked to compare the DNA from the samples taken from the victim's body with DNA taken from not just the defendant, but from one other person as well?"

"Yes, we did analyze samples from a second person."

"Were you aware at that time that the samples came from Joe Tolleson?"

"No."

"Now Doctor Alvarez, you said that the probability estimates that you used in stating your probability estimate were based on research done by the FBI. Would you say, as a theoretical matter, that the FBI would always be unbiased and objective in developing so-called scientific methods to put people behind bars?"

"No, but—"

"Thank you Doctor Alvarez. You represent the state's DNA testing facility. Would you say, as a theoretical matter, that the State will always be unbiased and objective in developing so-called scientific methods to put people behind bars?"

"I'm not sure what you mean."

"What is the name of this case," she said, handing him a document with the case name on it.

"The State versus Silas Wayne."

"And who operates the DNA testing facility?"

"The state."

"Thank you, Doctor Alvarez." Strassberg turned away from the witness and walked towards the defense table. She looked at some papers on the table. She turned, facing the doctor.

"Now, regardless of which probability you assign to any two DNA fragments matching, and regardless of how many DNA fragments actually match, you can never say that when two samples match, they could not have come from two different people. In other words, you can never say that the probability is zero that matching samples came from different people?"

"That's correct."

Strassberg spent an hour questioning Alvarez about the intricacies of DNA testing. She did not draw out any startling or damaging statements from the well-prepared expert and ended her cross-examination.

"Your Honor," Devore said, standing, "the State calls Alice Tolleson."

CHAPTER 23

▼

SACRIFICE

Although Alice Tolleson was well known in Hidden Falls, for the past six months she had seldom been seen in public. There were murmurs of shocked recognition as her appearance registered with the spectators. She had gained many gray hairs, many pounds and many worried wrinkles. She wore a loose fitting blue dress and low black, high heels. Her body craved the alcohol she had denied it for the last four days, and she tottered slightly as she walked to front of the courtroom. She stepped to the stand and the oath was administered. She gave her name, address and occupation.

"Mrs. Tolleson," Devore said, "you've heard your son's testimony and your husband's testimony about what your son told you on the night of November the eighth of last year. To save the court's time, I will merely ask you if your memory of that evening is any different from theirs?"

"No."

"Your son has said that neither you nor your husband believed his story. Is that correct?"

"Yes."

"Why didn't you believe your son?"

"I didn't believe Silas could have done what Joe said he did. I thought Joe had wandered into the old church and had scared himself with something he thought he saw."

"Mrs. Tolleson, were you ever in love with Mr. Wayne?"

A murmur ran through the courtroom. Judge Longworth banged his gavel. There was a long pause, but she did not answer.

"Mrs. Tolleson, were you ever in love with Mr. Wayne?"

"Yes."

The only time she had ever been in love.

"When did you first meet him?"

"In high school."

Those high school memories had an immediacy and poignancy that never faded. She was the only girl ever to be head cheerleader her sophomore, junior, and senior years. She stood on the sidelines, performing her routines. Her flowing, wavy blond hair bounced and her blue eyes sparkled. The dimples at the corners of her mouth that formed when she smiled fit exactly between her perfect nose and perfect chin and emphasized her high cheekbones. Her short skirt highlighted her long, slender legs as she moved with a dancer's natural grace. She knew Coach Tyson reprimanded his players for watching her instead of the game and she knew they eventually turned away, but not because of anything he said. She was unattainable; they were frustrated.

"When in high school did you meet Mr. Wayne?"

"My junior year."

Silas was different—like Joe is different. Silas had been as untouched by her beauty as he was by everything else. He never smoked or drank or drove out to the parking lot at the falls with a girl—he didn't need any of that. There was no adolescent confusion in Silas; he knew who he was, what he wanted and how he was going to get it. He took his religion seriously. Other kids were faking it; they wanted people to pay attention to them. Silas didn't need anyone's attention—that's why she had fallen in love with him.

"And what were the circumstances of that meeting?"

"Objection," Catledge said, "this little exposition is irrelevant to the case at hand."

"Your Honor," Devore responded, "we're going to show that Marsha Walton is not the first woman whose life the defendant has destroyed. If the witness is allowed to proceed, we believe that her story will illuminate some relevant character traits of the defendant, especially his attitude towards women. Recall the testimony of Joe Tolleson, who said that the defendant at one point said 'poor Alice' when the defendant and Tolleson were underneath the church, and talked about how Mrs. Tolleson loved him."

For the first time in the trial, Judge Longworth took several minutes to make a ruling. Finally, he said, "overruled, the witness's testimony may proceed."

"Mrs. Tolleson, what were the circumstances of your first meeting with the defendant?"

It was a week into her junior year. She was curious about him—he was the only boy that mattered who hadn't tried to ask her out during her sophomore year.

"I met him in the library. He was reading and I sat down at his table and began talking to him."

"What was he reading?"

"*Crime and Punishment.*"

The courtroom erupted in laughter. Judge Longworth banged his gavel.

"Did you discuss that novel?"

"Objection," Catledge said, "what on earth does this have to do with anything?"

"Just bear with us and it will be clear."

"Overruled, but let's get to the point, Mr. Devore."

"Did you discuss *Crime and Punishment?*"

"Yes, we did."

He had told her about Raskolnikov, who wanted to be like Napoleon—above all moral laws. Unfortunately for Raskolnikov, the Russian judicial system didn't consider him above its laws. He was arrested, convicted and sent to prison. He repented and, with the help of the woman he loved, returned to his simple faith. Silas's voice conveyed an irresistible certitude, talking about *Crime and Punishment.*

"And were you attracted to Mr. Wayne?"

Attracted—such an ordinary word for such an extraordinary feeling. A wonderful, electric sensation that seemed to affect all five of her senses, heightening their powers. With him, she felt intensely alive. He had assumed her interest in ideas when he talked to her that day. Her looks and popularity were irrelevant—he spoke to her mind, a novel experience. And when he smiled, a tremor ran up and down and her legs. A dangerous smile.

"Yes, I was," she said.

"Did you see him again?"

"Yes I did."

She saw him that night, as she lay in bed, unable to sleep—the object of innumerable fantasies. She wanted to shatter that austere reserve, to see passion in those gray-green eyes. With her eyes opened or closed, she saw his eyes and his lanky frame, black hair, narrow face and sharply defined features.

"Did you date him steadily from that point?"

"Yes I did, until the end of our senior year."

"Did you ever have sexual relations with Mr. Wayne?"

"No. Nothing beyond a few good night kisses."

His restraint made her love him that much more. Spiritual love. Silas cared about the human soul. He talked of good and evil and man's capacity to know God, sounding neither foolish nor dogmatic. Their long conversations left her filled with religious fervor.

"What were your plans after high school?"

"I wasn't sure. I had been in some local shows and had received a scholarship to an acting academy in New York. But I didn't know if I wanted to leave Hidden Falls."

"Why not?"

"Because I wanted to marry Silas."

"Did you talk to him about your dilemma?"

"Yes, I did, towards the end of my senior year."

They sat on a bench in the schoolyard during their lunch break. She told him about her scholarship and her desire to marry him, hoping that he would insist that she stay in Hidden Falls and ask her to marry him.

"How did he respond?"

"He told me that he couldn't offer me any advice, that it was a decision I had to make with God's help."

"Did he say that he would marry you?"

"No."

"Did he say that he wouldn't marry you?"

"No."

"What did you decide to do?"

She made up her mind about a week after that conversation, late one night walking along a backcountry road. She liked walking at night, alone with her thoughts, under the canopy of darkness and pinholes of light. People in cities had no idea how stars shimmered in the clear country air. She could be a star someday, but could she leave Silas? With men, ambition was stronger than love and with women, the opposite held true. Her dreams had a self-centered grandiosity that didn't fit the awesome, still silence of the night. She belonged to that country night, to Hidden Falls, and to Silas Wayne.

"I decided to stay in Hidden Falls."

"So you declined the scholarship?"

"Yes."

"What were Mr. Wayne's plans?"

"He was going to the seminary to become a minister. He would return to Hidden Falls and work with the Reverend Ames for a few years, until Reverend Ames retired. Then he would become the minister at the First Christian Church."

"Did you tell Mr. Wayne that you wanted to marry him when he returned from the seminary?"

"Yes, just before he left."

They sat under a tall pine. The late summer air was warm and filled with the night noises of crickets and cicadas. Somewhere in the distance they heard a group of children playing. Scents of honeysuckle and jasmine perfumed the air. A not-quite full moon hung halfway up in the northern sky.

"What was his response?"

She had looked in his eyes, not understanding his expression. She saw both an infinite, pained sadness and an unyielding hardness—a saint being led to his martyrdom.

A solitary tear trickled down her cheek. "He said that if personal desire were the only consideration, he would marry me. He said he loved me and that there was no rule against ministers marrying. However, he believed that God required an extra measure of sacrifice from him. He said that he had to remain celibate, like Christ. He had to give his heart completely to the Lord, so he couldn't marry me."

"What was your reaction to this?"

A trap door had given way—she had felt a tightness around her neck and a dryness in her throat.

"I couldn't talk—I started crying. I asked myself why he couldn't have told me this before I turned down my scholarship. I couldn't marry him and I didn't have my scholarship. He took me in his arms and stroked my hair and kissed my forehead." She could not continue. Devore handed her a glass of water.

"Did you reproach him?"

She took several sips of water, composing herself. "No."

"Why not?"

She had looked into his eyes. He had returned her gaze, knowing what she was thinking. Now he was resolute—a knight departing on a crusade. The reproach went the other way.

"I suddenly felt like I was being selfish. I wasn't thinking about the sacrifice he was making—I was too concerned with myself. So I told him I respected what he was doing and I admired his commitment to his beliefs."

But she had felt a sensation beyond identification—something inside her hurriedly taking flight. A faint voice had whispered: you're making the only offering on the altar of sacrifice. He held her for a long time, and they did not speak. She heard the cicadas hum and the crickets chirp. She looked at his face in the moonlight and he returned her gaze. She said, "I love you, Silas," and gave him a long, passionate kiss. He closed his eyes and said, "I love you, too, Alice, but I love God more." Then he gently separated from her, stood and walked away.

"He went to the seminary?"

"Yes."

"After Mr. Wayne went to the seminary, you met your husband, Jack Tolleson?"

"Yes."

She was working at a cafe in Hidden Falls as a waitress. She had been on a break, sitting at a corner table and staring out the window. Jack approached her table. She knew Jack, who had been in her graduating class, but not well, although they were part of the same clique of popular kids. He was of medium height and stocky build, with straight reddish blond hair, blue eyes, fair skin and a sprinkling of freckles on his cheeks and pug nose. He had been the senior class president and captain of the baseball team, and had the unflagging congeniality and persistence of a good salesman. Like most good salesmen, he knew how to be liked without being particularly likeable. He had an uncanny ability to remember peoples' names, faces and idiosyncratic details about their lives. He got them talking about themselves, earning a reputation as a good conversationalist. He had a quick smile, which was ingratiating, but not a quick wit, which would have been threatening.

"How long did you date before you married?"

"Objection," Catledge said, standing, "are we going to get Mrs. Tolleson's entire life story?"

"If the defense promises not to make an issue of why Mrs. Tolleson didn't believe her own son, we won't attempt to explain why she did so," Devore responded.

"Mr. Catledge?" Judge Longworth asked.

"Objection withdrawn."

"You may answer the question, Mrs. Tolleson."

"We dated for almost three years before we were engaged."

Somehow, Jack saw through the cloud of pain and self-pity that enveloped her that day in the cafe, and over-looked the twenty pounds she had gained since Silas left. He got her to talk and he listened. He made her forget about Silas. She liked his self-confidence. He scorned their classmates who had gone to college, saying that higher education was for people who wanted to spend their lives working for somebody else. He was working at Ray Dolan's Chevy dealership, and he planned to buy the dealership when Dolan retired. After two months he was already the top selling salesman. She agreed to go out with him.

"Did you have the same feeling for Jack Tolleson that you had for Mr. Wayne?"

She looked at her husband in the gallery and then low-ered her head. "Do I have to answer that?"

"You're on the stand, you have to answer."

She hesitated before responding, "no."

What she had felt for Jack was not an all consuming passion, it was more like that comfortable feeling she had for her dog or her old woolen sweater. She felt relaxed with him; he was neither a martyr nor a knight. He made her feel desirable; she dieted and exercised until she lost those twenty extra pounds. He asked her to marry him about a year after they started dating.

"Why did you agree to marry your husband?" Devore asked.

"I was hoping…I was hoping…It was just before Silas came back from the seminary. Jack had asked me many times, and finally I said yes. I went to Silas the day he returned, to tell him what I had done. I was hoping that he would reconsider, that it would force him to ask him to marry me." She glanced towards her husband and quickly looked away.

"What was Mr. Wayne's response?"

"He just smiled…that ice cold smile. He congratulated me and told me how appropriate it was that our wedding would be the first one he performed. He told me that I had found the right man, that Jack was going places. I guess he was right about that." Several tears ran down her cheeks, which she dabbed with a Kleenex.

"Mr. Wayne performed your wedding?"

"Yes."

"And your husband was successful in business?"

"Yes."

Tolleson Chevrolet, Tolleson Toyota, Tolleson Buick, Tolleson Auto Parts, Tolleson Hardware, Tolleson Manor Hotel, Tolleson Rental and Storage—within ten years it seemed like Jack owned half of Hidden Falls. There were investments—stocks and bonds, interests in both local banks, a real estate development firm and several office buildings and warehouses. A multimillion-dollar fortune built in the blink of an eye.

"And you worked with your husband until Joe was born?"

"Yes."

"Did you also see Mr. Wayne?"

"Yes."

"How often?"

"Well, every week at church. I also did a lot of charity work, and he was involved in all that. I saw him at least two or three times a week."

"And you still had feelings for Mr. Wayne?"

"Yes."

"Did you enjoy the life you were leading?"

"Yes."

It was almost the truth—she led a good life. They were rich, they had plenty of friends, and she was at the center of Hidden Falls social life. Silas was unattainable, but at least she saw him. Only occasionally did she remember the dreams of her youth.

"How old were you when Joe was born?"

"Thirty-three."

"Were there complications when he was born?"

"Yes. I was unable to have any more children."

"What was Joe like as a child?"

"Very bright, very active, but solitary—he didn't really play with the other kids. He was always asking me questions that I didn't know the answers to. But he knew when you were bluffing, even when he was a child, so I would tell him I didn't know."

"Did you feel particularly close to your son?"

"No. It was hard to. He was always doing something—playing with his computer or his piano, or building something or tearing it apart, or reading. He loved to read. He just never slowed down."

"You said your son was solitary. Why do you think he didn't have a lot of friends?"

"Well, he was too smart for the kids his age; they kind of bored him. And I think he became disappointed with adults."

"Why do you say that?"

"There's a lot of games among adults, a lot of pretense. From an early age he saw right through all of it. He doesn't like the kind of things we all do to smooth out relationships. I remember once Joe asked Jack why he took a man out to dinner, a man Jack had called a 'jackass' the week before. Jack was trying to do business with him, but Joe didn't care for that explanation. Joe lives in a black and white world."

"Given what you just said, how could you not believe his story about what happened in the church?"

There was a long silence. Her voice was barely above a whisper when she spoke. "I think I did believe him, deep down inside, but I couldn't bring myself to face the truth about Silas. When Joe wouldn't go to confirmation classes, when he rejected Silas, I felt like I had to make a choice. I had to choose between Joe and the life I was living. I had chosen that life, I had accepted that life. If I believed Joe, it would be admitting that it was all a lie. I'd have to go all the way back…all the way back to admitting that Silas wasn't what I thought he was. I just couldn't do that then."

"But you can now?"

"I'm trying."

"No further questions. Your witness."

Catledge stood and approached the witness.

"Mrs. Tolleson, did the defendant at any time ask you to marry him?"

"No."

"Did he ever indicate that he was going to ask you to marry him?"

"No."

"Did he ever ask you to decline your acting scholarship?"

"No."

"I have no further questions."

"Your Honor," Devore said, "we have no further witnesses at this time."

"The witness may step down." Judge Longworth looked at the clock on the wall. "It's four-thirty. It's too late for the defense to start presenting its case, so let's adjourn. The jury will remain sequestered throughout the weekend. Court is adjourned."

CHAPTER 24

THE DEFENDANT

"Silas Wayne is a lamb, an innocent lamb. He did not; he is incapable of, committing these crimes. I have known Silas for over twenty years; we attended the seminary together. I have seen his love for those whom only God has not forgotten and his unyielding commitment to truth and righteousness. He has prayed for those who have wrongly accused him and we shall do the same. Jesus forgave those who nailed him to the cross. We must forgive Silas's accusers."

The Very Reverend Wilbert Weathin was the guest minister at the First Christian Church of Hidden Falls. The church was packed and television cameras recorded the service. Weathin was used to ministering before the cameras; he was famous around the world, with a large and faithful following. A man of impeccable integrity, he had avoided the temptations that beset many of his fellow televangelists. Whether conducting services for the high and mighty or preaching at a slum church, his manner never changed—each person was a unique child of God. Lines of wisdom and concern tempered his chiseled, tanned, telegenic face. His blue eyes had a constantly changing quality—one moment radiating profound compassion; another moment looking inward, seeing a private vision; then changing again—intently focusing, judging; and sometimes widening in childlike wonderment, contemplating God's earth and its treasures. He stood at Silas's pulpit, addressing Silas's flock. He ran his hand through his brown hair, now running to gray, and continued his sermon.

"It is fashionable to suspect the worst of religious figures. It is a sign of our corrupt times that we are suspicious of anyone who forswears the transient pleasures of this life and instead starts down the hard, endless road to God and moral perfection. Our cynical press gleefully reports every accusation of perversity and depravity against priests, ministers and rabbis who have made their faith their life's work. Lives are ruined and although many of the accusations are either not proved or disproved, it is not reported—they're on to the next alleged scandal. Look at how many out-of-town news organizations are here reporting this trial. Through this ordeal, Silas is fortunate to have received the great blessing of his congregation's love and support."

He raised his open right hand, making a waving motion to emphasize his words. "I spent last night with Silas in his jail cell. He was neither frightened nor bitter. Silas has always had a serene sense of peace with himself. He knows who he is and he believes in God's plan for his life. He told me that his time in jail had given him an opportunity to pray and that he'd never felt closer to God. I held his hands and we prayed for many hours together. Finally, I stood before him and looked him in the eye.

"'Silas,' I said, 'this week I will testify, before God and man, that I know you and that you could not have raped and murdered Marsha Walton. God is in this cell, Silas. You cannot lie to him and you cannot lie to me. Look me in the eyes and tell me that you didn't rape or murder this girl. By my faith in God, I know that you cannot bear false witness.'

"The cell filled with light as Silas stood and clasped my hands. He looked directly into my eyes and said, in that steady, magnificent baritone that has called so many to Christ, 'Bert, with God as my witness, I swear to you that I didn't rape or murder Marsha Walton. When you testify for me, your heart, your mind and your soul will be pure. I am innocent.' At that moment, I felt God's presence. I was filled with his joy and I knew that my brother Silas was innocent. We embraced and wept in exultation. Silas settled into an untroubled sleep and I sat beside him through the night. Now I stand before you and say, once again, Silas Wayne is God's innocent lamb."

Weathin moved from behind the pulpit, raised his left hand and pointed angrily at one of the cameras. His voice rose with anger. "Some of the news accounts say that DNA tests 'prove' that Silas committed these crimes. How long are we going to be led by the false prophets of science? Surely no age is more rational, more scientific, than our own, and surely no age is more evil. We have replaced faith in God with faith in technological progress. What has it brought us? Nuclear weaponry enables us to scientifically murder the population of the entire world. We are destroying God's earth in our pursuit of profit. Millions of children, trapped in obscenely violent cities, will never know the joys you people of Hidden Falls take for granted—fresh air, clean water, open spaces, rivers, mountains and forests.

"Yes, God gave us each a mind and yes, we must use it to its full power. However, I say to you that the power of the mind is nothing compared to the power of faith in God. I do not care that a high priest of science declares that there is only a one in two hundred and fifty million chance that somebody other than Silas Wayne raped and murdered Marsha Walton. I do not care that some sort of child prodigy, a prodigy, I might add, who has spent very little time in this church, says that Silas Wayne committed these crimes. Prodigy and prodigal are often the same thing. I know what I know in my heart, and no evidence, presented in a fallible human court, will convince me of anything other than Silas Wayne's innocence. God will judge Silas Wayne and he will judge those who accuse him. Let us pray for those who accuse him."

The congregation leapt to its feet and thunderous applause filled the old church. The worshippers cried and embraced each other. They believed in Silas and the Reverend Weathin had given voice to that belief. It was a matter of faith and they were not going to believe in science, law or courts. They believed God's truth, as revealed to the Reverend Weathin in the Reverend Wayne's jail cell.

*   *   *

"The defense calls the Reverend Silas Wayne," Preston Catledge announced. Catledge wore a gray, tailored suit, white shirt with gold cufflinks and a red tie with a geometric pattern. As always, his ramrod straight posture and his tall, slender frame, graying hair and scholarly horn-rimmed glasses conveyed the desired image—the distinguished courtroom attorney. It was Monday morning, the beginning of the second week of the trial.

Silas Wayne walked to the witness stand. He appeared composed. His face no longer had the closed, tight expression he had adopted during the presentation of the prosecution's case. He wore a dark blue suit with a white shirt and a solid burgundy tie. His dark hair, streaked with gray, was cut short and combed to the side. He swore out the oath and took his seat in the witness stand.

Joe Tolleson watched Silas Wayne from a seat on the bench behind the prosecution table. He had not attended the trial after his own testimony, but he could not miss Silas's testimony. Mr. Mendolsohn, the high school principal, had given him permission to skip class, although it was only two weeks before final exams.

"Would you please state your full name, address and occupation," Catledge said.

"My name is Silas Zachary Wayne. I live at the parsonage at 410 Main, Highway 38, by the First Christian Church and I am the minister of that church."

"Thank you, Reverend Wayne. Please tell the court where you were on the afternoon of November the eighth, last year?"

"I was in the study of the parsonage. November the eighth was a Friday and I was preparing my sermon for the service that Sunday."

"Were you inside the church that day?"

"No, I was not."

"Did you leave the parsonage in the late afternoon or early evening?"

"No. I started work on my sermon at about two-thirty and worked straight through until dinner, at about seven o'clock. I fixed dinner and watched the news on television while I ate. After dinner I completed my sermon. Then I read for a couple of hours and went to bed."

"Did you know Marsha Walton?"

"Yes."

"How long did you know her?"

"About eight years. I met her when she was a small girl, maybe six years old. I met her when I met her mother, Nancy."

"What was your relationship to the Walton family?"

"Well, I was their friend, I helped them out. Several years ago, I heard that Ron Walton had deserted the family. Nancy attended my church. It was just before Christmas and I brought Marsha and her sister, Janice, a few small presents. I may have given Nancy some money, I don't remember."

"Did you see the Waltons after that?"

"Yes. Nancy would bring the girls to church occasionally, and sometimes I'd stop by their house. Nancy didn't work in the mornings, so I'd come by and we'd have a cup of coffee."

"Did you ask Marsha to attend confirmation classes and become a member of the First Christian Church?"

"Yes. She refused and the matter never came up again."

"After that, did Nancy Walton ask you to talk to Marsha?"

"Yes, she did. Marsha was having some problems in school. I talked with her, alone, for about half an hour one day at the Walton's house."

"When was that conversation?"

"Early last fall, September or October."

"Did Marsha tell you that you were 'full of shit'?"

"No. However, she was hostile and I'm afraid our conversation didn't go very well."

"Did you bear any animosity towards Marsha Walton because of that conversation?"

"No, not at all. She was fourteen. At that age children are rebelling against everything; I didn't take it too seriously. Marsha was a bright, high-spirited girl. I knew she would get past her adolescent growing pains. Nancy loves both her daughters and is a good mother. I told her to keep the lines of communication open with Marsha and to call me if she needed to talk."

"On the morning of November the eighth, did you receive a phone call from Lou Santori, the bartender at the Starlight Lounge?"

"Well, I didn't, but my answering machine did. I was out that morning, at the hospital. When I returned, I checked my machine and Lou had left a message. All he said was that he needed to talk to me, but that it wasn't urgent."

"Did you save that message?"

"No, I erased it. I made a mental note to stop by the Starlight Lounge."

"Why would Santori have your card with the phone number of the parsonage written on the back of it?"

"Half of Hidden Falls has my card with the parsonage phone number on the back of it. Anytime I meet somebody I give them my card. Part of my job is to be available for people."

"Did you visit the Starlight Lounge?"

"Sure, I went in there a few times."

"Did you think it was appropriate for a man in your position to visit a cocktail lounge?"

A gentle smile played across the minister's face. "Jesus sat down with prostitutes and tax collectors. I'm a minister to people—I go where they are."

"Did you talk with Mr. Santori at the Starlight Lounge?"

"Yes."

"Did you talk with him about Nancy Walton?"

"I'm sure we did, she was a mutual friend."

"Did you ask Mr. Santori to call you if Nancy Walton left the bar with a man?"

"No, Nancy wouldn't have appreciated that."

"Why would Mr. Santori call you on the morning of the eighth?"

"I don't know. He had mentioned he was having some problems with his girlfriend, maybe he wanted to talk about that."

"Why would Mr. Santori say that he talked with you that morning?"

"I don't know, because he didn't talk to me, he talked to my answering machine. I wish I had saved the message."

"Mr. Santori never communicated to you that Nancy Walton had left the Starlight Lounge with a man the previous evening?"

"No."

"Who were you visiting in the hospital that morning?"

"I wasn't visiting anyone in particular. I stop by the hospital almost every morning to talk to the doctors and nurses and see the patients. It's part of my ministry."

Catledge walked to the witness stand and placed his right hand on the rail. He looked directly at Wayne. His voice became severe, almost harsh. "Did you see Marsha Walton at all on November the eighth?"

"No."

"Did you abduct her sometime during the day and take her to the First Christian Church?"

"No."

"Did you rape Marsha Walton?"

"No."

"Did you kill Marsha Walton by hanging her from a rope tied to a rafter in the choir loft of your church?"

"No."

Catledge moved away from the witness box to the defense table. He turned and faced Wayne. "Did you know Joseph Tolleson before November the eighth?"

"Yes, I did."

Some of the spectators looked towards where Joe was sitting. He ignored them; he was focused on Silas.

"Before November the eighth, when was the last time you saw Joseph Tolleson?" Catledge asked.

"I don't recall. I saw him a few times around town, maybe at his father's hardware store. He didn't attend church."

"Did you ever see Joe Tolleson attempting to pick the locks on the doors of the church?"

"No."

"Did you ask Tolleson if he wanted to attend confirmation classes and become a member of the First Christian Church?"

"Yes, when he was twelve years old. He refused. Jack and Alice invited me to dinner one night to discuss it with Joe. Joe didn't want to discuss it, he walked out of the room."

Catledge again advanced toward the witness box. "Did you see Joseph Tolleson on November the eighth?"

"No."

"Did you confront him in the choir loft?"

"No."

"Did you try to apprehend him, and did he elude this attempt by jumping over the rail in the choir loft?"

"No."

Joe stared at Silas, but the minister did not look his way.

"Did you subsequently hide the corpse of Marsha Walton in a room under the church?"

"No."

Catledge moved away from the witness box. "Reverend Wayne, let's shift to the Sunday following November the eighth, the tenth. Did you have a conversation that day with Edna Mayhew?"

"Yes."

"Did she tell you that the ice machine was missing from the recreation room kitchen?"

"Yes."

"What was your response?"

"I said that I didn't know where the ice machine was, but that perhaps it had been taken in for repairs. I told her I would check and see what had happened to it."

"Reverend Wayne, you saw Mrs. Mayhew's videotaped deposition. She said that you told her you had taken it in for repairs. Why would she say that?"

Silas paused for a moment and placed his hands together in front of his chest, as if he were going to pray. He moved them up and down several times. "I don't know, because I wouldn't have taken it for repairs; Jasper Wooters would have. Keep in mind, though, poor Edna's health was failing. I've seen enough dying people to know that their memory and hearing often go. I think she either didn't hear what I said at the time or her memory of the conversation is faulty."

"Thank you, Reverend Wayne. Now let's move to a week after the alleged incident in the church, to Friday, November the fifteenth. Where were you that night?"

"Early in the evening I was at Dave Owens' ranch, presiding at his and Dorothy Flagle's marriage. I stayed for part of the reception, then I came back to the parsonage."

"Did you enter the church that evening?"

"Yes."

"Why?"

"Chester Matlock's funeral was the next day. I went into the church to set up the altar and make sure there were enough hymnals and Bibles in the holders in back of the pews. I was also going to put the programs for the service on the table in the vestibule."

"When you entered the church, Mayor Matlock's casket was already in the church, is that correct?"

"Yes, it was."

"Why was it brought to the church the night before the funeral?"

"That was Sarah Matlock's idea. She said she wanted Chester to spend his last night in a church. It was unusual, but I saw no point in arguing with her."

"What happened after you entered the church?" Catledge walked to the defense table and sat down.

Silas shifted slightly in his chair. "I was in the pews when I heard a noise coming up through a grate on the floor. I ignored it, thinking it was rats or something under the church, but then I heard it again. I knew there were tunnels underneath the church—I had discovered them shortly after I became the minister at the church. It sounded like somebody was walking on the gritty tunnel floor beneath the church floor. I got a little nervous, so I went back to the parsonage and got a flashlight and my revolver. I've always kept a revolver because I'm isolated, living on the outskirts of town.

"I returned to the church, went to the tapestry and opened the door to the tunnels underneath the church. At the bottom of the stairs, I didn't turn on my flashlight; I just stood there, listening. I knew someone else was there; I could hear footsteps. I tiptoed down the tunnel and heard the footsteps coming towards me. When it sounded like they were very close, I turned on my flashlight and took the revolver out of my pocket."

Silas paused, and for the first time, looked directly at Joe. "Joseph Tolleson was standing about ten feet in front of me, carrying a body wrapped in plastic. He had a flashlight, but it wasn't turned on. I could tell that I had scared him. He tried to talk. His mouth moved, but he couldn't say anything. I asked him what he was doing and he wouldn't speak. I took a couple of steps towards him. I had the gun and I guess this sounds foolish, but I didn't think he was dangerous. Joe looked like a deer caught in the headlights. I stared at the body in the plastic wrapping. I think Joe noticed that I was looking at the body and he lunged at me and dumped the body in my arms.

"I panicked. I dropped my flashlight and Joe dropped his as well. I fired a shot, which fortunately missed Joe. We were standing at an intersection of two tunnels and I heard Joe running down the crossing tunnel, to my right, away from me. I fired two shots down that tunnel and then waited. I didn't hear anything, but I was afraid to walk down that tunnel. I leaned against the wall and thought about what I should do. Finally, I heard some noises coming from the tunnel, so I knew Joe was alive. I was relieved that I hadn't killed him.

"I didn't want to leave to get help because Joe would have escaped. Still, I was afraid to go after him because it was completely dark and I didn't know if he had a weapon. I had only been under the church a couple of times and I wasn't familiar with the layout of the tunnels. I thought that if I went after Joe, he might run down another tunnel and escape. I sat there for many hours, knowing that I was blocking the tunnel that led to the only stairway. I was hoping that Joe would give himself up. However, I didn't hear any sounds from the other tunnel for a long time and I started to worry about Joe. I was afraid that I might have wounded him."

Silas paused and pointed at a pitcher of water on the defense table. Catledge filled a glass and brought it to him. He took a drink and handed the glass back to Catledge, who returned to the defense table.

"I walked slowly down the tunnel Joe had gone down. I kept calling out for him. I guess that's how he knew I was coming. I reached a point where I felt a draft coming from my right side, so I figured I had reached the intersection of another tunnel. I called Joe's name and that's when he hit me on the head with his pipe. My legs started to go and he hit me on the head again. After that I went unconscious.

"I don't know how long it was before I came to. I was woozy and nauseated. I called out, but there was no response. I felt around for my gun, but I couldn't find it.

I walked back to the intersection of the tunnel with the main tunnel. The body was gone and I ran up the stairs and through the church. When I opened the door, Joe was running across the parking lot, carrying the body. I chased him out to his car, but I was very weak and I didn't catch him. He drove away and I went back to the parsonage. I think I was still in shock because I passed out on my living room couch. I didn't wake up until the police arrived."

Joe stared at Silas, astounded. The minister did not look at him. Which was worse—the lies, or the hope that they would be believed? The lies were there; Joe knew how he would proceed if he were cross-examining Silas. What would Silas achieve if, by some miracle, he were believed? He would stay out of prison, despising those who believed and despised by those who didn't. Of course, there would be no miracles, nobody would believe. Anyone paying attention to Silas could find the holes in his testimony. Joe turned to see how the gallery and jurors were reacting to his testimony and something sank inside him—the weight of his own belief in human rationality.

They believed. He could see it in their eyes and faces. Both the jury and the spectators had succumbed to the magic of the deep, compelling voice that filled the room. Silas's words were to be felt, not considered. Consideration had floated out the courtroom, vanquished by fog. Silas was a liar with an accomplice—a willingness to believe that overrode any desire to know the truth. Joe felt the same terror as the night he told the police and his parents about Silas's crimes. What experience, what corruption, was responsible for a decision to ignore the truth? Perhaps all the people are fooled some of the time, but why would they deceive themselves? How could such deception lead to anything but pain? Joe shook his head. Perhaps Silas could answer his questions.

As Silas described the police arrival at the parsonage, Catledge stood and advanced towards the witness stand.

"Thank you, Reverend Wayne. Did you ever tape or glue hair to the tapestry over the door to the subterranean tunnels and rooms to the wall to alert yourself to an intrusion?"

"No."

"When you went under the church, you kept your flashlight off until you heard that the intruder was very close to you. You didn't hide in a side tunnel and wait for that person to pass, you confronted that person face-to-face, correct?"

"That's correct."

"You didn't grab the intruder, who turned out to be Joe Tolleson, from behind?"

"No."

"Did you ever tell Joe Tolleson that you had raped and murdered Marsha Walton?"

"No."

"Did you call Marsha Walton a 'heretic,' or a 'witch'?"

"No."

"Did you ever say anything about Tolleson's mother, Alice Tolleson?"

"No."

"Tolleson dropped the body in your arms and ran down the perpendicular tunnel. Then for a long time, neither one of you did anything. Did you at any time go to the room where Marsha Walton's body had been kept and turn on the light in that room?"

"No."

"So when you went down the tunnel to find Tolleson, it was completely dark?"

"Yes."

"Tolleson knew your location because you called his name?"

"Yes."

"He hit you twice on the head and you passed out. Were you aware of him holding your gun to your head?"

"No."

"You probably also were not aware of Rachmaninoff's Third Piano Concerto?"

The spectators laughed until Judge Longworth banged his gavel.

"No."

"After you came to, you chased after Tolleson. Did you know that he had the gun?"

"I thought he might, but I wasn't sure."

"After you failed to apprehend him, you went back to the parsonage and passed out until the police arrived, correct?"

"Yes."

"You didn't call the police?"

"No."

"One last question. Did you devise a scheme whereby you led Alice Tolleson to believe that you would marry her, so that she would decline her acting scholarship?"

"No."

"Thank you. I have no further questions at this time, your Honor. Your witness, Mr. Devore." Catledge returned to his seat at the defense table.

Devore stood, making a conscious effort to control his nerves. He had to show that Silas Wayne was lying. Wayne's testimony had gone well and he was too smart to be trapped into an outright admission. Somehow, Devore had to cultivate seeds of doubt in the minds of the jury. If he didn't, his career in Hidden Falls was over. He approached the defendant.

"Mr. Wayne, you have testified that you were in the parsonage for the entire afternoon and evening of Friday, November the eighth. There is nobody who can verify your whereabouts, is that correct?"

"Yes, it is."

"You have testified that you had an answering machine at the time. If somebody called you while you were at the parsonage, was it your usual practice to pick up the phone?"

Silas's eyes narrowed. "Yes."

"So if somebody called and heard the answering machine message, they could assume that you were not in at the time?"

"Yes, that's correct."

Strassberg whispered to Catledge, "let's hope Devore doesn't produce a rebuttal witness with a phone bill testifying that he called the Reverend Wayne Friday afternoon, November the eighth and reached his answering machine."

"You deny having entered the church at all on November the eighth. Did you see or hear anything that would indicate that anyone else was in the church on that day?"

"No."

"How long have you known Joe Tolleson?"

"Since he was a small child."

"You said that he did not attend your church and he refused to be confirmed. Did he attend church before he refused confirmation?"

"Occasionally, at the insistence of his parents."

"But after he refused confirmation, you only saw him around town and once when you went to the Tolleson's for dinner, is that correct?"

"Yes."

"Did he ever exhibit any hostility towards you?"

"Well, like I said, he didn't want to talk about his refusal to join the church."

"Yes, but would you characterize that as hostility towards you? Did he threaten or abuse you, personally?"

"No."

"Marsha Walton also refused to be confirmed as a member of your church, is that correct?"

"Yes."

"So one person who refused confirmation in your church is dead, and you're virtually accusing another person who also refused confirmation of the murder. How many other children have refused to attend your confirmation classes?"

"Oh, I don't know, there have been several."

"Can you name any of their names?"

"Uh, no, not right off the top of my head. If I had some time I would probably remember. It's not—"

"Thank you, Mr. Wayne. Let's talk about Lou Santori, Sarah Matlock and Edna Mayhew. Your account of certain events is, in some respects, at variance with theirs. Is Mr. Santori a member of the First Christian Church?"

"Yes, he is."

"You had gone into the Starlight Lounge and had several conversations with him. Were those conversations friendly?"

"Yes."

"They must have been. Didn't you say that he mentioned some problems that he was having with his girlfriend?"

"Yes."

"And you gave him your card with your phone number written on the back?"

"Yes."

"So given this amiable relationship, why would Mr. Santori try to discredit you by saying he talked to you when you claim he talked to your answering machine?"

"I don't know."

"Why would he say that you asked him to call you about Nancy Walton, when you say that you didn't?"

"I don't know."

"Thank you. Was Edna Mayhew a member of your church?"

"Yes, she was."

"Did she regularly attend your church?"

"Yes, she did."

"However, there was a long stretch, after her husband died, when Mrs. Mayhew did not attend your church?"

"Yes, there was."

"Weren't you instrumental in convincing her to return to church and getting her reinvolved with church activities?"

"Yes, I was."

"Would you characterize that as an act of friendship?"

"Yes."

"And would you say that your relationship with Mrs. Mayhew was a close friendship?"

"Yes, I would."

"Then why would she so emphatically insist that you had told her that you had taken in the ice machine for repairs? Surely it wasn't out of animosity towards you?"

"No, as I said earlier, I think that with her illness she lost either her hearing or her memory."

"But you saw the videotape, and didn't she rebuff that suggestion when it was made by Mr. Catledge?"

"She did, but by the time that videotape was made—"

"Thank you, Mr. Wayne. Is Sarah Matlock a member of the First Christian Church?"

"Yes."

"And have you had a close relationship with her?"

"Yes, I have."

"To the extent there are differences between yours and Sarah's version of who had the idea to move the coffin to the church, it casts doubt on your version. However, Sarah Matlock would have no reason to want to cast doubt on your version, would she?"

"No."

"The night before Chester Matlock's funeral, you went into the church to prepare it for the funeral. How long did you estimate that your preparations would take you to complete?"

"A half hour, forty-five minutes."

"What time was the funeral the following morning?"

"Ten-thirty."

"So you would have had plenty of time to do all that the next morning, if you had wanted to?"

"Yes, but I wanted to go to bed knowing everything was taken care of."

"Of course, if you were going over to the church to put Marsha Walton's body in Mayor Matlock's casket and dispose of the rest of the evidence, wouldn't that have taken considerably longer?"

"I suppose it would have."

Devore took a step backwards, towards the prosecution table. "Once you were in the church, you said you heard noises coming from below the church. Where were you when you heard these noises?"

"I was in the pews, checking the hymnals and Bibles."

"You said you heard the noises through grating on the floor?"

"Yes, I did. I don't know why they are there, perhaps for ventilation, but there are four holes in the church floor. The holes are about one square foot and they are covered with a steel grate that allows air, and in this case noise, to come through."

"What did the noises sound like?"

"At first I thought rats, but then it sounded like someone walking on the gritty surface below the church."

"You were aware of the tunnels and rooms below the church?"

"I was aware that there were some tunnels under the church. I didn't know about the rooms."

"How long had you been aware of the tunnels?"

"From the first time I had the tapestries cleaned. I found the door when I removed the tapestry from the wall."

"Did you go beneath the church after you discovered the door?"

"Yes."

"How many times?"

"Just that one time. I only walked a little ways down the tunnel, the one that's labeled main tunnel on your drawing. It was dark, and I don't particularly like those kinds of areas—sometimes they have rats and spiders."

"You said in your direct testimony that you had been under the church a couple of times." Devore walked towards Wayne, put his hands on the witness box railing and looked directly at him. "Now you say that you had been under the church just one time. Were you lying then, or are you lying now?"

There was a noticeable pause before Silas responded. "Uh, yes, well counting that evening I had been under the church twice."

"I see." Devore nodded. "You also said in your direct testimony that since you had only been under the church a couple of times, you were not familiar with the layout of the tunnels. You said you sat in the main tunnel for many hours, knowing that was the only tunnel that led to the stairway, to prevent Joe Tolleson from escaping. If you were unfamiliar with the layout of the tunnels, how did you know that the stairway was the only way out from under the church?"

There was a longer pause and Silas moved back in his chair. "I didn't, I just assumed that it was."

"That seems like a risky assumption, given the danger that Tolleson might have escaped." Devore paused and stepped back from the witness stand. "Did you ever take a can of metal sealant and a length of pipe under the church?"

"No."

"Do you know who would have done so, and why?"

"Maybe the Reverend Ames wanted to repair a leaky pipe. I would think there would be access to the plumbing for the church in those tunnels somewhere."

"Going back to the night of your confrontation with Joe Tolleson, you said you heard a noise and went back to the parsonage?"

"Yes, I did. If someone was under the church, I wanted to have a flashlight and my gun."

"Why would a minister own a gun?"

"I've owned that gun for fifteen years. The church and parsonage are on the outskirts of town. Right behind my house is a wooded area. I've shot a couple of snakes and scared away some raccoons going through the trash. There's nothing in the Bible that says that you can't protect yourself."

"So you returned to the church and went underneath it. You said you didn't initially turn on your flashlight. Why?"

"I was afraid that if I turned on the flashlight, I would alert the intruder to my presence. I wanted to get an idea of where the intruder was. When I heard footsteps coming towards me, I turned on the flashlight."

"Did Joe Tolleson have his flashlight on?"

"No."

"Doesn't it strike you as odd that he didn't have his flashlight on?"

"No, considering what he was doing there."

"I see. Now Joe Tolleson was standing in front of you with the body of Marsha Walton in his arms. You said that very little was said between you. Did you in fact have some sort of relationship with Alice Tolleson when you were in high school?"

"I'm not sure I would call it a relationship, at least not a romantic relationship. We were very close friends. She told me she wanted me to ask her to marry me. I couldn't because of the nature of my calling to Christ. However, I've been close to both Alice and Jack since they were married. I performed their marriage ceremony."

"Did you at any time tell anyone about your relationship with Alice Tolleson?"

"Well again, I don't think relationship is necessarily the right word. I never told anyone that she wanted me to ask her to marry me, but there was no secret that we were close friends in high school."

"How do you think Joe Tolleson learned about his mother's past relationship with you?"

"Not because I told him. However, as I said, it was no secret that Alice and I were close friends in high school and we've remained close friends through the years. Any number of people, including his father, could have told him that."

"You testified that Joe Tolleson dumped the body towards you. Did you actually catch the body?"

"Well, I don't fully remember, but it seems to me that I must have, since I dropped my flashlight."

"So you did handle the body?"

"Yes, I did."

"And you fired your gun once?"

"Yes."

"And then you fired twice at Joe Tolleson as he ran down the tunnel?"

"Yes."

"But he was running away from you?"

"Yes."

"And did he appear to be unarmed?"

"I didn't know if he was armed or not."

"But he didn't fire back?"

"No."

"So Tolleson didn't pose a threat to you?"

"Well, he had dumped the body in my arms."

"Yes, but then he ran away from you, correct?"

"That's correct."

"But you were so shaken that you fired blindly, in the dark, down the tunnel in which he was running?"

"Yes."

"Now, during this entire time, it was dark, pitch black, right?"

"Well, yes, after Joe dumped the body in my arms we both dropped our flashlights."

"But there was another light available. In the room where Marsha Walton's body had been kept, there was a light bulb hooked up to the generator. However, you never went in that room, did you?"

Silas paused for a second and looked towards Preston Catledge. Catledge looked towards Judge Longworth and then at his wristwatch. The judge seemed to take the hint. "It's noon, we'll adjourn for lunch," he announced.

Catledge and Strassberg stayed at the courthouse, in conference with their client. Devore and Benewski walked to Brigg's Diner. Devore was excited; as they sat down at their reserved table, he could barely contain himself.

"Did you catch that signal between Wayne, Catledge and Longworth? Wayne was in trouble and he wanted Catledge to help him out. I'm surprised Judge Longworth went for it. It doesn't matter, though. The light bulb, in the room—that light bulb is the key, Gary. It's going to blow Wayne's story apart."

"How?"

"I'll show you."

He took a yellow legal pad from his briefcase, and for the next half hour diagrammed the progression of his questions for that afternoon, accounting for each possible answer by the defendant. Benewski ate his cheese-bacon-onion burger.

"I see what you're going to do," Benewski said when Devore had finished. "And I see why you're so excited. You haven't touched your hamburger, though."

"I don't feel like eating," Devore said, picking up his soggy hamburger and then putting it back on the plate. "Its time to go back." They paid for their lunch and returned to the courthouse. When the afternoon session resumed, Devore picked up where he had left off.

"Mr. Wayne, let me repeat my question from before lunch. According to your own testimony and that of Joe Tolleson, both of your flashlights were inoperative after the confrontation. However, there was another light available, the light in the room where Marsha Walton's body had been kept. You never went in that room, did you?"

"No."

"Mr. Wayne," Devore said, stepping closer, "I'm going to pose some hypothetical questions, and I just want you to give me the answers that seem most logical to you. Let's say the light had been on in that room when you came down the stairs and that the door was open. If Joe Tolleson was advancing down the main tunnel, wouldn't he have seen you before he got close to you?"

"Objection," said Catledge, standing. "What is the relevance of these hypothetical questions?"

"Your Honor," Devore responded, "we think the defendant is lying. Our questions will illustrate how he's lying."

"Overruled."

"Do you need me to repeat the question, Mr. Wayne?"

"No. If a light had been on in the room, Tolleson would have seen me."

"And if that were the case, he probably wouldn't have kept walking towards you, he probably would have dropped the body and run away, wouldn't he?"

"Probably."

"But if he had done that, then your fingerprints probably wouldn't have been all over the plastic wrapping around the body, would they?"

"Probably not."

"And if the light had been on, sometime during the night that you spent under the church, don't you think you might have gone and looked in the room where the light was coming from?"

"Probably."

"And if you had done that, wouldn't it be likely that you would leave your fingerprints somewhere in that room?"

"Well, since we are dealing in hypothetical situations, I might have tried not to leave fingerprints so as to avoid disturbing evidence of an apparent crime."

Devore walked to the witness stand and put his hands on the rail. "Well, you might have, Mr. Wayne, but remember, you were pretty shaken up. After all, you shot twice in the dark at Joe Tolleson as he was running away from you. It seems to me that you wouldn't have had the presence of mind to be that careful. However, your fingerprints weren't found in the room, and you say it is because you were never in the room, correct?"

"That's right."

"This is just an aside, Mr. Wayne, but don't you think it's odd that the only fingerprints found in the room were Joe Tolleson's? Detective Baerwald testified that it was impossible to lift fingerprints from the circular light switch, but don't you think he should have found some other prints on the church recreation room ice machine and the table that apparently came from the recreation room? Doesn't it seem odd to you that he didn't?"

"I don't know."

"It almost seems like somebody wiped every item in that room for prints, and did so before Joe Tolleson was in the room, doesn't it?"

"I don't know."

"Of course, you were never in that room, were you?"

"No."

"Okay, here's another hypothetical situation. If the light wasn't on when you entered beneath the church, but you were somehow aware of the room and the light, you probably would have turned the light on when you went to find Joe Tolleson, wouldn't you?"

"Probably."

"But you couldn't be aware of the light in the room, since it had only been recently hooked to the generator, presumably by Marsha Walton's murderer, correct?"

"Yes."

"You couldn't say that you first found the room after your initial confrontation with Tolleson, because if it was dark you would have stumbled around and left some prints in the room before you found the light switch. So it had to be dark when you went looking for Joe Tolleson. You say he knew where you were because you were calling his name. Would you say that it was completely dark, pitch black?"

"Yes."

"Let's conduct an experiment, Mr. Wayne. Would you please close your eyes?"

"Objection," Catledge said, "what is the relevance of this exercise?"

"Your Honor, if I can have the court's forbearance, I think the relevance of this exercise will become apparent."

"Overruled, proceed Mr. Devore."

"Thank you. Please close your eyes, Mr. Wayne. Thank you." Devore took five steps backwards. "How far am I away from you?"

"About seven feet."

Devore stood where he was, but raised his voice. "How far am I away from you now?"

"You are closer to me than you were before, maybe five feet."

Devore took two steps towards the defendant, but lowered his voice. "How far am I away from you now?"

"You are farther away, maybe eight or nine feet."

"Thank you, Mr. Wayne. You can open your eyes now. Mr. Wayne, you gave me the wrong answers simply because I raised and lowered my voice. You say it was completely dark underneath the church, but you say that Joe Tolleson was able to tell where your head was just by the sound of your voice. Isn't it amazing that he was able to pinpoint the location of your head such that he could deliver two blows with a pipe, one of them a knockout, from the sound of your voice, yet, you were unable to tell, from the sound of my voice, where I was standing when you had your eyes closed. What do you think accounts for his ability to detect location from sound and your inability to do so? Or do you think he eats a lot of carrots and has extraordinary vision in the dark?"

There was a long pause. "I don't know."

"Thank you, Mr. Wayne. Why did you go after Joe Tolleson at all? You were under the church all night, why didn't you just wait until people started showing up for the funeral, rather than risk going after Tolleson?"

"Well, I had no idea what time it was, so I didn't think about waiting it out. I was also concerned about Joe. I hadn't heard any noises for a long time. I was worried that he might be hurt."

"You were worried that he might be hurt, but you had shot at him three times earlier?"

There were scattered chuckles. The judge banged his gavel.

"Yes, I was worried that he might be hurt."

"Why didn't you go after him earlier?"

"Well, it was dark and I was afraid he might attack me or that he might escape."

"Were you aware that he was carrying a pipe?"

"No."

"And you still had a gun with three bullets in it, didn't you?"

"Yes."

"Hypothetically speaking, if you were responsible for Marsha Walton's rape, murder and subsequent mutilation, the last thing you would want would be for Joe Tolleson to remain alive and for people to see the scene under the church, correct?"

"Objection," Strassberg said, "the question asks the defendant to assume his own guilt and thus, indirectly violates his Fifth Amendment privilege against self-incrimination."

"I'll withdraw the question," said Devore before Judge Longworth could rule. "Mr. Wayne, after you regained consciousness, you chased Joe Tolleson to his car. Why did you chase after him?"

"I wanted to catch him and hold him for the police."

"You didn't want to catch him because he had a key piece of evidence against you—the body—and he would be able to testify against you?"

"No."

"However, once he drove away, you went back to the parsonage and passed out. You chased after him so you could catch him and turn him over to the police, but once he left you didn't call the police, is that correct?"

"Yes, but—"

"I have no further questions, your Honor."

"Does the defense have questions on redirect?"

Catledge looked expectantly at Strassberg. She wondered if anyone it the courtroom, besides the other attorneys, appreciated Devore's performance—he had done a great cross-examination. He was a hard guy to get a handle on. His intensity and powers of concentration appeared to match her own. Many people had told her that she was too cerebral, that she thought and analyzed too much. Devore had probably heard the same sorts of criticism. How was one supposed to turn off one's brain? Years of single-minded dedication to trials—meticulous preparation, attentive listening, thorough cross-examinations, all-night review and strategy sessions, never ending attention to detail, a ruthless will to win and the constant self-discipline of staying alert and focused—produced a personality that perhaps could only be understood or appreciated by other trial lawyers. Catledge's whisper brought her attention back to the case at hand.

"What do you think, any more questions?"

She shook her head. "No, let's not give Devore another shot at him. Get him off the stand."

Catledge stood. "Would the Reverend Wayne please complete his answer to Mr. Devore's last question?"

"I intended to call the police when I got back to the parsonage, but I passed out on the couch before I could do so."

"Thank you, we have no further questions, your Honor."

"No further questions, your Honor," Devore said.

"The defendant may step down."

Joe watched Silas as he returned to the defense table, but Silas never looked at him. Joe glanced at the jury box and saw twelve expressionless faces. At least Devore had figured out the discrepancy about the light. Would his expert cross-examination outweigh the magic of Silas's voice and words? Maybe not. He walked out of the court-room, reflecting bitterly on Diogenes' quest.

CHAPTER 25

THE DEFENSE RESTS

Strassberg and Catledge conferred and agreed that Devore had done some damage—Silas's image needed repair. Catledge stood and announced, "the defense calls the Reverend Wilbert Weathin."

The world's most famous televangelist stood and walked from his seat to the witness stand. If Judge Longworth had not prohibited cameras there would have been a barrage of flashes. Weathin placed his hand on the Bible and recited the oath, his well-known voice reverberating throughout the courtroom. He took his seat on the stand and Catledge walked towards him.

"Reverend Weathin, how long have you known the Reverend Wayne?"

"I first met Silas when we were students together at the seminary."

"What was your impression of his character?"

"His devotion to his calling, his zeal in pursuing his religious studies, was what stood out. Nobody took the coursework more seriously than Silas—he had both an emotional and intellectual commitment to his faith. I think that's what everyone remembered about him.

"However, there was another, hidden, side to Silas. I may have been the only person in seminary who knew about it. Professor Albright announced that he was going to host a special seminar on the philosophy of Christianity at his house on Wednesday evenings. Everyone assumed that Silas would attend because of his interest in the subject. We were all surprised when he wasn't at the first meeting. I asked him why he hadn't gone and he just smiled; he wouldn't give me an explanation. It was a mystery, but I got to the bottom of it. Silas and I were roommates that year and one night I skipped the seminar to see if I could find out why Silas didn't attend. He didn't know it, but I watched our room and then followed him from campus to the hospital. He stayed there several hours and after he left I went in, talked to a couple of nurses and discovered that he was visiting with patients almost every night. Later, I found out that he was also spending a lot of time at the orphanage."

"Have you kept in contact with the Reverend Wayne since you were at the seminary?"

"We frequently write to each other and we talk on the phone. We also see each other at the annual meeting of the regional conference. He was elected chairman two years ago."

"Reverend Weathin, it's clear that the Reverend Wayne has a deep commitment to his religious calling. Would you say that he has a problem with people who either are not as devout as he is, or who reject his religion entirely?"

"No, I haven't seen that at all. A minister that can't tolerate disbelief is going to have a difficult time of it. I've talked with Silas; we've always regarded those who choose not to hear God's call as a test of our own faith. Silas will talk with nonbelievers for hours. He's very patient, he doesn't get angry."

"What would be his reaction if a child refused to attend confirmation classes for his church?"

"I think he would attribute it to the inexperience and obstinacy of youth and he would pray that the child would eventually find his way."

"You said that you were impressed in the seminary by the Reverend Wayne's devotion to his religion. Is that still his primary motivation?"

"Absolutely."

"In your opinion, could the Reverend Wayne rape and murder a fourteen-year-old girl?"

"No. I would believe myself more capable of doing such a thing than Silas."

"Thank you, Reverend Weathin. I have no further questions."

Devore stood, but did not advance towards Weathin.

"Reverend Weathin, were you in Hidden Falls on the day of November the eighth of last year?"

"No."

"Were you in Hidden Falls on November the fifteenth of last year, or any day from the eighth to the fifteenth?"

"No."

"So you cannot testify as to the whereabouts or actions of Silas Wayne during that period?"

"No."

"Thank you. I have no further questions."

Weathin left the courtroom. Through the afternoon and the following morning, witness after witness testified about the Very Reverend Silas Wayne's good deeds. The jury heard about late night visits at homes, jails, and hospitals to console the troubled or grieving; loans for which repayment was never requested; efforts to find jobs for the unemployed or companions for those who had lost their mates; counseling for alcoholics and drugs addicts; baptisms, confirmations, marriages, funerals, charities and other civic activities. Silas's unselfish sacrifice was the leitmotif of every story. Each witness held an obviously sincere belief that the defendant could not have raped and murdered Marsha Walton.

Devore would ask a few questions to establish that the witness had not been at the old church on the nights of November the eighth or the fifteenth and so had no firsthand knowledge concerning Marsha Walton's rape and murder. These brief, contrary footnotes for the jury did little to interrupt Preston Catledge's skillful canonization of Silas Wayne. After the last character witness, the widow Reeves, stepped down, Judge Longworth recessed for lunch.

After lunch, Strassberg called the first of the defense's two experts on DNA testing, Professor Harold Boranian. According to Boranian's published articles, DNA testing was a valuable forensic tool, but it had been oversold as an irrefutable means of proving a defendant's connection to a crime. The exaggerated claims made for DNA testing allowed critics to point out certain theoretical and practical shortcomings, and the resulting controversy roiled the courts. Strassberg had challenged DNA testing in prior cases—the trick was to find an articulate, forceful critic who could play off latent technophobia within a jury and inculcate a mistrust of the procedure.

The professor was sworn in and responded to Strassberg's question about his credentials by rattling off an impressive list of degrees, professorships and articles in professional journals. He looked like a distinguished professor. He had a neatly trimmed black and gray beard and wore a tweed coat with suede patches on the elbows. His descriptions of the conceptual basis and methodology of DNA testing were similar to Dr. Alvarez's. However, he parted company with the prosecution expert in his evaluation of the efficacy of the procedure. He was not quiet as impressive as Alvarez had been—he had a stiff, formal manner of speech, but he was still effective.

"Professor Boranian," Strassberg said, "would you please tell us what you regard as some of the deficiencies of DNA testing?"

"The first difficulty with the procedure is one of semantics. DNA testing is sometimes referred to as DNA fingerprinting, which is misleading. No two sets of fingerprints are identical; each person has unique fingerprints. This is not true with the fragments of DNA strands that are analyzed in DNA testing. Two individuals, even unrelated individuals, can have identical fragments of DNA. In fact, most of one's DNA is identical to everyone else's DNA— that identity is a defining characteristic of the human species. Only fragments of the long chain of DNA are different from individual to individual. This group of fragments is what makes each individual unique. However, two individuals can have identical fragments, even among the group of fragments that vary across the population. That is why DNA tests typically analyze and compare a number of DNA fragments. Although the probability that DNA from two samples did not come from the same source shrinks as the number of matching segments increases, theoretically, it is never possible to say that probability is zero."

As if he were giving a lecture, he paused and surveyed the courtroom, trying to determine if his listeners were properly attentive. Apparently concluding that they were, he continued. "Compounding this theoretical problem are several practical issues. If an analyzed DNA sample at the scene of a crime is old or decomposed, the resulting records of the fragments, which are called autoradiographs, may be of poor quality. Also, faulty gathering of either the scene-of-the-crime sample or the suspect's sample can lead to invalid results. It is my understanding that there was such a problem in this case, necessitating a second round of tests. Finally, the probabilities for matching various segments from the DNA were developed from FBI data. My colleague, Professor Lamson, will have more to say about shortcomings in that work, but I will say that those probabilities are based on an assumption that subjects are not related. The probability of matching segments increases when the samples are taken from related parties."

"Thank you, Professor Boranian. I just want to make sure that one point is clear. You have said that unlike fingerprints, it can never be conclusively stated, with complete certainty, that DNA taken from a sample from the scene of the crime is the same DNA as a sample taken from a suspect, no matter how many segments match. Is that correct?"

"Yes, it is."

"I have no further questions, your witness."

"Professor Boranian," Devore said, standing and advancing toward the witness, "have you had an opportunity to examine the autoradiographs in this case?"

"Yes, I have."

"What is your opinion as to their quality?"

"They are good."

"How many fragments of DNA were analyzed?"

"Five."

"Would you agree with the conclusion of Dr. Alvarez of the DNA testing facility that the five autoradiographs from the samples taken from the victim's body match the samples taken from the defendant, Silas Wayne?"

"No."

"You would not? Would you say that the autoradiographs are similar?"

"I would say there are some similarities."

"Why would you not say they are matching?"

"I believe the term 'matching' conveys a precision that is impossible to achieve with this procedure."

"I see. Have you had an opportunity to examine the blood tests of Joseph Tolleson and Silas Wayne?"

"Yes, I have."

"Based on those test results, is it possible that Silas Wayne is Joseph Tolleson's father?"

"No, he cannot be his father."

"You mentioned that the probabilities of DNA matching increase among related parties. However, that would not be a factor in this case, since there is no possibility that the defendant is related to Joseph Tolleson, is that correct?"

"That is correct."

"Is there any 'similarity' between the autoradiographs for Joe Tolleson and for the samples taken from Marsha Walton's body?"

"No."

"What is your estimate of the probability that the five segments of DNA selected from the samples taken from Marsha Walton's body and the five segments of DNA from the samples taken from Silas Wayne would be substantially similar, but that the DNA would not be from the same source? In other words, what is the probability of substantial similarity without both sets of samples being from Silas Wayne?"

"I refuse to say, because I don't think our work on this technology has advanced to the point where we can assign such probabilities with any degree of accuracy."

"Thank you, I have no further questions."

Devore walked back to the prosecution table. As he sat down, he whispered to Benewski, "damn it, why did I ask that last question? I knew he wouldn't answer it."

"You also forgot to ask him if was paid as an expert witness," Benewski said. "I thought you were saving it for the end, but you quit your questioning so abruptly I couldn't remind you." Devore winced.

The defense's final witness was Professor Cynthia Lamson, another expert in genetics and microbiology, with special expertise in population statistics. She was young for a professor, in her mid-thirties. She had blond hair and was only a couple of inches taller than five feet. Her looks probably went unnoticed in the laboratory, but sitting on the stand, wearing contact lenses instead of safety glasses and a burgundy dress instead of a white lab coat, she was quite attractive. She reviewed her credentials and her experience with DNA testing.

"Professor Lamson," Strassberg said, "you have published several articles on statistics and the FBI population studies that are used as a basis for quoting probabilities in connection with DNA testing. Could you please summarize what you have written about those studies?"

"The FBI studies are based on blood samples from several thousand people. Those samples are used to ascertain a probability that any given DNA fragment would match the corresponding fragment of another, unrelated individual. With each DNA fragment, there is a finite probability of sampling error. It is standard procedure to say, when summarizing the results of statistical sampling, that the probability of matching two corresponding segments drawn from unrelated individuals is a number, call it X, plus or minus some factor which accounts for this sampling error. However, the way the FBI tests have come to be used, no account is made for sampling error and a probability is quoted for individual matching fragments. The error is then compounded as the probability of multiple matching fragments is derived by multiplying the individual probabilities. On that basis, astronomical probabilities are quoted that DNA from the sample taken at the scene of the crime is from a different source than the DNA from samples taken from a criminal defendant."

"So there is always a measure of imprecision in statistical sampling, and saying, as an example, that the probability of two individuals matching corresponding fragments is one in one hundred, does not accurately convey this imprecision, is that correct?"

"That is correct, it does not reflect the possibility of error inherent in any sampling procedure."

"Furthermore, when such a probability is multiplied with another probability to determine the possibility of two individuals having two matching corresponding fragments, the possibility of error is multiplied as well, is that correct?"

"Yes, it is."

"So you would not be able to accurately quote a probability of one, two, or five matching DNA fragments, and the magnitude of the potential error in such a probability grows larger for each successive set of DNA fragments, is that correct?"

"Yes it is."

"I have no further questions, your witness."

"Professor Lamson," said Devore, advancing towards the witness, "regardless of potential sampling error, as a theoretical matter there is a probability that any particular segment of DNA drawn from one person will match the corresponding DNA segment drawn from another person, is that correct?"

"Yes."

"And as a theoretical matter, the probability of two matches will always be equal to or smaller than the probability of one match, and the probability of three matches will be equal to or smaller than the probability of two matches, and so on, is that correct?"

"Yes."

"Have you previously testified as an expert witness for criminal defendants?"

"Yes, I have."

"How many times?"

"This will be my sixth time."

"Are you paid for your testimony?"

"I am reimbursed for my expenses, and I receive compensation for my time away from the university."

"Thank you, I have no further questions." Devore walked back to the defense table and sat down.

Two experts testifying about the statistical nuances of DNA testing was not how the defense attorneys had wanted to finish their case—it was an anticlimax. Their original plan had been for the Reverend Weathin to be the final witness, but Devore's cross-examination of Wayne had inflicted damage they wanted to fix immediately. Strassberg disliked flat conclusions, but hoped she could restore some drama with her closing argument.

"Your Honor," she said, "we have no further witnesses. The defense rests."

"Mr. Devore," Judge Longworth said, "does the State have any rebuttal witnesses?"

"No, we do not, your Honor. The State rests."

"I want to complement both sides for your experts' testimony," Judge Longworth said. "You managed to make your points without overwhelming the court with minutiae. It's a little early, but let's adjourn. Tomorrow we'll have the closing arguments and my instructions and then the case goes to the jury."

CHAPTER 26

▼

CLOSING ARGUMENTS

Gary Benewski stood before the jury. He wore the same dark gray suit and silk tie he had worn during his direct examination of Joe Tolleson. It had taken four days to pick the jury— ten women, six men (the jury would consist of twelve people, but four alternates had to sit through the trial). By occupation there were five housewives, an accountant, a shopkeeper, two teachers, a clerk at the electric company, a postal carrier, a construction worker, a golf pro, a retired executive, a rancher and a writer. They all came from towns in Merton County other than Hidden Falls, where virtually everyone knew Silas Wayne. During jury selection, Benewski and Devore had tried to get intelligent jurors with a scientific bent. Strassberg and Catledge wanted jurors who might be swayed by emotional appeals and the reputation of the defendant. Inevitably, the jury that was chosen represented a compromise between the opposing strategies. Benewski was to make the first part of the prosecution's argument—summarizing the facts of the case. Devore would present their argument and rebut the defense's.

"On the afternoon of Friday, November the eighth of last year, Joe Tolleson picked the lock on the front door of the First Christian church and entered the church. He walked through the vestibule and into the nave, where he heard a creaking noise coming from the choir loft of the church." Benewski proceeded to review the case. Although he tried to vary the inflection of his voice and to look at individual jurors, his delivery was unexciting. At one point in his summation, he paused and turned towards the spectators' gallery, surveying the crowd. Behind the prosecution table, in a front row bench, sat Joe Tolleson—hands folded, gaze intent, demeanor solemn. Benewski walked to the prosecution table, poured a glass of water and took a sip. An encouraging smile flashed across Joe's face. Benewski turned, advanced towards the jury, and continued.

"One noteworthy aspect of this case is the insight and ingenuity of Silas Wayne. When he strangled Marsha Walton, he laid out a plastic sheet under her dangling body to catch her bodily fluids. He stuck a hair from the wall to the tapestry that concealed the hidden door—if the hair was broken, he would know that the door had been discovered. After Joe escaped from the choir loft, he coolly decided that his reputation within Hidden Falls would be all the protection he would need. He said to Joe: 'Welcome to hell, young Joseph, you're about to find out why I'm the Very Reverend Silas Wayne.'

"Wayne's assessment was nearly correct. When Joe told his story to the police, they didn't believe him and wouldn't investigate. The defense has disingenuously suggested that there was nothing wrong with this refusal to investigate. On cross-examination, they suggested that Joe's remarks were defamatory and that Joe committed crimes when he entered the church. Defamation is a civil, not a criminal matter, and virtually all accusations by one person that another person committed a crime are defamatory—they injure the reputation of the one accused. It is not the job of the police to squelch defamation; it is their job to investigate the truth or falsity of the accusation. In this case, they failed, as Wayne suspected they would. Wayne was also correct that Joe's life would become a hellish nightmare.

"Unfortunately for the defendant, the physical evidence is entirely consistent with Joe's story. The autopsy revealed that Marsha Walton had been raped and that the cause of her death was strangulation. The layout of the room in which her body was stored matches Joe's description. Joe's fingerprints, but not the defendant's, were found in the room. Joe and Wayne's fingerprints were found on the plastic wrapping around Marsha Walton's body. Two flashlights were found where Joe confronted Wayne. Three bullets were found in locations consistent with Joe's account. Urine stains were found where Joe waited through the night and bloodstains were found where he ambushed Wayne and hit him twice with the metal pipe. Joe and the defendant's footprints were found in the area where Joe parked his car. Finally, a DNA analysis reveals that five segments of DNA strands taken from foreign skin tissue found under Marsha Walton's fingernails, from foreign hair found in Marsha Walton's pubic hair and from semen taken from Marsha Walton's vaginal cavity match segments from DNA samples submitted by the defendant. Thank you."

Benewski returned to the prosecution table. Devore had polished his glasses during Benewski's speech. He put them back on and nodded. Benewski had done his share of the argument perfectly. He had presented an adequate summary of the facts of the case, but had never mentioned the defendant's testimony, thus giving the defense no idea how the prosecution would attack that testimony. Defense counsel would have to anticipate, rather than respond to, Devore's argument.

Was Rachel Strassberg up to the challenge? Many had questioned the wisdom of using an expensive defense attorney from New York. Anticipatory murmuring ran through the gallery as she advanced towards the jury box. She stood silently for a moment before the jury. She wore a blue suit, white silk blouse, blue hosiery and pumps, and diamond earrings. Her voice was low as she began her argument; several jurors leaned forward.

"Jack the Ripper could have found somebody to say something nice about him at his trial. There is undoubtedly a remnant of virtue in even the most depraved individuals. However, the witnesses we called testified not to some residual decency in the Reverend Silas Wayne, but to a lifetime of demonstrated concern for his fellow human beings. This concern is not some abstract love of humanity; it has been a personal commitment to helping real people—the people of Hidden Falls—with real problems. A cardinal element of any criminal case is the defendant's potential motive. The Reverend Weathin and the other witnesses testified, not in vague, glowing terms, but with concrete example after concrete example, to actions by the

Reverend Wayne that are wholly inconsistent with, and indeed are antithetical to, the motivations of a rapist and a murderer. A fundamental weakness of the prosecution's case is that the only motive offered to explain our client's alleged crimes is that the victim once rejected his offer and refused to be confirmed in his church.

"Does anybody in this courtroom believe that the Reverend Wayne hasn't been the target of abusive language during twenty plus years of working with children and adolescents, or that some of them would refuse to join his church? As the Reverend Weathin testified, it comes with the territory; it's part of the job. The experience of Joe Tolleson rebuts the defense contention that the Reverend Wayne couldn't tolerate those who questioned him and his religion. He refused confirmation as a member of the First Christian church and would not explain his reasons to the Reverend Wayne. The Reverend Wayne's reaction was sorrow tempered by a hope that Tolleson would change his mind, not murderous fury. Four years after he refused to become a member of his parents' church, Tolleson was alive and well, and able to fabricate his story about what happened on those two Friday evenings."

Strassberg turned away from the jury, towards Joe, and took a step towards him. "One of the leaps of faith in this case is believing the amazing story of Joe Tolleson," she said, gesturing at him with her open hand. She turned back towards the jury. "Mr. Benewski asserted that the physical evidence supports Tolleson's story. The prosecution's chief witness said that he confronted the Reverend Wayne in the choir loft of the First Christian Church after discovering the naked hanging body of Marsha Walton. How does the physical evidence support this story? There is no physical evidence. The prosecution never introduced fingerprints from the choir loft of either the witness or the Reverend Wayne, never introduced a rope, or Marsha Walton's clothes, or traces of bodily wastes or the plastic sheet that supposedly was used to catch those bodily wastes. Detective Baerwald was unable to find any evidence that a rope had hung from the rafters above the choir loft.

"All the prosecution has concerning the alleged confrontation in the choir loft is Tolleson's story. Like any good story this one has a hero, but like many bad stories the storyteller is the hero. According to his story, it was too dark for him to see the choir loft from the floor of the church, so he went up to investigate. He turned on a light in the hall and claims he saw the hanging body of Marsha Walton. However, he claims that the defendant shut the door to the hall so that there was then no light. One would think that a sixteen-year-old, under those circumstances, would panic. If he were going to jump out of the choir loft he would do so immediately after realizing that the probable murderer was there with him. Our intrepid witness, however, waited until the person who closed the door was close enough so that he could recognize, in the near darkness, that person's face.

"He says that once he saw that it was the defendant, he rolled over the railing and fell to the hard stone floor below. Miracle of miracles, he didn't land on one of the pews, he landed in an aisle and miracle of miracles, he fell fifteen feet like a cat—landing on his feet with no broken bones. Of course, he didn't immediately run from the church, he claims he hung around to listen to some prophetic, quasi-Biblical intonation from the defendant."

Strassberg paused for a moment, surveying the jury, trying to make eye contact with each juror. "Mr. Tolleson then went to the police station, where we he told his story to Sergeant Ruprecht and Chief Marsh. The prosecution has implied that there was some sort of sinister motivation underlying their decision not to pursue an investigation of Tolleson's story. However, given all the implausible elements of that story, is it any surprise that they didn't believe it? Is it any surprise that Tolleson's parents didn't believe it? Not only was he asking them to suspend their critical faculties, he was asking them to believe that the most respected man in Hidden Falls had committed two horrible crimes. Sergeant Ruprecht, Chief Marsh, Jack Tolleson and Alice Tolleson were prosecution, not defense witnesses, but they all testified that they didn't believe Tolleson's story because they couldn't conceive of the Reverend Wayne doing what Tolleson said he had done. Their actions are more eloquent testimony than even that of our character witnesses concerning the relative credibility of Tolleson and the Reverend Wayne.

"There is conflicting testimony about some of the events during the week between Tolleson's first and second alleged confrontations with the Reverend Wayne. Mrs. Edna Mayhew recalls telling the Reverend Wayne that an ice machine in the church recreation room kitchen was gone. Mrs. Mayhew, an elderly woman whose health was rapidly failing, recalls the Reverend Wayne saying he had taken it in for repairs. The Reverend Wayne does not remember making that response. Such a response would have been unlikely since the caretaker, Jasper Wooters, would have taken in the machine. Similarly, the bartender, Lou Santori, says that the Reverend Wayne asked Santori to inform him of the comings and goings of Nancy Walton, while the Reverend Wayne denies ever doing so. Santori says that he talked on the telephone to the Reverend Wayne on the day of Marsha Walton's disappearance. The Reverend Wayne says Santori talked to his answering machine. Finally, there appears to be some confusion about whose idea it was to move Mayor Matlock's casket to the church the night before the funeral. What is clear is that the idea emerged in a conversation between the Reverend Wayne and Sarah Matlock.

"A week after Tolleson and the Reverend Wayne's alleged confrontation in the church choir loft, they had another confrontation underneath the church." She forced herself to look towards Tolleson. He was staring at her. She momentarily held his glance, then turned back towards the jury and smiled. "Now hold on to your seats, folks, because if Tolleson's first story requires a leap of faith, his second story requires a triple jump. How did Tolleson deduce that the body was hidden in the church? Mr. Benewski told him that he had watched one night as the Reverend Wayne went from the parsonage to the church, and Tolleson overheard his parents mention that Mayor Matlock's casket was being taken to the church the evening before the funeral. From these two unconnected pieces of information, he supposedly figured out that the defendant was going to dispose of Marsha Walton's body in Mayor Matlock's casket. Instead of conveying this astounding conclusion to anyone else, he drove to the church by himself to find the body, knowing that the defendant could return at any time.

"For you see, our hero was not just extraordinarily bright, he was also extraordinarily brave. And extraordinarily

lucky—he happened to lift one of eight tapestries and *viola!*
a secret door. He says that he noticed a hair stuck to the tapestry, but this is another one of his assertions that is not supported by physical evidence. Detective Baerwald could find
no tape or glue residues on the tapestry."

Strassberg turned away from the jury and walked back
to the defense table. She poured a glass of water and took
a sip, glancing at an outline of her speech. She returned to
the jury and resumed her argument. "At this point, you
must choose between the Reverend Wayne's and Joe
Tolleson's version of events. The Reverend Wayne testified
that there was no light in the tunnel and he confronted
Tolleson face-to-face as Tolleson was carrying the body.
He testified that there was almost no conversation
between them before Tolleson dumped the body in his
arms. Tolleson has a different story.

"As you decide which story you believe, ask yourselves
two questions. If the Reverend Wayne took the body of
Marsha Walton to the room under the church, eviscerated
it, placed the organs in bottles of alcohol, drained the
blood and preserved the body on ice, why was there not a
trace of his fingerprints in that room? The prosecution will
maintain that he always wore rubber surgical gloves, from
the box found in the room, but isn't it strange that there
weren't any detectable fingerprints on that box of surgical
gloves or the rolling switch to the light bulb? The prosecution will say that he was smart and careful and wiped all
his prints.

"However, consider the second question. If the
Reverend Wayne was that smart and careful, why, when he
confronted Joe Tolleson, did he stand there and confess to
the crime and allow himself to become so distracted that

Tolleson was able to dump the body in his arms, as Tolleson claims? If the Reverend Wayne is the meticulously ruthless killer the prosecution portrays, why didn't he just shoot Tolleson and be done with it? When it suits the prosecution's purposes, we're asked to believe in the Reverend Wayne's brilliance, and when it suits their purposes we're asked to believe that he's an idiot.

"From this point, Tolleson and the Reverend Wayne's testimony are similar. Tolleson dumped the body into the defendant's arms and the defendant fired his revolver. Tolleson ran down the darkened side tunnel and the defendant fired twice more. Then the two settled into a long wait. Finally, the Reverend Wayne, concerned about Tolleson, went to look for him. The Reverend Wayne says it was completely dark. Tolleson says that the light in the room was on, providing some illumination. It wasn't clear what point the prosecution was trying to make with their exercise during the Reverend Wayne's cross-examination, but it seems that they want you to believe that Tolleson would have been unable to see well enough in the dark to strike the Reverend Wayne twice on the head with a metal pipe. Keep in mind that the prosecution also wants you to believe that Tolleson could see well enough in the dark to determine that it was the defendant who came after him in the choir loft. If you believe their version of events, a sixteen year old jumps out of that choir loft, deduces the location of a body, enters a church at night when he knows that the murderer could return at any time, finds a secret door and retrieves a body that has been brutally mutilated, but can't tell from the sound of a voice the location of the speaker's head. Just as we are asked to believe that the Reverend Wayne is both a genius and an idiot, we are

asked to believe that their chief witness is either a super-
hero or an ordinary human being, depending on what
suits their purposes."

She paused for a moment and surveyed the jury. They
were listening attentively.

"Rachmaninoff's Third Piano Concerto will always
have a special place in the heart of the Reverend Wayne—
it apparently saved his life after Tolleson hit him twice on
the head and knocked him unconscious. Tolleson decided
not to kill the Reverend Wayne, influenced by a mystical
rendition of that concerto. After that, Tolleson says he
went back to the small room, took the body from the tub
of ice, turned off the light and carried the body out of the
church. Although pursued by the defendant to his car, our
hero made his escape in the nick of time. Of course the
Reverend Wayne pursued Tolleson—he thought that
Tolleson would abscond with the body. Then he returned
to the parsonage. In his cross-examination, Mr. Devore
tried to make an issue of the Reverend Wayne's failure to
call the police. However, a man who has been knocked
unconscious after being hit over the head with a metal
pipe and then has chased the person who hit him for a
quarter of a mile would have a difficult time thinking
clearly, and it's understandable that he passed out again."

Strassberg slowly paced in front of the jury box,
stopped, faced the jury and spread her arms outward.
"Which story best comports with the evidence presented
in this court? No evidence supports Tolleson's account of
the events in the choir loft. No evidence supports his contention that a hair was stuck to the tapestry and the wall.
There were no fingerprints of the defendant's found in the
room where Tolleson claims that the defendant mutilated

Marsha Walton's body and prepared it for burial—the only fingerprints were Tolleson's. The Reverend Wayne's fingerprints were found on the plastic around the body, but there is no dispute that Tolleson dumped the body into his arms, thus, the Reverend Wayne touched the plastic. There is no dispute that the defendant fired his gun three times, that Tolleson hit him twice on the head, that Tolleson left the church with the body and that the defendant chased him to his car. A point of contention is whether the light was on or off when the defendant approached Tolleson, but the light was off when the police investigated below the church.

"You must be guided by your assessment of the relative credibility of the Reverend Silas Wayne and Joe Tolleson. As you make that assessment, remember how other people in Hidden Falls judged their trustworthiness. Sergeant Ruprecht, Chief Marsh and Tolleson's own parents refused to believe Tolleson's fantastic story, they knew that the Reverend Wayne couldn't brutally rape and murder a young girl.

"The prosecution implied that the defendant had figuratively done to Alice Tolleson what he is accused of doing to Marsha Walton. Mrs. Tolleson's tears aside, her story sounds like the story of probably everybody in this room—she loved someone who didn't love her. She was a close friend with the Reverend Wayne in high school and she had hopes. They were never physically intimate. He never promised to marry her. He never told her to abandon her acting scholarship. Mrs. Tolleson was and is a very attractive woman, but the Reverend Wayne didn't love her and he didn't want to marry her. Somehow, we're supposed to believe that he, and not Mrs.

Tolleson's overactive imagination, is responsible for her disappointments. It's an offensive notion that a woman with Mrs. Tolleson's gifts didn't determine her own fate, that the Reverend Wayne decided the course of her life. The Reverend Wayne has, at all times, behaved honorably toward her. Indeed, he performed Mr. and Mrs. Tolleson's wedding ceremony.

"The most eloquent, most telling, example of the regard that the people of Hidden Falls have for the Reverend Wayne was provided by Marsha Walton's mother, Nancy. When she asked him to preside at her daughter's funeral, he was officially a suspect in her rape and murder. Nancy Walton knew that the man who had helped her and her family so many times couldn't have done what he is now accused of doing."

Strassberg slowly passed by the jury box, looking at each member of the jury. "Actions speak louder than words and Sergeant Ruprecht, Chief Marsh, Jack Tolleson, Alice Tolleson and Nancy Walton have shown, with their actions, that they believed the version of events that is most clearly supported by the physical evidence found at the church—the Reverend Wayne's. That's why the DNA tests are so important to the prosecution. If one accepts the results of the DNA tests, it is the only evidence they have that might implicate the defendant. Police, detectives and district attorneys are always searching for an evidentiary Holy Grail—some infallible technique or test that will clearly establish guilt or innocence. They think that DNA tests have ended their quest. The men and women in white lab coats testify that there is only an infinitesimal chance that someone besides the defendant committed the crime and presto—automatic guilty verdict.

"Unfortunately for the prosecution, other men and women of science come along and point out the obvious—that no scientific technique is infallible. The tests must be properly administered. The DNA tests in this case had to be performed twice; the administration of the first tests was flawed.

"Like any testing procedure, DNA tests incorporate certain assumptions and they are only as good as the subject material. The background probabilities from FBI studies assume an unrelated population and are derived from imperfect statistical sampling techniques. As Professor Lamson testified, the probability quoted so authoritatively by the prosecution's expert could be off by one, two, three or more orders of magnitude. The one in two hundred and fifty million probability could be a one in twenty five million probability, a one in two and half million probability, or a one in two hundred and fifty thousand probability. Autoradiographs, like any other graphical representation, are subject to interpretation. In response to Mr. Devore's question, Professor Boranian would not state that the autoradiographs from the samples taken from Marsha Walton's body definitely matched those taken from the defendant.

"These are matters that are argued by the experts, but ultimately resolved by you, the members of the jury. To resolve these issues, you must address a philosophical question. Judge Longworth will instruct you that the defendant is presumed innocent and must be proved guilty by the prosecution. There must be no reasonable doubt in your minds that the Reverend Wayne raped and murdered Marsha Walton if you are to decide that he is guilty of those crimes. Is a probability compatible with the absence of reasonable doubt?

"Probabilities and statistics are not exact sciences. Consider the prosecution's probabilities with a healthy skepticism and remember, the source material for those probabilities comes from governmental agencies that have an incentive to overstate them. The men and women in white lab coats can't replace your judgment. Before you decide the guilt or innocence of a man who is loved and venerated throughout Hidden Falls, who has dedicated his life to Hidden Falls, make your own assessment of the relative credibility of that man and his accuser. As you make that assessment, consider the evidence that was presented in this courtroom and consider the evidence the prosecution was unable to produce. You must perform a difficult duty and reach a difficult conclusion, but ultimately there is only one conclusion you can reach. There is more than a reasonable doubt that the Reverend Silas Wayne raped and murdered Marsha Walton. The Reverend Wayne is innocent. Thank you."

She once again surveyed the jury, making eye contact with each member, returned to the defense table, whispered to Preston Catledge and walked up the aisle. The spectators were murmuring and she heard an older lady say "that was fantastic" as she exited the courtroom. She walked quickly down the hall to the women's restroom. Alone in the restroom, she stood at a sink dabbing small beads of perspiration from her forehead and upper lip with a Kleenex. She grasped the sink for support and forced herself to take several deep breaths, trying to still the churning, nauseated sensation in her stomach. She stared at the mirror above the sink. That face—pallor evident through the makeup, a picture of ordeal—was it hers? Wondering if it mattered, she closed her eyes and struggled to regain the order in her thoughts.

She had done closing arguments for many defendants she either suspected or knew were guilty, but this one was different. Different because of Joe Tolleson. He was a confederate in a battle she had fought all her life. He might not yet recognize the enemy or the issues, but they were on the same side. They were soldiers in a battle against something vast and amorphous, something recognizable but impossible—like nailing Jell-O to a wall—to define; its meaning suggested by a string of banalities masquerading as wisdom, a strand of lusterless pearls: "it's not what you know, it's who you know," "it's better to be lucky than smart," "life isn't fair," "you can't fight city hall," "if something can go wrong, it will," and so on. The best and the brightest rejected the bromides and met life's challenges head on. They assumed risks, bearing the consequences of failure and reaping the rewards of success. Mostly what they wanted from other people was to be left alone.

Arrayed against them was an army of mediocrities whose sole weapon was the word "no." No, they said, to thought, to experimentation, to risk, to dreams, to desire, to ambition, to work, to achievement; no, they said, to self. The no was rarely explicitly stated, it was often disguised as a yes. They praised humility, acceptance, conformity, selflessness, reputation, prestige, duty, faith and obedience. Don't question, don't challenge, don't protest, and don't fight—believe, accept, resign and die. She despised Silas Wayne, a lieutenant in the army of no. Throughout history, the foot soldiers had found succor, organization and leadership in religion. Holy men had led, and often won, the fight against individual initiative and achievement.

Drafting her closing argument the previous evening, she had recognized a growing sensation of moral doubt—something inside collapsing downward into an anxious void. Was she betraying her own cause? She had carefully outlined the argument with Catledge at his offices and then returned to her hotel room to complete it. She rejected those who mocked virtue, who met any attempt to rise above the ordinary with sarcasm or derision, but she tortured herself knowing that was what she would do to impeach Joe Tolleson's credibility. She went back and forth with herself. Twice that night she had picked up the phone and started dialing Catledge's home number to ask him to do the closing argument. She replaced the receiver both times before she finished dialing, held back by a thought she could not formulate. She returned to the closing argument, struggling with each word and phrase.

She had thought of her father. What would he say? She could almost hear him. Nazi Germany had made him a libertarian. Governments were the real danger in the war on enlightenment—armies to religions' battalions. It was terrifying when the two joined forces, but religion was a matter of private, voluntary choice—governments were organized coercion. Yes, she was fighting a man she admired and helping a man she despised escape punishment for his crimes, but that was an inevitable consequence of a decision she had made long ago. She could let Catledge do the closing argument—he believed in Wayne and she did not. However, she was a better attorney, and would make a better closing argument, than Catledge.

Wayne was entitled to their best. The presumption that one accused of a crime is innocent—that the government must prove guilt—is empty when the accused is without the benefit of zealous advocacy. The law school cliché was no less true for being a cliché—that presumption was the bulwark of civil liberties. There were no defense attorneys in Nazi Germany, because there had been no individual rights to protect. After her second aborted phone call to Catledge, she decided to stay the course. Still feeling uneasy, but vowing to do her best for her client, she had finished her closing argument around 3:00 o'clock in the morning and had gone to bed for a few hours sleep.

Now, standing at the courthouse restroom sink, she opened her sleep-deprived eyes and looked in the mirror. Her closing argument had been one of her best, in spite of the emotional toll it had taken. Reviewing the previous evening's struggle was oddly steadying—her stomach was not in great shape, but she no longer felt nauseated. She did not know how long she had been standing at the sink. She wet a paper towel, wiped her face, repaired her make-up and returned to the courtroom. She entered just as Mike Devore began his closing argument. He stood before the jury, wearing a dark blue suit, starched white shirt, red patterned tie and black winged-tip shoes. His voice was clear and calm and his tone was friendly.

"Ladies and gentlemen of the jury, let's not waste time addressing issues that are not in dispute. The prosecution will concede that the defendant has been known as a respected citizen of Hidden Falls. We won't argue with the Reverend Weathin, Archie McDaniels, Samantha Foster and the rest of the witnesses who testified to the good deeds he has performed. We're not going to say that there was no basis for Chief Marsh, Sergeant Ruprecht, Jack and Alice Tolleson and Nancy Walton to doubt that he raped and murdered Marsha Walton.

"The point we're not going to concede, though, is that Silas Wayne did in fact rape and murder Marsha Walton. Nobody on the defense's long list of character witnesses was present at the First Christian Church on the evening of either Friday, November the eighth or Friday, November the fifteenth. Joe Tolleson was in the old church both nights, and he told this court what happened.

"Ms. Strassberg artfully maintains that Joe Tolleson's account of the first night, when he saw Marsha Walton's body in the choir loft, is not supported by physical evidence. It would have been nice of Mr. Wayne to leave us the rope, the plastic sheet used to catch Marsha Walton's bodily fluids, and her clothing, but he was a little smarter than that. He disposed of that evidence and he's shown no inclination to tell us where—we'll probably never find it. However, that doesn't mean that there's no physical evidence to support Joe Tolleson's story. Joe saw a girl's body hanging from the choir loft rafter, and the girl had apparently been raped. Sure enough, we have the body and the autopsy report on that body. The report confirms that Marsha Walton, a fourteen-year-old girl, had been subjected to sexual intercourse before her death, that the sexual intercourse was consistent with rape because there were numerous bruises on her body and around her genitalia, that she had died of strangulation and that there were marks and bruises on her neck consistent with hanging by a rope. Perhaps the defense forgot about this physical evidence, which supports Joe Tolleson's eyewitness account of the night of the eighth in every particular."

Devore paused momentarily. He had watched the jury during the trial and had decided that an intelligent looking, middle-aged woman, an accountant, would be its most influential member. Now he looked directly at her. "Joe's account of that night hasn't varied in even a detail since he told it to Chief Marsh and Sergeant Ruprecht, then his parents, then Mr. Benewski, and now in open court. If it had, you can be sure that the very capable team of Strassberg and Catledge would have pointed it out. Ms. Strassberg argued that the police department's refusal to investigate Joe's story was understandable, given Silas Wayne's reputation. However, shouldn't the police always investigate an accusation of a possible rape and murder, regardless of the comparative social position of the accuser and accused? In this case the refusal to investigate was incomprehensible. The accuser is the valedictorian at Hidden Falls High School and has never been in trouble at school or with the police.

"Ms. Strassberg mentioned motives, so let's talk about motives. The question of motive arises concerning the bartender, Lou Santori. The defense has not contested that he apparently had a cordial relationship with the defendant. Wayne came into his bar several times; they talked and Santori even told him about some problems he was having with his girlfriend. Santori was a member of the First Christian Church. What possible motive, then, would he have for inventing a story about Wayne asking him to keep tabs on Nancy Walton and to call him if she left the Starlight Lounge with a man? There is none, so the defendant has to stonewall. The defendant claims he never asked Santori to check up on Nancy Walton and that Santori did not talk to him on the morning of the day

Marsha Walton was raped and murdered. However, the defense never suggests why Santori would perjure himself under oath in open court.

"It's a crucial matter because if you believe Santori, Silas Wayne knew that Nancy Walton had left the Starlight Lounge with a man on the night before her daughter's murder. Wayne knew that it upset Marsha when her mother brought home men and that she had run away twice before in similar circumstances. He knew there was a high probability that if Nancy Walton left the bar with a man and went home with him, she would upset her daughter. If that were the case, Mrs. Walton and anyone she talked to about the matter would think Marsha's disappearance was another attempt to run away. Wayne could abduct, attack, rape and kill her, and Marsha Walton would become just another face on a milk carton."

Devore turned away from the jury and took several steps towards the defense table. He looked at Silas Wayne, who did not look away. Devore turned back towards the jury.

"Unfortunately for Wayne, his plans for the perfect crime went awry when Joe Tolleson saw Marsha Walton's dangling corpse above the choir loft. Sunday, two days after that incident, Wayne had a conversation with Mrs. Edna Mayhew. The ice machine in the room below the church came from the kitchen in the recreation room annex. It was missing when Mrs. Mayhew brought her Sunday school students to the recreation room. You saw Mrs. Mayhew's videotape; she clearly recalls telling Wayne that the machine was missing and she clearly recalls his response. She said that he told her the ice machine was in for repairs. He says that he told her that he didn't know what had happened to the ice machine, but that the caretaker, Jasper Wooters, might have taken it in for repairs. Wayne ascribes the difference in his and Mrs. Mayhew's recollection of the conversation to her failing health and memory.

"You saw Mrs. Mayhew adamantly reject this suggestion by Mr. Catledge on the videotape. On the videotape, it did not appear that her memory was in any way impaired. If it was not, the only thing the defense can argue is that she fabricated the story. Again there is a question of motive—why would she lie?" Devore held up his hands and gave a mock shrug.

"Among the scores of good deeds Wayne has performed was helping Mrs. Mayhew recover from the death of her husband and getting her reinvolved with church activities. It was clear on the videotape that she was troubled by the implication of her conversation with him; she regarded Wayne as a close friend. If he said the ice machine was being repaired, he misspoke—the defense has offered no proof that the machine was being repaired. If he misspoke, it was because he was lying and knew that the machine was in a small room beneath the church, hooked to a generator to produce ice to keep Marsha Walton's body cold. That is why the defense clings precariously, but tenaciously, to the thin reed that Mrs. Mayhew's recollection of the conversation was erroneous. Anyone who watched that videotape can't reach the same conclusion."

Devore paused and walked back to the prosecution table for a sip of water.

"A macabre aspect of this case is the mutilation of Marsha Walton's body. Why did Silas Wayne cut the body down the middle of the abdomen, remove the organs and drain the blood? On the Tuesday following the Sunday conversation between Mrs. Mayhew and the defendant, Mayor Chester Matlock passed away. We don't know when Wayne first conceived of putting Marsha Walton's body in Matlock's casket, but it certainly was an ingenious idea. The defendant slowed the decomposition of the body by keeping it on ice and by removing the blood, and he made it as light as possible by removing the organs. Matlock was a large man with a large coffin. After the defendant performed his grisly mutilation, Marsha Walton's body weighed about eighty-five pounds. There was room in the coffin for that extra body and nobody would notice the additional weight. The defense has admitted that the idea to move the coffin to the church arose in a conversation between the defendant and Sarah Matlock, Chester's widow. They had to admit this because they couldn't impugn Sarah Matlock's credibility or her motives and Silas Wayne was aware that the coffin would be moved to the church the night before the funeral.

"Again, Wayne was unfortunate; Joe Tolleson figured out his plan for the disposal of Marsha Walton's body. Much has been made of Joe's supposed good fortune in this case, most particularly his luck in finding a door to the tunnels and rooms underneath the church. However, was it luck that he found the door? Where else was he going to look? He knew the body was in the church and he had examined the entire area by the chancel. He lifted the tapestry and found the door, but any reasonably intelligent person looking for what Joe was looking for—a hidden door concealing a hiding place for a corpse—would have eventually done the same thing."

Devore paced before the jury box, making eye contact with the jurors. "There are, of course, conflicting stories about what happened beneath the church. The trick for whoever is lying is to make his story consistent with the physical evidence. Fact number one that Wayne must deal with is that his fingerprints were not found in the room where Marsha Walton's body was kept. If he had not raped and killed her, he would have left fingerprints if he had entered the room. If the light was on in the room, he would have been aware of the room and sometime during the all-night standoff he would have entered it. Furthermore, if the light were on in the room, Joe Tolleson would have seen him from a distance as he was leaving the room with the body, before Wayne could confront him. Joe says that the light was on and Wayne stood in a darkened tunnel and grabbed him from behind.

"So Wayne has to say that the light was off—it's the only way he can maintain that he was ignorant of the room and thus, left no fingerprints. Here the defendant is tripped up by his own cleverness. He carefully planned to kill Marsha Walton at a time when nobody would be surprised by her disappearance. He had the patience to wait and not to make a mistake by prematurely trying to dispose of her body. He intended to make sure that it was never found by burying it with Chester Matlock. Unfortunately for him, he was too careful when he used surgical gloves and wiped all his fingerprints from the room where he stored the body. It is not surprising that he took those precautions; it would have been more surprising if he hadn't. However, by not leaving fingerprints, he couldn't claim that he had ever been in the room. The only way he couldn't have been in the room was to claim that he was unaware of its existence, and the only way he could be unaware was if no light came from the room.

"However, if no light came from the room, how did Joe Tolleson hit Wayne flush on the head, not once, but twice, with enough force to knock him out?" Devore held up one, then two fingers as he spoke. "Think about the impossibility of seeing anything in pitch blackness, much less hitting a moving person in the head twice. Yes, Joe is an extraordinary individual, but neither he nor anyone else could do what Wayne claimed he did—it's simply not possible.

"And so the defendant's story breaks down. Wayne went under the church, knowing from the broken hair on the tapestry that his hiding place had been discovered. He saw the light coming from the room and hid in the darkened tunnel, waiting for the intruder to pass. He grabbed Joe from behind and then proceeded to tell him what he had done to his mother and to Marsha Wayne. Ms. Strassberg argued that if the defendant is as smart as we say he is, he wouldn't have stood there and told Joe about his mother and Marsha Walton. However, remember one well known aspect of the criminal psyche—the compulsion to confess. Wayne could satisfy that compulsion, seemingly without danger to himself, because he had a gun and he intended to murder Joe Tolleson. If he didn't intend to murder him, why did he shoot three times at him as the unarmed youth ran away?"

Devore looked out at the gallery. Like the jury, their attention appeared to be focused on him. "Returning to the issue of motive, the most important motive in this case is that of the defendant. Ms. Strassberg and the Reverend Weathin make the point that ministers must be able to tolerate dissent and the rejection of their religion. Certainly a minister in the normal course of his duties will encounter disbelief and must learn to deal with it rationally. That presupposes the minister's rationality. Men who rape and murder are not rational—they are psychotics. Recall that the defendant could not remember the name of anyone, besides Marsha Walton and Joe Tolleson, who had refused to take his confirmation classes. We can't look into the soul of Silas Wayne, but from what he told Joe Tolleson about his mother, from Alice Tolleson's testimony, and from what he did to Marsha Walton, we can speculate that he hated females who possessed a certain independence of spirit. Something about them provoked an irrational need to either control or destroy. Alice Tolleson and Marsha Walton were victims of that psychotic need.

"Keep in mind the unimpeached testimony of Joe Tolleson, the damaging conflicts between Wayne's version of events and those of Tony Santori and Mrs. Mayhew, the internal implausibility of Wayne's story about what happened under the church, including the defendant's confusion on the stand about how many times he had been under the church and the layout of the subterranean tunnels, and finally, all the physical evidence that was presented as we turn to Ms. Strassberg's claim that the DNA tests are the only things we have to support our case. We will make another concession to Ms. Strassberg—DNA tests are not a Holy Grail. They are, however, another advance in forensic science, used by criminologists who have no ax to grind against any particular defendant, but want a method to better ascertain the guilt, or innocence, of all criminal defendants. There's nothing sinister about the fact that this advance was developed by the government; its the government's job to apprehend and punish criminals and to develop methods of determining guilt and innocence."

Devore walked back to the prosecution table, picked up a bound report, and displayed it to the jury. "What do the DNA tests demonstrate in this case? Simply stated, they demonstrate that the autoradiographs of five segments of DNA extracted from samples taken from Marsha Walton's body match the autoradiographs of the corresponding five segments of DNA taken from samples submitted by Silas Wayne. Whatever the problems of ascertaining the probability of segments matching, the likelihood of two sets of segments matching is less than the likelihood of one set matching, the likelihood of three sets matching is less than two, and so on." Devore placed the report back on the prosecution table and advanced towards the jury box. "We will concede that as a theoretical possibility, it can never be stated with complete certainty that a DNA match of segments means that the DNA comes from the same source. However, in a case such as this one, where the evidentiary samples are of good quality and the autoradiographs are clear, and where there is not a question of related parties, the possibility that five segments match, but that the DNA is not from the same source, is infinitesimally small.

"Implicit in the defense of Mr. Wayne is the contention that we should be pursuing the only other person previously suspected of committing these crimes—Joe Tolleson. However, consider this point. If there is perhaps a remote possibility that it was not Silas Wayne's DNA that was found on the body of Marsha Walton, despite the matching autoradiographs, there is no possibility at all that it was Joe Tolleson's. He submitted samples and there is not one match between the evidentiary autoradiographs and his.

"No, the only thing the defense has on Joe Tolleson is a lot of sarcasm and a sneering incredulity. How many times did Ms. Strassberg call Joe a hero? On this point, the defense and the prosecution are in perfect agreement—Joe Tolleson is a hero. Our age doesn't believe in heroes, or believes that everyone is a hero, which is the same thing. Both beliefs negate the idea of heroism. The heroic is the extraordinary, the difficult to attain. How else can you characterize what Joe has done? Granted, he took his father's lock picking tools without permission and entered the First Christian church. However, at twilight, a time of shadows and mystery, he overcame his trepidation, investigated a noise from the choir loft and discovered Marsha Walton's hanging body. Then he was nearly caught by Silas Wayne, and only barely made his escape by rolling over the railing and falling to the floor below.

"Joe's effort to tell his story, in the face of disbelief, hostility, and orders from both the police and his parents to keep silent, was extraordinarily persistent. His deduction about Wayne's plans for the disposal of the body was brilliant. He demonstrated exceptional courage and resourcefulness going to the church, finding the body and then confronting and outsmarting Silas Wayne. Once he turned over the body to the police, his resolve could have crumpled when he became a suspect, when he was incarcerated, when he faced unrelenting pressure from most of Hidden Falls to drop his accusation against its most influential citizen, or when his father threatened to withhold funding for his college education if he testified. His resolve didn't crumple. In fact, he seemed to become more stubbornly insistent on telling his story."

Devore paused for dramatic emphasis, took several steps towards the jury box and placed both hands on the railing.

"Why did Joe persist? Ladies and gentlemen of the jury, you are the answer. Joe Tolleson did what he did because he believed that if the evidence was presented and he was allowed to tell the truth in open court, twelve impartial, rational jurors would render justice. There are heroes and there are villains, and this trial has made it clear who's who. After all the testimony and all the evidence, there is no reasonable doubt that Silas Wayne is guilty of the rape and first degree murder of Marsha Walton. Thank you."

Devore walked back to the prosecution table and took his seat. Benewski leaned over and whispered "good job."

"I hope it's good enough," Devore whispered. "It's going to be close."

At the other table, Catledge asked Strassberg, "What do you think?"

"It's going to be close."

Judge Longworth adjourned the court for lunch. Joe left the courtroom and drove back to school. He would like to have stayed for the jury instructions, but he had to attend an important literature class—the teacher was reviewing materials for the final exam.

After Devore and Benewski left the courtroom, Devore fought through TV cameras, reporters, and spectators and caught up to Rachel Strassberg outside Brigg's Diner. He tapped her on her shoulder.

"Ms. Strassberg?"

"Yes, Mr. Devore."

"I've seen many closing arguments, but I just wanted you to know that I thought yours was exceptional."

"Thanks, I knew I had to rise to the level of the competition."

"Thank you." He held her glance momentarily and then went to the table reserved for him and Benewski. As he sat down he said, "I hope the jury was distracted by her looks." Benewski smiled at Devore's attempted levity.

As they ate lunch, all four of the attorneys felt the same emotion—a slow melting away of the tension that had gripped them throughout the trial. They had done all they could; now the matter was out of their hands. The judge would instruct the jury. The jury would make its decision. The four attorneys would be in suspense until that decision was announced, but the nervous energy that had propelled them for the last three weeks was quickly giving way to overwhelming exhaustion. Tonight would be their first good night's sleep since the trial began.

After lunch, they returned to the courthouse and settled at their tables to listen to Judge Longworth's jury instructions. They had worked many hours on their requested jury instructions, which were an exercise in subtle persuasion. They had to accurately state the law so that the judge would use their instruction, but also to state it in a way that sounded favorable to their side. The judge was free to use or discard an instruction, or to use his own instruction, but it was reviewable on appeal and it had to be a correct statement of the law.

Judge Longworth asked both sides for their requested instructions. This was a formality since both sides had submitted their instructions at the end of the previous week. He put the instructions under his own and surveyed the courtroom. He pulled a black case from a pocket in his robe, removed his reading glasses, put them on and adjusted them, and began his instructions.

"First degree murder is conduct on the part of the defendant that is the legal cause of the death of the victim, accompanied by a 'malicious' state of mind, premeditation, and deliberation. 'Conduct,' in this definition, means an affirmative act, or an omission to act where there is a duty to act. A 'malicious' state of mind is either intent to kill or do serious bodily injury; a depraved heart; or intent to commit a felony. Second degree murder lacks the elements of premeditation and deliberation. Manslaughter lacks premeditation, deliberation and also a 'malicious' state of mind. Thus, the determinative factor in distinguishing between first degree murder, second degree murder, and manslaughter is the defendant's state of mind. If you find the defendant not guilty of first degree murder, you may consider whether he is guilty or not guilty of second degree murder or manslaughter.

"Rape is the act of sexual intercourse committed by a man against a woman without her consent, committed when the woman's resistance is overcome by force or fear, or under other prohibitive conditions. Even if you do not find the defendant guilty of rape, you may still consider whether he is guilty of statutory rape—having sexual intercourse with a woman under the age of sixteen."

Judge Longworth reviewed the elements of first and second degree murder, manslaughter, rape and statutory rape. Benewski and Devore had weighed adding a charge of attempted murder, for Silas's three shots at Joe under the church, but decided that that Silas could make a plausible claim of self-defense and it would distract from the two main charges. As the judge droned on, the prosecution and defense attorneys watched the jury. The jurors had been impassive during the trial closing arguments, as if they had taken a vow to maintain a collective poker face. This did not change during the jury instructions. Despite Judge Longworth's drone, they listened intently, and aside from occasional twitches their faces did not change expressions.

The judge detailed the complexities of the law on the presumption of innocence and the prosecution's burden of proof, and defined a "reasonable doubt." He admonished the jury to consider only the evidence that had been presented in the courtroom and instructed them to appoint a foreman from among themselves. He then remanded the jury to the care of a sheriff's deputy and administered an oath to him. The sheriff stood and announced, "this court is recessed until the verdict of the jury or the further order of the court."

Judge Longworth went to his chamber. The defendant was escorted back to his jail cell. The jury filed out of the jury box and into the deliberation room. The courtroom erupted in a cacophony of anticipation and speculation as the gallery benches emptied. The attorneys were the last to leave the courtroom. When they returned, it would be to hear the verdict.

CHAPTER 27

▼

THE VERDICT

Silas Wayne's first memories were of a dilapidated shack on the outskirts of a dirt poor, shitkicking little town. He did not remember his father, who disappeared shortly after the birth of his younger sister, Rebecca. He vaguely remembered his slatternly mother, but only for her indifference to her children. He remembered his misshapen foot and the ugly black corrective shoes and leg brace that the relief agency doctor made him wear. He remembered the taunts and abuse he and his sister endured from the other children for their tattered clothes, dirty faces, runny noses and squalid poverty. He remembered their insults about the brace and orthopedic shoes. And he never forgot the many nights—cold, hungry, huddled in a small bed with Rebecca—that he cried himself to sleep.

The first blessing in his bleak life came when he was six years old—his mother died. He and Rebecca moved to

Hidden Falls, where their mother's sister, Ethel, took them in. Aunt Ethel was tall, thin, with sharp brown eyes and a Grant Wood face, her gray hair pulled back in a tight bun. Caring for her sister's children was a religious duty. She never smiled, never demonstrated affection or warmth, but she did manage to keep Silas and Rebecca fed, bathed and clothed on her widow's pension and her small income as a seamstress. Her strict edicts were obeyed without question.

Rebecca quickly made friends and was happy with the move to Hidden Falls. Silas was miserable. Although he was freed of the brace and orthopedic shoes shortly after they arrived, he had another handicap that made it even more difficult for him to fit in—he was smarter than the other children. He wanted desperately to belong, but felt awkwardly foolish playing games and seeking friends. The other children had an instinctive sense of his insecurity and mocked his clumsy shyness. Once he picked a fight with a boy to impress a pretty classmate, Jane. He, and his fragile psyche, took a beating. Jane and her friends followed him home from school, laughing. He hated them all.

There was a room in Aunt Ethel's house, at the end of the hall, which he was forbidden to enter. One day, when he was ten, he opened the door and found a sanctuary. Dust covered everything—the large leather recliner, the small desk by the window and the books on the shelves lining the walls. As a memorial to her late husband, an omnivorous reader, Aunt Ethel had kept his library exactly as he had left it. Aunt Ethel never read anything except the Bible and religious tracts. Silas removed a book, *Tom Sawyer*, from a shelf, sank into the dusty recliner and read for many hours. He did not hear Aunt Ethel call him for dinner; she eventually found him. Seeing his happy absorption in the Twain classic, she did not reprimand him for entering the library, but told him to wash up. The next day she cleaned the library and gave him permission to use it.

Every day he would hurry home from school and retreat to the library. What he read—literature, histories, biographies, and books on science, philosophy and art— reflected his wide range of interests and his exceptional mental abilities. The awkward boy who could not talk with his classmates experienced the world through the written word, and so began to formulate his ideas about that world. He figuratively emerged from his library-sanctuary about four years later, greatly changed. Gone was the insecure clumsiness. Conscious of his posture and his maturing body, his tall, erect carriage conveyed an imposing gravity, unusual for an adolescent. Ostensibly giving up his pursuit of acceptance and popularity, he adopted a quietly stern demeanor. His classmates might never like him, but they were going to respect him. And bend to his will. Believing that the first step to control of others was control of self, he became a model of restraint, never experimenting with tobacco, alcohol, or other drugs. He admitted his chastity as a matter of pride, not shame, in response to other boys' boasts about their first experiments with the opposite sex. When he was fifteen, he told Aunt Ethel that he would study for the ministry. Her tears of joy were his reward for the way he had shaped his personality.

He gradually won the moral authority he craved. The truth, he discovered, could be a powerful weapon. Seeing through adolescent pretense, he began stating his judgments to the small, but growing, group who sought his views. Coupled with the truth were moral pronouncements. Phyllis needs those flashy clothes to hide her insecurity— real assurance and security comes through God and Christianity. Bill's confused, but he brags about sex and dating because he's overwhelmed by his desires, which only God can help him control until they find their proper expression within marriage. Ted mocks his parents and wants to establish his independence from them, when he should be submitting to their love and authority—the family is the basis of God's society. Truth and guilt were his faithful sheepdogs, effectively herding his little flock in the desired direction. When Alice, the most desirable girl in Hidden Falls, fell in love with him, it only increased his stature among them.

As they approached graduation from high school, his acolytes began asking him what they should do with their lives. Silas always had an answer. It usually involved shunning one's first love and either staying in or returning to Hidden Falls after further education or military service. He used the same sleight of hand that had worked so well with Alice. Frank Marsh was advised to forget his dream of becoming a pilot, and to stay with his ailing mother and join the Hidden Falls police force. He counseled Preston Catledge to avoid writing—it was too uncertain a career— and to go into the law, which would still afford him opportunities to write.

Silas followed his own advice and returned to Hidden Falls after the seminary. With painstaking effort, he insinuated himself into the lives of the townspeople. Although few really knew or liked him, as the good deeds piled up, he eventually won the veneration he sought. He had a secure place in their hearts and minds and a secure grip on their souls until that terrible Friday afternoon in the choir loft. Then he found the truth, the dagger he had used so well against others, poised against his own breast.

The truth was the truth.

Silas sat on his cot in his cell, two days after the jury had began deliberations, on another Friday afternoon. His head was bowed as he ran his fingers through his hair. There were no other prisoners in the cellblock. His thoughts were erratic, fragmentary strokes, painted on a canvas of doubt and anxiety. The truth was the truth. After consideration of many alternatives, he had fashioned the most plausible lie. It best fit the known facts with the least deviation from the actual truth. And it had almost worked, except for the light. Constructing his lie, he had mentally journeyed through a maze, exploring every passageway and always returning to one impassable barrier— the light. If the light in the room where he stored Marsha Walton's corpse was on, how could he not know about the room? If it was off, how could Tolleson see to hit him on the head twice with the metal pipe? If he hadn't wiped the room of his fingerprints, he could have told his story with the light on. The truth was the light, and the light was truth. He bitterly regretted wiping the room for fingerprints, and not killing Tolleson immediately after discovering him under the church. Those were his only regrets.

The best liars believed their own lies. He didn't. He divided the world into two groups—the gullible, who needed to believe somebody's version of the truth; and the sophisticated, who held that the truth was relative, or a political choice, or unknowable, or did not exist. He directed his efforts towards the former—there was power in numbers. The latter were well served by university professors and other so-called intellectuals. He had lied and lied effectively, but he'd never believed his own lies. That's what made the difference this time. He could fool the Bert Weathins of the world, but he couldn't fool himself. He couldn't produce the mental fog necessary to becloud his own mind. If he could have made himself believe, like he'd made so many others believe, then maybe Devore would have believed...and Strassberg.

The problem with Devore was a perpetual problem with political figures—they could be bought, but they didn't stay bought. Silas had known that Benewski wouldn't see the discrepancy concerning the light, but he had feared that Devore would. Devore owed his position to the minister. From the beginning, Silas wondered if he would stay bought. He realized with Devore's first question about the light bulb in the room that he would not. Things had gone too far and the ambitious Devore couldn't afford to lose. Silas had erected his prevarication on a cracked foundation, hoping that Devore would not undermine it. The district attorney's question had dashed his hopes.

In a more subtle way, so had Strassberg. Not that he could fault her courtroom tactics or her brilliant closing argument. However, some time during the trial, he began sensing a certain antipathy towards him, and a certain affinity for Tolleson. There was nothing overt, but an unshakable feeling developed that, unlike Catledge, she was not really with him. He wondered if the jury sensed it as well.

What if all he had with the jury was his reputation? Reputation was, as Napoleon once said about history, a set of lies agreed upon. Trapped in his cell, he felt as if he were looking across a wide, deep gorge, to his freedom on the other side. If his reputation was his defense, then the bridge across the gorge was a crude rope affair, riddled with rotted planks and frayed rails. The discrepancy about the light, the conflicts in his testimony with that of Sarah Matlock, Lou Santori, and Edna Mayhew, Joe Tolleson's testimony, and the DNA tests, left him precariously balanced on the bridge, wondering if he could make it across the gorge. What would be the decision of the twelve? Could they see a shadow of doubt? Shadows require some light and lies require some truth. Was there enough light in his dark lies to cast the necessary shadow? When he told his story, he had seen in the courtroom the same desire to believe that filled his church every week. Would it be enough?

The thought of the courtroom and the jury inflamed the acid pit that was his stomach. He had not fully digested a meal for weeks. Food passed through a digestive system that was too preoccupied with his worries and doubts to do its job. The churning never stopped, even when he tried to sleep. The occasional thought, which surfaced in spite of his best efforts to suppress it, that he might be executed or spend the rest of his life in prison sent a knifing, searing pain slicing through his entire abdomen. The guards had grown used to his many requests to go to the bathroom. He wished his sister were still alive; Rebecca would have been a comfort. When would the jury return its verdict? Was it a good or bad sign that they had deliberated for two days?

The door to the cellblock opened and the guard who had escorted him to and from the courtroom approached his cell. The guard was a small, wiry man with a perpetually embittered expression. Now Silas detected a remote twinge of some other emotion, perhaps anticipation.

"Reverend Wayne," the guard said, "the jury has reached a verdict."

*   *   *

On the Wednesday afternoon the case went to the jury, a woman who worked in the branch college front office handed Joe a note as he was leaving his physics class. The note said that Barbara Martel, his calculus teacher, wanted to see him. Joe walked over to the high school and found Martel's classroom. She was teaching a class, so he waited about ten minutes until she finished her lecture and the classroom emptied. He entered the classroom. She was standing at the front of the room, erasing a blackboard.

"Hello, Mrs. Martel. I got a note that you wanted to talk to me."

"Thanks for dropping by. I heard on the radio in the teachers' lounge that Silas Wayne's case has gone to the jury."

"Yes, it did."

"Joe, I don't know how the verdict will go. Sometimes a criminal can be guilty, but it can't be proved beyond a reasonable doubt. I just wanted to tell you that no matter what the verdict is, I believe you. I must be one of the few people in this town who doesn't know Silas Wayne. I know you, though, and I know that you tell the truth. I also want to apologize for not saying something to you sooner. This must have been an incredible ordeal, and it might have helped you to know that someone believed you."

There was a long silence; Joe did not trust himself to speak. In a voice barely above a whisper, he said, "thank you, Mrs. Martel."

The next two days were an agonizing paradox for Joe. Each interminable moment of waiting for and wondering about the verdict seemed separate and distinct, but later, when he looked back, he could not recall a single thing he did, said or heard during that time. He knew he had conversations with people, listened to lectures and prepared for exams, but the only thing he remembered was his anticipation and anxiety about the verdict. Wednesday and Thursday nights he did not sleep, awakening every time he began to doze. As he sat in his last class of the week Friday afternoon at the branch college he felt disappointed. If the jury did not reach a verdict that afternoon, they would adjourn through the weekend, assuring at least two more days of waiting. With about fifteen minutes left in class, there was a knock on the door and a lady from the front office entered the room and approached Ms. Amstad, the professor. They talked briefly. Ms. Amstad motioned for Joe. He walked to the front of the class.

"The jury's reached a verdict, Joe," the woman from the front office said.

"I think you're going to want to go to the courtroom," Ms. Amstad said. "You may leave."

Joe forgot to say thank you and he ran to his car. His stomach was a knot and he could feel rivulets of sweat running down his underarm and back. He was too agitated to drive, but it was only a mile to the courtroom. The courthouse parking lot was full, so he had to find a space on the street. As he approached the courthouse, he fought his way through hordes of reporters, photographers and

TV cameramen. He walked into the courtroom, which was already packed. Silas Wayne and the two defense attorneys were at their table and the two prosecution attorneys were at theirs. Gary Benewski waved at him—he had saved him his seat in the first row, directly behind the prosecution table. Joe sat down and Judge Longworth banged his gavel.

"Bailiff, bring in the jury."

The woman that the jury had chosen as their forewoman, the accountant Devore had focused on his closing argument, was the first to enter the jury box. The other eleven jurors filed in, found their seats and sat down. There was a rush of excited murmuring in the gallery.

Judge Longworth banged his gavel again. "I warn everyone here not to interrupt the announcement of the verdict and the polling of the jury or risk expulsion from the courtroom. Thank you. The clerk will proceed."

"Members of the jury, have you agreed on a verdict for each of the crimes charged in the case of the State versus Silas Wayne and if so, who will read the verdicts?" said the clerk.

The forewoman stood and said, "I will announce the verdicts." Her voice quavered and her face betrayed her tension. The courtroom was silent. The incongruous laughs and shrieks of children playing in a schoolyard nearby were the only sounds.

"The defendant will rise and face the jury," said the clerk. Even his voice trembled.

Silas Wayne stood and turned towards the jury, his expression grim.

"What are your verdicts?"

"We, the jury in the above entitled action, find the defendant, Silas Zachary Wayne, guilty of the crime of murder in the first degree. We, the jury in the above entitled action, find the defendant, Silas Zachary Wayne, guilty of the crime of rape." The forewoman closed her eyes and bowed her head.

The verdict had been as anxiously awaited and mercilessly quick as the drop of a guillotine blade. Judge Longworth broke the stunned silence. "Members of the jury, your verdicts as recorded are that the defendant, Silas Wayne, is guilty of first degree murder and rape. Is that your verdicts?"

Each member of the jury nodded and said, "yes."

The courtroom erupted in noise. Joe stood and looked toward the defense table, where Silas Wayne had sat down and was now slumped in his chair, staring vacantly into space. You lost, you poor son of a bitch, you lost. He exchanged a quick glance with Preston Catledge and a longer one with Rachel Strassberg, conscious that Gary Benewski and Mike Devore were both trying to shake his hand. He turned around, towards the courtroom, noticing that his legs were wobbly, feeling many emotions—exhilarated vindication, relief that his ordeal was over and overwhelming gratitude towards the members of the jury. His glance at the jury box was a silent salute to their attentiveness and integrity—you can't fool all the people all the time. They stared at him. He turned and looked for what seemed a long time at his parents. His father was watching him and slowly nodding his head. His arm was around his mother and she was crying, wiping her eyes with Kleenex. He saw Nancy Walton crying uncontrollably into the shoulder of a female friend. A sense of expectation, focused on Joe, hung over the courtroom, which grew strangely hushed. A door had closed between them and him. Sliding past the other people in his row, he walked up the aisle and out of the courtroom, alone.

     *   *   *

For the first time since Hidden Falls High School began holding commencement exercises, the valedictorian was not invited to address the graduating seniors. He had been the first to file into the school gymnasium, as was traditional, and he had taken his seat in the first chair in the first row of chairs on the gymnasium floor, also the tradition. However, he did not give a speech. There was no explanation in the program, but everyone knew why he did not fill the customary slot between the guest speaker and the high school principal, Art Mendolsohn. Mendolsohn finished his speech, on the promise of the future, and waited for the applause to die down. He cleared his throat.

"Thank you. It is now my pleasure to present the diplomas to our graduating seniors. I will call their names—first the valedictorian, then the salutatorian, then the honors graduates—the top ten percent of the class— and then the rest of the senior class. Mr. Carsdale, the vice-principal, will hand the graduates their diplomas. Please hold your applause until after all the names have been announced." He looked down at his list of graduates. "This year's valedictorian is Joseph Samuel Tolleson."

Joe walked to the front of the gymnasium and stepped up to the speakers' platform. As he received his diploma from Mr. Carsdale, a big man at the back of the gymnasium stood and clapped. Everybody recognized the man from television and from his pictures in the newspaper. Mendolsohn looked as if he wanted to say something, then thought better of it. The man's clapping grew louder, but no one joined him.

Joe stopped at the end of the platform and surveyed his fellow graduates and the audience. Soon he would leave Hidden Falls. Would he ever return? You can't go home again to a home that never was. He had destroyed their icon, but they would find another. Why they needed icons was the mystery he hadn't solved. A seamless web, they all believed because they all believed. The arachnid that spun the web which ensnared their souls; that engulfed them in its deadly casing of popularity and prestige; that pierced them with concern for everyone else's opinion, injected them with dreary conformity, sucked out their dreams, their integrity and their lives and then unhurriedly crushed the remnant (indistinguishable from the other remnants) of their personalities—that spider came from within. But one could brush aside the web—Joe had. He smiled his secret smile and returned to his chair, noticing as he descended the stairs that Mrs. Martel and his parents had joined Benewski and were standing and applauding. They were the only ones to do so.

CHAPTER 28

A PHONE CALL

Joe opened the door to his spacious apartment and heard the phones ringing. He picked up the nearest one, on a stand by the living room couch.

"Hello."

"Hi, Joe," said Gary Benewski. "We were notified this morning that the Supreme Court won't hear Silas Wayne's appeal. It's all over. Silas will spend the rest of his life in the state pen."

Joe sunk into the couch, overcome with exhilaration and relief. The possibility that Silas Wayne, represented by Rachel Strassberg, might have his verdict overturned on appeal had been a dark cloud on his horizon for three years.

"Joe…Joe, you still there?"

"Yeah. That's great news."

"I tried calling you all morning, but you were out. You'll have three messages on your voice mail. I called both your mom and dad, to let them know. Your mom said they're going to see you in Hawaii next month."

"Yeah, dad booked us into a resort on Maui for two weeks."

"You still won't come back to Hidden Falls?"

"No."

"That means I'm going to have to come out your way. I think that can be arranged. There's one other thing. After we found out about the Supreme Court decision this morning, I got a call from Rachel Strassberg."

"What did she say?"

"She congratulated Devore and me, and then she asked about you."

"What did you tell her?"

"I told her that you had gone to college, then quit and started a successful computer networking company with two of your professors. That's all I said. She asked for your phone number and your address. I told her I would have to ask you before I gave her your number or address. She left her number. Do you want me to call her back?"

"No, I'll call her myself. What's her number?"

"2125550404. I guess it wouldn't be like you to use an intermediary."

"No, it wouldn't. I have to go to New York on business in a couple of weeks. I'll look her up."

"Good luck. My buzzer's buzzing; I've got an appointment. Let me know how everything turns out. Keep in touch."

"I will. Good-bye, Gary."

"Good-bye, Joe."

About the Author

Robert Gore was born in 1958 in California, and grew up in Los Alamos, New Mexico. He graduated with honors from UCLA in 1980 with degrees in economics and political science. He graduated from the UC Berkeley in 1984 with Masters degrees in business and law. He is an inactive member of the California Bar. He currently trades bonds and is the partner in charge of fixed income investments at a Southern California securities firm. His main hobby is writing. The Gordian Knot is his first novel. He lives in Los Angeles with his wife, Roberta, and his son, Austin.